'The undisputed queen of crime writing'

Erwin James

MARTINA COLE

Author of 22 novels – and counting…

14 No. 1 bestsellers

4 screen adaptations

3 stage shows

Over 15 million copies sold across the world

Stay in touch for film and TV news, book releases and more…

🐦 @MartinaCole
f /OfficialMartinaCole
www.martinacole.co.uk
#geteven

GET EVEN

MARTINA COLE

headline

First published in Great Britain in 2015 by
HEADLINE PUBLISHING GROUP

First published in Great Britain in paperback in 2016 by
HEADLINE PUBLISHING GROUP

1

Cataloguing in Publication Data is available from the British Library

ISBN 978 1 4722 0101 0 (B-format)
ISBN 978 1 4722 3260 1 (A-format)

Typeset in ITC Galliard Std by Palimpsest Book Production Ltd,
Falkirk, Stirlingshire

Printed and bound in Great Britain by Clays Ltd, St Ives plc

Headline's policy is to use papers that are natural, renewable and recyclable
products and made from wood grown in well-managed forests and other
controlled sources. The logging and manufacturing processes are expected
to conform to the environmental regulations of the country of origin.

HEADLINE PUBLISHING GROUP
An Hachette UK Company
Carmelite House
50 Victoria Embankment
London, EC4Y 0DZ

www.headline.co.uk
www.hachette.co.uk

For the Fredster and baby Chris,
my beautiful daughter and grandson.

And for my Clarkie boy!
My big grandson and Nanny's boy.

Prologue

God be merciful to me a sinner.

Luke 18:13

Prologue

Sharon was drinking a glass of wine and wondering how her wonderful, charmed life had been reduced to this. She had once been the envy of all her friends. But the reality could not have been more different to the illusion.

She closed her eyes and pictured her first husband, Lenny Scott, in her mind's eye. She had started going out with him at thirteen and married him at seventeen, much to her parents' chagrin. But they had been so happy together – they had had two sons and that had cemented their relationship.

Then he had been brutally murdered, found tortured and battered to death one night – and that was it.

That same night she had also uncovered his secret – the secret he had kept from her and everyone around him for so many years. A secret that would have caused untold aggravation and upset in the world of Faces, affecting her boys' lives into the bargain, if it had ever been revealed.

But what good had keeping the secret done them

really? Today she had visited her sons in prison, and they had acted like being there was just a game. They had killed someone and they thought it was funny. How had she allowed that to happen? How had she not realised that they were broken and turning into fucking thugs? Because that was all they were. They weren't even true Faces; they had just beaten a man to death for no reason. She couldn't believe that her two boys, who she had had such hopes for, could have turned out so wrong.

She swallowed down her tears, because tears were useless. Life was shite, really. No matter how great you thought it was, it could always creep up and bite you on the arse when you least expected it. Well, fuck it! She had never known the reason behind her Lenny's death. She had lived all these years in ignorance – until tonight the one man left in her life that she trusted had told her the truth. And now there was no going back.

She gulped at her glass of wine. She needed the alcohol to get through this. Tonight she was going to right some wrongs. No matter what danger it might bring to her door, there was no stopping what was about to happen.

Young Lenny Scott and his little brother, Liam, were laughing raucously together. They were a handful, as the POs would say – protected, not just by their father's name, but by the man who had become their stepfather;

the boys knew this as well as the POs did. They more or less had a free pass – it was galling, but it was the truth. Being on remand for the first time was an adventure, but one of the older prison officers, Eric Marks, could tell from experience that they were not as hard as they thought they were.

The younger one was not taking to prison life quite as easily as his older brother. Liam Scott was not cut out for the regime prison insisted on: slopping out, eating at set times, early fucking nights. Unlike his older brother, Lenny, he appeared to be losing interest in this 'adventure' on an hourly basis. The fact that their mother had cunted them into the ground in front of everyone on a visit earlier that day had not helped matters either. Now they were being laughed at – just not to their faces. They might be in for murder, but they had clout and that could guarantee them a short sentence. It was such a waste, because they were clever, handsome, well-educated lads, and with a few quid behind them. Shame they didn't think about that – and their mother who had buried their father after he had been killed. Eric would lay money that that horror had left its mark on her, and probably on those lads as well.

He sighed heavily. Twenty years in this job and he was still continually disappointed in Mother Nature. Murderers, he had decided early on in his career, were a breed apart. Some of them had good reason, or were provoked, but he still saw so many lives ruined thanks to a drunken fight or a drugged confrontation that had got out of hand. And then there were the young Lennys and Liams of the world who simply thought it was all a joke.

One thing Eric would give their mother – she, at least, knew that what they had done was wrong and she had told them as much that afternoon in the visiting room. Maybe, just maybe, there was hope for these lads yet. Not that he would hold his breath, of course.

Sharon's daughter, Kathy, was frightened and ashamed. Everything had blown up in her face, and she finally realised the seriousness of what she had done – and what she had caused.

She felt the tears coming again, hot and wet. She had always been a good crier, and normally that was enough to make her dad give her what she wanted. But not tonight. Tonight she had known what it was to go too far; her mum and dad were not going to make it all right again as they normally did when she fucked up. This time her actions could cause actual murder. Worst of all, her father would never look at her in the same way again. She had let him down badly, and her mum. Her dad had always given in to her – it had been her mum who had been the bad bastard, telling her a big resounding 'no' when she didn't think she deserved or had earned whatever it was Kathy decided she wanted. Now she saw that all these years her mum had been trying to look out for her; Kathy had hated her for that when Sharon had simply been trying to help her daughter to help herself.

Kathy picked up her mobile and tried the number again, but there was no answer. She threw the phone at the wall in frustration. It was so unfair. Well, fuck him! He was always ignoring her calls so let him deal with her father himself. After all, that's what she'd had to do.

Reggie Dornan was so angry he felt that he could take on Man Mountain Dean with one hand tied behind his back and come out on top. He had been mugged off, betrayed in the worst possible way, and there was no chance he was taking this lying down. Tonight was the end. And please God in His heaven it all worked out because that would finally make him feel that he had seen through his promise to look after Lenny Scott's family. He owed Sharon because he had broken her heart once. Oh, he owed her fucking big time. He would do everything in his power to make sure that Lenny Scott would be remembered. And Reggie Dornan always paid his debts.

Sharon held Kathy in her arms but she was still furious with her; her daughter was a spoiled brat and that needed to be addressed.

'I am so sorry, Mummy. Please believe me. I am so very sorry.'

Sharon looked down at her beautiful face. Kathy

was just like her father: what she wanted she took, no matter who got hurt or who might have to pay the price for her enjoyment.

'You're not really sorry, Kath! You are just sorry it all fell out of bed.'

She pushed her daughter away from her and left her crying bitter tears. It amazed Sharon how dispassionate she could feel at her daughter's obvious distress. But, then, was it really surprising after what she had heard this night? Her daughter's predicament was nothing to her right now. Maybe tomorrow, if it all worked out, she would have the time and energy to try and help her out of the corner Kathy had finally painted herself into. But now she had other things on her mind.

Downstairs, Sharon looked around her beautiful home – the house she had furnished and decorated with such love and care. It was as if the place was mocking her, making her see that material objects meant fuck-all in the grand scheme. Oh, hindsight was a fucking wonderful thing. She'd had only two men in her life: one had been murdered and the other . . . Well, that remained to be seen. As her old mum used to say, where women were concerned, they never got mad if they were clever – they went one better and they got *even*.

When the call finally came she felt such relief that she could have wept. After all these years, she was finally in control of her own life. She only hoped it wasn't too late. One thing she did know for sure was that she was going to see this through to the bitter end. It was all she could do for herself and her children. She wanted payback for what had been done to her and hers.

She felt a calmness wash over her. *This* was what she had been waiting for. She would do what needed to be done – no matter the consequences.

Book One

Deep in my soul that tender secret dwells,
Lonely and lost to light for evermore,
Save when to thine my heart responsive swells,
Then trembles into silence as before.

'The Corsair', Lord Byron (1788–1824)

Chapter One

1984

'You stupid little mare! I knew it!'

Sharon Conway rolled her eyes with the irritation typical of her youth, which did not calm her mother's fury in the least. In fact, it was like a red rag to a bull.

'Roll your eyes at me, would you? You idiot – tied to that fucking thug for the rest of your days. Honestly, Sharon, I wonder if you have even one iota of fucking intelligence in that made-up, backcombed head of yours. If you had actual brains you would be up that clinic getting the thing out of you faster than Billy Whizz. But not you! Oh no, Clever Bollocks, *you* think you can change him, *you* think he will become Mr *Perfect*. Well, I will let you in on a little secret: he won't fucking change. *You* will, you daft fucking mare! You will be tied down for the rest of your life with that ponce, and you will never get shot of him once you produce his offspring.'

Sharon had already tuned her mother out. She knew exactly what she was going to hear, and experience told her that the best way to deal with her mum was just to pretend to listen and let the silly old cow get it all out of her system. It was pointless to argue; her mum was the queen of arguing – everyone in the street knew that. If it was an Olympic sport, Ivy Conway would be world fucking champion by now.

Sharon's father, Derek Conway, known as Del, continued to read his paper as if the house was as quiet as a monastery. He had learned to ignore his Ivy early in their marriage. It had either been that or throttle the fucker to death and, in fairness, when she wasn't arguing, she was a great girl. But light the blue touchpaper and she was like a banshee – she could howl all fucking night.

He drank his tea. He had seen this coming and so had Ivy, though she had done everything in her power to prevent it. But their Sharon had been mad on Lenny Scott since they had started going out together when she was thirteen and he was fifteen. Now, four years later, he was the father of her child and they were going to get married. At least Lenny *wanted* to marry her – that in itself was a turn-up in this day and age.

Derek winked surreptitiously at his daughter in support but, unfortunately, her mother caught him in the act.

'Oh, I see! You think this is fucking funny, do the pair of you? Well, you will be laughing on the other side of your face, lady, once reality sets in. You mark my words . . .'

Sharon made a suitably contrite face and tuned her mother out once more. At the end of the day, she knew that Ivy was not going to let up, and she accepted it. What her mother didn't allow for was the fact that she was adamant she was going to marry Lenny Scott – no matter what she, or anyone else, might have to say about it. Sharon Conway was determined. Her mum wasn't the only stubborn fuck in this family, as she would soon find out.

Sharon held her hand up with a finality that actually stopped Ivy Conway in her tracks. 'He will be here soon with his mum and dad, who are not pleased about the situation either, but unlike you, Mum, they see me and my Lenny as making the best of it. You would have more to say if he didn't want to marry me. But he does. We both want this wedding and, yes, it's a bit sooner than we planned, but there you are. It's happened. So get over it.'

Derek Conway was gobsmacked when his Ivy actually did shut that big galloping trap of hers. He had never believed that he would see the day.

Chapter Two

'Oh, son, are you sure about this? You don't have to marry them these days, you know. It's a different world.'

Lenny Scott was embarrassed and it showed. 'Honestly, Mr Johnson, I wanted to marry her anyway. It's just a bit sooner than we anticipated, that's all. We've been together four years now. She's a good girl, my Sharon, and I love her.'

He was blushing to the roots of his hair, and Jack Johnson couldn't help but smile. He liked Lenny Scott a lot; he was a good kid with plenty of nous, and he knew how to do a day's collar. He was a heavy, but Jack felt he had a bit more going for him, young as he was. He could add up like a fucking calculator – he knew exactly how much a person owed on a loan, could work out the take in seconds if necessary. And he never tried to have anyone over. Jack Johnson had seen too many in Lenny's position rip off the customers, swearing they hadn't paid, when Jack knew they had, and expecting the poor fuckers to pay again. Jack might be a loan shark, but he prided himself on being a reasonably honest one. And this was a very lucrative business – some of the council estates were into him for hundreds of thousands of pounds.

Jack had plans for this lad. And now, with a baby in the mix, he wondered if it might make Lenny more amenable to learning the seamier side of the business. Always look for an angle – that was Jack Johnson's mantra.

'Well, son, I wish you all the best, then. As long as you are sure you're doing the right thing, that's all that matters, mate.'

Lenny grinned. 'I'm sure. But the thing is, Mr Johnson, I need a few quid extra, like. I've got to get a place, with a baby on the way. You know the score.'

Jack Johnson was happy to help. 'You're preaching to the converted, son. I will be happy to sort something out for you.'

Lenny Scott was thrilled. 'I can't thank you enough, Mr Johnson. I will knock me pound out for you, I swear.'

Jack already knew that, and he smiled. 'Once the kid arrives you will be knocking your pound out on a regular basis, mark my words. I wish you all the best and, I tell you what, I'll give you a grand now to get the wedding underway. You're a good kid, Lenny, and I think you will go far.'

Lenny watched in utter amazement as Jack opened his small safe and took out a thousand pounds in cash. As Jack handed it over, Lenny felt the urge to cry.

The man was such a big-hearted character. Lenny swore his undying allegiance to him there and then – as Jack Johnson knew he would. It was about keeping your eye on the main chance, but also, as Jack admitted to himself, he genuinely liked this kid. Lenny Scott had a bright future, there was no doubt about that in his mind. And Jack Johnson had always prided himself on finding talent and putting said talent to work. It was why he was a rich man.

He had big plans for young Lenny Scott; the lad was that rare mixture of brawn and brains and, in Jack's game, that was a fucking gift. Lenny had his head screwed on – he knew the score, he had a nice nature – and he was grateful. The latter was an important attribute. Jack Johnson knew only too well how many nasty little fuckers were out there, with no integrity whatsoever and a God-given belief that life owed them a living. He blamed the welfare state – it had made people weak. The dole was supposed to tide you over till you got a fucking job. It was never meant to be your fucking main earn.

That was why Jack admired this lad so much – he didn't sign on for a poxy few quid on top of his wages. Lenny was kosher. He understood, as young as he was, the need to keep as far away from the government as possible. He kept himself well under the radar and earned his coin with his own graft. He was a man after Jack's heart.

Chapter Three

'*How* much?'

Lenny could hear the incredulity in everyone's voices and he laughed delightedly as he took the wad of money out of his pocket and threw it on to the kitchen table.

Ivy's eyes nearly popped out of her head at the sight of it. His own parents were quiet; his father, Big Lenny Scott, was chuffed for his boy, but his mother, Lesley, a tall, thin woman with a face like a broken watch, remained tight-lipped. As his dad would say, she felt too close to God to make her comfortable with Lenny's association with the likes of Jack Johnson.

Lesley liked Sharon, and felt she was good for her son. What she *didn't* like was her son's occupation. She believed he was bright enough to go to university, and she saw his intelligence as a wasted asset. She would work on Sharon to get him out of the life he had chosen and on to a path that was much more fitting. He had the makings of a businessman and Lesley intended to move heaven and earth to see that he reached his full potential. In fact, that was her main aim in life where this boy of hers was concerned. He needed something to work for – work towards – and she hoped at least that this girl and the child she was carrying would be just what Lenny needed to put him on track. Lesley Scott had great plans for her only son, and she would make sure Sharon understood the importance of them.

'That was generous of him, son. Jack was always good for a few quid if you worked hard for him.'

Lenny beamed at his father; he was made up and it showed.

Lesley kept her peace as they were not in their own home, but her opinion was obvious from the look on her face.

Ivy Conway watched the other woman warily; she wasn't sure about Lesley Scott. She had a reputation as being a hard woman to cross. She didn't go out drinking often, and she didn't play bingo either. She was also a God-botherer by all accounts, never off the church doorstep. Ivy was a good Catholic, but she didn't feel the need to traipse a path to the local church on a daily basis.

Del Conway was smiling as he poured the men another glass of whisky. Lenny sipped at his, but his father knocked his own back quickly.

'To the young couple.' Del raised his tumbler and toasted his daughter and his soon-to-be son-in-law happily. The women smiled and raised their cups of tea.

Ivy was secretly annoyed because she would have enjoyed a drink herself but because Lesley Scott had declined the offer – as if she'd been offered a glass of poison from Lucrezia Borgia herself – she thought it best to do the same. Big Lenny didn't seem to take any notice of his wife's behaviour and Ivy secretly admired him for that. Big Lenny Scott liked a drink, that was common knowledge.

Sharon Conway was looking at her intended with such love in her eyes even Ivy was impressed and grudgingly admitted to herself that the boy appeared to genuinely care for her pregnant daughter. Still, she maintained her opinion that they were young and fucking stupid. But the die was cast, and all they could do now was make the best of a bad situation.

Chapter Four

'I know you didn't want a council flat, Lenny, but it's in a nice block and my mum thinks we would be mad not to take it.'

Lenny sighed heavily. He could see the logic but he just didn't want to start his married life in a place like this.

Sharon smiled coaxingly. 'Private accommodation costs the national debt – this is much cheaper, Len, and we can save and eventually buy our own place. Plus it's near me mum and, after the baby, I'm going to need her help. Especially if I'm going to get a job.'

Lenny shook his head. 'No wife of mine is going to work!'

Sharon laughed, but there was a steely edge to her voice as she said, 'Oh, get back in your TARDIS, the Dark Ages are missing you! 'Course I'm going to work. Not immediately, but after a few months. The sooner we get saving, the sooner we can buy our own home.'

Lenny knew she was right but he wasn't happy about

it at all. He walked into the ground-floor flat and looked around sheepishly. He had to admit, it was a lot nicer than he had expected. The council had been in and revamped the whole place as the previous tenant had been lying in his bed dying for a year. The place had been so filthy even the kitchen had had to be replaced. But it looked bright and welcoming in the morning light and Lenny Scott was pleasantly surprised.

'It's got a bit of a garden and all, Len – overgrown now but we can soon sort that out.'

Sharon opened the Crittall doors that led outside and saw Lenny frown as a posse of young lads screeched past on their bikes.

'I won't swallow a lot of that, I can tell you, Shaz. Fucking noisy little bleeders.'

Sharon laughed. She knew she'd won him round. It was done. She felt that all her Christmases and birthdays had come at once; she loved this little flat and she was thrilled to be near her old home, because deep down, happy as she was, she was also terrified. She was only seventeen and the thought of having her first child was a scary prospect. Not that she would tell this lump beside her that. He seemed more frightened than she did at times. But her mum said that was just men, and that was why women had the kids – a bloke couldn't cope with any of it, especially not the pain. It was really the pain that was terrifying Sharon; the way her mum talked, it sounded like shitting a rugby ball.

She shuddered and Lenny hugged her to him tightly. 'This will do us till we get on our feet, I suppose.'

He was resigned to the flat and that was enough for Sharon Conway for now.

Chapter Five

The pub was packed out, and the smell of beer and cigarette smoke hung heavily in the air. Lenny's stag night was going well, and he was now drinking a yard of ale. His friends were clapping and egging him on and he was loving the attention, enjoying this night out.

Lenny wasn't a drinker really – he didn't like the taste, if he was being honest, and didn't understand how people could drink the shit night after night. But, for once, he was getting pleasantly pissed and actually the taste wasn't that bad after a while. It was his wedding the next day and he was secretly worried he might fuck up somehow – not least by being in no fit state to attend. But the more he drank the more those fears receded. Lenny Scott usually thought everything through; he was careful in that respect. But the buzz that the alcohol was giving him felt good tonight. After all, it was his last night of freedom, as everyone kept reminding him.

Their little flat was furnished and ready for them to

move into and, as of tomorrow, it would be their home. He was excited at the thought. 'Playing at grown-ups', according to Ivy Conway, which had annoyed him when she'd said it. He pushed the thought from his head and carried on drinking, the atmosphere making him feel relaxed and excited at the same time. After tomorrow he and Sharon could do what they liked, when they liked. It was a heady feeling. Being able to take her ripe body at any moment of the day or night, with no worry about anyone interrupting them – that was going to be the best bit of marriage. They were adults at last, soon to be parents. He hoped Sharon was carrying a boy. God, but he wanted a son.

He downed the last of his yard of ale to the sound of clapping and cheers from the boys. One of them – Keith Smith, a tall, bony-looking lad in possession of a large hooked nose and known for his jokes which were funny as well as nasty – shouted out clearly and loudly, 'Strippers are here, lads.'

The men looked around, waiting expectantly for the females to come into plain sight. There was a lot more cheering and shouting from the young ones, while the older men were laughing nervously, knowing that when their wives found out there would be murders.

Suddenly, a huge older woman with a heavily made-up face came into view from a doorway behind the bar, as the music boomed out of the speakers. She was laughing delightedly as she wobbled out on to the bar-room floor wearing a red and black basque and high-heeled stilettos. Her stockings had rolls of fat hanging over the tops and she began gyrating alarmingly as she shouted out good-naturedly, 'All right, boys, which one of you is the groom?'

Lenny Scott couldn't believe his eyes; the woman was grotesque. In his drunkenness all he could hear was the laughter around him. He found himself being pushed towards her and, as she raised her arms up to put the feather boa around her neck, the sweet smell of sweat and deodorant made him feel sick. He looked around and saw everyone laughing, even his dad. But the loudest laughter was coming from Keith Smith, and Lenny sensed instinctively that this was down to him. Keith Smith had arranged this. It was just the kind of nasty stunt he would pull – he was always trying to make everyone around him look a cunt.

Pushing the woman away from him roughly, making her overbalance on her high heels, he lunged himself at Keith Smith. Never in his life had Lenny felt such a powerful anger, and never before in his life had he had so much to drink. He wasn't aware of picking up a pint glass from the crowded bar. The only thing he remembered was smashing it with all his might into Keith Smith's face.

The real strippers, a blonde and a brunette who had just walked in, watched in morbid fascination with the rest of the pub, before putting their coats back on and exiting to their waiting car quick-sharp.

Big Lenny Scott was rooted to the floor. He had

never in his life seen his son act like this. He saw
Lenny's friends dragging him to the floor, eventually
sitting on him to try and contain his anger. He shook
his head slowly in abject disbelief at his son's actions.
His boy could have a row, there was no doubting that,
but he had never been vicious for the sake of it. And
tonight of all fucking nights! Lesley would have his
balls for this. He was still feeling thunderstruck when
the Old Bill arrived – along with the ambulance.

Chapter Six

'My Lenny? Are you sure that it was *my* Lenny?' The incredulity in Sharon's voice was clear.

Ivy Conway was standing behind her in the small hallway, in her rollers and a candlewick dressing gown, unable to believe what she was hearing.

'Well, that's fucking lovely, that is! Arrested the night before the wedding. Augurs well for the future that does, my girl!'

Sharon wasn't listening to her mother; she was reeling from the news Big Lenny had delivered. She couldn't believe it. Her Lenny was a gentle giant – everyone knew that. He was one of the gentlest people she knew. But now her husband-to-be was banged up in Barking nick.

Sharon picked up the phone and dialled a number quickly. It was Jack Johnson's. She was near to tears as she told him the events of the night.

On the other end of the phone, Jack Johnson was thinking fast. He calmed her down as best he could, then he rang off. But, like the young girl who had called him, he was having trouble believing that any of it was true. He hoped it wasn't, because uncontrolled violence wasn't what he was paying that lad for. He could get a thug on any street corner. He had admired the boy's acumen, his level-headedness – it was the main part of his charm. *That* was what he paid the little fucker for, not to go round glassing people in his spare time.

Jack sighed heavily, and started to make some phone calls of his own. Wonders would never cease. It was fucking outrageous, that's what it was, and it meant he might have to have a serious rethink where the lad was concerned.

Chapter Seven

Lenny was sheepish as the wedding party stood in the church waiting for his bride to arrive. He had the hangover from hell, and he was still unable to believe his actions of the night before. He put it down to the drink – that was the only thing it could be. He couldn't hold it, didn't even like it. He was deeply ashamed and, even though Keith had refused to press charges and Jack Johnson had somehow managed to get him back out on the pavement, he still felt he had got off too easy. Keith Smith might not have been his favourite person, but he knew the stripper had just been a joke. Normally he would have seen the humour of the situation, but last night it was as if he had been possessed by a devil. As his dad said, that's why it was called the 'demon drink'! He felt so embarrassed, and the worst thing of all was he had shown himself up in front of Sharon's family. Her mum wasn't exactly his biggest fan as it was – now she would use this against him at every opportunity. He closed his eyes in distress.

The music started and he opened them to see Sharon walking down the aisle towards him. He could sense the fear and disappointment in her lovely blue eyes. Well, that was it now – he wouldn't be drinking again any time soon, he swore that to everyone in his orbit. As Lionel Richie sang 'Hello', Lenny looked into his bride's face and hoped against hope that she could see the genuine sorrow there.

Chapter Eight

Lesley Scott was eating a small plate of sandwiches and she felt like she was chewing on sawdust. The fact that her son, her Lenny, had been able to inflict that kind of damage on another human being had really hit her hard. As she looked around the Irish club in Ilford, at the young ones dancing, and the older ones settled at tables with large drinks before them, she felt the urge to scream. Oh, Ivy Conway would be loving this! She had not wanted this wedding, but then, neither had Lesley really. But Lenny was besotted with young Sharon, and she was a good girl – she couldn't take that away from her. Hopefully she would be a steadying influence on her son. Like her husband, Lesley blamed the drink for Lenny's actions. Lenny was like her: she had never liked alcohol, not the taste nor the feeling of abandonment it gave to a body. Coming from Irish stock, she knew the trouble it could cause if you got a liking for it. It destroyed people's lives.

She looked around sadly. Her husband was propping up the bar with Jack Johnson and his other cronies.

He had a large Scotch in his hand and he was laughing loudly. It was as if last night had never happened. She was pleased to note her son was drinking a shandy. She had not been looking forward to this day; if she was honest, she didn't hold out much hope for these two. For all their proclamations of undying love and affection, they were just kids playing at grown-ups, as Ivy Conway had succinctly put it. But Lesley nailed a smile on her face – after last night's debacle she was determined to front this out. She saw young Sharon slip her arms around her new husband's waist, and watched as he smiled gently and kissed her, holding her to him tightly. For some reason the sight made Lesley feel tearful. She was a nice lass, young Sharon.

The Irish club was packed by eleven o'clock, and even though he hated the fact, Lenny could see he was being hailed as a hard man for his antics the night before. Keith Smith wasn't a popular guy – he'd rubbed too many people up the wrong way.

He was relieved that everything had gone off very well, considering. Sharon looked lovely in her white dress; it was simple but it suited her down to the ground. She was a great little dresser, was his Shaz, and she had the figure for anything. The dress, which had been purchased from a stylish new shop in Ilford, fitted her like a glove and, even though there was nothing revealing, she looked sexy. She wasn't showing yet, but her breasts had filled out nicely. Lenny felt the pull of her, and decided it was time they went back to the flat; he was looking forward to his wedding night. He watched her with her friends, dancing to Wham! and he felt a surge of pride. She was his wife, she was having his baby, and he loved her.

Jack Johnson came up to him and pulled his arm gently. Lenny followed him out into the night air, nervous now.

Jack lit a cigar noisily, and puffed on it for a while before saying harshly, 'Look, son. I like you, you know that. But last night had better be a fucking one-off. Because I ain't bailing you out again, do you hear me?'

Lenny had the grace to look sheepish, and this endeared him to Jack all over again.

'I can't have loose cannons, son, not in my line of work.'

Lenny nodded; his whole demeanour was contrite, sorry-looking. 'I know, Jack . . . I mean, Mr Johnson. I can only say again, it was the drink. I ain't a fucking drinker. I don't even like it. I could cut me hands off. It is not me, that kind of carry-on . . .'

Jack held his hand up. 'All right, all right, I get the picture. Some people can't hack a drink. You are obviously one of them. But this is a warning, OK? I had to lay out some serious fucking bunce last night. Consequently, I ain't a happy fucking bunny. Do you get my drift?'

Lenny nodded, another wave of shame washing over him. 'I can't thank you enough, Mr Johnson . . .'

Jack Johnson sighed. 'Relax, son. But you need to make me believe you are a changed boy. You're on a warning, son, OK?'

Lenny nodded. 'I promise you, I will work my bollocks off.'

Jack smiled then. 'See that you do. Now, get that wife of yours home. I want you in bright and early tomorrow.'

Lenny nodded gratefully, aware of just how lucky he was.

Chapter Nine

Sharon lay in bed beside her new husband, listening to the sound of his breathing. It was a wonderful feeling being married, and having her own home. But she couldn't deny that the events of the night before had frightened her. Not that she would ever have *not* married this man of hers, but it had shown her a side to him she had not known existed. Unsurprisingly, her mum had been *very* vocal about her feelings; Sharon had just kept her head down and not risen to the bait.

She shivered suddenly. The old saying of someone walking over your grave came to mind, so she settled into her handsome new husband's body and, like many a bride before her, wondered at what the future would bring. She loved Lenny Scott with a vengeance, and she would do everything in her power to make sure their marriage worked.

Nevertheless she was unable to sleep. She put it down to being in a new home, in a new bed, with her new husband. But she was still awake as the sun came up and the estate came to life.

Chapter Ten

'They said you ain't pursuing charges, Keith, and I can't thank you enough, mate.'

Looking at Keith, Lenny Scott felt shame washing over him once more. He had really made a mess of this bloke's face and head.

Keith shrugged. He had not been an oil painting to start with, but he now looked like something out of a Hammer Horror film. Jack Johnson had offered to pay for his plastic surgery, but he would be left with a glass eye. It was hard not to hold a grudge, but what could he do? Lenny Scott was an up-and-coming Face, and Keith had to live round here. But it still burned him. Jack Johnson had referred to it as 'an unfortunate accident'; he had warned Keith off, simple as that. He had slipped him a couple of grand and wished him well. If only Keith could shrug it off so lightly. His whole life was ruined, and there was nothing he could do about it. That was the bugbear.

'Look, Lenny, it happened. Let's get over it, eh?'

Lenny Scott knew how hard those words had been

for Keith, and he admired his stoicism. He wasn't sure he could bring himself to be that magnanimous if the boot had been on the other foot. He shook the man's hand and was glad to get away from him, if truth be told.

Chapter Eleven

At six months pregnant, Sharon Scott had just a tiny bump; but, according to the midwife, the baby was fine and a fair size. Sharon felt she had been short-changed; she hardly even looked in the club. She was full of energy and she looked amazing. Her skin was glowing, and her hair was thick and shining. She had not had any morning sickness after the first two months and she had never felt better in her life.

She and Lenny were building a lovely home for themselves, and she was delighted that they were managing to save as well, thanks to her new job. They both wanted to buy a property – it was their dream. She was working in a small betting office in Green Lane and she loved it. The hours were perfect and she knew most of the clientele now. The owner, an old Jewish man called Isaac Templeton, was a dote. He thought the world of her and he trusted her implicitly. She was good with numbers and could work out a bet in her head – something that had surprised her. She had taken to the job like the proverbial duck to water.

She cashed up the till and locked the money in the safe in the office, then she went through the slips and sorted out who would need to be paid out the following day. This was her kingdom, and she loved it here. It was a good little gig for her; Isaac pretty much left her to her own devices and she enjoyed her days.

She was aware she had been offered the job through Jack Johnson and she was grateful to him. Since that terrible night before the wedding it was clear that Lenny had been doing everything in his power to show Jack that he could be trusted.

She pushed those events from her mind – she hated to think about any of it, and she knew that, without Jack Johnson fighting their corner, Lenny could have gone away for a few years.

Even though she was relieved that the charges had been dropped, she still couldn't quite get it out of her head. That Lenny was capable of such a brutal attack frightened her. Of course she knew his job was not without violence, but the debt collecting was controlled violence, more about the threat of it really – or so Lenny assured her on a daily basis. She knew he would never hurt *her*, but it lingered there between them, and that bothered her. She guessed that Lenny sometimes sensed her reticence with him now, and he was heartbroken to have caused that.

She locked up the betting office and made her way home, wondering what to cook for dinner and whether

to start painting the bathroom. Anything so she didn't
have to think of the one thing that plagued her at all
times of the day and night – especially the nights.

Chapter Twelve

Jack Johnson was over his annoyance with young Lenny Scott's actions. If anything, his mad half-hour had only enhanced the lad's reputation. Far from hindering him, it had been a great help. People were mentioning him with a different tone of voice. Jack had even observed some of the older men who worked for him giving the lad his due. No more of the good-natured ribbing – now he was an equal.

Jack had a little job for Lenny and he was interested to see if he was willing to do it. It was a bit out of the ordinary, but he needed it done fast and with the minimum of fuss. Not everyone would take it on, but he had a feeling that Lenny would. He was determined to show willing, bless him. But this was a tricky situation and would need to be handled with great tact and diplomacy. Jack poured himself a large Courvoisier brandy and sipped on it thoughtfully.

Ten minutes later, he heard Lenny's car pull into the yard, bang on time as always. You could set your watch by this kid. He was a Brahma, there was no doubt about that. Jack sat back in his chair and waited for the lad to come into the offices.

Lenny entered with his usual sheepish smile, and Jack was reminded just how good-looking he was. Yet he was all loved up with his little wife. Jack had asked around and there was not a hint of scandal about this boy taking up with any strange whatsoever. He was genuinely on a love job, by all accounts.

Lenny placed a Waitrose carrier bag on the desk, filled with money. It was a big drop – over twenty grand. He took out the bundles of notes and then he carefully folded up the carrier bag and put it in his pocket. Jack Johnson watched him, marvelling at the lad's concise movements. He moved like a boxer, fluid for all his size.

'A Waitrose carrier bag?'

Lenny laughed as he said, 'That's the Fagans for you. No wonder they have to borrow so fucking much. But it's the wife – she spends money like fucking water. They've got the biggest TV Dixons can provide – they could hardly get it in their own front room!'

Jack shrugged, smiling at the boy's incredulity. It was the Fagans of this world that kept them in bread and butter.

'What we like to hear in this game.' He didn't offer Lenny a drink; he knew he would refuse. 'Sit down, son. I need a favour from you, a favour you will be handsomely paid for. I will genuinely understand if you refuse and there will be no ill will. But you're my first port of call.'

Lenny sat down, intrigued.

Jack sipped his brandy before saying quietly, 'Be honest with me, son. Have you heard anything untoward about Billy Mason?'

He saw Lenny's face close up. It was what he expected – the lad was loyal to him as well as his co-workers, of that Jack was convinced.

'In what way, Jack?' Lenny asked carefully.

Jack smiled then, a nasty smile. 'Where shall I start, eh? My nose told me he was taking the piss somehow, I just couldn't work out how. So I had a little bird I know go round to his earns and have a chat. I then found out he was undercutting my loans and giving them loans himself. I deduced this, Sherlock, by how much they were paying him. Less than they would be paying me. Now, I am all for free fucking enterprise – as long as it ain't taking the food out of my mouth, so to speak.'

Lenny nodded. 'I thought he was up to something too, I just wasn't sure what, Jack. I wasn't about to come running to you until I had sussed it out.'

Jack could see the logic of that, and he liked that the boy hadn't come telling tales before he had the facts.

'So, what do you want me to do?' Lenny asked.

Jack Johnson was thrilled. This kid never disappointed.

'I want you to take that cunt out, that's what I want.'

Lenny Scott frowned, weighing up what had been said. 'Kill him, you mean?'

Jack grinned. 'No. I just want a really good example set. If we kill him, he's won. I want a walking reminder of his folly. I want people to know that he tried to have me over and what the consequences of such behaviour will be should they embark on such a quest. It's simple really. You fuck *me* over, I will fuck *you* over big time.'

Lenny nodded in agreement. 'Cripple him, or blind him?'

Jack laughed. Lenny was a fucking diamond. 'Bit of both, son.'

Lenny stood up and said seriously, 'I know you will reward me handsomely, as you put it, Jack.'

''Course, Lenny. And this will enhance your standing with the rest of the workforce. It means you're my main man. That in itself will make sure the collecting of your debts will be much easier. But it also means you will be the victim of envy and malice. Are you prepared for that?'

Lenny grinned. 'What do you think, Jack?'

Chapter Thirteen

Sharon had cooked a steak and kidney pie and she was very happy with how it had turned out. The pastry was perfect and it smelled divine. She was really getting good at this cooking lark, and more of a surprise was that she quite enjoyed it. She glanced at the clock and saw it was nearly seven. That meant her Lenny would be in any minute. She still felt a shiver of excitement at his arrival. She loved him so much.

She rushed into the bedroom and brushed her hair and reapplied her make-up. She made sure she always looked nice when he came home from work. Some of the girls on the estate were only a couple of years older than her and already looked like their mothers. She sprayed herself with Blue Grass perfume and she was ready for her husband's return.

As she started to plate up the meal, she heard his key in the lock and she smiled happily.

Lenny shouted from the small hallway as he took off his overcoat, 'That smells fucking handsome, Shaz. I could eat a scabby horse between two mattresses.'

She smiled. He said the same thing nearly every night, even when her food had been an absolute disaster, but she loved him for it.

He washed his hands in the bathroom and then made his way into the kitchen. The house was spotless, and the table was laid like a restaurant: napkins, the works. She was funny like that, his Sharon – she even refused to have red sauce in the house. She said it was common. He had to go along with it. The house was her domain.

The pie and mash, peas and gravy looked delicious. She was getting to be a really good cook. Even his mum was impressed, and that wasn't an easy thing to accomplish. As his dad was often heard to say, she would have found fault at the Last Supper.

They chatted amiably and ate together in complete harmony. Sharon wasn't a girl who forced opinions on you; she was quiet, willing to listen to her husband's chatter. But Lenny knew there was steeliness inside her. If she thought she was in the right she would not back down. It was one of the things he loved about her.

'Here, Len, Isaac is thinking of selling the betting office. He's had enough, I think. He is getting on, bless him.'

Lenny stopped chewing at her words. 'How much does he want for it?'

Sharon shrugged. 'I dunno. Why?'

Lenny grinned. 'Just wondered, that's all. It's a nice little earner.'

Sharon opened her blue eyes wide as she said, 'It's that, all right. I should know, I do the takings.' She carried on eating, her lovely face intent on her food.

'Listen, Shaz. I have a bit of business tonight. I will be out late. But it will bring in a good few quid.'

Sharon nodded. 'Okey-doke.'

He smiled. He loved that she never questioned him. She accepted everything he said at face value. Most girls would have wanted the ins and outs of the cat's arse. *Where you going? Who with? How long will you be out?*

'I will be back as soon as possible, babe, you know that.'

She smiled again and nodded happily. 'I know that, Len. I'm going to have a long bubble bath and an early night. I feel tired today.'

He was immediately concerned. 'You all right, babe? I can stay here, darling.'

She rolled her eyes in irritation. 'I'm pregnant, not suffering from fucking terminal cancer. I'm just tired, mate. Plus I want to watch *Dempsey and Makepeace* without you making remarks all the time.'

He laughed at her, she was such a strong character. 'OK. If you're sure, mate.'

She cut him another huge piece of steak and kidney pie as she said, 'I will be fine. Just you be careful, OK?'

He nodded. She knew he wasn't going out to wish anyone well. She was aware he was up to some kind

49

of skulduggery, and she was a woman who understood that the less she knew about his nefarious businesses the better. She was a real fucking diamond was his Sharon, and he couldn't believe his luck.

Chapter Fourteen

Billy Mason was a man who always had to have *just that little bit more*. No matter how good the earn, he always felt it should be greater. Greed was a prerequisite for a criminal lifestyle, but that depended who you were nicking from. Banks, building societies, big houses or Post Offices were seen as fair game. Council flats were seen as off limits, unless you were a junkie piece of shit. No one with half a brain nicked off their own. Billy Mason should have known that better than anyone – he had been in the Life long enough.

But Billy lived by his own rules; he prided himself on that fact. He also had a belief in his own God-given right to take any earn that he saw fit. He was confident that the men he worked alongside were too frightened of him and his reputation to even consider giving him the hard word. He was happy with his life, and he was coining it in.

Billy Mason's big mistake was that he was a creature of habit. A large man with a beer gut and Denis Healey eyebrows, he wasn't exactly the answer to a maiden's prayer, but what Billy had going for him was money and a sense of humour. He could laugh a woman into bed. He genuinely loved them – all shapes and sizes. He could find something complimentary to say to any woman he came across, even if it was only that she had nice eyes or a good set of teeth. He frequented Tiffany's in Ilford every Thursday for Grab-A-Granny night, or if you were a female, Grab-A-Granddad.

As he tripped out of his house in Manor Park, bathed, shaved and smelling of Old Spice, he was nonplussed to see young Lenny Scott on his doorstep.

Lenny smiled graciously and said respectfully, 'Sorry, Billy. Can I come in a sec, mate? I need to discuss a rob I heard about. Thought you might be interested, like.'

Billy Mason was always up for a rob of any kind, and he liked this kid. Smiling, he said jovially, ''Course, son.'

He held the front door open and followed the lad inside. Billy's house was like him – old but well looked after, all Axminster carpets and Dralon furniture, smelling vaguely of beeswax polish and Flash liquid.

Lenny went into the through lounge-diner with him; it was a typical Ilford house – practically on the pavement and no garden to speak of. High ceilings, though, and nice cornices, with the original fireplaces. Lenny approved of it.

Billy was eager to get going – it was nearly half past ten, and all the birds would be turning up at Tiffany's after the pub. It was free for women before ten thirty. He liked to get in early and stake his claim. Still, he was all smiles as he asked, 'Is this the robbery at Lloyds Bank in the high street? Because I never shit on my own doorstep.'

Lenny sighed heavily, and slipped an iron bar out of the sleeve of his raincoat.

Seeing it, Billy shouted angrily, 'You cheeky little fucker!'

Billy Mason could have a row, no one would dispute that. But young Lenny Scott could have a better one. He concentrated on the man's eyes and legs. When he left twenty minutes later, Billy Mason was barely functioning.

Lenny stopped at a phone box and called an ambulance; he had left Billy's front door ajar so they could gain entrance. He went to a mate's and washed up there – burned his clothes and changed into a new set.

He was home and in bed by twelve fifteen. He hugged his young wife to him, and she snuggled into him naturally as she slept contentedly in his arms.

Chapter Fifteen

Jack Johnson was over the fucking moon. The fact that Lenny had done a perfect job was just the icing on the cake – carrying it out that same night was an even more pleasing surprise. Lenny Scott just did what he was told, no questions asked. Not yet twenty years old and he had the nerves of an old hand. From what Jack could gather, old Billy Boy was half-blind and would walk like he was on a fucking carousel for the rest of his life.

That was the result he wanted. Never leave an enemy with the means to come back at you, but make them serve as a reminder to everyone just what your retribution would be if they decided to fuck you over. Billy Mason was a treacherous cunt. Jack had given him a serious earn but he had always suspected that Billy Mason would one day want more; he was a greedy ponce. Well, he would regret his covetous nature now. Jack took a few deep breaths to calm himself down, but it still rankled. He had trusted Billy once. He had given him a good lifestyle but that had not been enough for him: he still wanted the main chance.

Lenny drove into the yard, satisfied. He was happy with his night's work, and felt that he had done a good job. He had liked Billy Mason, but he had been given a task and he had done it to the best of his ability. He hoped that Jack was pleased with him, though he was suddenly filled with trepidation as he walked into his office. Maybe he'd gone too far. But he had been asked to teach the man a lesson and he had done just that.

Jack was smiling as if he'd just won the pools and Lenny immediately relaxed.

'You fucking little fucker!' Jack was out of his seat and pulling out a chair for Lenny. 'Sit down, son, you earned it.'

Lenny Scott was embarrassed; he had not expected this. Jack Johnson appreciated the boy's reticence – he wasn't crowing about his job like many others who would have given him a blow-by-blow account, acting like it had been a fucking royal event, trying to prove they were indispensable. Young Lenny just did it, and that was that. He had seen this boy's potential and Jack loved it when he was proved right.

'You've done good, Lenny. I'm impressed. I told you what I wanted and you did it without fear or favour.'

Lenny smiled sheepishly.

'Who did you bring on board?'

Lenny frowned. 'No one. I thought this was best kept in-house, so to speak.'

Jack grinned; this was just getting better and better as far as he was concerned. 'What, you did it on your Jack Jones?'

Lenny nodded. ''Course, Jack. I wasn't sure you would want it done mob-handed, like. It was just me. I gave him the business, though. He ain't going anywhere for a long time.'

Jack Johnson sat back in his comfortable chair and wondered at a lad like this; he was clearly a fucking one-man war machine. Billy Mason was no easy mark. He could take care of himself – that was why he had worked for Jack in the first place.

'Well, Lenny, I can't tell you how fucking impressed I am. Especially as you went all on your tod. I want you to know that I won't forget this. I am going to bung you a serious drink – ten grand cash. And, listen to me, son, if you ever need anything you just have to talk to me, all right? I will give you the earth on a plate. You proved yourself to me, mate, not just as a worker, but also as a man I would be honoured to have running my businesses.'

Lenny Scott felt almost tearful at Jack's words. This was what he had dreamed of, what he had always wanted – the big in, the rite of passage.

'I think the world of you, Jack, you know that. You gave me the opportunity to have a serious earn. I will never forget it.'

Jack Johnson looked at the huge young man sitting before him. The lad was humble, he was grateful. And evidently he was also a dangerous little fuck.

'Son, listen to me. You're on the road to greatness, and I want you right beside me.'

Lenny nodded his huge head, and he smiled as he said, 'Thank you, Jack. Appreciate that.'

Jack Johnson looked at Lenny Scott and thanked Christ and all the saints for dropping this boy into his lap and not someone else's.

Chapter Sixteen

Ivy Conway was fit to be tied and her daughter was already sick of listening to her.

'He apparently crippled a man, nearly blinded him. It is all over the pavement.'

Sharon Scott sighed. Lenny had explained everything to her, as he had guessed she would hear about it eventually. He had shown her the ten grand cash and said that it was just a means to an end, that Billy Mason had had Jack over and it was a lesson needed. It had all sounded very reasonable the way that Lenny explained it. At least that is what she chose to tell herself anyway, even if there was a bit of her that found it very frightening. But it was her husband's business not hers, and the sooner her mother realised that, the better for everyone.

She turned on Ivy and shouted, 'Oh, give it a rest! It's his fucking job. If you want to keep coming round, Mum, my advice to you is to keep your opinions to yourself. Lenny is my husband. I love him, and I will not hear a bad word about him, OK?'

Ivy Conway was so shocked she actually stepped away from her daughter.

'I mean it, Mum. He is trying to give us a good life. You know as well as I do that he works for Jack Johnson, and that means he will never be a choirboy.'

Ivy Conway looked at her beautiful daughter and realised that she had lost her. Her beautiful baby was as caught up in Lenny Scott's world as he was. She also knew that no good could come from it; everyone had to pay the price for their sins one day. Sharon looked into her mum's eyes as she said seriously, 'I mean it, Mum. Lenny is my family now. I will *not* have a word said against him.'

Chapter Seventeen

Lenny Scott's standing in his community had only grown since the incident with Billy Mason. He felt himself how everyone he came into contact with treated him with respect. But Lenny, being Lenny, didn't let it go to his head and that too was noticed and appreciated. He still gave people their due, and that was something the men in his world really *did* respect. Too many had made enemies when they had gained their reputations. It was a pleasure when a person remembered that good manners cost fuck-all, and it went a long way.

Lenny was at the betting office picking up his wife, and Isaac was all smiles as he invited him into the office for a chat. Lenny was only too pleased to accommodate the old man – he had been very good to his Sharon.

'You know I am selling up?'

Lenny nodded. 'Yeah, Sharon said. Nice little earner. I wouldn't mind it myself.'

Isaac grinned. 'Good. Because it's yours, son.'

Lenny looked bewildered. 'Sorry?'

Isaac grinned again, and he was genuinely pleased as he said, 'It is a gift, from Jack Johnson. It will be all yours by the end of the month.'

'Fucking hell!'

Isaac laughed delightedly as he said, 'I hope they do, son. I ain't had much fucking luck up here.'

Chapter Eighteen

Big Lenny Scott was made up for his son. He was so young and he already had the world by its balls. Big Lenny was as proud as punch. Lesley, on the other hand, was, as usual, the prophet of doom.

'I can't believe it, Dad, it's all in my name. It's mine – well, mine and Sharon's, obviously. She will run it, you know, do the day-to-day. It's a fucking right little earner. I reckon we will be able to start looking at houses within the year.'

Lesley looked at this son of hers who she loved with all her heart, and feared that she'd lost him to the Life. 'So, you get this betting office for nearly killing a man, is that it?'

Lenny looked at his mother and said quietly, 'Yeah, Mum, that's about the strength of it. But do you know what? I am going to tell you what Sharon told her mum. Keep your fucking nose out. I don't live here any more. I'm a grown man with a family and I will earn for my wife and my kid in any way I can.'

He looked at his father, pleased to see that he was

of the same mind. Nevertheless, Big Lenny chastised him. 'No need to swear at your mother, son. But I admit you are in the right. I admire you. You're a big lump with a quick brain. A lethal combination in our game. I'm made up for you.'

Lenny grinned. 'This is just the start, Dad. I really love my job, you know. Jack Johnson's so good to me. I trust him. He's a good man, a decent man.'

As Lesley watched her husband and son talking, she realised that her boy was as far gone from her as if he had been struck dead. That he could talk to her like that! Her husband was acting like he was the Christ Child, and everyone was treating her as if she was visiting royalty. She was devastated. Her handsome son had had the brains to go to university, and he had thrown it all away. Now he was a thug, no more and no less. And a vicious thug at that.

He had crippled a man and he had not even had the excuse of the drink. Keith had been because of alcohol – she had made herself believe that. But this last one she couldn't justify to herself, however hard she tried.

She watched as her son talked about his plans, and she wondered at a future that was based on violence. Never in her life had she felt so low, so disgusted with her family. Even Sharon, who had turned a blind eye to what Lenny had become. It was as if Lesley had never really known her son. Her dreams were dead, and all she had now was the promise of a grandchild to give her any hope for the future.

Chapter Nineteen

Ivy was delighted with things. After her initial shock at the Billy Mason incident, she had done what Sharon had asked and accepted the situation. If she was honest, it was mainly because Ivy was enjoying her newfound celebrity as Sharon Scott's mother. She loved the way people who had never given her the time of day before broke their necks to ask how she was and how her daughter was. It was heady stuff.

Sharon was on her time now, and she looked amazing. She still had a tiny bump and loads of energy. She was training up a girl to manage the shop while she was off with the baby, but she was saying how she would be in and out, keeping her eye on 'the business', as she called it. It was a dream come true in many respects. Just eighteen and she had a lucrative career and the world at her feet.

Ivy would always have her reservations about Lenny Scott but, in fairness to him, he had the makings of a good provider. He was a nice lad and he loved her girl – that was evident.

'I can't believe it, Mum. And Isaac, bless him, kept it quiet. He is made up for me and my Lenny. Reckons I can run the place with my eyes closed. Said I was a natural because I can work out the bets in me head. But, honestly, once you get the knack, it's easy as pie.'

Ivy looked at her husband and they laughed together for once. It was good to see their girl so animated and so happy.

'You got a fucking good one there, girl, but I don't need to tell you that.'

Del Conway had asked around and he knew that young Lenny wasn't putting it about; he had nothing but a good rep in every way. For all the boy's grandiose notions, if he hurt his girl, Del would shoot the fucker dead – that was a given. His daughter was his flesh and blood, and no one would ever make a cunt out of her, no matter who they were. The hardest fuck in the world couldn't argue with a gun. He genuinely liked young Lenny and, as long as taking care of Del's baby girl was his main agenda, they would get along like a proverbial house on fire.

'We can start looking at houses now, because we have a legitimate earn, like. It is so exciting.'

'I bet. Lenny has really made his mark, Sharon. Honestly, everyone is talking about how well he's doing.'

Sharon preened. She was so proud of her husband. 'I better get home – he likes his dinner ready, does

65

my Lenny! Tonight I am doing him liver and bacon, his favourite.'

Ivy nodded. 'Liver is good for the baby, darling, plenty of iron.'

Sharon was amazed to hear that. 'Really? Oh my God. I love it! Wait till I tell my Lenny.'

She left her mum and dad and they both watched her with love in their eyes.

'Well, Del, I will hold me hand up. I was wrong about that lad.'

Derek Conway hugged his wife to him, as he said seriously, 'Time will tell, Ivy. Time will tell.'

Chapter Twenty

Jack Johnson had made the decision to give Lenny Scott the job of overseer. The boy was good with numbers, and he was good with people, given his knack for treating everyone with the utmost respect. He was being given the chance of a lifetime – it was unheard of in this business. He was big, he was handsome and he was liked, even by the punters. That was a bonus. Lenny Scott could charm the money out of people. He was so nice he could make the usual rabble feel bad about trying to give him a swerve. Jack Johnson had big plans for this boy. He had known he was worth something and he had been proved right.

Not one person had felt the urge to retaliate about Billy Mason, which spoke volumes. He was liked, was old Billy, but he wasn't respected. He had mugged off too many people for that to ever happen.

Now Jack had this lad who he could mould, who he could teach his craft to. He knew he had a one-off in young Lenny Scott. He was that rarity: hard as fucking nails when he needed to be, but a regular

John in his everyday life. Men like Lenny were few and far between, thank fucking God! The world was his oyster, and Jack envied him the life he had ahead of him. But he knew Lenny admired him, respected him, and was grateful to him. It meant the world that Lenny Scott revered him – it showed him the boy's loyalty, and it also made him feel good about himself. Jack Johnson liked that he was seen as a man of stature, not just by the general populace – the majority of them were prize cunts – but by someone like young Lenny; it meant a lot.

The phone rang and he picked it up quickly. It was Lenny Scott apologising for not being able to make the meet. His wife was in labour and he was at the hospital.

Jack laughed loudly as he said, 'That's exactly where you should be, boy. I wish you luck.'

Truth be told, he appreciated that the boy put his family first. It said a lot about him, about his priorities and about his decency. Jack hoped the baby was a boy; he understood that was what Lenny wanted. He deserved a son – he was a man who would appreciate a male child.

Chapter Twenty-One

Lenny Scott Junior was born at eleven fifteen at night; he weighed nine pounds and had the look of a mini sumo wrestler. Lenny Scott was overwhelmed with the feeling of love as he held his son in his arms for the first time.

His Sharon had just got on with it, like she did everything else in her life, with hardly a word out of her. As he had watched her push his son into the world, he had been genuinely amazed at the power of women. Seeing his son's head emerge, he had finally understood the strength of the female sex. There was no fucking way on earth a man could have lived through something like that. It was brutal, it was violent and it was the most beautiful thing he had ever witnessed in his whole life. His Sharon was stronger than most men he knew. She had shat his son into the world and acted like it was nothing. He was so proud of her. Seeing her like than, so brave, with her legs in stirrups and his son appearing amidst the blood and the gore – his heart had burst with love and pride.

'He is fucking beautiful, Shaz. You did a real good job, girl.'

Sharon Scott laughed at her husband's words. It had been painful but she was amazed at just how easy it had been. According to her mother it was the most traumatic thing a woman could ever experience. She had enjoyed it in a funny sort of way. Childbirth was a means to an end, and what an end! She had a fine, handsome son. It had been worth every second of her labour, especially seeing her husband's absolute amazement at the child they had created. This was one of the best days of her life. They were here, they were together and, most importantly, they were finally a real family.

Sharon Scott had never felt so valued, so needed in her whole life. It was as if she had lived every moment for this, for this child and for the chance to make a family for herself. This is what she had dreamed of since she was thirteen years old. Since she had fallen in love with Lenny, all she had wanted was their baby, their own child. Now they had him. Leonard Derek Scott. She had had trouble talking her husband out of calling him Leonard Scott the Third. Imagine the shit that would have brought him at school! But she laughed at her husband's obvious pride in his son and heir, as he kept referring to him.

The grandparents were also doting, as they should be, of course. After all, he was the first grandchild on both sides.

Ivy was overwhelmed with the love she felt for the tiny scrap of humanity her daughter placed into her arms. Never having had a son, she was shocked at the rush of love he engendered inside her.

But it was watching Lenny with his son that really warmed everyone's hearts. He was absolutely besotted with the child, even getting up with Sharon while she breastfed the boy, making her cocoa and tea and watching in amazement as she nourished their son.

'I never imagined, Sharon, how fucking fantastic nature is really. I can't get over seeing him attached to you like that, and I don't even feel jealous!'

She laughed with him, pleased that he was so interested in the baby and still so in love with her. She felt blessed. If anything, this child had brought them even closer together.

Chapter Twenty-Two

Jack Johnson was giving Lenny more and more responsibility, and Lenny was rising to the challenge. It was as if becoming a parent had made him grow up even faster. He had the look of a man now, a grown-up, fully fledged male. He was getting bigger as well, filling out even more, if that was possible. Jack saw the way the women looked at him, but he had never seen the lad once take the bait. Sharon was a lovely little thing, but if he were Lenny's age he would be off with anything remotely pretty with a pulse. That was Jack though – Lenny was obviously a much better man than him. Or a complete cunt; it depended how you looked on it really. Jack was a man who thought that youth and opportunity went hand in hand. As his old mum used to say, one day you would be old for the rest of your life – many a true word and all that.

As he looked at young Lenny, he felt a moment's envy for the boy's youth and happiness. Everything was possible when you were his age – the world was your oyster and the years were still passing slowly.

'You know that you're going to be given a piss-up for your birthday, don't you?'

Lenny nodded and smiled. He had large, white, strong teeth, and when he grinned he looked like a model in a toothpaste advert.

'I know. I hope it ain't a late one. I like to help with the baby. You want to see him, Jack. Bigger every day. He's smiling as well now – and it ain't just wind!'

Jack laughed. 'You're getting a right fucking Mary Ann!'

Lenny grinned. 'I can't help it. He fascinates me.'

Jack raised a bushy eyebrow. 'So it would seem!'

Lenny got the message that it was time to talk about other things than his boy.

'Anyway, I'll be there and I'm going to put a few quid behind the bar. Do the fellas good to have a night out with no women to tie them down and, as it's Sunday the next day, they can all sleep in.'

Lenny nodded. He wasn't really looking forward to it if he was honest. He wasn't happy about leaving Sharon and his newborn son. But then she had her mum who was never off the doorstep and if Jack wanted to give him a birthday night out with the men, he couldn't refuse it. Plus, Jack was right – the lads deserved a night out occasionally, and this would cement his place as head of the firm, after Jack. His quick mind combined with his sheer size was something only a few of the men possessed. His accuracy with mathematics and fractions was something most of the workforce now depended on him for. He knew how lucky he was, and he was not going to nause it up.

He would have a great night; after all, it was his birthday.

They busied themselves sorting out the money paid, and the problem payers who might need a bit of an incentive. They sent round different men for different problems. But there was one family that was starting to get on Jack's tits, and he wanted young Lenny to pay them a call personally. He had had enough shillyshallying; they were taking the fucking piss now. Lenny assured him he would sort it on his way home. Jack smiled happily. That was exactly what he wanted to hear.

Chapter Twenty-Three

The Dornans were one of those families that seemed never-ending. There were Dornans all over the show; they were numerous, and they were troublesome – especially the ones who still lived with their mother.

Jane Dornan was a big, blowsy blonde, with a constant cigarette hanging from her mouth and the manners of an Irish navvy. No one really liked her on the estate, but everyone was wary of her and her extended brood of children. Janey, as she was known, kept a filthy home that was jam-packed with all the latest gadgets, and her children were dressed in designer clothes, all obtained thanks to thievery and loans. Janey's children were what the police called a 'one family crime wave'. If the older ones weren't drug dealing or on the rob, it was the younger ones terrorising people and generally wrecking anything they came into contact with.

Lenny and Sharon lived on the same estate as them, although they were on the other side, so the Dornans were not too much of a nuisance. Plus everyone knew who Lenny was and who he worked for, so he and his were automatically given a swerve. Even so, Lenny Scott was no fool, and he had asked one of the younger lads, Cyril Brock, to accompany him on the visit. The eldest son, Reggie Dornan, was twenty-five, and had a rep to be wary of. He had just come out after doing a three for malicious wounding. Lenny parked the car outside the council house and sighed in annoyance. These were actually nice houses. Built after the war, they were spacious and had good-sized gardens. Most of the homes were well kept, but the Dornans' place looked like an abortion. The windows were wide open, with loud music blaring out into the early evening twilight. There was rubbish piled up out the front, and two ferocious-looking dogs barked over the dilapidated fence. Lenny remembered what his nan used to say: people make slums not houses. She knew what she was talking about all right.

'What a dump, eh, Len? It's like something from a documentary.'

Lenny laughed at the truth of Cyril's statement. 'Let's hope Old Mother Dornan is dressed today. Usually she's got half her business hanging out, and that is not a pretty sight!'

They got out of the car and stood on the pavement, surveying the dogs warily. Lenny hated people who used animals for intimidation. These were German Shepherd crossbreeds and were fine-looking animals. Going to the boot of the car, he took out a small stun gun which looked like a torch. All you did was pull off the top where the light was supposed to be and you were left with a perfectly reasonable-looking but dangerous weapon. He set it to high, and took both the dogs down in seconds. Their screeches of dismay were loud enough to bring the music to a stop and the Dornan family out of the front door mob-handed. Lenny was pleased to see a young girl rush to comfort the dogs. At least one of the family seemed to have their priorities right.

'What the fuck you doing?' This was from a dark-haired boy of about eight years old with a pierced ear and a New Romantics haircut.

Janey was watching warily; she recognised Lenny Scott and she wasn't about to queer her own pitch until she had to.

Her eldest son pushed her out of the way and, cuffing his little brother hard around the head, he yelled, 'What have I told you about keeping your big fucking trap shut?' He looked at Lenny and his worker and nodded respectfully. 'Can I help you, Lenny?'

Lenny smiled that charming wide smile that made him look so amenable and handsome.

'I hope so, mate. Reggie, ain't it?'

The man nodded. He was big, this Reggie, and he had obviously been working out in the nick. He was dark-haired and brown-eyed, good-looking in a gypsy-type of way. Lenny imagined the women loved him; he had the look of a rogue, and a lovable one at that.

'It's you I need to talk to really, Janey. You are into us for over seven grand, and Mr Johnson likes regular payments, see? Now he has asked me to politely request said payments.'

Janey felt sick to the pit of her stomach. She knew her Reggie would hit the roof over this little lot; he was a funny fucker like that. He couldn't stand what he called 'unnecessary aggravation'.

'I will have it next week with a bit off the back, I give you my word.'

Lenny laughed. 'Oh, well, that's all right then. You hear that, Cyril? She is giving me her word.'

Cyril Brock laughed on cue. 'You're off the books now, Janey. No more loans of any description. You pay double every week until this debt is cleared. If you miss one week I will be back and this time I will be mob-handed and I will take the debt in kind. Do you understand me?'

Janey had to nod in agreement; she knew the neighbours were listening and enjoying seeing her brought low like this. Seeing Lenny Scott himself told her that she had taken the piss about as far as she could. It was Reggie who was worrying her now. He'd obviously read too many books inside. Since he had got out of the nick, he was like a born-again choirboy, talking about serious earns and convinced that it was better to maintain a low profile and keep the Filth at bay. He didn't want her to bring unnecessary attention to the house; it was a show-up, if only she could see that.

And now Lenny Scott and his trained monkey were putting the hard word on her in front of the whole fucking street. She could quite happily cry with the frustration of it all.

Reggie was fuming; he stepped forward and, looking into Lenny's eyes, he said quietly, 'Seven grand?'

Lenny nodded. 'Three grand is fucking late-payment fees. She is her own worst enemy. It ain't like she ain't got the dough. She just never wants to pay.'

Reggie sighed a deep, angry sigh and Lenny felt a moment's sorrow for him. He couldn't imagine being dragged up by someone like Janey.

'I will sort it, mate. I know what she's fucking like. Give me a week and I will try and get a good lump paid off, bring the debt down.'

Lenny smiled and held out his hand. Reggie shook it firmly and, strange as it seemed given the circumstances, they both realised they liked each other.

'Listen, Reggie, pop round my drum tonight. I might have a bit of work to put your way, if you're interested.'

Reggie smiled and said, 'About eight OK?'

Lenny nodded and, giving Janey Dornan one last ferocious glare for good measure, he left the scene as quickly as possible. He had done his job, and all was right with the world.

Chapter Twenty-Four

Lenny Scott sat at his kitchen table holding his sleeping son in his arms. Reggie Dornan was sitting opposite him, sipping a bottle of Sol. They were chatting amiably when Sharon came in to take the baby; it was time for him to go to bed. Reggie watched as Lenny kissed the sleeping child gently, and saw the smile he exchanged with his young wife. He felt a stab of jealousy at the way this man lived. The flat was decorated beautifully and spotlessly clean. There was really nice furniture and fittings everywhere, and even homemade cake visible under a glass dome on the counter. It was certainly an eye opener.

'Right, my little man's off to bed, the wife will be watching that pile of shite *Dallas*, so you and I can have that chat in peace.'

Reggie smiled; he felt at ease with this man, which was strange considering how they had met.

'That was nothing personal today, and with respect your mum . . .'

Reggie held his hand up to indicate he understood exactly what Lenny was trying to say. 'Honestly, Lenny, you are preaching to the converted where she is concerned. I mean, I love her – I have to, she is my mum – but she is a fucking nightmare at times.'

Lenny nodded in sympathy; he wouldn't like a mother like that.

'Thing is, she was only fifteen when I was born. She's only forty and she's had eight kids. My nan – her mum – is not exactly what you would have called a good role model. Mum was dragged up, and she is now dragging us lot up.' He laughed ruefully. 'Some of the stunts she's pulled. You wouldn't believe the half of them. Once, she locked the gas bloke in the cupboard, in the pitch dark. He never came near again. She had boyfriends over the years who always disappeared with her purse, the telly or, in one strange fucking case, a fish tank full of tropical fish!'

Lenny was laughing now; it was said in a really jokey, funny way and he understood that this was Reggie's way of coping with it all. If you could laugh, it couldn't hurt you too much.

'She has had a hard life really, Lenny. No one to depend on, you know? Never had anything or anyone that lasted. Except us kids, of course. She can be a really nice person when she ain't had a drink. I mean, whatever people say about her, she loves her kids.'

Lenny didn't know what to say. This was getting a bit deep for him now.

81

Reggie took a long pull from his bottle of lager and said quietly, 'So what's this business you were talking about?'

Lenny sat forward in his chair and looked intently at the other man. He was clearly genuinely thrilled at the prospect opening up for him. He felt instinctively that Reggie Dornan wouldn't waste any chances he was given – he was far too shrewd for that. Lenny had asked around, and word on the pavement was he had kept his head down and done his bird without a murmur. He was also said to be close-mouthed and that was imperative in this game.

Lenny opened another couple of beers and Reggie smiled to see him carefully binning the used bottles. His old woman had him well trained, and why not? He lived there too.

Lenny settled himself back in his seat and said seriously, 'Whether you take this job or not, you don't tell a fucking soul I asked you, OK?'

Reggie nodded impatiently as if that was a given.

'I have been given a debt that will be difficult to reel in. They are being seriously slippery, but I have tracked the fucker down, and I need someone the person concerned doesn't know to lure him out and give him the business with me.'

Reggie digested this bit of information before saying quietly, 'Who is it?'

Lenny grinned mischievously before answering. 'Jason Prior.'

He saw Reggie's eyebrows shoot up and understood that this was something he needed to think about. Well, he could wait.

'Fucking hell, Lenny. He's a fucking nutter.'

Lenny nodded his agreement. 'He is also into a friend of Jack's for forty grand. Jason has it – he is a fucking premier drug dealer, for fuck's sake – but he is also a gambler. Never liked gambling myself, a fucking mug's game. Some of the stories my Sharon tells me about the cunts that frequent the betting shop. Anyway, I digress. How do you feel about it?'

'Shooters?'

Lenny laughed then, a genuine belly laugh. ''Course! No one would go near that ponce without being tooled up.' Lenny sipped his beer daintily before saying, 'Jack bought the debt for five grand. That means he owes us forty-five smackeroons. Your cut will be about five grand – danger money, if you like. But I understand if you don't want any part of it. He is, as you say, a fucking nutter.'

Reggie took a deep gulp of his beer before saying, in a sunny manner, 'Fuck it, that's good poke. I'm in.'

Lenny grinned and stuck his hand out. 'Put it there, mate. Now we have to strategise. See how we can lure the fucker out into the open.'

'I can actually help with that, Lenny. He is knocking off my little sister Geraldine.' He saw the amazement on Lenny's face and he laughed then. 'He's trying to get her on the bash, I think. This is working out well for us all.'

'Let's drink to that.'

And they did.

Chapter Twenty-Five

'Oh, Mum, will you stop fucking going on!'

It was Saturday night, Lenny was out with the lads, and Sharon's mum was doing her head in. Anyone would think Lenny was out every night of the week to hear Ivy Conway go on. He rarely went out without her – they had a babysitter and he would take her out for meals or to a nice wine bar. She was pleased he was out with his mates; it made a nice change for her as well. She could watch what she liked on TV instead of bloody *Match of the Day*, and she could have a relax in a nice bath and catch up on her beauty regime.

Ivy Conway didn't like it. She was a woman whose own husband had been and done whatever he liked because she had not had the sense to nip it in the bud. She didn't want Sharon to make the same mistake – that was all she was trying to say. But Sharon was having none of it.

'I'm sorry to get cross, Mum, but I am a married woman now. I have my own home, a baby. It's up to me what I think and how I choose to live my life. And Lenny is bloody good to me.'

The problem was, Ivy knew the girl was speaking the truth. Lenny Scott was a wonderful provider, and he adored his wife and his little son. There had never been a hint of scandal about him. It occurred to Ivy that maybe she was a bit jealous of this daughter of hers. Sharon already had more than Ivy had ever hoped for. There was a small part of her that resented this and Ivy felt ashamed.

'Do you want a glass of wine, Mum? I'm having one as soon as this little sod goes to bed.'

'That would be lovely, darling.'

She watched her daughter take her grandson from the room and sighed heavily. Sharon had turned the council flat into a palace, all big TV sets and sound systems, wall-to-wall carpets and expensive drapes. It looked like something from a magazine. Well, it had been copied from a magazine! She pushed the thoughts away, but there was no denying that her daughter was certainly a very lucky girl. A very lucky girl indeed. Del thought the sun rose and set on this pair, and he doted on that child. So did she – she loved her grandson. But this feeling that her daughter was getting it all a bit too easy plagued her. No one could be this lucky. Happiness came at a price; everyone with half a brain knew that.

Sharon came back into the room with two glasses of ice-cold Chardonnay and, giving one to her mum, she clinked their glasses gently as she said happily, 'Cheers.'

Ivy sipped her wine, and wondered at how her daughter had developed this habit of drinking wine in the evenings. Honestly, she was like something off *Play for Today*.

But she drank the wine anyway.

Chapter Twenty-Six

Geraldine Dornan was a very good-looking girl with a spectacular figure, and a mouth like a Tilbury docker. Lenny could certainly see what had attracted Jason Prior, especially if he was looking to rent her out. She had the face of an angel, and the body of a porn queen – a lethal combination by anyone's standards. She was on the ball though; she was listening intently to her brother as he explained what she had to do, and he respected the fact that she asked how much she would be getting paid for it.

Jason Prior surrounded himself with the lowest of the low. And so even though he might be mob-handed, none of the people with him would put themselves in danger to save his sorry arse. He lived just off the Railton Road in Brixton, in honour of his black roots. He was a mongrel – a bit of Jamaican and a bit of Mexican, with a white mother. He had grown up a troubled boy and he was now a seriously damaged man. Jason was known as a good earner; he could get his hands on literally any pharmaceutical known to man, which he did regularly.

The downside of Jason Prior was that he was a degenerate gambler and, like all true gamblers, he had no conscience. When he lost large amounts, he was not inclined to pay the debt. He would be angry with himself for losing, and with whoever gave him the means to blow said money. He would be granted the honour of writing a chit, promising to pay the poke back within fourteen days, and he would then tip whoever had given him the tick a resounding bollocks. He was fast running out of people to borrow from, even though they knew he was good for it. His failure to pay had caused a lot of bad feeling and resentment. Jason was a man for whom that upset meant absolutely nothing – he genuinely didn't care. Or, in his words, he didn't give a flying fuck. If they wanted their money, let them come and get it, simple as that. If they were mug enough to give it to him, then that was their lookout. Jason was a ferocious man, with an even more ferocious temper, so the odds on that happening were slim. He was a bona fide nutter, and that had always been his biggest asset as far as he was concerned. But now he was finally going to pay the price for his bad behaviour and, as the word was coming from Jack Johnson this time, Jason needed to wise up. Jack only asked once.

This was what was going through Lenny's mind as

he saw Geraldine waiting outside Jason's house. It was a nice drum – with three storeys it had the look of a substantial property. Lenny was waiting over the road, his shotgun hidden by his long overcoat. He nodded towards Reggie who was opposite him. They had agreed it would be best to come at Jason from the front and the back to give him no chance of escape. He was a slippery fucker at the best of times.

As Jason tripped happily down his front steps, smiling widely at Geraldine, both Reggie and Lenny moved into place. Geraldine started running away and Jason stopped short for a few seconds, wondering what the fuck was going on with her. It was then that he saw Lenny Scott and the shotgun. For a few seconds his face registered shock, and then he dropped to his knees, pulling out a weapon of his own. As he took aim, both Lenny and Reggie started blasting him. He didn't have a chance. No one on the street took any notice – they just moved away as quickly as possible.

While Lenny kept an eye out and watched the dying man at his feet, Reggie ran into the house and collected all the money he could find. Within ten minutes it was over. The money and the guns were in the boot of the car, and Lenny and Reggie were laughing their heads off; they had pulled it off without a hitch. It was a great feeling. The euphoria was infectious and they were almost hysterical.

When they got back to Jack's yard they were still high as kites. It was such an adrenaline rush. Neither of them cared that Jason was dead and gone. In truth they were pleased. Jason Prior had been an accident waiting to happen. He had mugged off too many people, laughing while he did it. No one would be mourning him.

Chapter Twenty-Seven

'You took a fucking chance there, Len.'

Lenny shrugged; he had expected this from Jack.

'Reggie is a good bloke, plus his share of the earn is going to pay off some of his mother's debt. I'd heard good things about him, thought I would give him a try-out.'

Jack Johnson grinned. 'A nice fella, I admit. Must be hard coming from a shower of shite like that lot.'

Lenny nodded. 'Thing is, he ain't been seen around because he was obviously banged up. So I put him nearest to Jason, thinking if he noticed him he wouldn't click anything, you know? Jason would expect trouble from me, but not from an unknown face. And Reggie looks like butter wouldn't melt.'

Jack nodded. 'Good-looking lad, no doubt about that. And your hunch played out.'

Lenny grinned. 'I think we can use him, Jack. He's got a bit of savvy. Knows the score. He is willing and all – appreciates the chance we are giving him. We need some new blood. No disrespect, but a lot of the blokes are getting on a bit, and the younger ones ain't exactly fucking contenders for *Mastermind*, if you get my drift. We could do with a few team leaders. He is good with people as well, very respectful.'

Jack laughed loudly. 'Fuck me, when's the wedding? All right, you've convinced me. And, joking aside, you have a point. Time fucking rushes by, son – remember that. Old Sammy is sixty-five this year and still at it. Sounds like a fucking sewing machine when he has to run away. But he's still game. I wouldn't fancy my chances with him in a straightener, old as he is.'

Lenny knew Jack spoke the truth. But this was a young man's game, and the older blokes still thought it was the 1960s. They had no finesse whatsoever. He was wise enough to keep that little gem to himself though – Jack wasn't exactly a spring chicken either and Lenny knew his place.

'There was eighty-five grand taken from Jason Prior's residence. You did good, son. I will make sure you and Reggie get a decent bonus. It will be all over the Smoke now, and that can only be good for business. People will be on the blower, selling off difficult debts, which is just what we want. That's where the big earn is. I think you and that lad can sort them.'

Lenny nodded his agreement. It was exactly what he had been hoping for.

Chapter Twenty-Eight

The pub was packed with men celebrating Lenny Scott's birthday. The atmosphere was all friendly camaraderie and jokes. Big Lenny looked around and felt pride in this lad of his. He had really made his mark on the world. He watched as the men were respectful to his boy, and saw how respectful Lenny was in return. He always gave people their due. He had a great nature – though, as everyone knew, he wasn't a man to cross. Now he had taken out Jason Prior and that just added to his mystique.

He was a son to be proud of, in every way – he was a good provider, a wonderful father and he was also a fucking nice man. Big Lenny Scott was thrilled with his boy, and he didn't care who knew it either.

The drink was flowing and the men were starting to get raucous now. Lenny was still known to not really be a drinker except for a few beers and so he was not offered serious alcohol – everyone remembered the Keith incident too well. But he was happy for everyone else to indulge and he liked a laugh and a joke.

One lag, Freddie Forester, was regaling them with stories of his sexual exploits when he had been a youngster. Freddie had been, by his own admission, a seriously good-looking fucker, and there were still traces left in his old face. He had a magnificent head of hair and, though he was heavy these days, he looked fit for his age.

'This bird had tits like fucking rugby balls. The face on it wasn't anything to write home about, but the body . . .' Freddie rolled his eyes and everyone laughed at him. 'So, there I am, going at it like fucking no one's business, and her fucking dad walks into the room. Straight up! I nearly fucking passed out. And she goes – all bored, like – "Your tea's in the oven." I nearly missed me fucking stroke! I finished up and was straight out of there, I can tell you!'

The men were roaring with laughter and Lenny joined in although he caught Reggie's eye and smiled, shaking his head at the way Freddie carried on. Reggie Dornan was laughing hard with everyone else but Lenny could see that, like him, he found the story irritating really. These kinds of tales were outdated now. Nevertheless, Freddie could make a cat laugh and that was his secret: he was a genuinely funny man.

Lenny walked outside to get some air. It was like a sauna in the bar, and he felt the need for a bit of quiet. He had drunk more beer than he usually did and he felt light-headed. Reggie followed him, and they stood round the side of the pub, smoking together.

'I just wanted to say thanks, Lenny. For giving me the chance, like. I needed a fucking job, you know? I was boracic.'

Lenny shrugged. 'Plenty more where that came from, mate. You did good. Jason Prior wasn't an easy first. But it did the job in more ways than one, see? Jack is inundated with difficult debts now. That will be me and you sorting the harder ones. You are up for this, I take it?'

Reggie looked into Lenny's eyes and smiled slowly. 'What do you fucking think?'

Lenny grinned.

'My mum's over the moon, so I had to put the hard word on her. I don't think I will ever make her exactly respectable, but I told her to sort herself and the fucking kids out. She had them – she has no choice but to take care of them. I was fuming that Gerry – my sister Geraldine – was nearly put on the bash by that cunt Prior. I really gave Mum hell to pay over that. But she is what she is.' He shook his head.

Lenny knew Reggie was ashamed of his family and he was trying to let Lenny know that he was aware of their status. He was doing everything he could to try and bring some kind of normality into his brothers' and sisters' lives. Lenny would have done the same thing. He grabbed the man's shoulder and squeezed it, saying, 'You are a good bloke, and now you're in with us lot you should find it easier to get things done. As for your mother, she is a lost cause, I think. You will have to concentrate on the kids – that's all you can do.'

Reggie put his hand over Lenny's and squeezed it gently. 'I do appreciate this, mate.'

It was said low, and Lenny pulled away quickly. He felt embarrassed suddenly and, laughing, he said loudly, 'Bit pissed, I think, don't you?'

Reggie smiled and nodded, and went back inside the pub. Lenny stood there and lit another cigarette. His hands were shaking. He had never felt such a powerful pull towards anyone before in his life. He shook his head, as if trying to clear it. That could not have just happened. But he knew that something *had* happened and he didn't know what to do about it. He wasn't a fucking shirt-lifter. It was the drink – he was never good with alcohol. It was just a misunderstanding. All the same, his mind was asking him why was he sorry that Reggie Dornan had gone back inside the pub? Why did he still want to feel his touch on his skin? What the fuck was wrong with him? He had a wife and a child, that should tell him everything he needed to know.

He went back inside, so shaken he decided to order a large brandy. He noticed that Reggie was nowhere to be seen. Swallowing the burning liquid down quickly, he stood and cheered with the other men as the strippers started their routines. He loved his wife and he was just drunk. That was all it could be.

He kept his eye out for Reggie all the same, but he had clearly gone home. Lenny was disappointed, and that bothered him more than anything.

Chapter Twenty-Nine

'Let me do that, darling. You will have the baby up with this racket!'

Sharon was happy enough to cook her husband a bacon sandwich when he got in. After all, she was his wife, and it meant less clearing up as well! He was one messy fucker, and the place would look like a pikey camp if she didn't take over.

Lenny sat at the kitchen table and watched as Sharon made his sandwiches and a pot of tea. He loved her; he loved her with all his being. So what had happened to him to make him feel like he had earlier in the evening?

'Did you have a good night, Len?'

He nodded. 'Rather have been at home with you, darling.'

She smiled happily at his words.

'How was the little man?'

Sharon sat at the table. Now she had cleared the kitchen, she could relax. 'He was as good as gold, Len. We are lucky with him, you know. Some of the horror stories I hear about babies not sleeping!'

He listened to her prattle on, but all the time he was thinking about Reggie Dornan. About his face, his eyes, his physique. Even his hands, feeling the thrill once more as their skin had touched briefly. What he couldn't understand was why he had not beaten the man to within an inch of his life. Surely that is what he should have done?

Sharon Scott looked at her big, handsome husband and, leaning over, she kissed him softly on his lips. Then, suddenly, without any preamble, Lenny was picking her up bodily and the next thing she knew they were naked and he had her on the kitchen table. The excitement was overwhelming and she enjoyed his attentions, glad that he still had this need of her as powerfully as she did him. She had heard that after a kid men often lost interest in their wives, but this was not the case with her Lenny. She closed her eyes and let the good times roll.

Chapter Thirty

Reggie Dornan was lying in his bed awake and he was a worried man. He should not have drunk so much tonight – then he would not have made a pass at Lenny Scott. But he sensed that Lenny – whatever he might be telling himself – was as up for it as he was. They had had a rapport from the minute they had clapped eyes on one another.

Reggie felt sick with apprehension; he knew that many men denied their real instincts. Christ Himself knew, *he* had tried to push his feelings aside for years. It had taken a stint inside for him to admit what he really was and, in that way, it was the best thing that could ever have happened to him. But that didn't mean Lenny was likely to embrace the truth of his real nature.

He lay there with his arms behind his head; he knew that sleep wouldn't be coming to him any time soon. But he couldn't stop pictures forming in his mind – pictures of Lenny naked, of kissing him, feeling the sheer strength of him, his hardness.

Over the other side of the estate, Lenny Scott was lying with his wife asleep in his arms, thinking the exact same things, and hating himself because of it. The baby cried and Lenny got up to see to his son, glad of the distraction. As he quietened him down and felt the love he had for his child, he wondered again at what kind of man he really was. He was an unnatural bastard, and that frightened him. What other weaknesses had he lurking inside him? He sat in his son's bedroom holding him tight, and he cried bitter tears.

Chapter Thirty-One

Lenny Scott was waiting outside Reggie's house and he watched warily as Reggie climbed into the passenger seat of his BMW. He noticed that the house was already looking better – tidier at least. Janey Dornan waved in a friendly manner but Lenny didn't bother to acknowledge her. She wasn't in the least put out and that made him stifle a smile. She really was a piece of work. He drove away quickly. Reggie didn't even say a good morning, just sat beside him quietly, waiting to see his reaction to the events of the night before. Lenny felt that was a good move.

He glanced at the man beside him quickly. He was good-looking, with thick, dark hair and piercing eyes. They had a look of each other in some ways. Both were big, muscular and dark. He could smell Reggie's aftershave and underneath that was the smell of his fresh sweat. It was heady stuff for him suddenly. It was as if now Lenny was acknowledging this other nature he had, his eyes had opened to everything about Reggie Dornan he felt attracted to.

Lenny took a deep breath before saying, 'So, come on then. Explain what all that was about last night.'

Reggie laughed quietly. Then, lighting up two cigarettes, he passed one to Lenny.

It was the intimacy of the act that threw Lenny. A part of him knew he should be putting the cigarette out on Reggie's face, not accepting it without a second's thought. But he pulled on it deeply as he waited for Reggie to explain to him. He was in a quandary because this was so far away from his usual behaviour – he wasn't sure what he was supposed to do, how he was supposed to act, to be.

'Look, Lenny, you know as well as I do what was happening last night. And I think somewhere inside you have known since we first met what was going to happen at some point.'

Lenny didn't answer; he manoeuvred the car on to the A13 and drove out towards Essex.

'Where are we going?'

Reggie sounded nervous. And so he should; he had no idea what Lenny might think, say or even do in the cold light of day.

'Southend. I have to see a bloke about a debt that Jack needs pulled in. As I told you, Jason Prior has opened the floodgates. Debts that were once liable to be written off are now seen as viable again. That is good news for Jack, ergo, that is good news for us.'

Reggie nodded. He liked the 'us' in that sentence, and he relaxed a little. He looked out of the car window, but he could feel the pull of the man beside him and hated that he was this way. It was so difficult in the world they inhabited. It was seen as a weakness, as an aberration of sorts. He should never have tried it on with Lenny, even though he believed it was something they both wanted. He had guessed that Lenny Scott had never acted on his impulses. People like Lenny lived a life of normality as a matter of form. Now Reggie had stirred him up, and this could go either way. Lenny was quite capable of killing him over this, so great would his fear be about anyone finding out the truth.

Reggie had been celled-up with a lag from North London; the old boy was doing a lump and a half. They had some good times, and he had made Reggie see that it wasn't unnatural. How could it be, if they were both quite happy to indulge? But he had also warned him that in their world it was a definite no-no. Men had been scalped for less, and he made sure that Reggie understood that fact. Reggie had also learned that some men were only queer in prison and, once they stepped back out through the gates, they were as straight as an arrow once again. With him it had just been sex though – he had liked the fellow, but he had not felt like he did now about Lenny Scott, who had filled his mind day and night since they had first crossed paths. And Reggie was sure that Lenny reciprocated those feelings, whatever he might try to tell himself.

'I've been there you know, Lenny. Denying what I really was. What I felt. I have been fighting these feelings since I was fourteen. God knows, in our world, our environment doesn't exactly make it easy for us—'

Lenny interrupted him angrily. 'What are you fucking on about? We were pissed. That is all it can be. I have a wife I love, and a little boy I fucking adore. This cannot ever be a part of my life. Think about it – I have a family and responsibilities, for fuck's sake! If my Sharon ever even thought . . . That's without Jack Johnson and the others . . .'

Reggie was quiet for a few seconds before he said gently, 'Who are you trying to convince, Lenny? Me or you?'

Lenny sighed heavily. This was so far out of his remit it was almost impossible to believe. That he was even considering it . . . But there were no two ways about it – considering it, he was.

Chapter Thirty-Two

Sharon was happy. As she busied herself with sorting out the small betting office, she wondered at just how fantastic her life was. Her mum loved having the baby while Sharon worked and she actually appreciated her time away from her little boy. She enjoyed being back in the real world, and being a productive member of the family. It felt good to earn money, and it was all for their benefit, so they could buy a decent place. They had discussed it over and over: they would wait and buy a house that they could do up and stay in as a family until the kids – and they wanted more kids – grew up.

It was a dream come true and sometimes she had to pinch herself at just how lucky they were, her and her Lenny. Then, last night, that amazing sex had proved to her once again that they were meant to be. God, but she did love her Lenny, no matter what her mum tried to insinuate. Ever since that misunderstanding with Keith Smith, not to mention Billy Mason, her mum had had a hard-on for Lenny. In fact, at times Sharon almost felt that her mum was a bit jealous of her, even though she would never admit it.

She had her dad working with her in the betting shop now – that had been Lenny's idea. He worried about her there alone and she understood that. They did brisk business, and it was all cash, so she knew the dangers that presented themselves in the world they inhabited. But, as her dad said, 'Who would be cunt enough to rob Lenny Scott? They would have to be on a death wish', which made her laugh, but also pleased her. She felt safe being Sharon Scott. People treated her well, and even the hard women on the estate were pleasant to her. It felt good to be so looked after, so taken care of in every aspect of her life. Unlike her mother, she didn't think that luck had to be paid for at some point. She didn't feel that every time something good happened to her she should look over her shoulder.

Her mum really pissed her off at times. Her dad said because her mum was a pessimist she always felt that something bad might happen, but Sharon felt that it went deeper than that. She could almost sense the resentment in her mother every time they purchased something for the house or they talked about their plans for the future. They had plans – big plans – and they would work together as hard as they needed to see them come to fruition. Unlike her mum, Sharon was a working partner in her marriage – and she had a knack for the betting shop. She had been taught well by old Isaac, and he was pleased to see the young couple have the opportunity to better themselves. Unlike her mother, of course, who seemed to think this was all a precursor to a mighty fall. It hurt Sharon to think that her mum wasn't thrilled to see her only child doing so well, and at such a young age too.

She sighed heavily. She knew she had to forget about it. That was her mum, a prophet of doom. Her dad said she was always the glass-half-empty sort, his old woman, never half-full. It was her nature, and there was no changing her. Fuck knows, he had tried over the years. Catholic guilt, that was what was behind it apparently. But it still hurt and, though she loved her mum, Sharon had to be honest and say she was starting to get on her nerves. She wondered why, when everything was going so well, there was always something to bring you back down to earth. Without realising it, Sharon was echoing her mother's thoughts entirely.

Chapter Thirty-Three

Southend was empty. It was the end of the season and in the dim daylight it looked scruffy and unkempt. The seafront only ever really looked good when the night fell, and all the flashing lights and glamorous colours attracted the eye.

'We're early, Reggie. Let's go to the cockle sheds and get something to eat in the Crooked Billet. They do a handsome fish and chips in there. Sharon and me used to come here a lot when we was courting.'

Reggie stifled a smile; it was such an old-fashioned word, 'courting', but then he knew that Lenny had an old-fashioned streak. As they drove back towards Leigh-on-Sea, the North Sea looked grey and ominous in the darkness of the day. It was going to storm, and a few drops of rain started to hit the windscreen. When they got to Marine Parade, the heavens opened and a flash of lightning lit up the sky. The thunder was rumbling and they knew that soon the storm would be overhead.

'You and Sharon have been together a long time, haven't you? I mean, considering your ages.'

Lenny nodded, not at all sure he was happy discussing his wife with this man who was his . . . His what? Potential friend? Boyfriend? Lover?

Reggie understood his predicament and changed the subject. 'Look, Lenny, I apologise if I was out of order last night. If I got the wrong signals.'

He was offering Lenny an out and they both knew it.

Just then a tremendous clap of thunder crashed overhead and they both laughed as it had made them jump.

'Right fucking pair of hard men we are, leaping out of our skins over a thunderbolt!'

Reggie laughed with him; the atmosphere between them was changing, getting lighter. Lenny pulled up in a narrow back street and they got out of the car. They went up a small pathway and Lenny opened the front door of the ground-floor flat with a key. It took him a while to do it, the rain was so heavy. They both stepped inside quickly. The place was a wreck, and Reggie looked around him in wonder. He felt a stab of fear suddenly. Was Lenny going to take him out here over what had happened, in case Reggie told anyone?

Lenny could almost see the thoughts as they flashed through Reggie's mind. Peeling off his wet jacket, he threw it over the arm of a dilapidated armchair, and then slowly he started to take his clothes off.

Reggie, realising what was going on, went to him

111

and held his huge hands either side of Lenny's head. Then he pulled him towards him and kissed him deeply.

Lenny kissed him back, amazed at the strength of feeling washing over him. It was done now; he had burned his boats. And, by Christ, it felt fucking good.

Chapter Thirty-Four

Jamie Ryan was in his fifties, but he looked good on it. He was much taken with expensive suits and hand-made shoes. From Irish stock, he had the dark good looks of his forefathers. He had also inherited their strength and sense of purpose.

He had started life as a bank robber, and had the good sense to invest his money in clubs, pubs and other drinking establishments. He could pass for legitimate and that was exactly what he wanted to do. He very rarely made a mistake and, when he did, it rankled with him. Now he had made a major one and the knowledge had been eating at him like a cancer.

He was sitting in the back of one of his clubs on Southend seafront and he was setting about rectifying said mistake. He liked the look of these two, and he had heard good things about Lenny Scott. If Jack Johnson trusted him, then that was good enough for him. Jamie and Jack had known each other for years; they had run about the streets of East London together, their arses hanging out of their trousers and bombs dropping overhead. Oh, they went way back.

He smiled at the two huge young men, envying them their youth, and the future that lay ahead. He didn't like getting older, and he was well aware he was a laughing stock, as his girlfriends seemed to be getting younger.

'So, I hear great things about you, Lenny. The Prior business was a coup, all right.'

He liked that the lad acknowledged his words with a small nod, without feeling the urge to discuss it, especially his part in it. That told Jamie this kid could keep his trap shut.

'Can I get you boys anything?'

Lenny shook his head. 'No, really we are fine. We had lunch in Leigh-on-Sea.'

He looked around the office, impressed despite himself. This was what he wanted – this kind of legitimate set-up that would bring him money and respect.

'OK, then. The business I want to discuss goes no further than us and that is imperative.'

Lenny and Reggie nodded in unison and Jamie had the thought they could be brothers.

'I did a cuntish thing a few years ago. A very cuntish thing. I lent eighty grand to a man I thought was a mate. He took the money, and he ran with it. Invested it wisely, and then stiffed me for my stake. He was last seen on his way to fucking Colombia, and I am sure we are all aware of what the attraction was there!

Anyway, I hear through the grapevine that he is back, only he is in Marbella. Built a stonking great big drum and base for himself and living the proverbial life of fucking Riley. New wife – a Colombian tart, apparently – the usual bollocks. I want him taken out and I want my poke back. Now, no one is willing to do this little errand for me because of the man's reputation with the South Americans. Like they would give a flying fuck – they deal with whoever is available! There is no sentiment in the drug trade, believe me. Now, are you interested?'

'How much?'

'You keep the eighty grand, and I put twenty on top. You have my word.'

Lenny digested this information for a few seconds before saying, 'Who is it?'

Jamie Ryan looked him straight in the eye. 'Christopher Steel.'

Reggie was heard to whisper 'Jesus Christ' under his breath.

Lenny Scott leaned forward in his seat and said seriously, 'You arrange flights, accommodation, et cetera. I might want to bring a couple more lads out there, and I will need time to plan it properly. I want to be located outside of Marbella, in the countryside. I think the only way to get this done is to lure him out to us.'

Jamie Ryan couldn't believe his luck. 'You're up for it, then?'

Lenny grinned. 'Oh, yeah. I'll be in touch within seven days, and I'll talk you through what I have decided to do and how much it will cost you to bankroll it all.'

He stood up, and held out his hand; Jamie Ryan was impressed at the firmness of the lad's handshake. If he pulled this off, his future would be secured for ever. But he knew that Lenny Scott was as aware of this as he was, so the thought was left unsaid. He admired the lad's bravery, because Christopher Steel was not a man to cross lightly. He was a vicious, violent cunt, and that was when he was in a good mood. They had been friends for years, and to think that he had had him over was one of the biggest irritations of Jamie's life. Steel would not be expecting this little get-together, and he hoped that it worked out in Lenny Scott's favour. Which would then mean, of course, that he had got his revenge. It was a win-win for Jamie; all he had to do was pay out if, and only if, the trip paid off. He was thrilled at his own acumen. Minimal outlay, maximum benefits – the kind of deal he had always liked. He had written off the eighty grand, so he would wipe his mouth and let that lad collect it. If he managed to take that cunt Steel out, it was worth every fucking halfpenny.

In the car, Lenny was smiling grimly. 'We can do this job between us, Reg, and we can make some serious bunce. And, on the plus side, we get a few days in sunny Spain in an isolated farmhouse.'

Reggie couldn't believe the way things had turned out for him. On the one hand he was thrilled to bits, but there was another side to all this that was only just beginning. They had to be careful, so very careful. He shrugged mentally. That was a worry for another day. Placing his hand on Lenny's knee, he squeezed it gently and, when Lenny placed his hand over his, that seemed to settle it for both of them.

Reggie was happier than he had ever been in his life. He looked at Lenny Scott and felt the pure maleness of him, and he knew that he would take any chance to be with this man.

Chapter Thirty-Five

'You and Reggie are like the fucking Thompson Twins, all you need is Snowy and Tintin.'

Lenny grinned easily; he was used to people remarking on their friendship. It was funny really, but because they were both so masculine no one even suspected anything untoward was going on.

Jack Johnson picked up his brandy and knocked it back in one, then he motioned to the barmaid to refill his glass.

'I know. But we have a lot in common. Plus I trust him, Jack. He gets what I mean, and he is shrewd. Natural, really, I suppose.'

Jack nodded sagely. 'Oh, yeah. You are a great fucking team. I like him, he's a good kid.'

They were in The Volunteer pub in Barking. Reggae was blasting out from Flanagan's Speakeasy, the club attached to the side of the public house, but they were in the lounge bar with a few other men having a business drink. The trip to Spain was completely hush-hush, so that was not on the agenda this evening.

Reggie came back from the men's and slipped into his seat quietly. He had fitted into the firm perfectly: he was good-looking, could have a fight, and he was liked. His friendship with Lenny Scott had been noted and taken on board. Reggie Dornan was going places, simple as that. Tommy King and Davey Boy Harris were with them tonight. Both were good collectors who concentrated on the council estates.

Two young men walked into the bar; both were dressed like New Romantics and had glitter on their faces and eyeliner on their eyes. Lenny judged them to be about eighteen years old.

Tommy King looked at them in disgust. 'Fucking real, ain't it? Fucking shit-stabbers out with normal people.'

Jack laughed at the man's outrage.

'In my day, Jack, they'd have never got past the fucking door. Fucking animals.'

Davey Boy was nodding in agreement. He was a small man with a big temper and an ill-fitting wig that no one ever mentioned.

'You're right, Tom. You seen these adverts for this Aids fucking malarkey? That was brought here by that lot. Fucking poof's disease. I can't believe they have the front to walk about like they do. Imagine your son putting on make-up! You would knock the cunt out, wouldn't ya?'

Reggie laughed, then he said, 'I think that's just the fashion now, guys. It don't mean they are queer as such.'

119

The older men looked at him askance and he turned to Lenny for help.

Lenny was laughing loudly as he said, 'He's right. It's the fashion.'

Davey Boy started laughing too. 'Can you imagine going round to collect a debt dressed like that?'

Tommy waved his hands in annoyance. 'You telling me that Boy George ain't an iron hoof, Lenny?'

Reggie grinned. 'Even I would have to give you that one, Tom.'

Jack spluttered through his laughter, 'And what about Liberace? My mum loved him but I'm sure he's queer as a ten-bob clock.'

Tommy was still annoyed. 'They should be put down, it's unnatural. Even the fucking Bible condemns it.'

Lenny grinned cheekily as he said, 'It also said "Thou shalt not steal or covet thy neighbour's wife"!'

Everyone knew that Tommy was a robber in his day, and that his wife had caught him in bed with the next-door neighbour. They were all laughing now, even Tommy.

'Don't remind me! She brings it up twice a week, and it was over ten fucking years ago! She still earholes me about it.'

The talk went back to matters of business, but Reggie and Lenny were reminded of just how precarious their positions would be if their secret came out. Lenny could not believe that he was willing to take such a chance just to be with a man he had known less than two weeks. It was unbelievable really. He caught Reggie's eye and they smiled slightly at one another. He knew Reggie was thinking the exact same thing.

Chapter Thirty-Six

'Oh, that smells handsome, Shaz. You got enough for Reggie? His mum's idea of cooking is to raid the fucking chippy.'

Sharon grinned happily. ''Course. There's plenty, mate.'

Reggie smiled his thanks and sat at the table. He looked at the little boy propped up in his highchair gnarling on a crust of bread and butter. His whole face was shiny from the spread and he gave them all a gummy smile. A few minutes later, Sharon placed huge platefuls of Irish stew in front of them and Lenny and Reggie tucked in immediately.

'This is good, Sharon. I wish my mum bothered to cook. It is so nice to have a proper cooked meal, you know?'

Sharon sat down; she had mashed up a small bowl of food for the baby and, as she was blowing on it to cool it down, she said, 'According to your sister Geraldine, you're the cook in your house. A good one too, from what I've heard.'

Reggie busied himself seasoning his food for a few seconds. 'Nothing like this, Sharon – I wish.' But actually he knew he was a better cook than she would ever be. Trying to make sure his younger siblings had a decent plate in front of them had perfected his skills.

Lenny got up and opened them both a beer. Reggie took his gratefully and watched as Lenny poured his wife a glass of wine. This house was so civilised, it was like being in a TV programme.

'I've got to go away, darling. A bit of business. If anyone asks, you have no idea where I have gone, OK? This is important, Shaz. It is a lot of money if I can pull this off – enough to get us looking for a decent property.'

Reggie watched as Sharon nodded at her husband without a second's hesitation. She trusted this man with her life, that much was obvious.

'Oh, Len, have a guess what I heard today? The cab rank by the betting office is going up for sale. The Greek bloke who owns it has had enough. But it's a good earner – I nipped in with me dad and looked at the books. Cash business, so you can imagine how much he must take under the table.'

Lenny looked at his wife with interest. 'Who would run it?'

'Well, we would, of course. But I thought we could stick your dad in there. Keep it in the family, like.'

'Fair enough. Look into it. If I am still away, you talk to Jack and he will set you right, OK?'

Sharon was over the moon and, as she fed the baby, she felt a feeling of complete happiness wash over her. She was so very lucky. She had a beautiful baby, a beautiful home, a handsome husband who loved her and now she would also have two businesses.

'How long are you going to be gone?'

Lenny shrugged. 'Not sure, darling. But I will call you often.'

'OK, mate.'

Reggie was amazed at just how compliant she was. No *where you going? Who with? What for?* This was a girl who trusted her husband completely. If only the poor cow knew.

Chapter Thirty-Seven

Sometimes Sharon wondered at her friendship with Geraldine Dornan. They were such different people yet they got on like a house on fire. She wondered if it was because of the friendship between Lenny and Reggie. They had become best mates overnight it seemed. She was pleased about that though. Reggie wasn't one for going out drinking all the time and he was not a womaniser either. Sharon understood that in the world they lived in womanising was the norm for a majority of the men. She knew that Lenny loved her and, in the years they had been together, he had never once caused her a minute's upset.

Geraldine had got involved in a bad situation with Jason Prior, and she had explained everything to Sharon; about how exciting he had seemed at first and how she had finally realised that he'd been using her all along. That had hurt her so much, because she had believed he cared for her. Geraldine had a way of explaining things that made them feel normal – not scary. She was sensible, Sharon supposed. She certainly didn't sugar-coat anything though – she said it the way it was.

Sharon wasn't a fool; she knew that her husband had taken Jason Prior out, but she did what she always did with unpleasant facts and just tried not to think about it. After the Keith Smith incident it was the only way she'd been able to live with the knowledge. As far as she was concerned, Lenny had his reasons, and that was pretty much good enough for her. Unlike her mother, she didn't feel the urge to go in and out of the cat's arse looking for hidden agendas. Plus she trusted her husband; he would always make sure she was well cared and provided for.

Geraldine was making little Lenny laugh, and Sharon smiled at her son's obvious pleasure. Gerry was very good with him, and he had more than taken to her.

'I would love a baby of my own. It must be great having someone who loves you unconditionally, you know? So dependent on you.'

Sharon laughed and said in the voice of a much older woman, 'You don't think that when they are up all night teething. Though, to be fair, my Lenny does his share. I am lucky with him in that respect.'

Geraldine grinned. 'Wish he had a brother!'

They both laughed at that.

'You will find someone, a good-looking girl like you!'

Geraldine smiled, but she knew her family name would be off-putting to most men. It was hard living her mother down. She said as much and Sharon felt for her friend.

'None of that matters if a bloke really cares for you, Gerry.'

Geraldine sighed heavily. 'I love me mum, but sometimes I fucking hate her. Especially when she's out in the street fighting with the neighbours! Honestly, her mouth!'

Sharon couldn't help smiling. 'She is funny though at times, Gerry.'

Geraldine Dornan grinned then, and her beautiful face was shown to its best advantage. She really was a good-looking girl.

'I laugh, Sharon, but deep down I could fucking muller her myself. But, you know, for all her shouting and swearing, she loves us lot. She ain't had the easiest of lives, as Reggie is always pointing out. Thankfully, since he's been home she has calmed down a lot.'

Sharon busied herself making a pot of tea; she could hear the pride Geraldine felt for her brother in her voice.

'Him and my Lenny have really hit it off. I've never known Len to have such a close mate before. I think it's good for him, you know? I suppose it is because they are such similar people.'

Gerry was holding the baby up in the air and she said loudly, 'They even bleeding look alike. Everyone remarks on it.' She laughed in a naughty way as she said, quietly, 'Here, you don't think Mr Scott slipped my mum a length do you? I mean, she was hardly fucking Snow White in her day!'

Sharon laughed; she felt a bit guilty, but Geraldine was funny, there was no doubt about that.

'Don't let his mother hear you say that, she is such a Holy Joe!'

She realised what she had said and she was surprised at herself. But Geraldine did that to a person. She made you as irreverent as she was.

'I don't know how you stand it. She's like the voice of doom all the time. She could take the joy out of winning the pools, that miserable old bag.'

They were laughing again and, as Sharon placed the teas on the table well out of baby Lenny's reach, she said seriously, 'Fancy a day out shopping tomorrow?'

Geraldine nodded in appreciation. 'That sounds right my cup of char.'

Sharon smiled as she said, 'And no thieving, all right?'

Geraldine rolled her eyes as she said placatingly, 'I promise.' Then, looking down at the baby on her lap, she said in a childish voice, 'Your mummy is so straight! What on earth is she doing married to your daddy?'

They were laughing again; Geraldine was as good as a tonic, and Sharon loved having the company, especially while her Lenny was away.

Chapter Thirty-Eight

It was hot in Spain, and the farmhouse they were staying at was remote and well equipped. They also had use of a 4x4 and a small family car – something that would blend in, and had Spanish plates. It was the first time abroad for both of them and they were like schoolboys. They had applied for one-year passports at the Post Office and, before they knew it, they had been on their way. It was an education for them both. Marbella was starting to take off, and it was a paradise to the likes of Lenny and Reggie.

They had found their mark in no time, and were amazed at the lack of security around him. Even his villa was approachable. It was absolutely outrageous that a man could put himself on display like that. But, as Lenny reasoned, Christopher Steel thought he was untouchable what with his Colombian contacts, etc.

They were sitting outside at a small table, eating bacon and eggs that had been cooked by Reggie. They were enjoying the time alone together; it was like a honeymoon and they could forget the rest of the world for a few hours at least. Lenny had never felt like this in his entire life. It was as if he had been asleep and had finally woken up to the real world. He looked at Reggie as he wolfed down his food; he was tanned and muscular, as Lenny was himself. There was a pool that they were delighted with, and where they had already had a few encounters that left Lenny flushing red at the thought of what he was capable of with this man. This handsome man who he could talk to for hours, and whose body felt as if it was a part of himself. How could his life have changed so dramatically in such a small space of time?

If he had not met Reggie, would he have never known these feelings? Yet he still loved his wife, still desired her. It was confusing and exciting at the same time. He had not even really tried to fight his feelings, if he was honest with himself. He had wanted Reggie Dornan since the first time he had laid eyes on him; he just had not understood the attraction. If Reggie had not been so forward he wondered if it would ever have occurred to him that he had fallen in love with another man – fallen in a big way for his physique, his eyes, his hardness.

Reggie grabbed his hand suddenly and said happily, 'Stop questioning it, Lenny. Just enjoy it.'

Lenny smiled that crooked smile he had. 'You a fucking mind reader?'

Reggie fluttered his eyelashes girlishly and said in a high voice, 'I am where you're concerned.'

Lenny laughed and they finished their breakfast, happy in each other's company.

Chapter Thirty-Nine

Christopher Steel was dark-haired and dark-eyed. He was a tall man, without an ounce of spare fat on him because he worked out a lot and he was vain. He also liked the best of everything, and that included his women. He had a lovely wife – a Colombian associate's sister, so marriage it had had to be. No kids as yet, though he had a string of mistresses of every nationality. That is what he liked about Marbella: it was cosmopolitan. You could get a fuck with anything from a Russian bint with cement tits, to an Irish girl with red curls and green eyes. It was a wonderful life all right, and he was enjoying every second. Not that his wife, Maria, thought that, of course, and she was very vocal about it as well. She was a spoiled cunt, that is what she was. But her brothers were not men even *he* would chance making an enemy out of. They were important in their country and they loved their pretty little sister. Christopher wished he could say the same – her voice went through his head these days. He should knock her up really, give her a couple of kids. If ever a woman needed a hobby, she did.

He pulled on his linen jacket and adjusted the cuffs, admiring himself in the mirrored wardrobes. This villa was built on a grand scale like the ones in Colombia. He had learned a lot about how the rich should live. That was the great thing about dealing in such huge quantities: the money was phenomenal and also endless. It was all about supply and demand – and cocaine was very much in demand these days. It was the drug of choice for anyone who needed to give their night out a little lift. He wasn't averse to a snort occasionally himself.

The great thing about Spain was the Filth were more corrupt than Idi Amin, and there was no extradition with the UK. He was just a few hours away and the fucking Old Bill couldn't touch him. He was a lucky boy.

He walked through his spacious home and, as he descended the sweeping staircase, he saw Maria getting ready for a shouting match. Her big brown eyes were flashing hatred and, as she walked quickly towards him, he slipped around her and out of the front door. He was laughing his head off as he strolled casually towards his Mercedes.

He wasn't laughing when the gun was pushed into the back of his head and he was told to shut his fucking trap and drive. He could not believe the audacity of these fucking people. Then he realised the accent had been a London one, not Spanish, and his heart sank down to his boots. He had thought it was a kidnapping, and now he had a feeling he would have been better off with that scenario. For the first time in many years he felt a stab of fear, but he wasn't a pushover and this pair of fuckers would know that before the night was over. If he was going down, he wasn't doing it without a fight.

He glanced in the mirror and saw the large, dark man in the back was smiling at him slightly. He was amazed at how young the lad was, but he was a lump, and no mistake. Christopher drove where he was told. Outside of town he was ordered to pull over and he did. Then he felt a blow to his head and he was out like a light.

Chapter Forty

Lesley Scott and Ivy Conway were like a pair of harpies and Sharon was fed up with the both of them. They were united today on finding out where Lenny was and, as Sharon didn't know, she wasn't in a position to enlighten them. Not that she would have told them had she known anyway, and they were both old enough and ugly enough to understand that.

'Look, you two. For the umpteenth time, I. Don't. Know. Where. Lenny. Is.' She sighed heavily. 'What bit of "I don't know" don't you get?'

Lesley was annoyed at Sharon's obvious sarcasm and she wondered at how she could· *ever* have thought this girl would be a good influence on her son. It seemed she was the opposite, letting him run amok and do what he liked. Lesley was frightened for him; she knew he had made a name for himself and, even if her husband thought that was the best thing that could happen to him, *she* didn't. She knew that when people made it to the top of their game, there were ten more people waiting in the wings to take their place. It was the law of the pavement.

'So, if something were to happen to the baby, God forbid, you can't get in touch with him. Is that what you are telling me?'

Sharon closed her eyes in distress and nodded. She didn't tell her she would get in touch with Jack Johnson – this mad old cow was liable to turn up there and read him the Riot Act. Lenny would love that. Jack Johnson wouldn't be too pleased either, she would imagine.

Ivy looked at Lesley while the information she had been given sank in. She collapsed on to the nearest chair, and she looked beaten, vulnerable. For a few seconds, Sharon's heart went out to her.

'Whatever he's doing, it must be dangerous, if even *you* don't know where he is.'

Sharon put the kettle on again for yet another cup of tea.

'I never know where he is, and I don't ask, Lesley. It's a pointless exercise. If he wanted me to know, he would tell me.'

Her words annoyed her own mother, who said angrily, 'And you are happy with that, are you? He just waltzes in and out of here at his leisure and you don't question any of it?'

Sharon turned to look at her mother and her face was hard as she said slowly, 'That is *exactly* how it is, Mum. And, do you know something?' She was bellowing

136

suddenly at the top of her voice. 'That suits *me* down to the fucking ground! Now let it go, for fuck's sake.'

Both the older women were shocked into complete silence. This wasn't the Sharon they knew, the sweet girl who was all for a quiet life. This was a woman grown, who was telling them in no uncertain terms to mind their own business.

Ivy was the first to find her voice. 'Well, I never . . . That you could talk to me like that . . .'

Sharon held up her arm like a traffic officer as she said, in a very determined manner, 'Well, it is time you all understood that me and Lenny have our own home, a family, and we do not have to answer to anyone. *Anyone* at all. Am I making myself clear?'

She lit herself a cigarette and she took a long pull on it before saying evenly, 'Now, who wants a cup of tea?'

Ivy and Lesley exchanged glances and Sharon knew that she had made her point. It had needed to be said and her Lenny would back her to the hilt when she told him. She wasn't a schoolkid any more.

Chapter Forty-One

Maria Steel was asleep in her suite of rooms when her maid Consuela heard sounds from the master bedroom. She sighed, relieved. If the master was home, then the mistress would be happy the next day. This was a difficult household to work in; they were very volatile people and she was worn out with their antics. She went back to sleep unaware that there were, in fact, two men in her master's bedroom, and they were robbing the safe.

Lenny and Reggie were impressed with Steel's house; it was like something from a Hollywood movie. They had opened the safe easily enough, and were searching through the contents, finding two hundred grand and some good watches. They took the money but left the rest. They weren't gas-meter bandits, after all. Reggie glanced through the documents in case there was anything interesting, but they were just deeds to the house and paperwork for the cars – nothing worthwhile for them there.

They left the house as quietly as they entered it,

laughing once they were out of danger. It amazed the men that Christopher Steel was so bloody open to attack. Even a fucking amateur could have done him. No one could argue with a shotgun, no matter how fucking hard you might think you were – it was a known fact. He had gone down in their estimation. How could you respect a cunt? Reggie said as much.

Lenny laughed at his outrage. 'Well, we've done our bit. Now it's time for a holiday!'

'He was a hard fucker, though – fairness where it's due. Took two fingers off before we got the safe combination. I wonder what state he will be in when we get back to the farmhouse.'

Lenny shrugged. He didn't really care. 'Hopefully he'll have bled to death. The sooner he's gone, the sooner we can start to enjoy ourselves.'

Reggie grabbed Lenny's thigh and squeezed it contentedly. 'Are you happy, Len?' It was said quietly, with meaning.

Lenny smiled slowly and said, 'I am, as it happens. Very happy.'

Reggie grinned. 'Good.'

Chapter Forty-Two

Christopher Steel was lying on the filthy floor of the barn and he was fuming. His hand was screaming with pain; they had taken off his middle- and forefingers with bolt cutters and it had fucking hurt. It was throbbing and he was losing a lot of blood. All this over eighty poxy grand. He could have paid that fifty times over and not missed it. But his greed had been his downfall, as his old mum had predicted all those years ago when he had half-inched his little brother's birthday money. He felt the sting of tears and blinked them away hastily. But he felt such futility at how he had ended up, trussed up like a kipper and destined to die in a shithole like this. He supposed they would bury him deep and that would be the end of it. He tried to sit up, but it was impossible.

He heard the car outside and followed the reflection of the headlights as they played across the wall and ceiling. The lights of the car were left on and he waited for them to come for him. He saw a rat in the light; it was in the corner watching him and he felt his stomach lurch when he saw it was nibbling on one of his fingers. The two men walked in, and he was convinced that he was hallucinating. They looked like they were holding hands! If that wasn't the final insult – taken out by a pair of fucking pansies. He knew he had tucked Jamie up, but this was beyond the fucking pale.

'Are you a pair of fucking poofs?'

Lenny laughed loudly at the man's incredulity. He knelt down beside him and said, in a threatening voice, 'Yes. And we are going to bugger you to death!'

Christopher went white with fright, and Lenny smirked.

'Don't worry, Chris, you're not our type.'

He took out a small German-made Luger and shot the man execution-style in the back of his head. The grave was already dug and, once he was dead and buried, all they had to do was clean up the blood and that was the end of it. It had gone better than they could have hoped.

An hour later they were sitting by the pool, looking up at the stars and drinking cold beers. They looked like two mates having a little holiday in Spain. That was the best bit about being together – no one would ever suspect a thing. They were too hard, and too well respected for anyone to ever even harbour any kind of suspicion that they were more than friends.

They would travel back to England by sea as they couldn't take the money on an aeroplane. Instead they'd pick the boat up in Benidorm. They had arranged to have a few days' holiday before they left – they had earned it, Jack said. He had told them to have a few drinks, some good food and grab a bit of strange. Might as well enjoy the sunshine – it was raining in the UK, as fucking usual. Lenny knew Jack was well pleased with them. He couldn't believe he didn't want to hurry home to Sharon and baby Lenny. He wondered at how his life could change so quickly. He loved his wife, and he loved his baby, but he *needed* Reggie Dornan. That was the difference, he supposed.

They finished their beers and went to bed. Never had Lenny felt as content in himself as he did when he was with Reggie. It was as if a piece of a puzzle had finally been found, and now he was whole. He could have him *and* have his family; as long as they were discreet they were fine. It wasn't just about sex either, though that was amazing and came naturally to him. They talked for hours about everything and anything – that was the main attraction for him. In some ways, Reggie was like the brother he had never had.

As they lay together in the moonlight, the breeze drifting in through the open patio doors and the smell of sweat in the air, Lenny knew he had never felt such complete happiness before, and that actually saddened him. A part of him knew that Sharon was worth so much more than he could now offer her.

'You're quiet again, Len.'

He sighed in the half-light. 'I'm thinking about Sharon.'

Reggie stroked his stomach gently, and he closed his eyes. 'We won't hurt her, Lenny. How could we?'

'She was all I ever wanted, and now this has happened. It is hard to get my head round it you know, Reg?'

Reggie smiled slightly. 'I feel the same. But no one will find out. No one can *ever* find out. So there is no harm really, is there?'

Lenny supposed there wasn't and, as they fell asleep, he decided that he was just going to go with it. He had no choice really. The die was already well and truly cast.

Chapter Forty-Three

'Ooh, wait till Lenny sees you in that!'

Sharon blushed at Geraldine's words. She had bought some sexy underwear from a shop in Soho and she was going to put it on for her Lenny when he got home. She still had a good figure, not a mark on her really. She had carried such a small bump that there had not been too much to stretch. Her boobs were still full – that was down to the breastfeeding, she had heard – and her Lenny was all over her like a rash. He couldn't get enough of her. Look at how he had taken her on the kitchen table! She felt the pull of him as she thought of their reunion tonight. She was going to cook a nice dinner, with candles and everything. Then she was going to lead him to bed.

God, she had missed him so much.

'Earth to Sharon!'

She laughed at Gerry's scandalised face.

'I can guess what you were thinking about, dirty cow.'

They went into a Wimpy and settled at a table.

'I really missed him, Gerry. I suppose that is natural enough. We're still newly married after all.'

Geraldine Dornan felt a wave of affection for her friend; she looked so bereft without Lenny. It was lovely to see.

'You'll knock his eyes out with that underwear!'

'I hope so!'

They ordered their food from a young waitress with streaked blond hair and a nose ring.

As they settled in the booth, Sharon said seriously, 'Has Reggie got a regular bird?'

Gerry laughed at that. 'Not him. He's the love-'em-and-leave-'em type. Reckons he has got plenty of time for all that.'

'I suppose he has a point. If I hadn't got pregnant, me and Lenny would have waited a few years before we got married. Funny thing is, I've been with him since I was thirteen and he was fifteen. We knew even then that we were for keeps. That sounds mad, doesn't it?'

Geraldine shrugged. 'Not really. I mean sometimes it's just meant to be, I suppose.'

Sharon nodded sagely. She held out her hand and admired her wedding and engagement rings. To Geraldine she looked so young, like a girl playing at being a grown-up.

'We were meant to be, all right. I couldn't live without my Lenny.'

Geraldine slapped her hand in a playful way and said

seriously, 'Well, you won't have to, will you? Don't be so bleeding morbid.'

Sharon grinned. Geraldine was right, there was nothing to worry about with her Lenny. He adored her and their little boy. She was a very lucky girl; she knew that better than anyone.

Book Two

Death is the privilege of human nature,
And life without it were not worth our taking.

The Fair Penitent, Nicholas Rowe (1674 – 1718)

Chapter Forty-Four

1989

'Lenny, will you talk to your sons! They have been right little fuckers today.'

Lenny sighed. This was getting to be a bit too common for his liking. He saw his two handsome sons, blue eyes wide and worried-looking, and he felt the usual rush of love for them.

He put on a stern face and bellowed, 'What is it now, Sharon? What they done?' He had to stifle the laugh that was threatening to break out at the look of shock and awe on the boys' faces.

Liam, at three years old, was a natural-born bastard, as his dad would say. If he was walking in the Gobi Desert he would find a puddle of mud and fall in it. He was one of those kids who trouble seemed to follow around.

Sharon looked at her two boys and rolled her eyes in pretend annoyance.

'Where do I start? Oh, yes. Young Lenny swore in school – at his teacher, no less! And that Liam kicked over Mrs James's shopping. Bold as brass, he was. Then he down and out refused to apologise.'

Lenny gave his sons a ferocious look that made them cower and said, 'What have you got to say for yourselves?'

They were both silent, watching him warily.

Then little Lenny, always the first to break, said quietly, 'I'm sorry, Daddy.'

Lenny turned to his younger son, who was huge for his age and already had the air of a hooligan.

Liam looked him square in the eyes and, after a few beats, he said loudly, 'I'm sorry then!'

'Get to your rooms. There will be no sweets tonight, and no TV either.'

The lads stomped off together.

Sharon placed a cup of tea on the kitchen table and Lenny sat down, grasping the mug gratefully. It was freezing out.

'Honestly, Len. That Liam! It's like he has the devil in him.'

Lenny laughed. 'He is a fucker, all right. My dad was telling me he told my mum he saw a dinosaur looking in his bedroom window.'

Sharon grinned. She sat opposite her husband and grabbed his hand tightly. 'He has a good imagination, I'll give him that. But it's like he has no fear of anything.'

Lenny shrugged. 'He is only three years old. He will be all right.'

Sharon nodded and smiled. 'How was your day?'

'Nothing spectacular. I went into the cab firm and put the hard word on that Hassid bloke. He can't fucking pick and choose his jobs, and I explained that in words even he couldn't fail to understand.'

Sharon laughed. 'He was born and bred in Ilford. Why he talks like that I don't know. But thanks, anyway.'

He waved away her gratitude, but she saw he looked tired.

'Why don't I run you a nice bath after dinner, eh? We could have an early night!'

She was leering at him playfully and inside he groaned. The last thing he wanted was sex; even Arnold Schwarzenegger couldn't raise it for him at the moment. Not that he would tell her that, of course. She was still as eager as she had been when they first married, while he was getting to the stage where he was happy to keep it to once or twice a week. It was hard, sometimes, to pretend. But so much of his life was pretend these days.

He sighed once more.

'I said I would meet Reggie for a few beers. We need to strategise about something Jack wants us to do.'

Sharon looked suitably disappointed, but didn't complain. She was a good girl, his Sharon; she knew work was his priority. It was what had bought and paid for this lovely house that was her pride and joy. It was a nice drum, no doubting that, but she was forever decorating or changing the carpets. It irritated him at times, even though he knew he should be pleased that she took such a pride in her home. When he was being completely honest with himself he admitted too that, at times, Sharon herself irritated him. She had no real thoughts beyond her boys and her house. Oh, and him, of course. He wondered why he had never realised years ago just how small her world really was. But they had been kids then, and they had thought they knew it all. Now here they were, tied together for life, and that was all there was to it. He felt a moment's shame at his thoughts and watched as Sharon started to dish up their dinner. She was a good cook, a good mother and a good wife. It wasn't her fault that he had grown away from her in some ways.

At twenty-four he was now doing very well for himself, making a lot of money, and he also had serious responsibilities. Jack Johnson was leaving more and more of the day-to-day with him, and with Reggie as his number two he was enjoying the Life.

Reggie Dornan and their 'friendship', as they referred to it, was still going from strength to strength. It amazed him that he could still feel this deeply for anyone, let alone another man. Thankfully it was the very fact of their manliness that stopped people from thinking there was anything going on. They were simply held up as paragons of good friends. People talked about how close they were, and how well they worked together. It was amazing, but understandable given the world they inhabited. Poofs, shit-stabbers, whatever they might be called, were seen as Dick Emery-type figures to the criminal world. High-pitched voices and limp wrists constituted their idea of homosexual men. Hard men were not even suspected of anything untoward. Ronnie Kray had never really had the respect of his peers; he was seen as unnatural, as an aberration almost.

He remembered his dad warning him about a bloke on their estate. He was very effeminate, and Lenny was told *never* to speak to him, and *never* to go in his flat. His father, he now realised, couldn't differentiate between a homosexual and a paedophile. But that was the world Lenny lived in and he had to accept that. Reggie hated it as much as he did, but, like him, he had no choice but to bow down and hide their true natures from the people around them.

They had taken up deep-sea fishing and, out on the boat, they could do what they liked. They found time to be together, and they made the most of it.

What other choice did they have? But they couldn't escape the fact that it was wearing, constantly living a lie, living with the fear of being found out. And if anyone ever did find out they would be finished in more ways than one – not to mention if Jack ever got wind of his lucrative ventures outside the Smoke.

'You all right, Len? You were miles away.'

He smiled tiredly. 'Just thinking about work, darling.'

He pulled her on to his lap and squeezed her tightly. 'Tell you what, get a babysitter and I will take you out for a nice meal tomorrow night, eh?'

She kissed him full on the lips. 'Sounds good to me!'

She stood up and called the boys to the table for their meal, pleased that she was going to have a night out to look forward to with her big, handsome husband.

Chapter Forty-Five

Reggie Dornan had bought a flat in Kensington, and he loved it there. It was far enough away that no one dropped in unexpectedly and it had a doorman, so if anyone *did* arrive, he was warned well in advance if he was with Lenny. As he stepped out of his black marble shower he eyed himself in the mirrored tiles. He knew he looked good. He set about his ablutions carefully. He looked after himself, even used women's face creams, but he didn't care – he felt it was important. You have one life – you might as well enjoy it, was his mantra. Lenny laughed, saying he could just see the expression on Sharon's face if he started using Oil of Ulay.

Reggie sighed. He liked Sharon, but he felt such a jealousy of her at times, even though he granted it wasn't her fault. He felt the same about the boys. He resented the times when they had to take them out on the boat and actually fish. Yet he understood the importance of having to do that. They took some of the men sometimes as well so as to make it look normal – like a thing guys would do together.

He wrapped a towel around his waist, went into his lounge and poured himself a brandy. Then, sitting in a leather wing chair, he lit a cigarette and, pulling on it deeply, picked up his book. He was looking forward to tonight. Lenny was like him – tired out and in need of some R&R. He enjoyed their time in his home. It was perfect for them as a cover to others, but it also meant Lenny could keep clean clothes here, etc. They were just two mates having a game of cards and a beer. The phone rang and he picked it up.

'Hi, Reg. It's Lenny. Rain check on the beers, I'm afraid. Liam set fire to his bedroom.'

Reggie put the phone down and stared at it for a few minutes, wondering whether to laugh or cry. Those kids were bastards.

Chapter Forty-Six

'Get out of the way, Sharon. I mean it.'

Sharon was frightened; she had never seen Lenny like this before.

'Not until you calm down a bit—'

He grabbed her arm and pushed her roughly away from Liam's bedroom door. His son was terrified. White-faced, he was watching his father who looked huge at this moment in time, and scary too. Lenny picked his son up by his arm, threw him on to the wet, charred bedcover and laid into him, slapping him hard across his behind and legs.

'You fucking idiot! Do you know you could have died! Burned yourself badly? Are you a fucking moron, son? Don't you ever take a fucking second out of your day to actually think before you get up to bastardy?'

Liam was screaming now, in pain and in fright. Young Lenny was watching it all calmly, glad it wasn't him getting the good hiding. Sharon ran into the room and dragged Lenny off the terrified child.

'Calm down, Lenny, for Christ's sake!'

Lenny stared at his wife, the anger boiling up inside him again. 'I fucking blame you for this, Shaz. They are spoiled brats. He could have roasted us alive in our beds and you still want to fucking protect him? This is serious, woman! Are you as fucking thick as him? You can't see what the fuck he has done? How fucking stupid lighting a fire is?'

Sharon Scott was shocked by the vehemence of her husband's words. Never had he spoken to her like that before in her life.

'Look around you, you stupid mare! Look at his room. If this had happened during the night it would be a different fucking story. Well, that's it now. He has fucked himself, big time. No sweets, no telly and no playing till I say different.'

Lenny stormed from the room and down the stairs, his tread heavy and menacing to the two boys. He poured himself a large Scotch and swallowed it down in one. He was so angry he was shaking. When he had seen the flames he had nearly had a heart attack, and that fucking kid had been standing there watching as if there was nothing untoward going on, like it was normal to set fire to your bed. There was something lacking in that child, he would lay money on it.

He closed his eyes and willed himself to calm down. But he was fucked if he was going to apologise to Sharon; he had only said what needed to be said. It was time those boys of his knew that the days of

Mummy sticking up for them were over. They had to answer to him now. And by Christ and all the Apostles, they would do just that.

Chapter Forty-Seven

Sharon Scott was aware that something had changed with Lenny, and she was unsure what to do about it. Since the fire he had been like a different man. He was very cool towards her, and offhand with both her and the boys.

Ivy Conway was sorry for her daughter and her poor grandsons, and she said as much. 'He is too hard on them, Sharon . . .'

Her husband, who had been sitting quietly reading the paper, said loudly, 'That's shite and you know it, Ivy. Those boys, Liam especially, needed a firm hand. I'm with Lenny on this one.'

Ivy was annoyed. 'Well, you would be, wouldn't you? Lenny Scott can do no wrong in your eyes, can he?'

Del looked over his paper at his wife and she was amazed to see the anger on his usually friendly face.

'What is that supposed to fucking mean, eh?'

Ivy was nonplussed for a few seconds.

'That lad has given our daughter more than she could ever have hoped for. He makes sure I have a decent earn, and he asks very little in return. Just that his sons be given the sense to not fucking burn down houses, or fucking swear at their teachers. Or fight with everyone they come into contact with.' He looked at his daughter and said seriously, 'When was the last time they were invited to a birthday party?'

Sharon didn't answer her father.

'They don't get invited because people don't fucking trust having them in their homes. I watch them like a hawk when they are here. Face it, Sharon, they need discipline, not you and your mother breaking your necks to give them what they want, laughing off their antics. No, Lenny is right. They need a firm hand before it's too late.'

Ivy and Sharon were both quiet now. His words had a ring of truth to them and they both knew in their hearts that he was right. But it was hard for Sharon at times; the boys were a handful and it was easier to placate them than punish them. Truth was, they didn't listen to a word she said. They knew she was a pushover.

'That child is bruised from head to foot.'

Del laughed nastily at his wife's words. 'Not before bleeding time, if you ask me.'

Ivy shut up. She could tell that her husband was on the verge of blowing up and that wasn't something she was willing to let happen. For all her nagging, she had the sense to see when it was better to retreat. He didn't go often, her Del, but when he did, it was, without doubt, in a spectacular fashion.

Chapter Forty-Eight

Jack Johnson was laughing his head off.

'Pair of fuckers you got there, Lenny. Christ, they must run the two of you ragged.'

Lenny allowed himself a small grin. 'Worst of all, is little Liam. He honestly can't see what the problem is, Jack. He asked me last night if he was so naughty then why didn't God step in and stop him. He is not yet four and he wanted me to go into a discussion about free will. Sharon told him God was everywhere and could see him wherever he was. "Not if I'm behind a wall," he said!'

Jack was laughing once more. 'Clever kid, to be fair.'

Lenny nodded and sighed heavily. 'I am so angry though, Jack. All joking aside, between her and the grannies they are fucking destroyed. Ruined.'

Jack was aware Lenny had referred to Sharon as 'her' a lot lately. He seemed very discontented with his life, and that wasn't like Lenny. He adored his family.

'Look, I know this latest escapade probably frightened you, but that's boys for you. They are dangerous, kids. They don't realise that, of course.'

Lenny sat down and lit a cigarette. 'It's not just this latest aggro. Honestly, Jack, I feel at times like I don't know what I am working for, you know? Sharon is a good girl, I know that. It's just sometimes she bores me.'

Jack Johnson looked at his young protégé and said seriously, 'Are you playing away from home?'

Lenny shook his head. 'No! 'Course not. Fucking hell, I have enough with Sharon!'

Jack watched him closely. 'Look, Len, it is none of my business, but remember all marriages go through hard times. That is natural, really. Being with the same person can get a bit wearing, you know? But don't throw everything away. Think long and hard about that. The grass is rarely much greener; take it from someone who knows.'

Lenny nodded. 'Thanks, Jack. Now what about the Wilson brothers? Any news?'

Jack shook his head. 'They have disappeared off the face of the earth. No one has seen hide nor hair of them since last Monday. That's four days.'

Lenny frowned at his words. 'Do you think someone has taken them out?'

Jack shrugged. 'What else could it be?'

Lenny stood up then and pulled on his overcoat. 'I will get busy, Jack. See what I can find out.'

'You do that, son. If something untoward has befallen them two, I want the culprit fucking bang to rights.'

Lenny nodded and left the office.

Chapter Forty-Nine

Reggie and Lenny were in the pub waiting for an old lag who often knew more than people realised. Alan Moore kept his ear to the ground and made himself a good living by knowing things that other people might be interested in. He was a small man, with a bald head and a great thirst; he could put away ten pints and still have a reasonable conversation. That was how he gathered his information.

Lenny saw him outside and they left the pub and walked him to the car. He got into the back seat and waited for them to speak. Alan was a shrewd man, a decent bloke, who was well liked and trusted. He knew when to speak and when to keep his trap shut.

'You heard a whisper about the Wilson brothers?'

Alan shrugged slightly. He had a feeling this was what they would be after. 'It will cost you. I could get in serious trouble for this.'

Lenny opened his coat and threw an envelope with two grand inside it on to Alan's lap.

Alan opened it and smiled. 'All I know for sure is,

they had an altercation with the Carter twins. I don't know what it was about but, knowing the Carters, it was probably something to do with the old Persian rugs.'

Lenny and Reggie looked at one another and sighed.

Lenny turned back to Alan as he said, 'That it?'

Alan nodded and left the car.

Reggie swore under his breath. 'Fucking idiots. I knew there would be trouble along the line with them. The Carters are not exactly known for their friendly natures.'

'It would be Kevin Wilson who would start something like this. He has too much fucking pride. Well, I think we can safely assume they are dead.'

Reggie nodded. 'We better give Jack the bad news, eh?'

Lenny started the car and drove off. He was fuming, absolutely fuming. This was the last thing they needed.

Chapter Fifty

Jack Johnson could not believe what he was hearing. The Wilson brothers were serious earners and they were also under his protection. The Carters taking them out was like a declaration of war.

Lenny was shaking his head as Jack ranted and raved. 'Look, we don't know the story yet, do we? Let me and Reggie take a couple of the lads and go and have a chat with the Carters. See the lie of the land.'

Reggie nodded his agreement. 'This could simply be over Kevin saying something untoward. You know what he can be like, Jack. It doesn't mean the Carters are trying to muscle in on our territory. Lenny is right – we need to talk to the Carter brothers and see what's what.'

Jack nodded, but he was still annoyed. 'If those Carters think we will roll over, they had better have another fucking think.'

Lenny placated him as best he could and finally left with Reggie to go and hunt down the Carter twins. But his heart wasn't in it. Unlike most people, he got on with them. He was in the minority he knew, but, in all fairness, what you saw is what you got – there was no side to them. They were just a pair of naturally antisocial fuckers.

Chapter Fifty-One

Sharon was ironing when Lenny walked into the house, and he forced himself to smile at her. He saw the relief in her face and felt a moment's sorrow. He held his arms out and, as she ran into them eagerly, he held her tightly to him. He could smell her perfume and her shampoo. She always smelled nice, did his Sharon.

'I'm so sorry, Len. You are right. Even my dad thinks so. I will really come down on the boys, I promise you.'

He kissed her head gently, swaying as he held her to him. 'I'm sorry for being such a hard bastard, Shaz. I know they are a handful, that's why we have to sort them out now. Leave it much longer and they won't have a chance.'

She saw Reggie in the doorway looking awkward, so she pulled herself free from her husband and said brightly, 'Can I get you fellas something to eat? How about a beer?'

'Some sandwiches and a cup of tea would be hand-some, Shaz.'

She went into the kitchen and started to make the food. The men followed her out there and sat at the big, scrubbed table that was her pride and joy.

After a few minutes Lenny said to her, 'I don't know what time I will be finished tonight, love, so lock up properly. I am going to stay at Reggie's. We have a lot of running about to do.'

She sighed. 'OK, mate. I want to finish the ironing, have a bath and then get to bed. I'm shattered, if I'm honest.'

'How have the boys been today?'

She placed a plate of sandwiches on the table and set about pouring the tea.

'Good. I think they know that they are on their last chance. I didn't let them have any treats whatsoever and now you have removed the portables from their bedrooms they seem to understand that this is serious.'

'I will go and check on them.'

He went up the stairs quietly so as not to wake the boys.

'When are you going to find yourself a nice girl, Reg? They must be lining up for you!'

Reggie smiled. This was par for the course and it irritated him but he had to play the game.

'You know me, Sharon, love them and leave them.'

'Typical bloody man. Good-looking fella like you should already be thinking of settling down.'

He bit into another sandwich to save having to answer her.

'Gerry was telling me that you rarely even go out with women! Says your mum is worried about you!' She was laughing as she spoke, but it occurred to her when she saw his face that Reggie didn't think what she was saying was funny.

'Look, Sharon, just because I don't discuss every aspect of my sex life with my sister and mum doesn't make me a bad person. I just prefer to keep my private life *private*.'

He was being short with her and they both knew it. Sharon was immediately contrite.

'I'm sorry, Reg. I was only having a joke, mate.'

He sighed and forced a wide smile on to his face. 'Honestly, Sharon, Gerry and my mum are always trying to marry me off. I have plenty of time for that. I am a man who needs to sow his wild oats!'

Sharon laughed with him, but for some reason she felt that there was more to it than that – yet for the life of her, she couldn't say why.

Chapter Fifty-Two

Lenny and Reggie finally tracked the Carter twins to a brothel they owned in King's Cross. It was a nice house in what had once been a pleasant road; now it was another casualty of bedsitterland. It was a substantial size and it earned them a good wedge. They had girls of all ages, shapes and colours for the punters' delight. The funny thing with the Carter twins was that, as bastard-like as they could be, they treated their girls with the utmost respect. Maybe that was why Lenny had always liked and got on with them.

They didn't suffer fools gladly, and they were very touchy where their dignity was concerned. Both were big, arrogant men, in their late twenties, balding, running to fat and married to a pair of dark-haired sisters who they worshipped and adored. They were strange fuckers, odd coves, but they were good earners and they were respected in their own way. They didn't suffer fools gladly though and the fact that they were always looking for the insult or the piss-take made them people to be wary of. A lot of Faces were guilty of the same thing – it was just that not as many felt the urge to murder over it.

Lenny and Reggie walked up the steps to the front door and went inside. It was a typical cathouse: it stank of perfume, grass and sweat, with the stench of baby oil and sex underneath. There were girls in various states of undress in the main lounge where a short black man was the bartender. The music playing was Alexander O'Neal; it was loud enough to drown out conversations but not so loud that you couldn't hear what your chosen partner was saying. The barman gave them each a beer and Lenny motioned to one of the bouncers, informing him he needed to see the twins. The man knew exactly who they were and nodded. He walked off towards the back of the house.

Reggie and Lenny saw the girls eyeing them up and both felt a wave of revulsion. How could men do it? Fuck knew who'd been through these women; it was the same with the rent boys who hung around King's Cross. A young woman of about seventeen, with a slim figure and heavy breasts, made to walk over to them, and Lenny waved her away as if she was contaminated. He was embarrassed by this kind of place; he didn't feel comfortable being there and it showed. The older women with more experience eyed them critically – and both men were aware they were found wanting.

Dicky Carter came seeping into the room, all expensive teeth and cheap aftershave. He had his arms out in welcome. 'What a fucking honour! What brings you two into my establishment?'

Lenny grinned as he said, 'Well, it ain't for one of this lot, Dick!'

The man laughed, a loud, boisterous laugh that belied his true nature. He came across as a buffoon and that was exactly how he wanted to be perceived.

'Come through to the back, boys. Dom is there – he's looking forward to saying hello.'

They followed him warily. This was when the Carter twins were at their most dangerous: when they were smiling and joking and laughing with you. Lenny had heard a story once where Dominic Carter had been telling a joke and, just before the punchline, he had cut a man's throat with a razor. The Carters had found that utterly hilarious but they were in the minority.

In the large kitchen they saw that Dom was already pouring them large whiskies. They sat down at the scruffy Formica table and accepted the drinks.

'So, what can I do for you two?'

Dicky was smiling as he spoke; Dominic was straight-faced and seemed genuinely interested in their answer, whatever it might be.

Lenny sipped the whisky and said easily, 'The Wilson brothers, as if you didn't know, you rascals.'

The Carter twins looked at one another for a moment

and then they both burst into loud laughter – real laughter this time.

'What did I tell you, Dom? Lenny Scott is a funny fucking man!'

Then the laughter stopped as quickly as it had started and Dom said seriously, 'It is not what you think, lads. They were into us for a lot of money. They were dealing outside your firm, and they thought they were safe because of Jack Johnson and yourselves. Well, they fucking well made a big mistake because me and my brother ain't scared of anybody.'

It was said not as a threat, but as a statement of fact.

'Where are they?'

This from Reggie, who was not as welcome as Lenny and should have remembered that. He immediately realised his faux pas.

Dicky sneered at him as he said theatrically, 'It fucking speaks!'

Lenny closed his eyes to regulate his breathing and his temper. He wasn't in the mood for game-playing tonight.

'Answer the question, lads.' His voice was low and he sounded genuinely interested in the answer.

'Nowhere you will ever find them. They are gone, mate.'

Lenny Scott nodded.

Dominic Carter leaned forward and said conversationally, 'Before they slipped off their mortal coils, they tried to tell us that you two were stuck up each other's arses. Said that you went off on a boat together for days on end. Nice people you had working for you, Lenny.'

Lenny and Reggie were both shocked at the words and it showed.

'They fucking what?' Lenny sounded suitably outraged, which, of course, he was.

The twins were laughing again now.

'I know. Honestly, by the time we were finished with them they would have said anything to get another few minutes on the earth. Pair of treacherous cunts. Reckoned they'd sussed it out a few months ago. Said there was something a bit iffy about you two and your *deep* friendship.'

Reggie and Lenny realised that the Carter twins believed it. Lenny nodded gently at Reggie, and they both pulled out knives from inside their coats.

It was all over in under two minutes. The Carters had had their mouths sliced open and their throats cut.

Lenny and Reggie watched them bleed out. That was the trouble with the serious nutters: they never thought anyone would ever take them on their own doorsteps. They had let their guard down, and paid the price for their big fucking mouths.

The men slipped out the back door, aware that this deed would be all over the Smoke by breakfast time. But what the twins had said had rattled them and they wondered who else had heard the same story. Both were quiet as they drove back to East London.

Chapter Fifty-Three

'You two had a lovers' tiff?'

Sharon's voice was full of fun so she was shocked when Lenny turned on her and shouted angrily, 'What is that supposed to fucking mean?'

She realised that he had been drinking, and remembered all too clearly that he was not a good drunk. She was stammering now as she tried to placate her big, powerful husband. 'I'm sorry . . . Look, Len, it was just a joke . . .'

Lenny, even drunk as he was, knew deep inside that he should not be bullying the woman who had done nothing to him. But he couldn't stop. The anger had been building inside him since the run-in with the Carters. And now, weeks later, it had reached boiling point.

Sharon felt cold dread wash over her as he advanced. The kitchen table was between them and, as she tried to run away from him, he leaned across it and dragged her by the jumper over the table towards him. All the while he was screaming and shouting at her, his words making no sense whatsoever.

'You and your smart fucking mouth! You can't keep it shut, can you!'

As he raised his fist, she pulled away from him with all the strength she possessed, and ran into the hallway. Lenny chased her, so drunk his huge body was banging against the doorway and the walls. He brought her down by the front door, sending the telephone table crashing to the floor. He hit her three times in the face and head before his sons' screams broke through his anger. He looked up the stairs and saw them watching, wide-eyed and white-faced, as he attacked their mother.

It was as if Lenny was waking up from some kind of nightmare. He looked at his Sharon, and saw the blood streaming from her nose and mouth. She was terrified and he pulled himself off her and staggered to the sink where he started to throw up the whisky and brandy he had been consuming all afternoon in the pub.

Sharon dragged herself from the floor; the shock of what had happened had barely set in, so she didn't even hurt anywhere yet. Seeing the blood dripping down on to her clothes, she stared at it in total amazement until her maternal instincts took over and she went up the stairs and gathered her sons to her. That was when the tears started.

Lenny could hear his wife and his sons sobbing

above him and he stood gripping the sink tightly, wondering at what he had turned into.

But he knew exactly what was wrong with him, and he couldn't admit it to anyone in the world.

He was frightened his secret was out.

Chapter Fifty-Four

Reggie was in his flat. It was three weeks since the Carter debacle and, though it had done their creds the world of good, there were still murmurings of what those shitbags the Wilson brothers might have said to people in their circle. It worried Lenny far more than it worried Reggie but he knew that he had to do what Lenny wanted – and Lenny felt they should not be seen so much together. Just for a while, he said, to see how the land lay. Reggie had no option but to go along with him.

He looked around his home and sighed; he loved it here. There were many reminders of good times in this flat – it was a haven for him and Lenny. He was frightened that Lenny was going to call it all off. He had not understood until now just how terrified Lenny was about them being found out. But then, he had a wife and two young sons, so he had a lot more to lose than just his street credibility.

The phone rang and he picked it up casually. Then after a few seconds he said urgently, 'I am on my way.'

Chapter Fifty-Five

Sharon Scott had been taken to the hospital for stitches, telling a story of falling down the stairs that no one believed. Reggie Dornan had held her hand and talked to her as the doctor fixed her lip and eyebrow. He was shocked at what Lenny had done to this poor girl who had done nothing to warrant such an attack.

In the car going back to the house, he said seriously, 'If I hadn't seen this with my own eyes, I would never have believed it, Sharon.'

She looked awful; her face had swollen up like a football and the bruising was already starting to go black.

Sharon spoke with difficulty. 'I don't know what it was over. I made a silly joke, that's all.'

She explained what she had said and he saw that she was watching his reaction; he was careful to give nothing away and instead simply sighed heavily. 'You know Lenny can't take a drink, Sharon. Anything can set him off when he is drunk. Silly cunt, he is. But I

will have something to say to him, don't you worry.
So will Jack Johnson . . .'

She grabbed his arm then and said quickly, 'You
can't tell anyone, Reggie. That's why I called you and
not my mother. No one can know about this.'

He could sense the urgency in her voice and he
wondered how a woman could stay with a man who
had hurt her, attacked her like an animal. Whatever
his feelings for Lenny, even Reggie knew that this
wasn't his finest hour. He supposed it was the bond
of having children together; but women were far more
forgiving than the male species, he realised.

'Sharon, love, how are you going to hide that away?'

She shook her head sadly. 'I don't know, but I will
sort something out.'

Then she started to cry again and, pulling the car
over, he shut off the engine and took her into his
arms, comforting her as best he could. For the first
time ever, he could cheerfully smack Lenny Scott right
across his handsome face.

Chapter Fifty-Six

Liam was sitting beside his big brother on the sofa, watching warily as their dad tried to explain that he had not meant to hurt Mummy. Young Lenny was looking at his father with a face full of hate and fear. He had heard his father shouting at their mummy before, but he had never seen him hurt her like that. It had been such a frightening experience, and nothing his daddy could say would make it right. Young as he was, he knew that this was all wrong and that his mummy did not deserve to be hurt like that.

The boys were relieved when the front door opened and Mummy came in with Uncle Reggie. They rushed to her, but Liam held back when he saw the state of his mummy's face. He burst out crying again and Lenny tried to pick up his son but the boy fought against him. He went to his mother and, grabbing her legs, he cried into her skirts as she soothed him, calmed him and rubbed his back.

Lenny, sober now, was looking in horror at what he had done to his wife's face. He stepped towards her, his arms out in supplication, as he said brokenly, 'Oh God . . . Shaz, I'm so fucking sorry. I could cut me hands off, darling . . .'

He was crying too now and Sharon felt a wave of pity wash over her for this man who she loved so much and who she knew could be unpredictable with a drink inside him.

Reggie watched as she pulled her son from her legs and allowed her husband to hold her against him tightly. It was as if they were alone now, both talking at once, Lenny begging her forgiveness and her forgiving him.

It was horrible to watch, and Reggie took the two little boys and shepherded them into the kitchen. He shut the door behind them and started to make the lads something to eat and drink. He guessed that what these two needed now was a bit of normality.

In the hallway Lenny was swearing on his boys' lives that he would never raise his hand to her again, and Sharon was believing every word he said.

Reggie stayed until everything had calmed down and then the family drove off to stay at a hotel in the Lake District until Mummy's face got better. Reggie cleaned up the house and set the burglar alarm before shutting the front door behind him.

As he drove back to his flat in Kensington, he wondered what the magic ingredient was that Lenny possessed to keep him enthralled as well as his wife, no matter what he did to her.

Chapter Fifty-Seven

'It was a spur-of-the-moment thing, Mum. We decided to have a bit of time together as a family.'

Ivy Conway wasn't so sure but she was too shrewd to say it. 'You're wearing a lot of make-up these days.'

Sharon sighed heavily. There was still a bit of bruising but nothing she couldn't cover with a decent foundation. She knew her mum was aware that something had happened, but she was fucked if she would give her the excuse to turn on her Lenny.

'Look, Mum, if you have something to say, then fucking say it, will you? If not, drink your tea and leave me alone, yeah? Think you could manage that?'

Ivy was more convinced than ever that something was radically wrong in this house and she also knew she would not get to know unless this little madam here decided to tell her. The two boys were creeping around like mice, not in their usual smashing-and-crashing mode she knew so well. It was normally like Casey's Court in this house, and now it was as quiet as a library, as if everyone was afraid to raise their voices. She loved this house; it was a detached four-bedroom with a large garden and she envied her daughter her beautiful home. Money was no object with this lot, and they lived in the best part of Manor Park. Suddenly she realised what had been bothering her since she came into the house.

'Where's the telephone table?'

There was a new one by the front door, and it was much bigger and more opulent than the one it had replaced. She had always admired the old one though and she said brightly, 'I'll have it, Sharon, if you've got a new one.'

Sharon smiled tightly and said quietly, 'The boys broke it, Mum, rough-housing in the hallway.'

Young Lenny looked at her with the eyes of an ancient as she lied to her own mother's face.

Ivy was upset. That table would have looked lovely in her hall. 'Break the house up around you, they will, those little sods.'

She frowned crossly at her grandsons as they played with their cars quietly on the kitchen floor. Young Lenny glared back at her and she shook her head at the cheekiness of the lad.

Sharon busied herself making more tea; she couldn't look her elder son in the eye. But she shrugged; what was one more lie on top of all the others she had told? She blinked back the tears that were threatening to come. She loved her Lenny so much and that love was so big it included hiding from the world what he had done to her.

The few weeks in the Lake District had been like a new beginning. Lenny had charmed her and charmed his sons. They had gone on days out together, fed the ducks on Lake Windermere and eaten Kendal Mint Cake. Lenny had been his old lovable self, and he had gradually brought them all back to normal. This was the man she had loved for half her life – not the monster he became when he had alcohol. He had sworn to her he would never have more than a few beers again and she had believed him.

She *had* to believe him. He was her husband and the father of her children and, God help her, she loved him more than life itself.

Chapter Fifty-Eight

'The wanderer returns!'

Jack Johnson was pleased to see Lenny back after his impromptu holiday. There was a story there, he guessed, but that was for Lenny to tell in his own time.

'All right, Jack? Hope you didn't mind my sloping off but we needed a bit of time as a family, you know?'

Jack nodded his understanding. 'Good break?'

Lenny cracked one of his endearing crooked smiles as he said with feeling, 'The best. I needed to be with my lads, Jack. They are only young once.'

Reggie was amazed at how easily Lenny could lie but he kept his own counsel.

'Reggie has been doing fine on his own. I know you two have been in touch by phone so you're up to speed. I think taking out the Carters was a fucking good move – even the Filth are pleased!'

They all laughed. Particularly mad Faces getting taken out by one of their own often made the police feel as if they had had their job done for them.

'They were asking for it anyway. Pair of cunts!' Lenny's voice was disgusted.

Jack laughed. 'That's what I like to hear, Len. Back in work mode, are we?'

'Who has taken their businesses over?'

Reggie grinned at him and Lenny felt his heart flip over in his chest.

'Believe it or not, one of their bouncers, Terry Cobb. He is doing a fucking good job too. Well liked, he will go far. Been fair with the wives – that's what I like to see. Honourable man, I think.'

Jack was nodding his agreement. 'Very reasonable type of person, and you can bet your life the Carters treated him like fucking dirt. From what I hear on the street their deaths were celebrated all over the Smoke. Never a good idea to make too many enemies in this game. Fuck knows, trouble can brew in an instant so why go looking for it?' Then he sighed heavily. 'Talking of trouble, Frank Barber has raised his ugly head.'

'What's that got to do with us?'

Jack waved his hand in dismissal. 'Nothing – yet. I don't trust him. He has been away a long time and he holds grudges. I had a few run-ins with him years ago.'

Lenny and Reggie exchanged glances.

'Keep an eye on him, and find out what he's up to, will you? You know the old adage, forewarned is fore-armed? Well, armed is exactly what you will need to be if Frank comes looking for you.'

'Do you want us to pay him a friendly visit on your behalf, Jack?'

Jack Johnson smiled at the loyalty Lenny had to him. He had chosen well with this lad – he'd never had a moment's doubt about that.

'Nah. Just keep an ear out – see what he's up to.'

Chapter Fifty-Nine

'God, I missed this, Reg.'

Reggie was sitting on the edge of his bed and they were having the egg sandwiches and coffee he'd made for them.

'I know the feeling. How was it really?'

'I can't believe what I did to her, Reggie. Every time I looked at her poor fucking boat race I felt terrible. The kids were scared of me . . .'

Reggie sighed. 'Well, you can't blame them. It ain't something they can brush off, is it? I mean, you really fucking lost it, Lenny.'

He nodded. 'It was so hard, Reg, trying to win them back, you know? But I did it and I even managed to do a bit of business on the side.' He laughed.

Reggie grinned sadly. He pushed Lenny's hair back off his face and caressed the back of his neck.

'I thought you might want to stop this.' He motioned around his bedroom. 'After what the Carters said, especially.'

Lenny bit into his sandwich with gusto and said through his chewing, 'No way. Fuck the Carters and the Wilsons. Fuck them all.'

Reggie was glad to hear him say that.

Lenny finished his sandwich in two bites and placed the plate on the floor. Leaning back against the pillows, he said seriously, 'I never would have believed that this would ever be me. But I am glad we have each other, Reggie.'

Reggie smiled. This was the nearest Lenny would ever get to saying, 'I love you'.

Reggie changed the subject, as he knew that Lenny found it difficult to talk about feelings, particularly *their* feelings. He still had the innate fear of homosexuality that was present in many men, especially those who denied their true natures.

'I wonder what Jack and Frank Barber got up to in their day?'

Lenny was lighting them up two cigarettes as he said, 'I wondered about that too. We will have to ask about, see what we can find out. Jack can be very close-mouthed when the fancy takes him.'

'I know. I heard a while back that he was a right handful when he was a young man.'

Lenny laughed at that. 'He could be a right handful now and all, I reckon.'

Reggie laughed with him. He saw Lenny looking at his watch and knew it was the sign he had to go.

Reggie stood up and said casually, 'I'll get the shower

going for you, and make you a fresh coffee before you go.'

Lenny was already up and out of the bed. Reggie hated this part of the evening, even though he knew this was how it had to be. He heard Lenny singing tunelessly in the shower as he rinsed out the cafetière in the kitchen.

Chapter Sixty

Frank Barber was not a big man by any means, but he was mean. He had the look of one who was unpredictable and who could be capable of great violence. It was as if he was trying to hold it inside him, and that communicated itself to the people around him and made them wary of him. He had grey hair that was thick and wavy, and his eyes were a greeny-blue that gave him a claim to good looks. When he had been a young man he had been a fine specimen. Now he was in his sixties, but he still got the odd look from women.

Frank Barber's saving grace was that he loved his kids with all his heart. His eldest son was severely disabled and Frank had taken him everywhere with him, as proud of him as he was of his daughters. His son had died while Frank was doing a nineteen and it was said that he'd cried like a baby. Then he had smashed the wing up and spent three months in solitary. One of the screws that had tried to contain him had lost an eye. He was a hero in the nick, but he had missed his son's funeral.

Now he was out on the streets, eager to get back into the game and, as he stood in the pub, he wondered at how the world had changed while he had been banged up. A few of his old cronies had come to pay their respects and Frank had been shocked at how they all looked. Thanks to his own fitness regime in the nick, he was still in pretty good shape for his age. He was holding court when two big, dark and handsome men came over and introduced themselves.

He had heard of Lenny Scott and he was pleased at the way the boy and his companion respectfully shook hands with him. He liked the way they were deferential to the older men there and that they wore decent suits and good shoes. Things like that were very important to Frank Barber. After wishing him well, they said their goodbyes and left the pub quickly.

One of the men there, Davey Foster, said sagely, 'That is Jack Johnson's blue-eyed boy.'

Frank nodded. 'I know all about him and that young Reggie Dornan. They are the new guard, mate. Nice enough lads, though.'

The men agreed with him, as they had to – whether they really did or not. Frank wasn't a man who took kindly to being mugged off in any way, shape or form.

'I hear Jack has done well for himself.' No one elaborated on what he said and he smiled. 'I'm going to see him soon. We go back a long way, me and Jack Johnson.'

Still no one said a word either for or against him.

'I think he needs a lesson in etiquette personally, and I might be the one to give it to him.'

Then he ordered another round of drinks and the talk changed to other subjects. Everyone had forgotten how mercurial old Frank could be. They wouldn't do that again in the future.

Chapter Sixty-One

Lenny was quite taken with Frank Barber. He admired the old fucker; he had done a nineteen without too much trouble and he seemed a nice enough bloke.

'I can't imagine being banged up for nineteen years, can you, Reg?'

Reggie laughed. 'Can I fuck! I've only done a few years and that was hard enough. But the thing is, Len, once you're in there, you got no choice, mate. You have to wipe your mouth and get on with it. It's a mindset really.'

Lenny nodded. 'I suppose so. If we had a capture for some of the stunts we've pulled, we wouldn't get out ever!'

They laughed together at the truth of it.

'If it did come to that, there'd be nothing for it but to knuckle down and make the best of it, I suppose.'

Reggie laughed again. 'Turn it off, Lenny! You're giving me the fucking heebie-jeebies.'

Lenny lit them both cigarettes and passed one to Reggie before saying, 'I had a chat with Dennis Dunmore last night. I met him outside the off-licence near my mum's house. Interesting man.'

Reggie frowned as he said, 'In what way?'

'Well, he didn't exactly come out with it, but I got the impression that Jack started his businesses on what was, in effect, Frank Barber's money.'

Reggie whistled through his teeth. 'That might be why Jack is so interested in seeing what Frankie Boy has in mind.'

Lenny nodded. 'Maybe. I don't like to think that Jack tucked someone up. I think we need to get the full SP before we start wondering about things that as yet don't even concern us.'

Reggie dropped him outside his house and they smiled at one another.

'Shall I pick you up tomorrow?'

Lenny shook his head. 'Nah. I'll drive meself. See you in the morning.'

Chapter Sixty-Two

Sharon was waiting up for Lenny again. As always, she had her hair done and make-up on; she still made the effort. He knew that he was lucky to have her, but if he had his time over, he would have waited before marrying her. He loved her, but he wasn't in love with her any more. They had been kids, as her mum had pointed out, playing at being grown-ups. But he loved his sons too, and he knew he couldn't leave her. Nevertheless, it was getting harder and harder to pretend that he was really content with this life at home.

'You look nice, Shaz. How was your day?'

It was what she wanted to hear and, as he sat and ate the food she had so lovingly prepared for him, he tuned her out. Reggie had once said that his sister Gerry prattled on, and that was exactly the word for Sharon's scintillating conversation. Prattling. He knew he was being unfair but couldn't help stifling a yawn. She instantly became quiet.

'Shall I run you a bath, Len? You look like you could do with an early night.'

He was overwhelmed with guilt again and so he said jovially, 'Only if you get in with me!'

He jokily leered at her and she laughed with genuine happiness.

'I think that could be arranged!'

He smiled once more. 'That's a date then, darling.'

She removed his empty plate and started to load the dishwasher. He watched her movements; she was still a good-looking girl. Suddenly he wanted her, wanted her underneath him. He stood up and, before she knew what was happening, he was inside her, pushing into her as she leaned against the sink.

She loved it when he was like this, when he took her without warning. It proved to her that he still desired her. That he still loved her.

He had to shush her as she started coming in case the two boys came down. They finished together and, as he held her to him, feeling her heart galloping in her chest, he wished he was anywhere in the world but his own kitchen.

Chapter Sixty-Three

Lenny got into work early. He had rung Jack and arranged to meet him at 7 a.m. and he was waiting for him when he arrived. They were both drinking large mugs of tea when Lenny asked him the question he needed the answer to.

'I heard through the grapevine that Frankie Barber was drinking down the road so I popped in with Reggie to pay my respects, like, and get a look at him. He seemed all right – a bit of a handful I should imagine if crossed – but he gave me my due and I gave him his. Now, I am asking this with all respect, Jack: did you have any dealings with him in the past that he might have a problem with?'

Jack Johnson laughed loudly. 'You mean, did I tuck him up?'

Lenny nodded. 'Did you?'

Jack stopped laughing. He said seriously, 'Truthfully? Yes and no.'

Lenny frowned at his words. Jack Johnson sighed. He knew he would have to explain himself. The strange thing was, he didn't want Lenny to have a bad opinion of him. Lenny was a straight arrow in many respects and, though he was capable of great violence and great cruelty, Lenny Scott was also what was known as an honourable man.

'It's a long story, son.'

Lenny grinned one of his crooked smiles and said, like a schoolteacher, 'Then let story time begin. I'll make us another cuppa first.'

Lenny was intrigued. He couldn't imagine Jack tucking anyone up. But, as his dad always said, you live and learn.

Chapter Sixty-Four

Reggie was waiting at Custom House to meet Detective Inspector Daniel Smithson. Reggie had been shocked to get the early morning call from him, demanding they meet in private. Seemed it was of the utmost urgency and only he could help him.

Reggie Dornan's healthy disregard for the police as a whole had come in handy and he had managed to make the man think he was doing him a big favour by giving him a half-hour of his time. Christ knew, they paid the fucker enough. But it was handy to have Old Bill beholden to them, and something personal could always be used at a later date. So, he waited, looking out over the Thames and wondering what the fuck could be so important he was out of bed at this ungodly hour.

It was the beginning of autumn and the cold was setting in across England. There was a grey mist over the water and he could see the faint lights of office buildings in the distance. Reggie heard a car pulling up and turned to meet Smithson. He didn't like the man, but that was neither here nor there. You didn't love a guard dog, but you fed it and you housed it because it could be useful to you.

Smithson got out of his car and Reggie could see the worry on the man's face as he walked towards him. He wasn't exactly the answer to a maiden's prayer; he was tall, thin and looked like he had not eaten a decent meal in months. His sparse, sandy hair was badly cut, and he always seemed to have an aroma of peppermints that Reggie and Lenny guessed rightly was to hide the smell of his serious boozing. He was scum as far as they were concerned, tucking up his own. But they wisely kept that opinion firmly to themselves.

Reggie shook the hand that was stretched out to him and then smiled diffidently. He wasn't in the mood for small talk and he let this be known. Smithson came straight to the point, as Reggie had hoped he would. He passed a brown envelope over to Reggie which, when he opened it, he saw was full of glossy eight-by-ten photos. He looked at a couple of them and made a disgusted face.

'I'm assuming these weren't developed in Boots,' he said, trying to lighten the situation.

Smithson didn't answer and Reggie saw that the man was genuinely terrified of the photographs and what they could mean for him and his career.

Reggie shook his head, as he said quietly, 'Fuck me,

but you are one ugly bloke. And she's not just young enough to be your daughter.'

Smithson still said nothing. He didn't know what to say.

'Where were these taken?' Reggie decided not to torture him just yet; there was plenty of time in the future for that.

Smithson finally spoke. 'At a house in King's Cross.'

Reggie's ears pricked up. 'The Carter twins' old place?'

The man nodded.

'What do they want from you?'

Smithson looked into his face and said dramatically, 'They want you. Or, to be more specific, they want Jack Johnson.'

Reggie was frowning now. 'What? Terry? He wouldn't fucking dare!'

Smithson shrugged. 'It ain't him you need to be worried about, Reg. It's that cunt Frank Barber. He walked in and demanded it as his right. Reckons he had an understanding with the Carters. He's been shouting about how you and Lenny took them out.'

Reggie was quiet. He needed to think. Putting the photographs in his inside pocket, he said seriously, 'Leave this with me. I will be in touch.'

Smithson was scared. 'What do I say? What do I do?'

Reggie rolled his eyes in exasperation, as he said nastily, 'What do you want me to do, you gormless cunt? Hold your fucking hand? Use your loaf for once in your fucking life.'

With that, he got in his car and drove away.

Chapter Sixty-Five

Lenny was amazed at the story that was unfolding. But he could see Jack's point of view all right, and he said as much.

'So your sister's child was Frank's?'

Jack nodded. 'We were great mates, me and him – like you and Reggie. When he got her in the club, he told her he would never marry her. Remember, this was the early sixties and that wasn't a bit like now. Those were the days when a pregnancy outside marriage was seen as a terrible thing, you know? The girl was looked on as a whore, especially if the culprit didn't marry her. And he was a lairy fucker, was Frank. My sister tried to top herself over it all – she was too scared to tell me or my mum and dad. She had the baby – a boy – and he was adopted. But she was never the same. Still a bit touched to this day, if I'm honest about it. Lovely looking girl she was too. I blame meself. I warned Frank off her, see? And that just made him more determined to have her.' He sipped his tea and saw the wide-eyed incredulity on young Lenny's face. 'I couldn't let the truth out, so I gave him the hammering of a fucking lifetime and I never paid him a penny of what he was owed from our earns. It was the least I could do to pay him back for what he'd done. Then he got a capture and a big lump and that was it. Till now.'

'Fucking hell, Jack, what a cunt. I feel like slapping him myself.'

It was what Jack wanted to hear but Lenny genuinely meant every word he said.

'This needs sorting out.'

Jack smiled slowly. 'My thoughts entirely.'

They heard Reggie pull up outside the yard in his motor and, twenty minutes later, they were drinking strong cups of tea and planning their attack. It seemed everything was falling into place.

Chapter Sixty-Six

Terry Cobb was annoyed, but there was little he could do up against an old Face like Frank Barber. Frank had his creds and, as old as he was, he could still fight his corner in a row. The Carters were gone – no one could say whether he had right on his side or not, so that was a fucking no-go. Plus, Frankie had given him his due in that he was happy for him to run things, and that would have to do to be going on with.

What Frank Barber had not allowed for was Terry's determination to keep what he saw as rightfully his – and that he would move heaven and earth to achieve that end.

Terry said all the right things and acted in an appropriate manner, but inside he was seething at the injustice of it all. He would put his plans into action and take back what was rightfully his. But he knew how to play the game, so for now Frank Barber would think Terry was full of gratitude to his benefactor.

Chapter Sixty-Seven

Little Liam was sitting on his mum's lap and colouring with her. He liked these moments when Lenny was at school and he had her to himself. He loved his mum and he loved it when she babied him like this.

'Did you have a nice time with Daddy on Sunday, darling?'

He nodded as he concentrated on keeping the colours between the lines. He was colouring in a car and he wanted to give it to his dad later on, with his name printed on it neatly. His dad set great score on neat writing for some reason.

'Uncle Reggie was funny, as well. He chased us round Uncle Jack's yard and let us pet the guard dogs.'

He saw his mum frown and wished he had not mentioned the two Dobermans. His mum was what his Uncle Reggie called 'a worrywart' and that word had made them all laugh, especially his daddy.

'Did you and Lenny have cakes and tea as usual? And see the cars?'

She knew that was the highlight for the boys when

Lenny took them to the scrapyard. They loved to see the machines and the crushed cars. Lenny wanted them to start their education very early about how much money there was in scrap. She agreed with him on that score, though she thought the yard dangerous for two little buggers like her boys.

'What else did you do?'

He thought for a few seconds before saying seriously, 'Me and Lenny were playing hide-and-seek, and I hid in the office.'

Sharon smiled happily, until he looked into her eyes and said honestly, 'That's when I saw Daddy kissing Uncle Reggie.'

Sharon Scott felt her heart stop in her chest at his words. As young as he was, Liam was clearly waiting for a reaction so, swallowing down her fear, she said lightly, 'You must have been dreaming!'

He looked steadily into her eyes as he shrugged and she realised that he had seen something he was still trying to make sense of in his own little head. He dropped his gaze and went back to his colouring.

He knew inside that what he had seen was wrong somehow, he just wasn't sure why and that was the reason he had not said anything to his older brother yet. Something told him this was not to be bandied about, as his Granddad Del would say. He didn't know why but he felt this was a secret, and the fewer people that knew about it, the better.

Sharon Scott stood up and placed her son on the

kitchen chair gently. Then smiling, she said gaily, 'Who wants tea and biscuits?'

As she filled the electric kettle she felt physically sick. Her mind was screaming 'No!' There was no way the child could have seen something like that. But instinctively, she knew deep down inside her that Liam was telling her the truth. He had definitely seen something. But what?

Chapter Sixty-Eight

Lenny and Reggie were with Jack Johnson, making plans for the demise of Frank Barber. There was no other choice – especially now they knew about Frank taking over the Carters' business and the trouble he would cause if he started a blackmailing scam. If he went after the likes of Smithson, then he would be party to all sorts of information that would augur well for no one. He had crossed a line and he needed to be reminded of that. This wasn't the old days where anything went – this was the world of the new criminal.

They wanted him outed and this was as good an excuse as any to do that. It was a win-win situation, especially for Terry, who would happily work with them to take back what he saw as his. He was wise enough to know he couldn't do it without Jack and his boys, even if he would forever be beholden to them now. But, rather the devils he knew, than the one he was currently working with – a cantankerous old fucker who still thought Frank Ifield was the height of sophistication.

He was quite happy to lead Frank Barber to his death. This would soon be over and they could get back to normal.

Chapter Sixty-Nine

'You all right, Shaz? You're quiet tonight.'

Lenny wasn't sure what was wrong with his wife but he sensed there was something bothering her.

Sharon looked at her big, handsome husband and sighed gently. 'Just tired, that's all. It's been a long day.'

He nodded almost imperceptibly. 'That right?'

He turned his attention back to his food and, as he bit into his steak, he watched her surreptitiously. There was definitely something bothering her and he wondered if she had heard a whisper about Frank Barber.

'Sit down and talk to me, woman. You're like a fart in a colander – all over the fucking place.'

Sharon hesitated a few seconds before sitting at the table opposite her husband. She watched him eat. He didn't look any different, and she still wondered why she thought there could be some truth in her young son's words. But the reality was, she had long sensed that there was something not

217

right about his friendship with Reggie Dornan. Things that had vaguely bothered her over the years were coming to the forefront of her mind. Gerry Dornan saying that Reggie should come out of the closet before he ended up in Narnia; at the time she had laughed with Gerry at her words. They had been said as a joke because he never seemed to have a girlfriend. She could not think of one instance where Reggie had ever brought a woman anywhere with him, even to the pub.

She thought of Lenny and Reggie going off on the boat for long weekends fishing together. If she was honest, she had always felt that he preferred Reggie's company to her own. But whatever her suspicions, she could never ask this man about any of it. Saying what young Liam had told her would cause untold trouble for everyone. And that was something she knew she had to avoid at all costs. There were some things that could never be brought out into the open, and this was one of those things. Deep inside she wasn't sure she even *wanted* to know the truth.

'Have I done something that I don't know about?'

She laughed at his absolute surety of this. She could see him racking his brains for some slight or unguarded word.

She shook her head slowly. 'Do you still love me, Lenny? Like you did when we were really young and first together?'

He sighed in relief. It was one of her 'tell me you

love me and desire me and need me above all others' days. He smiled at her. Putting down his knife and fork, he grabbed her hand and kissed it with his greasy lips.

Sharon felt an urge to drag her hand away from him and his touch. Did he touch Reggie with those same lips? She forced the thought from her mind. She looked over his shoulder to the windowsill above the sink; there was a photograph of Lenny and Reggie on the boat in their shorts, arms around each other's shoulders. They were both smiling into the camera and she felt the bile rising in her throat at what she was picturing, imagining.

'Seriously, you all right, girl? You don't half look white. You sickening for something?'

He was genuinely concerned for Sharon now and his eyes searched her face to try and work out what might be wrong with her.

She forced a smile. 'I'm fine. Just feel a bit off-colour, you know?'

He grinned. 'You ain't in the club again, are you?'

She shook her head in denial; the thought of having another child with this man was abhorrent to her at this moment.

'It's women's problems, Lenny. That's all.'

He nodded in understanding. He assumed she was having a heavy period or something 'womanly', as he had always referred to it. It was the one answer to guarantee he wouldn't pursue the conversation.

'I think I will have an early night, Len. Take a hot-water bottle up and have a rest.'

He smiled at her, and he was so handsome she felt her heart would break.

'I've got to meet Reggie anyway: we have got a bit of business to attend to.'

She nodded quickly and busied herself making the hot-water bottle, but she didn't feel easy in herself until he had finally left the house. She had a lot to think about as she sat in the bed she shared with Lenny and looked through the photos of him and his best friend. They were so happy in them, smiling and laughing at the camera, and she knew then, without a doubt, that what her son had said was true.

Daddy had been kissing Uncle Reggie.

She cried bitter tears as she wondered how the hell she would cope knowing what she did. Because there was no way in the world she could ever, *ever* let Lenny Scott know that his secret was finally out. She lay awake for a long time in the darkness, waiting for him to return home.

Chapter Seventy

Jack Johnson felt good about what was happening tonight. Frank Barber was getting exactly what he deserved and that was not something to worry him unduly. Lenny and Reggie had handled the details well; Terry would forever be in his debt and that wasn't a bad thing. He was a good bloke and he was sensible enough not to make aggravation for himself. That was the epitome of a good earner as far as Jack was concerned. Trouble came in their game anyway so it was pointless going out and looking for it like Frank Barber seemed to be doing. He was too long in the tooth to start this shit now. He had been away too long and he didn't understand the economics of the modern-day Faces. But that was his lookout. All Jack Johnson knew was that no one from the old guard was going to busy themselves for that silly old fucker. Time was when Frank Barber would have worked that out for himself. He was an old Moustache Pete, a joke to the new generation of men waiting to take what he had. In their world, there was no room for stupidity – that much was certain.

Jack sat in his home, drinking twenty-year-old Scotch and waiting for the call that would tell him it was finally over. He was feeling quite relaxed and full of bonhomie. But, of course, he reasoned that could just be the Scotch. Or the fact that the old bastard was finally getting his comeuppance. And not before time either. He was stronging it and that never boded well for anyone, really. There was nothing sadder than a fucking has-been.

Chapter Seventy-One

Frank Barber was pleased with himself. He liked that he had made his mark so quickly and so succinctly on the world he inhabited. He had done his time – and a fucking big lump at that – and he had done it with aplomb, even if he said it himself. He had put his head down and got on with it. He would like to see that scum Jack Johnson do the same, and do it as well as he had! He had made a place for himself as such and, when they had finally released him back into the wild, he had picked up the mantle once again. Now he was making up for lost time, taking back the nineteen years he had lost – and taking back his crown.

He saw Terry Cobb smiling at him as he entered the house in King's Cross. This was another thing he was making up for – and the women were getting their fill of him all right. He smiled at the thought. He wouldn't pay them either; he had never paid for a fuck in his life and he wasn't starting at this late stage. They worked in his house so the very least they could do was fucking humour him. He was the main man after all.

The story was already going round that he wasn't exactly nice to the girls, and that often upset the men who they worked for. This had been a good house until now, and the girls had been well looked after, first by the Carters, and then by Terry. They were wary and waiting to see how long the new bloke lasted, especially the younger girls, who seemed to be the preferred choice of Frank Barber. Young and childish was his taste; for them, it was like sleeping with their great-granddad. But he liked them to act as though he was the dog's knob and they had no option but to play along. It was laughable, and when they were together that is exactly what the girls did: laugh at him. It was the only way they could cope.

They watched warily as he passed through towards the back rooms – the main workplace of the owner was always in the huge kitchens that had once been the domain of the servants. It was like a rabbit warren back there and the girls were not encouraged to visit unless expressly requested. That suited them down to the ground. It was also suiting Terry and his cohorts as they led the man straight through to his own slaughter.

When Frank saw Lenny and Reggie waiting for him, he had every intention of putting up a fight. But when Terry took him down with a well-placed blow to the back of the head with a lump of lead piping, he realised it was all over for him. He was absolutely gutted. He remembered Eddie Richardson saying to him once that everyone is king, even if it is only for one fucking day. Never was a truer word spoken.

Chapter Seventy-Two

Jack was pleased, Lenny and Reggie were pleased, and Terry was 'over the bastard moon', as he kept telling them all repeatedly. It had been a hair-raising few weeks but now the future was set. It would be a nine-day wonder, like everything else in their world, and then things would gradually settle down and get back to normal.

They left Terry to make the final arrangements and, after a few drinks, Reggie drove them to Jack's house to finish the evening off properly. Jack would be interested in the 'nitty-gritty', as he called it, and they would be only too happy to fill him in on the details. This was a big night in many respects, and the two men were aware that, for Jack, it was the paying of a debt long overdue.

Chapter Seventy-Three

Sharon had bathed the boys and put them to bed amidst loud protests of 'another five minutes'. But she had looked particularly ferocious for some reason, and the boys had picked up on that fact, deciding eventually that bed might be the best place to be. After kissing them and threatening pain, torture and destruction if she heard a peep out of them, they had looked at her wide-eyed and nodded in agreement. They both guessed rightly it was something to do with Daddy.

Lenny had not been home for twenty-four hours and she'd not heard a word from him. This had happened before, but that was normally under much different circumstances. She was still reeling from what Liam had said to her the day before. It was at the forefront of her mind and she was unable to decide what she was supposed to do. In her heart she wondered if she would have the nerve, the guts, to tell Lenny what Liam had said. But she dismissed it. The thing was, once something was spoken out loud, there was no *un*saying it. This was what worried her so much.

If she questioned Lenny, what would be his reaction? But, if she *didn't* question him, how could she live with the wondering?

Every photo looked suspicious now. Times when he and Reggie had gone fishing on the boat for weekends seemed to be mocking her. She had a terrible feeling that Liam was telling her the truth about exactly what he had seen. This was something so far removed from her realm of experience that she didn't know what on earth she was supposed to do. She felt sick when she thought of them together, him and Reggie like man and wife. Or, more precisely, man and man. She knew what those kind of people got up to, everyone did. But she would never, in a million years, have believed it of the man she had married, the man who'd professed to love her for all these years.

She felt the hot sting of tears and was determined not to cry again. She knew this was something she could never tell another living soul. Imagine her mother if she heard something like this? Or her father. Not that he would believe a word of it. Even Gerry, who was the first to say that Reggie, her big, handsome brother Reggie, had no interest in women, wouldn't believe it. This was one time Sharon was completely on her own; she would have to find the solution for herself.

She looked up at the crucifix on the wall in the hallway. It was beautiful, made of carved oak with the body of Christ fashioned in solid silver, His eyes raised to the heavens as He died for the sins of the world. She wondered if a prayer would help, but she knew it wouldn't. Nothing could help because she still didn't know what the fuck she was supposed to do. Lenny would deny it; he had no choice in the matter. That was something she knew for sure – he would not sit down and pour his heart out to the woman he had married and given two children, beg her forgiveness and say it would never happen again. That wasn't Lenny's style, she knew that much. Lenny would accuse her of all sorts, be outraged and on his dignity. He would feel she had impugned his reputation and, of course, he would want to know who she had told her suspicions to. She felt that she could pick up a knife and stick it through his cheating, filthy black heart. But she would not do that either.

She wandered into her front room, the room that they were so proud of with its grey walls and deep-red furnishings and she poured herself a generous helping of brandy. Somehow she had a feeling that wine wasn't going to do it for her tonight.

Chapter Seventy-Four

Lenny was drunk and full of camaraderie. He had enjoyed taking that cunt out, and he had enjoyed explaining it all to Jack Johnson too. He loved Jack more than he could have ever thought possible. He loved his Reggie too, but tonight he needed a bit of strange to round off the excitement. Unlike Reggie, who he knew loved him and him alone, Lenny had found he liked a bit of a cottage – a good, faceless fuck – sometimes.

There was a place in Ilford where like-minded men would converge to partake of their certain brand of sex, with no questions asked and definitely no fucking morning-after remembrances. Lenny parked his car carefully – the last thing he needed was a fucking parking ticket. He walked past Tiffany's and took a short cut through to the big car park behind the club. At this time of night it was full of men just like him – men who were looking for a quick connection. He knew it was dangerous – that was half of the excitement as far as he was concerned – but he always took precautions. It was the whole concept of the strange that appealed; the different smells and tastes were the big draw for Lenny, something Reggie would never understand or even suspect.

He stopped as a large man came out of the shadow of the bins and smiled easily. He was big, dark and hard-looking – just his type. The man was smiling now as he walked over, and Lenny instinctively moved to meet him, craving the darkness and all that he knew it contained. As the man drew closer Lenny smiled back at him. Then the man brought up his hand and, before he could react, Lenny was on his knees, a terrible pain shooting through his body, and he knew that something was radically wrong. He was lying on the floor, unable to move even a finger, when the man knelt down and said softly, 'I just paralysed you, Lenny, but you will feel every cut and blow I give you. This is payback, you cunt. Eye out first, I think.'

Lenny lay there incapacitated and, as the man used the same sharp instrument to slice into his eyeball, he could not even scream out in pain. In the distance he could make out the sounds of traffic and people talking, the occasional shout and the high-pitched laughter of girls making their way into the clubs. The man was calm and collected and he took his time, inflicting the maximum pain and damage, so that when he finally started beating him with a metal bar Lenny Scott was almost relieved. He felt grateful that his ordeal was finally over – even if it meant his death. His last thoughts were for his boys, who would have to grow up without him.

Chapter Seventy-Five

Jack was in a quandary and he didn't know what to do about it. He had a call from a friendly Filth, namely Daniel Smithson, saying that a body had been found tortured and beaten to death in an alleyway in Ilford. It looked like it had been in a train wreck. But Smithson had said it seemed to be Lenny Scott.

The body had been found an hour ago at the back of a nightclub when the cleaners had come out to empty the rubbish into the bins. He had been there a while, and Daniel thought he should give Jack a heads-up. But it couldn't be Lenny, surely? And where the fuck was Reggie? What the fuck was happening? The men had left him quite happily the night before and he had told them he would see them Monday at the yard. It was now Saturday evening and he had assumed they were working, as per usual. Lenny normally picked up his money from the betting shop, and had a drink with his old man and Reggie – well, he assumed Reggie had gone out and ended up on the nest somewhere. With some old sort, no doubt – he wasn't exactly the marrying kind.

All Jack's instincts were telling him that it could not be Lenny Scott. Surely not Lenny? He picked up the phone and started ringing round; once he located him he would feel a lot better in himself. No matter how much he thought about the last few nights, there was not one person he could think of who would have dared to retaliate for Frank Barber. He was a Face in his day, admittedly, but now he was a fucking bit of a joke. No youngster would put themselves out. So what the fuck could be going on?

For the first time in many years, Jack Johnson was seriously frightened. He looked on Lenny like a son. He loved that lad like a son. Lenny was far too shrewd; no one would get near him. This had to be a fucking big misunderstanding. But there was a small part of him that knew that cunt Smithson would not have rung him unless he knew what he was talking about. Lenny Scott was dead and that was the truth of it.

Jack felt an inordinate need to cry. Lenny Scott had been everything to him, and he had been cut down in his prime, never to reach his full potential. It was a crying shame because that boy had been going places and he had been going to make sure of that personally. He was devastated as he carried on calling round; there was still a hope that ponce Smithson had got it all wrong. Fucking detective? He couldn't sniff out his own fucking arse! He was hardly the sharpest knife in the drawer. But as time went on Jack began to lose every shred of the hope he'd been clinging to.

Chapter Seventy-Six

Reggie was still reeling from the knowledge that Lenny Scott was dead. It was unbelievable. He loved Lenny like he had never loved another person in his whole life. It just could not be possible that he was gone from him.

As Reggie pulled up at Jack's yard, he checked his face in the mirror. He could see the shock and desolation in his eyes, and he felt the urge to cry once more. But that was a luxury he would have to forego until he was locked inside his own flat where no one could see him and could guess the strength of his grief. How would he live without Lenny: the one person who had made everything in his life make sense? And, more importantly, who had done the dirty deed? If it was anything to do with Jack's businesses they'd find out soon enough and exact retribution. But maybe Lenny had pissed off some fucker Reggie knew nothing about. He had to box clever, whatever the lie of the land. His hands were shaking as he lit a cigarette.

Chapter Seventy-Seven

'I think that's him, that's definitely his suit . . .'

Sharon felt like she was going to throw up. Her Lenny, her husband, the only man she had ever loved, was destroyed. He had been completely obliterated. She knew one thing for sure: this was not a random fucking mugging in any way, shape or form. The way the Filth were acting told her that this was a big deal.

Lenny's body was broken completely. It looked all wrong, misshapen, like he had been crushed. She could see it even under the white sheet the mortuary had covered him with. There was something very wrong and she could not voice her thoughts, not to the Old Bill anyway. That would come later. Much later. She would have to talk to Jack and she would have to talk to fucking Reggie.

Reggie Dornan, her husband's so-called best friend. Deep down she knew he was Lenny's biggest secret. There was something inside her that made her feel sure her son had told the truth. Whoever the culprit was she had to ask herself: had they actually done her a favour? Had they saved her from having to acknowledge that her husband had been living a lie all these years and that her marriage was nothing but a fucking sham? She felt sick again. She wondered if her life would ever again take on some kind of normality.

The policewoman held her as she cried, and she could feel genuine sympathy from this strange girl who made a career out of locking up other people. But she held on, and she cried bitter tears as she tried with all her heart not to feel anything but relief.

When Jack arrived she had never been so happy to see someone in her whole life. He took her home to her family, and he was so gentle with her that she felt sorry for the man who had looked on her husband as a son. Jack was devastated too and she clung to him for dear life, knowing that she would always quell any rumours that might begin to circulate about her husband's true nature. Her job now was clear: she had to protect her sons and she would do it even if it was the last thing she ever did on this earth.

Chapter Seventy-Eight

Sharon Scott was back at home, sitting in her kitchen nursing a glass of wine, still in a state of shock. Whoever had attacked Lenny had done a good job. His face and body had been destroyed. A 'sustained attack', they were calling it, meaning that he had been tortured too. Completely wiped out.

Sharon had answered all the questions from the police in the same way. She knew nothing of her husband's business dealings and, no, she didn't know anyone who might want to hurt him. He had been a very popular man. The police seemed to want to believe it was a mugging that had gone dangerously wrong. Like anyone could have mugged Lenny Scott and got away with it! It was fucking laughable, as her father pointed out over and over again, until she had screamed at him to shut the fuck up.

Lenny had been murdered, there was no doubt about that. Someone had beaten him to death. The question was: why? Was it business or personal? If she was honest with herself, she didn't want to know. There was a tiny part of her that was glad he was dead. She was glad that she didn't have to question her marriage or the man she had married any more. But that didn't mean that her heart wasn't completely broken because, when all was said and done, she had loved him, loved the very bones of him. She would honour him, as his wife and the mother of his children. That was all that was left to her now. She cried, but anger lingered and it was growing by the minute.

Chapter Seventy-Nine

Ivy Conway was worried. She knew there was something seriously wrong with her daughter and she had no idea what to do about it. Sharon had worshipped her husband. Now it was as if she was on autopilot, even refusing to speak at his wake and leaving the funeral preparations to his family. It was like she didn't want any part of it at all.

On one level her daughter was devastated, of course, and Ivy understood that. But she knew her girl better than anyone else and she felt there was a break somewhere along the line. Lenny had hurt Sharon somehow and she couldn't get to the bottom of it. All she could tell for sure was that her daughter seemed almost relieved at the turn of events. Her husband murdered, and she didn't seem to want to know any more than that. Ivy kept quiet about her misgivings, but she sensed there was something she didn't understand. One thing she knew for certain, though, was that everything came out in the wash eventually. She would help her arrange the funeral; what else could she do?

Chapter Eighty

Reggie was devastated. It was as if he had died himself. He felt the man's death more acutely than anyone else in their world could. It was unbelievable to him that Lenny had really gone, that he would not walk in as he always had, with that half-smile on his face and that look in his eyes that was only for Reggie. He had genuinely loved Lenny, and that was something no one could ever know. He had to grieve alone. But it was a hard road and Lenny's death had taken away everything Reggie had ever really cared about. He had loved him with a passion he never believed possible. Lenny Scott had been the man of his dreams and he had been taken away from him by some vicious fucker. No matter where he looked, who he asked, he couldn't find a trace of him.

Now, as Reggie stood in the church, he looked about in bewilderment. He could not believe the scene in front of him. He was in the first pew, as befitted his best-friend status, but Lenny had been far more to him than that and it grieved him that he could never let anyone know. He looked at the bowed head of Sharon and his heart went out to her and those two little boys who were the apple of Lenny's eye. He was heart-sorry for them all. They had lost someone that would have moved heaven and earth to give them a good life. Reggie would take on that mantle now and do whatever he could to ease their pain. It was the least he could do for Lenny; it was what he would have requested, what he would have wanted. Reggie would take care of Lenny's family as if they were his own.

As the Mass started and the priest began the preparations for Lenny to enter the Kingdom of Heaven, it took all of Reggie's willpower not to break down there and then.

But he mustn't do that. He felt Jack Johnson squeeze his hand in solidarity and that brought Reggie back to his senses. If he was happy about anything it was that no one had an inkling of the real relationship he and Lenny had shared and, for that, he could at least be thankful. He knew the ridicule that would come if that knowledge were to get out and he didn't want it for any of them. Especially Lenny, who wasn't there to defend himself.

Reggie tried to catch Sharon's eye but she kept her head down and her sons pulled into her arms protectively. She was a wonderful mother, as Lenny had always insisted. Reggie swore to himself once more that he would do everything in his power for those two fatherless boys.

Chapter Eighty-One

Sharon listened to the eulogies and wished for this farce to be over. Jack Johnson was visibly moved as he spoke of the man he had looked on like a son, and how his death was a reminder to them all of how fleeting life could be, and how important it was to pack in as much living as possible. He had smiled at her and her sons as he'd said that and she had felt cold hatred in her heart once more for the complete hypocrisy of her life with the man everyone was feting. It was hard not to feel the disgust at what he had *really* been.

Had he ever come to her after he had been with Reggie? She could not forget the times he had returned home late at night, smelling of soap and aftershave, and had taken her into his arms and loved her. He never could have really loved her. He was unnatural. He had wanted a man, not her. He had wanted Reggie Dornan, not his family.

She felt certain now that her life had been a lie. A great big filthy lie. But she would get this day over with for her sons and then she would decide what she was going to do with their futures. That was the only thing she could do, even though every bone in her body cried out with the urge to unmask the unnatural fuckers and tell people the truth. But, for the sake of her boys, she had to keep her silence and, for them, she would do that much. They were without a father now – she was all they had and it was her job to make sure they were protected; she would protect them until she drew her last breath. But it was a hard road she was walking, knowing that the man she had loved and adored had never really wanted her in return. That the man she had married had taken more pleasure from another man who was as masculine as he had been.

Well, she knew better now – she would not fall into that trap again. She wiped the tears from her eyes. Everyone would think she was crying for her husband, not because she had been duped by the man she had loved more than life itself. She remembered her nan telling her years ago about a headstone in Glasnevin Cemetery in Dublin. It said, 'Under this sod lies another one.' Never was a truer word spoken.

Chapter Eighty-Two

Jack was worried about Sharon. She looked awful. He had tried to talk to her earlier about Lenny but she had shaken her head in distress. He envied the dead man the love of such a good woman. She was white-faced and she had clearly lost weight. It was as if life itself had left her – he knew that sounded melodramatic but it was the only way he could describe her. Her troubles had somehow made her even more beautiful, and she was a beautiful woman already – no one could deny that. Lenny had worshipped her; there had never once been a hint of scandal about him with another bird and, in their world, that was seriously unusual. Women – or a certain type of woman – threw themselves at Faces for the kudos they possessed, and the money they could provide. But Lenny had never once strayed, not to Jack's knowledge anyway.

He glanced around the wake; everyone who was anyone was there. Wreaths of complete ostentation had abounded at the graveside, and that had pleased him. Jack knew it was important for Lenny's sons to remember this day as homage to their dead father. It was important for boys like them to know the high esteem in which their father had been held. He hoped they had all done Lenny proud. He felt the sting of tears again.

There had been nothing – not even a whisper – of why he had died as he had; it was unheard of, but that was the way it was. Jack had spread money all over the Smoke and still there were no leads. Not a fucking whisper, not even a rumour, and that was what he found so blatantly suspicious. The Filth might not know anything, granted, but there weren't even rumours among other Faces of any kind of fucking scenario that could have brought on such actions. That was something Jack couldn't believe. Someone some-where had to know what had gone down, and he would do all in his power to find out what that might be. Not just for Lenny and his family but because it was genuinely pissing him off now too. No one liked being out of the loop. Least of all Jack Johnson.

Chapter Eighty-Three

Reggie slipped outside to have a cigarette; it was too hot in the Irish club. He saw Sharon standing alone, smoking quietly under a street lamp, and he made his way over to her. He could have sworn she was ignoring him; she had hardly spoken to him all day.

He walked over and put his arm around her shoulder; he really was sorry for her loss. But she moved away from him as if she had been burned. The force of her feelings was such that even the most ignorant of men would have realised that she wanted nothing to do with him.

'Don't you *ever* fucking touch me, Reggie.'

He was shocked at the vehemence in her voice. She could see the confusion in his face as he looked at her. She laughed bitterly. Her heart was already broken; there was nothing left to hurt.

'I *know*, Reggie.'

He looked into her wide, blue eyes. Even now, as she mourned her husband, she was a beautiful woman and he could appreciate that fact. But her words were cold and to the point, and fear gripped his heart.

He looked at her for a long moment and she finally said quietly, 'Liam saw you. You and my Lenny. He saw you kissing! Kissing his fucking dad. As young as he is, he knew it was wrong! How fucking ironic is that?'

Reggie felt the shock hit him then and all he could do was stare at her, at the woman he knew he had wronged in so many ways. He grabbed her arm and pulled her round to face him.

'It is not like you think. He loved you—'

She laughed then, a nasty, vicious laugh. 'Oh, really? Enlighten me, please. I'm dying to hear what you and him thought you were doing together. Playing hide-the-fucking-sausage?'

He looked at her with such distress and pity that she felt the urge to rip his face open, to make him hurt as much as she was.

'I loved him, Sharon, just like you did. But he would never have left you or those boys. You have to understand that this was never about *you* as a person. He always admired you.'

'Oh, get the fucking violins out! He was fucking you. And, if he admired me so much, why did he hit me and hurt me like he did? Tell me that, Reggie. I'm so fucking interested in what Mr Library has to say. That's what he called you, Mr Library. Call you that in bed, did he? While you were fucking each other up the arse?'

Reggie suddenly lost all compassion. Physically dragging her away from the doorway, he pushed her into the car park and, grabbing her coat, he pulled her face towards his.

'You listen to me, Sharon. You're fucking hurting. I get it, all right? Well so am I, lady. I loved him. God help me, I fucking loved him. He was a treacherous cunt, we both know that. But if we have nothing else to build on, we have that much. I know you are hurting and, believe me, I would give *anything* to make your hurt go away. I love you, just like I love those boys, because you were part of him. He was my first love too, Sharon, and I know that you can't understand why he would want another man. I wish to Christ he had not wanted me, but what we had never could take away from what he had with you. You have to believe that. You and the boys were always his first priority.'

Sharon was actually beginning to feel sorry for him – for Reggie, who had fucked her old man! She needed to get away.

'Lenny worshipped you and those lads. Please, Sharon. Never forget that.'

She grinned again, and she knew that she was very drunk. 'Thank you, Reg. I feel so much better now.'

The sarcasm wasn't lost on him, and his anger nearly took over as he said quietly, 'I will never rest till I know who killed Lenny. I loved him and I will always be there for you and those lads. Remember that.'

She turned away then, and crushed out her cigarette

angrily. He knew he couldn't stop her as she made to walk off. But then she turned suddenly and said with quiet hatred, 'I'm glad he's dead. You unnatural fuckers.'

He watched her walk away and felt the sting of tears once more. It was up to her now. She could make or break him. *Oh, Lenny*, he thought, *how will I live without you?* And Sharon Scott was clearly thinking the exact same thing.

Reggie Dornan ran to her then, and said sadly, 'We both loved him and that is something we can never change. But, no matter how much you hate me, I will always be there, looking out for you and the boys. Whether you want me to or not. It's the last thing I can do for him.'

His voice was choked with emotion and it suddenly occurred to Sharon that he was hurting just as much as she was. That, like her, he was bereft. As his arms went round her she felt herself holding on to him and then the real tears came. The deep sobbing that she knew she had to allow before she could ever really start to heal.

'Oh, Reggie! Oh, God. He's really gone. He's gone and I hurt so much.'

He held her tightly, his own tears mingling with hers as he said over and over again, 'I know, darling. I know.'

Jack Johnson came outside and sighed sadly as he saw them. He thought for a fleeting few seconds how lovely it would be if they got together at some point. After all, they had both loved Lenny in their own ways.

Sharon cried into Reggie's chest and felt the stone of hatred gradually softening.

She knew she would need Reggie in the future, and that there was no way she could ever let on about what she knew. But now, at this minute, she felt safer in his arms than she had since Lenny's death. Reggie would always be there for her. His guilt would see to that.

Book Three

Behold, I come as a thief.

Revelation 16:15

Book Three

Chapter Eighty-Four

1991

Sharon Scott was fuming and both her boys knew why.

'Are you fucking stupid? Bringing all this to my door! Who do you two think you are, eh? You're always fighting.'

She searched their faces for some kind of answer but, as usual, there was nothing. Liam looked sorry, but she knew that wasn't because of the fighting – it was because he had vexed her and he never liked to hurt her in any way. He was sorry for making her sad, not for the fight that had caused so much trouble. He was a good boy in that respect and he loved her dearly. But, like young Lenny, he found trouble before it found him. She sighed in consternation. Lenny was his father's son – he would go his own road. They both would.

'You're suspended from school. I hope you are pleased with yourselves. Like I haven't got enough on my plate.'

She walked out of the room and left them to their

own devices. She really couldn't do this any more. They were too much for her. She poured herself a glass of wine and took a big gulp. This was her time – a bit of peace. The boys were ruffians; always fighting, always together. She had had enough. Lenny's father thought they were wonderful – chips off the old block. She gulped at her wine again, and savoured the taste. If only he fucking knew the truth.

All she did was work and be a mother – that was all that she'd thought she needed. But she was still a young woman and, as the time had gone on, she was beginning to realise that what she really needed was a man. But she definitely wanted a *real* man. She would not allow herself to be so stupid this next time around. He would be a real fucking man all right, in every way that mattered. She would make sure of that much.

She missed the closeness of sex before she had been so cruelly shown that the man she had married and loved – oh, how she had loved him! – had been no more than a liar and a cheat. He had wanted her in the beginning – she *had* to believe that. But after he met Reggie he had used her shamelessly. It still broke her heart to think of how he had duped her, how he had used her. Seeing the devastation on Reggie's face when the news of Lenny's death broke had been enough to convince her that she was right about her husband. How that had hurt. Yet even knowing what he'd done, she could not stop loving him. That was what really angered her.

How many nights had she lain there, going back over every moment of their life together and looking for clues that convinced her that she had been made a complete fool of? He had wanted a man over her – a big, handsome, *masculine* man. She closed her eyes and tried to force the images away. They would gain her nothing, except pain.

She finished the wine and poured herself another glass. She would drink this one slowly.

She heard the boys upstairs and knew they were getting ready for bed, even at this early hour. They always went to bed when they had upset her. And she was ashamed to say that she let them.

Chapter Eighty-Five

Lesley Scott was annoyed and her husband knew why. Since the death of his son it seemed that Sharon was making any excuse she could to keep away from them and keep the boys away from them too. Sharon was a shadow of her former self, even though she had never looked lovelier. He was a man and she was a good-looking woman – not that he would ever say that to his wife, of course. Sharon should be like a daughter to him, but that did not mean he did not see her obvious charms. She was a woman who needed a man. He suspected all had not been quite right between Sharon and Lenny before his son's death, but every time he had tried to ask her if things were OK, she had smiled and briskly changed the subject. He could only assume his Lenny had had a bird of some description. He was a realist. Lenny, God love him, would not have been the first and he would not be the last. But his death had obviously marked Sharon in some way.

Sharon had carried on with the betting shop and the loans and she had done a good job – Jack Johnson had made sure of that. He'd seen off all threats and had given her the best help available; that was a testament to Big Lenny's son's memory as far as he was concerned. He knew that Jack paid the lion's share of their wages and that he kept a close eye on Sharon and the boys. But she had changed so much.

He sighed as he listened to his wife argue how their daughter-in-law seemed determined to shut them out. There was more to this than met the eye; he'd lay money on it.

He wondered if he should mention to his wife that her overbearing nature could be part of Sharon's irritation. But she would de-ball him in nanoseconds if he dared to criticise her. Lesley Scott thought that only three opinions were valid: God's, the Pope's and hers. Obviously hers was the most important. Since they buried Lenny she had turned into a religious maniac. She took Communion every morning at six o'clock Mass. The priest bore the brunt of her grief and Big Lenny was relieved about that. He missed their boy as much as she did but, unlike her, he didn't feel the need to harass the priest about it.

He certainly couldn't tell her that his dead son's wife was becoming more and more appealing to him by the day. That he thought of her constantly. That he wanted her desperately. No, he was best keeping his own counsel about that. Sharon was like a drug to him. He knew it was wrong and yet he still wanted her.

Chapter Eighty-Six

Reggie was pleased to hear that Sharon was making a success of her businesses. In fact, behind the scenes, he had made sure that success would be hers, whatever happened. Like Jack Johnson, he was doing everything he could to make her life as easy as possible. Too many women in the Life were forgotten when they lost their men. It wasn't just losing a husband, but often a decent standard of living into the bargain. Reggie was determined that would not happen to Sharon or her boys. There had been that terrible moment after Lenny's death when Reggie realised she knew about them. They never again spoke about it explicitly, but he knew that she couldn't stand the sight of him. He kept his distance. He understood that she resented him, and he also appreciated that she had kept his secret. She could have quite easily destroyed him. But, in doing so, she would have destroyed her husband into the bargain and she would not do that to her sons.

She was an astute woman who understood the virtue of her silence. If the truth ever came out about Lenny, her sons would suffer as she would. Nevertheless Reggie was aware of how hard it must have been for a woman of her passion and temperament. He knew Sharon – how often had he discussed her with Lenny? He knew that Lenny had loved her and he wished he could remind her of that. Not that she would ever believe it now.

He still missed his friend and his lover. Lenny Scott had been all he had ever dreamed of, all he had ever wanted. The short time they had had together had been bittersweet. But his grief was aggravated by the fact that he had hurt Sharon Scott for no good reason. He had wanted her to live in ignorance, as had her husband. Lenny would have been devastated to know she'd uncovered their secret. Reggie had been an uncle to their sons and wanted the best for them. Why wouldn't he? He had never set out to hurt her – he liked and respected her. He had also been in love with the man she had married. Had he loved him more than her? Who could say? All he knew was that he would watch out for her and her sons as best he could, whether she wanted him to or not. It was what Lenny would have wanted too and Reggie would still do anything for him.

He walked into the Prospect of Whitby public house and headed to the bar. Jack wanted him to meet with a contact of his called Ray Donovan. He saw a huge, handsome man at the bar. The eyes of everyone in the place were on him, not just because he was new in town, but because he was a handsome fucker with a real presence. Even Reggie Dornan was impressed.

Ray Donovan had an easy charm that belied his size. He had a great smile that seemed to light up his face. He was dark-haired, blue-eyed and built like the proverbial brick shithouse. For Reggie, it was love at first sight. For Ray Donovan it was the start of a great friendship.

Jack had been looking for someone to take over Lenny Scott's businesses and look after Sharon and the boys and had asked Reggie to check him out. Twenty minutes into the meeting he knew this was just the man. Ray looked intimidating but he was easy-going and willing to do what was asked of him. Reggie was impressed that the man had done his homework and knew everything about Sharon, her family and their business connections; that told him he was dealing with a man of sense and discernment. Reggie had never been a queen-like homosexual, but he felt his heart hammering in his chest as Ray spoke. Not since Lenny had he felt like this about a man. But Reggie's gaydar was pretty good, and this man was straighter than the proverbial ruler. He still felt himself getting a hard-on as he looked at him though. It was clearly time for him to disappear and look for some entertainment further afield; he had no chance looking locally. Plus his tastes ran to the masculine, to men like himself: big, dangerous, up-for-it and discreet.

He brought his mind back to the man in front of him and explained the situation.

Ray Donovan seemed happy to listen and keen to take on the protection of Sharon Scott and her businesses. There had been a few overtures to take her cab ranks off her hands and, though she didn't want to be relieved of them, the man who had requested them was a new, young Face who had a reputation for violent confrontation. The combination of a big, handsome fucker like Ray Donovan, himself and Jack, might just be the answer to their prayers. Apparently Ray had his creds, he had done a lump and had done it with ease and without ruffling any feathers. He was well thought of up North and was in need of a change of scenery. He had tugged a big Filth so needed to leave his manor quickly.

Now all Reggie had to do was sell Ray to Sharon Scott; he had a feeling that she might not put up too much of a fight. The man was beautiful and he was a man's man. What Reggie Dornan wouldn't do to make him *his* man. Life could be fucking cruel.

Chapter Eighty-Seven

When Sharon let her father-in-law in she could see immediately that he had had a few too many. She opened him a bottle of Beck's, hoping he'd leave when he was done, and he drained it quickly. She was beginning to dread his visits. The way he looked at her made her feel uneasy. She sensed he wanted her and she was frightened. He was the grandfather of her boys – it was wrong.

He talked about Lenny all the time, pointing out how alike they were, saying that her sons needed a male influence. It was creepy and it was also something she didn't know how to deal with. Her father would lose it if she told him her fears. He would commit murder. And she had to think of Lesley, the sainted mother-in-law, who never lost a chance to tell her what she was doing wrong with her fatherless boys. She'd never believe it. She'd blame Sharon for stirring up lies.

Sharon sighed in consternation. She poured herself a whisky and looked at the man sprawled on her sofa.

She guessed he needed to be drunk to come to see her. Sober, he was a sensible man. But with a drink in him, he felt the urge to come to her and try, in his clumsy way, to tell her he loved her. It was so awful. She listened as he told her that she was a young woman still, how she needed an older man, a man who would keep her happy, who would be a mentor to her sons. Sons who needed a firm hand, a strong influence in their lives so they didn't go to the bad. She felt physically sick listening to him; she didn't know what to do. The last thing she wanted was a confrontation of any kind with her mother-in-law. That would cause too much hurt and bad feeling, and she didn't understand why this man couldn't see that. She didn't want him, and she didn't want the trouble and heartache that would follow if this ever got out. As if she would go near him! It was disgusting even to contemplate.

When she heard a knock at her door she was up and out of her seat with a mixture of relief and dread. She hoped it wasn't her mum or dad; her mum was astute enough to suss out the situation. She opened the door to Reggie Dornan and, for the first time in years, she was actually pleased to see him. She could see how shocked he was at his welcome and only hoped that he would immediately take on board what was going on. When she saw the man standing behind him, she was stunned into silence. He was the most beautiful man she had ever laid eyes on. He was big – bigger even than her Lenny had been – and he had deep-blue eyes and thick, black hair. She stood there for a long moment, her hand at her throat, as Ray Donovan walked towards her and, holding out his hand, said softly, 'I'm Ray.'

She opened the door wide and gestured for them to come into her home. She was bereft of speech.

Reggie watched them greet each other and felt a prickle of jealousy. He followed them into the house and felt a moment's anger; *he* should not be following Ray Donovan into Sharon's home – he was there to introduce them. He had to tread carefully where Sharon was concerned. He saw her as little as possible but he knew that Jack had noticed the animosity between them and wondered at why it was there. Like most people, he assumed that Lenny had been playing away from home and that Sharon had found out and blamed Reggie. Reggie never said a word either way – he was far too shrewd.

When they walked into the lounge, Reggie's heart dropped and he understood the reason for his unusually warm welcome.

Big Lenny, as drunk as he was, knew he had been caught out.

Reggie introduced Ray Donovan and he saw that Ray had taken in the situation immediately as well.

Big Lenny stood up and said haltingly that he was just leaving. It spoke volumes that no one insisted he got a cab and that they happily let him get in his Cosworth and drive himself home.

When he had gone, Reggie rolled his eyes at Sharon and she smiled sadly.

'Looks like we came at the right time, Sharon.'

She sighed heavily. 'You could say that.'

She offered them a seat and sat there quietly waiting to hear why they had called on her.

Reggie took the initiative then. 'Sorry to come here so late but I wanted to introduce you to Ray. Jack thinks you need him, Sharon. This is just to be on the safe side so don't get too worried, but having Jamie Brewer come after your cab ranks is serious. He won't go up against me, or Jack, obviously. He is, however, one devious cunt. So we have brought Ray in to give you a hand and a bit of muscle. He will be with you to help you run the show and to be there if anything should get a bit out of hand.'

Sharon realised immediately that Jack and Reggie must be genuinely worried if they were going to these lengths. She also realised that there could be real trouble in store. In all honesty, she had been going to let the fucker have the ranks but this man put a completely different connotation on the situation. She decided that she wanted Ray Donovan around for a while.

'Can I get you both a beer?'

She went into her kitchen and, as she opened the beers, she felt the pull of Ray Donovan. Even his accent was attractive. He was the antithesis of Lenny and that was exactly what she needed. Oh, he was big and he was handsome, and he was more man than she had ever seen in her lifetime. She also sensed that Reggie wanted him; she saw the way he looked at Ray, and that was enough for her to want him more. Let him see how it felt. As tears came to her eyes she went to the mirror and looked at herself. She knew she was a beautiful woman; men desired her. She had a lot to offer, not just in her looks – she also had lucrative businesses. She was considered a catch in their world but, until now, she had not wanted to be caught. This new development might force her father-in-law to give her a wide berth and that could only be a good thing.

Big Lenny had increasingly become a worry that she could do without. She felt it would not be long before he got up the courage to actually lay his hands on her. She had given him no encouragement at all. Why the fuck would she? He was a womaniser and, with a drink in him, he would eventually approach her. She was also shrewd enough to see that this Ray Donovan would be an asset to her in more ways than one: he could be the man to wipe away the memory of Lenny Scott and his fucking duplicity.

She brought the beers in to the men, and agreed with Reggie that Ray would start working for her the next day as her number two and, with that in mind, she went to bed for the first time in years a happy woman.

Chapter Eighty-Eight

Ray Donovan had looked at Sharon Scott and felt a tremendous – and unexpected – desire to look after her. She was a beautiful woman, but she was also very vulnerable. If ever a woman needed a man to look out for her then she was the one – alone with two young sons and no man on the horizon. Her husband, he knew, had been brutally murdered and that had left Sharon and her children bereft in all ways. He had never felt such a pull before, never felt such a rush of emotion as he had with this Sharon Scott. He sensed that she reciprocated his feelings – he wasn't a fool. Women liked him – they always had – but he wasn't a man to flit from girl to girl. He wanted something more than that. He wanted a woman he could love deeply and who he could respect.

He had known that Reggie Dornan was a queer. He had encountered enough in the clink and he could smell them from a mile off. He also knew that Reggie Dornan had to be very careful that no one in their world ever guessed about that part of his make-up. It wasn't as enlightened in the criminal world as things were on the BBC. Gay men were looked on with suspicion and it was still seen as a weakness. To the old guard it was looked upon as an aberration, something to be frightened of. Personally, he couldn't give a flying fuck. But he knew his world and, for men like Reggie Dornan, it was a dangerous path. He admired him actually because he knew how hard it was to live a lie. He knew that better than anyone.

Chapter Eighty-Nine

Sharon Scott opened her door at 7 a.m. to Ray Donovan. She was shocked once more at the sheer size of him. He walked through to the kitchen and she saw the awe on her sons' faces as he introduced himself. She poured him a coffee and watched delightedly as he conversed with her boys and they chatted back, perfectly at ease with this man who was going to be her minder. He was a natural with kids; he talked to them as equals and listened to what they had to say. It was good for her sons to have a man around, and she was pleased that she had already put on her make-up and dressed herself carefully. She liked this man and she had a feeling that he liked her.

For the first time since her husband's death, it felt as though things were looking up. She had needed someone to take her mind off things and this man, this Ray Donovan, was exactly the one to do it for her.

She cooked him eggs and bacon and, as she placed

the plate in front of him, he smiled at her and she knew that whatever happened she would be hard pressed to be without him already.

Chapter Ninety

Jamie Brewer was what was known as a fucker. He loved the epithet, and he lived up to it at every available opportunity. He was miffed, seriously miffed, that the cab ranks that were the property of Sharon Scott were not his to take. Oh, he appreciated that her old man had been a Face and that she had Jack Johnson and that arrogant cunt of a man, Reggie Dornan, on her side. But, as far as he was concerned, he needed those ranks to add to his growing empire.

Jamie was not that tall but he was broad and he had laughing, brown eyes and blond hair, the combination of which made women give him a second look. Jamie loved women; he had even considered fucking Sharon to get what he wanted. It appealed to him to fuck the widow of Lenny Scott, but one meeting with her had assured him she would not be swayed to his way of thinking. If he was honest, that had annoyed him too – women were usually inclined to fall at his feet. He was determined to get what he wanted, no matter what it took. If that meant frightening her, then that was what he would do. Jamie was a natural-born bully. He liked to intimidate and he enjoyed other people's discomfort. He relished their fear. He felt that anyone who had what he wanted should remember that he would move heaven and fucking earth to take it from them. It was what he had always done and he saw no reason to change his ways now. Jack Johnson was a fucking dinosaur and that cunt Reggie Dornan needed a fucking slap. Who did they think they were?

He would put himself out now to prove his point. Sharon Scott was a fucking female who wanted to live in a man's world. That meant she would have to be treated like a man. See how she liked that. As the old saying went, how could you trust anything that bled once a month and didn't die?

He was smiling as he made his plans. He would put the fuck on them all. This would be his Waterloo; he would make his point and he would do it with aplomb. He was a man who knew what he wanted and he was willing to take it, no matter what the consequences.

Chapter Ninety-One

Sharon walked into the office of the taxi rank in Ilford with Ray close behind her. She saw the stares of the drivers, and her controller especially. Margaret Avis was a woman of indeterminate age and she liked the men. Her eyes were nearly out on stalks as she looked Ray Donovan over from head to foot. Sharon had to suppress a smile.

In the office Sharon put on the coffee pot and, turning to Ray, she said seriously, 'Am I or my boys in any real danger?'

Ray looked at her and said quietly, 'Maybe. Jack thinks this Brewer wants to make his mark, and the best way to do that, in his mind, is to take what was your old man's. It's a ploy, fucking outrageous really. But he can bask in your old man's shadow if he takes on his businesses. It is a child's fucking game. So, don't worry – I will take that cunt out as soon as he rears his ugly head.' He smiled then, as he said quickly, 'I am assuming he is ugly! I don't know for sure.'

Sharon smiled with him. Ray was a really nice guy

and she was falling for him in a big way. His accent was music to her ears, he had a softness to his voice that she liked. She felt that he liked her too – at least that is what she hoped. She had not looked at another man since Lenny. When she had found out his true nature it had broken her heart. She had loved and trusted him and he had betrayed her in the worst way. Another woman she could have coped with, even forgiven. But a man? That was something that she had never even contemplated. Why would she? Lenny Scott had been a man, a real man. He had fooled everyone. Each time his mother extolled his virtues Sharon had felt sick because she knew the truth about the father of her two children – her handsome sons, so like him in looks and even in temperament – the man she had adored with all her soul.

She wondered briefly if Ray was hiding his true nature. She wasn't exactly a good judge, was she? She had had only one man in her life: Lenny Scott. She poured the coffees and forced the thoughts from her mind. That was then and this was now. She had to remember that Lenny was gone for ever. He was dead but she wasn't. This man had brought her back to life and she wanted him all the more for it.

Chapter Ninety-Two

Jack Johnson was pleased that he'd got Sharon Scott a minder because, when all was said and done, that was exactly what this Ray Donovan was. And he knew she needed one. It was good that he wasn't a local man – that would just cause more complications. Jamie Brewer was an arrogant little fuck, but he also had a few people on his side and that was why Jack and Reggie wanted to sort this with the least aggravation possible.

The Brewers were a big family that had managed to marry into other families. That meant that Jamie had good connections. But, as Jack pointed out to Reggie, that didn't mean he was liked. One thing they knew for sure about Jamie Brewer was that he was a reckless fucker. He had far too high an opinion of himself. He always, however, made a point of going after what he wanted with a vengeance. That was what they were so worried about.

'You think he is a new enough Face to give that cunt Brewer second thoughts?'

Reggie nodded. 'It will buy time, at least, Jack. She is safe with Ray until we can discover what Brewer intends to do. He has made a point of saying publicly that he wants the ranks. I am quite happy to take him out myself, as you know. But it's what goes with him we need to think about.'

Jack nodded sagely. 'I hate this kind of shite. Jamie Brewer is a little cunt with big connections. From what I can gather, though, his own family are not that enamoured of him. They see him as a loose cannon. I'm meeting with his mother's brother later on. I will try and sort something; I am not without my fucking own creds. I don't want to start a fucking war over taking out that useless cunt but by the same token I will not let Sharon be taken advantage of. She's under my protection so the fact he is stronging it is an insult to me, not to mention the insult to Lenny Scott. After all, she is his wife – or widow.'

Reggie knew how much Jack missed Lenny. He wished he could say how much he missed him too. They had had such fantastic sex, but they had also had fantastic conversations. They had been soulmates. If the world had been different they could have been the people they were meant to be instead of living a lie. For Sharon, Reggie was the reason she felt that her life had been wasted – her husband had wanted him over her. If only she could understand the truth of it all.

'I think bringing Ray in is a good move, Jack. He is a big fucker and he is loyal. He likes her, as well.

But then, what's not to like?' Reggie still acted the womaniser. What choice did he have?

Jack smiled. He was old school. He thought women needed a man in their lives; he believed they were not made to be alone for any length of time. Sharon had been without one long enough.

'She needs a man to put those kids of hers on the right track, if nothing else. Pair of fuckers they are.'

'There's something else too, Jack. Big Lenny is after her. I don't know what has come over him . . .'

Jack Johnson was seriously perturbed now. 'You are having a fucking laugh, surely?'

Reggie could hear the incredulity in his voice. 'I know what you're thinking but I saw it for myself. Let's say that me and Ray turned up just in time.'

Jack Johnson shook his head in disgust. 'What a complete cunt! Are you telling me he wants his dead son's wife?'

Reggie nodded. 'Sharon was so pleased to see me and Ray turn up last night. It was fucking embarrassing. I mean, in fairness to her, she has to tread warily. It's her kids' grandparents. Can you imagine Lesley Scott if she even fucking suspected?'

Jack shook his head as he said angrily, 'It would be fucking ambulances arriving! More fights than Mike Tyson! And, believe me, Lesley fucking Scott might act the Apostle of Christ but she can have a fucking row. In her day . . .' He shook his head in consternation. 'She is one nasty fuck if pushed. And you know what? I think she always resented poor Sharon for taking away her son.'

Reggie nodded; he knew that poor Sharon had resented him more for taking away her husband.

'Well, whatever, Jack. Ray Donovan will look out for her.'

Jack nodded. He was pleased because he had done what Lenny would have wanted. And Reggie knew exactly what he was thinking.

Chapter Ninety-Three

The cab drivers were nervous. This new bloke was a big fucker and there was obviously something going down. They all knew about Jamie Brewer and they were waiting to see how it played out. They liked Sharon; she was a good boss and she was fair. She even made sure that the airport runs were on a rota. But, at the end of the day, none of them wanted to be a fucking hero. They were cab drivers not fucking villains.

Cabbing in London was a dangerous occupation when you worked a patch like this. They were on Ilford High Road so they had pubs and clubs and all sorts of shit to contend with. The last thing they needed was upset in the rank itself. They had Tiffany's, they had Room At The Top – they had so many fucking places they were called to. It was a lucrative business. It was also a very dangerous one when fuckers like Jamie Brewer jumped on board. So, they sat and they waited to see how the land would lie when it was all over.

Chapter Ninety-Four

Ray had been given a flat in Mortlake Road and he decided it would do for the time being; he was only sleeping there, after all. He was still living out of a suitcase and he had welcomed the chance for a change of scenery. It had got a bit too hot for him up North. He liked Jack Johnson and Reggie Dornan. He had guessed about Reggie and wondered why others didn't sense it too. Maybe it was a southern thing. He shrugged and pushed the thought from his mind.

It was Sharon that he was interested in. She was a looker and she was a nice girl to boot. She was also the mother of two little terrors who he felt needed a firmer hand than she could give them. As for the father-in-law, that was a disgrace of epic proportions. His own son's widow? It was almost incest. What kind of personality would even consider something so heinous? Sharon Scott had looked terrified and he recognised as well as Reggie did that they had turned up at just the right moment. He wasn't a fool – some men would shag a fence if the opportunity presented itself. But to hit on your daughter-in-law – the mother of your grandsons – was disgusting. He would have to keep his wits about him where that man was concerned. He had proved that he was capable of anything. Ray was also shrewd enough to realise that in the sober light of day Big Lenny would be mortified, all the more so because he would remember that his humiliation had been witnessed. That did not augur well for future friendliness. No one liked to think that they had been caught out and that was exactly what had happened to Big Lenny Scott. Well, he was a man of stature, but to someone of Ray's temperament that meant nothing. He would wait and watch to see how things panned out there. But it was not a good beginning for either of them.

He turned his mind to this Brewer idiot. He had gathered as much information on him as possible and, after careful consideration, Ray had decided he wasn't too bothered about him. If push came to the proverbial shove he would just take him out. The man was a fucking menace – pure and simple. He understood that Jack was in a precarious position as the boy was more connected than the fucking crown princes of Europe. But that meant nothing if he wasn't liked. It seemed Jamie Brewer was seen as a pain in the arse by the majority of his relatives, though that did not alter the fact that he was related to some heavy people. You might not like your kin, but at the same time they were still your blood.

Ray's stint in prison had stood him in good stead where his reputation was concerned. He had done nine years behind the door and he had acquitted himself well, used his time wisely and made some good connections for himself. He had a solid reputation and he was respected for his stoic personality and his natural friendliness. Oh, he was all sweetness and light until someone put him out, then it was either fight or fucking die. He had always been that way, since he was a kid.

His mother had spent her life in police stations, headmasters' offices or visiting him in prison. She was a good woman, who, like Sharon, had been left alone to bring up a son who would go his own road. He was sorry to the heart for the trouble he had brought to her door, but he knew she loved him and he loved her. Life was what you made it, for good or for bad.

As he tossed and turned in the strange new bed, he wondered how he was going to fare in the next few weeks. Jamie Brewer would be aware by now that he was on the scene and why, so he had to be doubly careful in case he was blindsided. There was a good chance he might be taken out of the equation before it got too hot and heavy. But he was prepared for all eventualities: that was something he had learned in the nick. Never completely trust anyone was the main rule that he lived by and it had got him this far. He saw no reason to change now.

Chapter Ninety-Five

Jamie Brewer had a volatile temperament and he was known for his rashness and his tendency to lash out and think about his actions later. This had made him quite a few enemies. He had fallen out with every friend he had at some point so he was always running with different crowds. He was acquisitive and avaricious and he would literally stop at nothing to get what he wanted.

This was being relayed to Jack Johnson by Jamie's uncle, Pete, who was a decent and trustworthy individual. Jack listened with particular care to what he was being told, aware that Jamie had scarred the man's daughter for life during a family argument. A kettle of boiling water had been thrown and Pete's fifteen-year-old daughter had unfortunately been in the line of fire. It had missed her face but caught her on the chest and shoulders; it had been an accident of sorts, but one that had been caused by his nephew's temper. The incident had been smoothed over but, like any hurt to a child, it could never really be forgotten. Jack sensed that Pete Brewer would love nothing more than to see young Jamie get his comeuppance, and get it as violently as possible.

'You talked to your brother about the situation, Pete?'

The man nodded. 'He thinks you are right to be concerned but Jamie is still his son. Personally, I couldn't give two fucks what happened to the lairy little fucker. Someone's going to put him down eventually. That is inevitable.'

Jack nodded but he didn't say a word. What he sensed, though, was that Jamie Brewer, cunt or not, had a few of his family by his side. He sighed heavily. This could turn nasty all right. But he was honour-bound to look out for Lenny Scott's family. He would have to do whatever was necessary.

James Brewer Senior was the main man when it came to raves, bare-knuckle fights – or any outdoor entertainments, come to that. He was a serious lump and he had his creds. Jack liked and respected him, but that was put aside for the moment. If this went off then there would be bloody murders all over the Smoke. But sometimes that kind of conflict was par for the course. Wars were costly, time-consuming and – occasionally – necessary. He would have to think this through carefully. He must wait for the other side to strike the first blow which, from what he had heard about young Jamie, he had a feeling would not be long in arriving. He had no choice now but to wait for the inevitable. It was at times like this that he missed Lenny.

Chapter Ninety-Six

Jamie Brewer was in his sister Jackie's kitchen in Essex and she was listening avidly as he raved about her husband's treacherous conduct. An angry Jamie was a sight to behold and Jackie was always frightened of his tempers. She knew how vicious he could be, having been on the receiving end most of her life. Now it seemed her husband had committed the cardinal sin of putting the phone down on her brother after telling him to go and fuck himself. Her husband was not a wimp – Davie Bannerman could look after himself and that was something that Jamie often forgot. Like most people, Davie thought Jamie was a twat but, *unlike* most people, he didn't mind expressing this view – even to Jamie himself.

'Where is he, sis? I am going to fucking muller him.'

Jackie shook her head as she said carefully, 'I don't know, Jamie. I swear I don't know.'

Her two-year-old daughter was crying in the hallway. The shouting had terrified her, but Jackie was too nervous to bring the little girl into the same room as her brother in order to comfort her. Jamie was unpredictable like this – and the scalding episode was always in the forefront of Jackie's mind. If she had known where her old man was, she would happily have told him to get Jamie out of her house. She wasn't a coward by any means, but she knew what her brother was capable of when he was angry like this.

She was genuinely frightened.

Jamie turned and, pointing at the door, screamed, 'Shut that fucking kid up!'

Jackie burst into tears and she was relieved when her brother stormed out of her home, screaming obscenities as he went. Hearing his car screech off down her drive, she picked up her terrified daughter and, like her brother before her, she left the house as quickly as possible. She would go to her mate's, and wait there until all the fuss died down. She hoped he didn't come across her old man, because, when he was in a temper, Jamie was capable of anything.

Chapter Ninety-Seven

The cab drivers were nervous – a fact that easily communicated itself to the walk-in customers. There had been whispers, of course, that there was something going down so it was a quiet working environment these days, which was unusual in a cab rank. Normally there was plenty of banter and discussions about certain fares – whether it was an old man who stank of piss, or a particularly fuckable young mum. There would be a TV blaring and the sounds of the drivers calling over the radio. There was a cab drivers' mantra that went: if the wheels ain't turning, I ain't earning. They needed to get as many fares as possible to pay their weekly upkeep. Most cabbies were gregarious by nature; after all, it was a job where you dealt with the public. Even the ever-ebullient Margaret was looking decidedly shifty and the punters were all glad to leave the office and jump into the nearest cab.

Sharon came in at four in the afternoon with Ray and went through to her tiny office. She could sense the tense atmosphere and she was affected by it more than she would have believed possible. Even with the protection of Ray Donovan, she was feeling real prickles of unease. When Reggie Dornan and two other men turned up at five o'clock, she started to feel physically sick with dread. But she refused to leave; she understood that, whatever happened, she needed to be there or she would always regret it.

She was running three lucrative businesses: the cab ranks, the betting office and the loan company set up shortly before Lenny died. She was a woman in what was usually a man's world and she felt she had to show that she wasn't frightened of standing up for herself. True, the men were here to do the defending, but instinct was telling her to stay put and have her say.

She could feel Ray watching her and she knew that he thought she should go home to her children and leave the men to sort everything out. Whereas Reggie appeared to understand what she was feeling; she was shocked to realise that he admired her for her stand. The two heavies didn't really give a fuck either way, or, if they did, they were not sharing their opinions.

Sharon made endless cups of tea and coffee and Reggie kept the conversation going so everything seemed as normal as possible. The drivers, though, were more aware than ever of the tension in the rank and more than a couple went home, unwilling to be caught up in whatever might happen.

Sharon's mother had the two boys overnight in case anything kicked off at the house and Jack Johnson was never off the blower, getting regular updates and revealing whatever he could find out to them. Reggie and Ray discussed the situation in low voices when the need arose and Sharon, realising she had not eaten since that morning, wondered how people in war zones lived in this state of perpetual fear of violence. Inwardly she was trembling like a poplar; outwardly she was aware that she looked very calm.

It was seven in the evening when the first blow was struck. It was a drive-by and three shots were fired through the windows of the cab rank. It was a miracle that no one was seriously harmed. Margaret's screaming was heard all over East London, and it took an injection by the local doctor to finally shut her up.

Chapter Ninety-Eight

David Bannerman was like a man possessed after his wife explained what had occurred at his home. It was his good luck that, shortly after talking to her, he had a phone call from Jack Johnson who was asking around about the whereabouts of Jamie.

Davie was well aware that there was aggro between Jamie and Jack Johnson over Lenny Scott's holdings but, until now, he had not given any of it a second thought in relation to his family. But after that cunt's behaviour in his home, threatening his wife and terrifying his child, Jamie Brewer had become what he classed as fair game. Davie Bannerman would happily serve him up.

He assured Jack Johnson that his main aim in life was to see that filthy, rotten piece of dog shit Jamie Brewer six feet under and, if necessary, he would do the fucking job himself.

Jack Johnson guessed rightly that once again Jamie had shat on his own doorstep. He was almost smiling as he explained the latest turn of events to the irate man on the other end of the phone.

Chapter Ninety-Nine

Jamie Brewer was in The Volunteer pub in Barking, listening to his father as he lectured his son for the umpteenth time about the fact that he could not go around threatening his own family and shooting up fucking cab ranks willy-nilly.

James Senior was more than aware of his son's failings but, as much as he irritated him, Jamie was still his eldest son and he had to make sure he kept his own temper in check. Nevertheless, sometimes he felt he could quite happily take the fucker out himself. Like most people who knew young Jamie, he believed his boy was living on borrowed time because, eventually, he was going to upset the wrong person. But explaining that to someone who had no intention of listening to anything he saw as even remotely a criticism of his own good self was basically an impossibility. It did not stop the man from trying though. He was also warning him that Davie Bannerman was baying for his blood and was threatening him with immediate extinction on sight.

Young Jamie took all this in his stride. He was still on an adrenaline high from shooting up the cab office; he was hoping that he had hit someone – that appealed to his sense of melodrama. In fact, he was hoping that he had taken out the giant Northerner who had been given to Sharon Scott as some kind of bodyguard! For fuck's sake, she would need an army of Titans to protect her before he was finished. He had always wanted Lenny Scott's holdings and he would not rest until he had them firmly in his hot little hands.

James Senior watched Jamie as he completely disregarded everything he was trying to tell him and, eventually, fed up with his son's attitude, he walked out of the pub and drove himself home. He only hoped that Davie Bannerman got him before anyone else. He wouldn't have to avenge Bannerman's treatment of his son, that was family business and Jamie had stepped over the line. But with Jack Johnson and Co. it would be completely different.

Chapter One Hundred

Reggie Dornan was fit to be tied. Whatever they had been expecting, shots fired while the offices were open was definitely not part of it. How no one had been seriously hurt could only be put down to a miracle. There were just a couple of cuts and abrasions to attend to, which, considering the amount of glass that had been flying around, really was miraculous.

Sharon had been fantastic; she had calmed people down and dealt well with the police. Ray had made himself scarce before the arrival of the Filth and took the two heavies with him. There was no need to alert the whole world to their presence. The cab drivers were shaken but kept their traps shut. Everyone acted as if the shooting had been as unexpected as a vicar at an orgy. The police were not fools but they knew when it was pointless to push too much over certain matters.

By ten o'clock the windows were boarded up, the drivers had gone home and Sharon gratefully downed a large brandy with Reggie.

'You holding up all right?'

Sharon looked at the man and remembered that, at the first shot, he had thrown himself on top of her. That had to count for something.

She nodded. 'Thanks, Reggie. For protecting me . . .'

He knew how hard it was for her to say the words so he smiled widely – a smile that, frankly, he didn't think he had in him.

'Look, Sharon, I know how you feel about me . . .' He hesitated before saying, 'And Lenny.'

She held up her hands as if to ward him off. 'Don't! I mean it, Reggie – I will not discuss him with you.'

She felt the familiar disgust rising inside her and she wished that he had died too. If he had died she would never have had to think of any of this again. Just looking at him reminded her of her husband's treachery. She was ashamed of her thoughts but she could not deny them. It didn't matter how many Elton Johns or Lily Savages came on the scene. She could never forgive her husband for lying to her the way he had and for letting her live a life that was a lie for all those years. When she looked at Reggie she wondered at how powerful hatred could be. Because she hated this man with a vengeance.

'There's nothing you can say that will make anything different.'

Reggie knew when to retreat. He refilled their glasses and watched sadly as she gulped at her drink. Her hands were shaking suddenly and he saw the shock had finally set in.

'Come on. Drink up and I'll run you to your mum and dad's. You need a hot bath and a couple of sleeping pills.'

She sighed. 'What happens now?'

He shrugged nonchalantly. 'Now, Sharon, we hunt that cunt down and sort him out. Jack can't let this go and neither can I. He stepped over a line today and that is why we have to take him out of the game once and for all.'

She nodded almost imperceptibly. She had guessed as much. 'Maybe I should just have given him what he wanted.'

Reggie grinned and she saw how handsome he was, how like Lenny he looked, and she felt the sickness that always assailed her when she thought of him and her husband together.

'You don't give spoiled brats what they want, Sharon. Plus, if you had rolled over he would have taken everything you had. That's his personality, the kink in his nature that makes him so greedy for everything he sees. Do you know the worst thing? Every business he gets his hands on, he ruins. Runs them into the ground and fights with his workforce, his partners, whoever. He is a nutbag, plain and simple. And by tomorrow he will be a fucking dead one.'

Chapter One Hundred and One

Ivy Conway had been terrified for her daughter's safety and she hugged Sharon tightly when she finally walked through the front door. Del was relieved and he shook hands with Reggie, thanking him for bringing her home safely. Reggie left to go about his business and Del followed him out. He wanted to be a part of all this, no matter what Ivy might think about it.

Inside, Ivy was having difficulty believing what her daughter had been through. 'Is it true they shot at the rank, Sharon?'

Sharon nodded.

'Dear God in heaven. What has the world come to when a woman can't even run a legitimate business in peace?'

Sharon sighed heavily. She knew that this would be the general conversation from now on; her mother exclaiming over the events, and her wanting to forget them, for a short while at least. The fear at the noise of the shots and the sheer confusion that had surrounded the act was finally hitting her and she felt sick with apprehension. She wished she had just given Jamie the fucking lot and been done with it. But she had listened to Jack Johnson and, knowing he had her back, she had not been too worried about the outcome.

Now, though, it was a different kettle of fish altogether. She was frightened, seriously frightened. It was just sinking in that someone had shot at her, had actually picked up a gun and fired at her and her workforce. The enormity of it was hitting her. The sheer outrageousness of the act made her realise just what she was dealing with. Suppose Jack Johnson, Reggie and Ray couldn't sort this out? Where did that leave her and her boys? Her husband had been murdered – and they'd never found the killer – would she be next? Her hands were shaking violently.

Ivy went to the bathroom and, taking two sleeping pills out of a bottle, she hurried through to the lounge and forced Sharon to take them. Then she ran her a bath and helped her daughter into it. Finally she poured out two glasses of wine and sat on the floor of the bathroom, listening helplessly as her daughter cried her heart out.

Chapter One Hundred and Two

Davie Bannerman was still like a man possessed. He had tracked Jamie down to a local boozer on Brixton High Street. He had no qualms about letting Jack and his crew know his brother-in-law's location because he intended to be there to make sure that everything was done properly.

The one thing with Jamie Brewer was that he had extraordinary luck where saving his own skin was concerned. It was almost fucking demonic. He had been stabbed years before in a fight and, though the knife had pierced his heart, he had fucking recovered. As he had lain in the ambulance, the Old Bill had asked him who the culprit was and Jamie had told them in no uncertain terms to go fuck themselves. He had to be given creds for that. But he had defied everyone, the doctors included, by surviving and coming out of hospital as strong as he ever was.

Jamie had then knifed the boy responsible fifteen times.

Oh, he had the luck of the Irish all right, but tonight that luck was going to finally run out. Because he, David Bannerman, was going to see to it personally.

Chapter One Hundred and Three

Ray Donovan was raring to go. He was absolutely fuming over the night's events and he would not rest until that little fucker was in the ground. The sheer recklessness was his main concern. What kind of fucking Face put the public in danger like that? Men and women who were simply going about their daily business. This was London, not fucking Belfast. It showed just what kind of an imbecile they were dealing with. Ray didn't care how connected this ponce was. It was all over for Jamie now – no one would countenance such stupidity, no one of any worth anyway. Jack Johnson seemed to think that the lad's father was even willing to wipe his mouth. There was a maniac brother-in-law out for his hide as well. Jamie Brewer certainly seemed to have the knack for making enemies.

Ray got out of the car with Reggie and the two heavies and they made their way into the public house. This was Rastaland, and Reggie had taken the liberty of informing an old friend of his that they were coming.

Barton King was a huge Jamaican with thick dreads

and an easy smile; he was the undisputed main man in Brixton and Tulse Hill. He had already had a couple of run-ins with Jamie Brewer so he was only too happy to help take him down. He had agreed to make sure the fucker didn't leave the pub – by force if necessary.

Jamie was with his crew; they were drunk and stoned, and celebrating his big shoot-up of a widow woman's business. Barton watched him warily as did Barton's own crew. He had crossed the line when he had gone after Lenny Scott's widow – she had two young sons and a dead husband. People like her were entitled to be left in relative peace.

Jamie Brewer was laughing when the four men walked into the boozer. Desmond Dekker was on the jukebox and, within seconds, the pub was cleared of its usual clientele who all had a terrible urge to suddenly walk down the high street and finish their drinking elsewhere. It wouldn't take Albert fucking Einstein to work out that some serious business was going down. For the first time Jamie felt a prickle of fear. His posse moved instinctively away from him, and he sensed the anticipation in the air. All his life his family had protected him. He had done exactly what he had wanted to and never had a thought for the consequences.

When his brother-in-law walked in and locked the doors of the pub he felt his stomach clench and he understood that he was on borrowed time. He looked up into the faces of Ray Donovan and Reggie Dornan and saw that they were determined to finish him.

'Hello, Jamie.' Reggie's voice was soft but in the quiet of the pub it sounded like a gunshot.

Jamie looked at his crew and saw the same fear etched on to their faces. Barton King was smiling that easy smile of his and, going behind the bar, he started to set up some drinks. Then Ray Donovan took out a machete from under his coat and they all watched in fascination as Jamie Brewer was dismantled before their eyes.

David Bannerman was the first to shake Ray Donovan's bloodstained hand and then a party atmosphere ensued. Jamie's crew were told to pick up their mate and deliver him to his home. They were given black bags to carry him in. Then the men sat down and, while Ray cleaned himself up, they chatted amicably.

The only comeback from James Brewer was to take out the two heavies who should have protected his son. Minor cogs was how he saw them. That satisfied his revenge and kept him in good stead with his colleagues. Something had been done – or had been seen to be done anyway. He knew better than to try and take it too far; even he wouldn't relish taking out his own daughter's husband. But, if he was honest with himself, he never really liked David Bannerman after that night.

Chapter One Hundred and Four

Ray Donovan and Barton King became good friends after the murder of Jamie Brewer and they were regularly seen together drinking. Ray always laughed and said it was because he favoured a machete, which was often the weapon of choice for Jamaicans.

It was three months after Jamie's murder that Ray brought Sharon with him to see Barton and his wife, Jamella. The two women had been friends at school and had wanted to meet up and reminisce. It was also the night Ray realised that he was in love with Sharon Scott. As they sat in the restaurant eating curried goat and rice, he watched her as she smiled and laughed with her old friend and he knew then that he would do everything in his power to protect her and her two little boys. He had never felt like this about a woman before and he liked it.

He liked working with her too, enjoyed running the loan operation, which was getting bigger and bigger by the day. Who knew there was so much money in poverty? But, as Sharon pointed out, they didn't charge as much as the other lenders and they didn't threaten violence if the money was in arrears. The secret was not to lend out money the person couldn't afford to pay off – though that was not how many of the other lenders worked.

They had expanded to other areas and they had good collectors working for them – even some women, which was unheard of in their game. But Sharon made sure that there was always a stunning array of bedding and clothes to offer on the tally, as well as electrical goods and homeware. That was where she believed the real money would be and she seemed to be right. She was astute in her own way. She was everything Ray wanted in a woman and he wished he could tell her how he felt. But the first move had to come from her, of that much he was sure.

Sometimes he caught her watching him with what he thought was a softness in her eyes, but he honestly didn't know if that was just wishful thinking on his part. The main thing he was pleased about was that the haunted look had left her, and for that he thanked God. After the trouble with the Brewers, she had seemed to lose a lot of her sparkle. But he had seen her gradually coming back to herself now that the immediate threat was gone.

James Brewer Senior, in a gesture that had thrown everyone – even Jack Johnson – had gone to see her personally and had assured her that he was heart-sorry for her troubles, offering her his protection or his help if she or her sons ever needed it. It was an empty promise, as she had Jack, Reggie and now Ray himself looking out for her, but the fact he had expressed it spoke volumes. He had certainly gone up in people's estimation since. Though cynics like himself, Reggie and Jack believed it might have had more to do with the man finding out that the little fucker had been robbing him blind right, left and centre. His own son! Who would have believed it? It seemed that Jamie Brewer was willing to thieve off anyone, family included, which spoke of the moral fibre he possessed.

As they were ordering their liqueurs, Ray's hand accidentally came into contact with Sharon's and he felt her draw back from him. But when he looked into her eyes she was smiling shyly at him and he answered that smile with one of his own. It was an intimation that she was ready to take their relationship a step further; at least he hoped so.

Barton and Jamella watched the display, both wondering why it was taking this pair of idiots so long to see that they were made for each other.

Chapter One Hundred and Five

Sharon Scott was nervous and she didn't know why. It wasn't like she didn't know Ray Donovan; she spent the best part of each day with him. He had even taken to running her sons to school, which they loved. They saw in Ray a surrogate father, and that could only be a good thing. He took them on jaunts as well, joked with them about supporting Manchester United instead of West Ham, though he supported Newcastle. He made sure they did their homework and questioned them about their lives. Something Lenny had never really done.

Lenny had assumed they would follow in his footsteps; in fact, that was what Lenny expected, whereas Ray talked to them about education and what opportunities there were if only they were willing to work hard. These conversations pleased her because she thought along those lines too. She could never bury her sons like she had her husband, and like James Brewer Senior had buried his boy. She was determined to keep her boys as far away from villainy as possible.

She knew first-hand the horror it could bring to the women involved, as well as the men. She wanted more for them.

Ray kept them in hand; they were already quieter, more ready to listen to reason because of his influence. When Liam had been fighting again, Ray refused him the opportunity to go on an outing, only taking young Lenny, and that had given the boy food for thought. Ray said the best way with kids was to praise good behaviour and punish the bad. It was as simple as that. Then he added ruefully that it had not worked in his case, but then his mother had been a lone parent like her. Boys didn't listen too hard to their mothers it seemed.

Now, as they drove home, Sharon hoped fervently that he would at least attempt to kiss her. She had been looking at herself lately with critical eyes. She had given birth to two sons but her body was still in pretty good condition. Maybe she wouldn't pass muster in broad sunlight, but she looked good enough considering. Plus she wanted this man, and that had to be a good thing, surely? After Lenny, and what she had found out, she wasn't sure she would ever have wanted or trusted another man again. But lately she had begun to change her mind.

She watched Ray closely, noticing the way he smiled when he was talking to the boys. She saw how his thick, dark hair curled into his neck. She liked that his eyes were deeply blue and had a sparkle in them.

Sharon Scott understood that she was falling in love with this man. He was another Lenny in some ways – a villain, a man who made his money off criminal activities. She knew he had been in prison for nine of his thirty-six years, yet she still saw him as the answer to her prayers. And, even knowing everything she did about him, she still desired him.

She had observed him intently with Reggie and, though they got on well and had a deep mutual respect, she sensed that was all it was. Gerry Dornan had nearly fainted at the sight of Ray and kept telling her she should de-trouser him at the earliest opportunity. She was a card, was Gerry. She was also a very beautiful girl, yet never once had she seen Ray treat her with anything other than friendliness. Gerry dressed with her assets always shown to their best advantage, but Ray had never let his eyes linger on her for too long. Sharon Scott hoped that she was right about this man because she really could not imagine her life without him in it. It was getting harder and harder to get into that great big bed and not think about what she could be doing in it with Ray Donovan. She blushed at the thought and saw that he was smiling at her, as always.

She invited him in for coffee and was inordinately pleased when he said yes. As they went into the house she felt the trembling inside her. The only man she had ever been with was Lenny Scott. They had courted from when she was thirteen years old and married at seventeen. She felt like a teenager again, not a mother of two sons. She was so nervous she felt ill!

In the kitchen she went to put on the coffee but he stopped her, saying quietly, 'Sit down, Sharon. I think this might be the time for a brandy, don't you?' He could sense how nervous she was, and he knew why she was feeling that way. He wanted this to be perfect, or at least as perfect as he could make it. He followed her into the lounge and as she perched on the sofa he poured out two generous brandies. When they were sitting side by side he smiled at her and she felt the pull of him; it was almost a physical pain she wanted him so much.

'Look, Sharon, I know you were happy with Lenny, and I don't want you to feel that I will, in any way, denigrate the man who married you and fathered your children. But I have to tell you, before we go any further, that I have fallen for you, in a big way.'

She felt the tears come into her eyes. Oh, the big-heartedness of him, the kindness of him.

'I am looking for a real relationship. I think the world of your boys, as you know. I think they like me too. At least, I hope they do. But I need to know how you feel about me . . . About us.'

She felt so shy again, and she wished she had more experience. But she guessed that, had she had the experience, he might not be so enamoured of her. Ray was a man who would not love lightly. For a start he had never been married, but that might be because he was banged up for nine years. She understood the world he lived in. He grabbed her hand and she felt the love inside her like she had never felt it with Lenny. Lenny had broken her heart; it was hard on a woman to find out she had lived what she believed was a good life with a man that, in reality, she had never really known. It still bit into her and hurt her. Now, though, the hurt came more from the knowledge that she had been duped by Lenny, that he had believed she was so naive she would never cotton on. She wouldn't have known anything if it had not been for Liam.

She looked into Ray's eyes and said honestly, 'We weren't that happy, Ray. Not when he died.'

He looked at her and waited for her to go on but she didn't say anything else. She just looked at him with her big blue eyes and he felt his heart beating a tattoo in his chest.

He had never wanted a woman so much in his life. But there was so much he could never tell her about his life. The telling could destroy her. He would never intentionally hurt her. He had fallen madly in love with her; he had heard people say that they loved but he had never understood it till now. It had been a very strange experience for him, as he had always believed that he would never feel such emotion for another person. He wanted this woman on any terms, but he would be as honest as he could without hurting her.

So he said softly, 'I know about Lenny.' He saw the

way her face paled at his words, but he went on. 'Liam told me.'

She didn't know what to say and she just sat there bewildered. 'Told you what?'

It was a whisper and he felt so heart-sorry for her. 'About what he saw with Lenny and Reggie.'

She was starting to panic and he took her in his arms and held her to him. She could hear the steady beat of his heart and it calmed her.

'Look, I can't imagine what it must have felt like to discover something so shocking. I ain't defending Lenny when I say that, in the world we occupy, this is not something anyone with half a brain would broadcast. He suppressed it, I suppose, and from what I can gather he loved you with all his heart. As I do.'

She was frightened of his words and he understood why. This wasn't something she would relish being spoken of by people in their world.

'I just want you to know, Sharon, that I understand how it must have hurt and I want to take that hurt from you, darling. I want to make you see that you are a beautiful and desirable woman. I just want to love you, if you will let me.'

And she let him. Twice.

Chapter One Hundred and Six

'Oh, Sharon Scott, you are a jammy bitch!'

Sharon laughed at Gerry's obvious delight. She had never felt so alive. Ray might never have been married but he was certainly not backwards in coming forwards. It was the best sex of her life, and that had been a revelation in itself. It had been a whole new experience for her. Lenny had satisfied himself; Ray wanted to satisfy her. She felt lighter inside somehow.

When she had found out about Lenny and Reggie it had made her feel less than a woman, especially when she remembered how vicious he could be with a few drinks in him. It amazed her to think just how under his influence she had been. She had lived her life only around him and her boys. She felt as if she had woken up suddenly and the world was a much brighter place. Her only worry was how the boys would react to the relationship with Ray, now it was on a more permanent footing.

Ray had told her that he loved her and wanted to be with her and the boys as a proper family. She loved that he had said that he did not want to take Lenny's place. He had been their father and they would never be allowed to forget that fact. But Ray was willing to be a good stepfather to them. He said he already loved them because they were from her body – they were a part of her, so how could he not want the best for them?

Her other worry was Big Lenny. They had never really got back on any kind of good footing and she knew that Lesley blamed her for that and felt that she was trying to keep the boys away from her. How could she tell her the truth of it? How could she confide in someone who thought she had the voice of God in her ear twenty-four hours a day? Who would be mortified to think that her husband had tried to have a relationship with her dead son's wife, insinuating that she needed a man and he was the man for the job. To make matters worse, Big Lenny knew that Reggie had sussed him out and that did not augur well for any of them. She sighed with sadness. Why couldn't life be easier? Why did it have to always throw her a fucking curveball when she least expected it?

She busied herself making more tea for her and Gerry. She would put the shit that had accrued since Lenny's death from her mind. She was happy and she intended to stay that way.

Chapter One Hundred and Seven

Ray Donovan felt like all his Christmases and birthdays had come at once. The night with Sharon was the best night of his life. In prison, he had dreamed of a good woman, a decent woman, someone he could love, respect and trust, and he had found her, under the most unusual circumstances. He was amazed that it was a woman who already had two sons and had been married to a piece of shit like Lenny Scott. Because, when all was said and done, Lenny Scott was scum, he now knew that better than anyone. He was a man who should never have married and especially not a girl like Sharon. She had been with one man and she had trusted him to do right by her. Lenny Scott had tried, Ray did not doubt that, but his nature had made sure that he could never really love her. Ray's heart broke for her; for a beautiful woman to find out she had never really been wanted was a terrible situation to be in. But now she had him, and he would make sure that she never doubted herself again.

They had talked into the night and she had explained

how her husband's actions had almost destroyed her. Even little Liam still had the memory fresh in his mind. For a child to see that? It was tragic.

He had left her that morning a happy man. The boys had stayed at her mother's and that had given them time together. He was thankful for that and he hoped that they would accept him. But they still remembered their father and he understood that it might be difficult for them at first. They would soon learn that life was hard even when you had more than most people.

He was nervous of seeing her today, and he wondered why. They were perfect together. He hoped against hope that she would not regret letting him into her life. It was all he had wanted from the first time he had seen her. That was the strange thing about life: you never knew what was going to happen next. It was what made it so exciting, and now he had Sharon Scott he would never let her go. He would grow old with her, and that thought pleased him. He loved everything about her, her face, her body, her personality – even her smell. He had never felt like this about anyone before.

Chapter One Hundred and Eight

Big Lenny was ashamed and annoyed in equal parts. If he was honest, he had always harboured feelings for Sharon Conway, but while his son had been alive, he could keep them in check. Seeing her alone with those two little boys, he had begun to think that he could be the answer to her prayers. She was so innocent, and he felt she needed a man of the world to look out for her. He still believed that she needed someone who could be a father to her sons and a man with her.

As far as he was concerned, Reggie Dornan and the northern ponce, who now seemed to accompany her everywhere, were out of order. She was his son's widow and that gave him rights. What those rights were even Big Lenny wasn't sure, but one thing he was sure of was once she understood where he was coming from, she would know it was the right thing to do, not just for her but also for those little boys.

Lesley had guessed that there was something troubling him, and he hated deceiving her. But she was old; old and boring. He was still a virile man and Lesley had never really been that hot in the sack – it had been the fucking missionary position their whole life. He envied the young men these days; they were pursuing women and girls who knew that sex was not just for the procreation of children. They liked a good time too.

He swallowed down another shot of vodka and immediately poured himself the next. It was Dutch courage. He knew that all Sharon needed was persuasion. She was ripe for a man, and that was something a girl like her would need explaining. She needed a real man. Which is exactly what he was.

Chapter One Hundred and Nine

Ray had settled into the London scene well. He was liked and that meant a lot. Unpopular people, especially if they did not originate in the Smoke, could often find their lives very difficult. Doors would be closed to them, and disrespect would be rife. Unless, of course, they had a killer reputation – then it was a different kettle of fish. Then they were vilified behind their backs until an opportunity came to see them off.

Ray Donovan, however, through his treatment of Sharon Scott, was seen as a man's man by everyone. He made a good impression and he didn't presume, which was always a good idea with Londoners. His friendship with Barton King also helped. They were an incongruous pair, but the genuine camaraderie was easily apparent. Barton was known as a man who did not suffer fools gladly, so this Ray Donovan had to have something going for him. Reggie Dornan and Jack Johnson were also giving him his due; all in all, Ray's life was settled.

Now that he had Sharon Scott he felt a very blessed

man indeed. In fact, he was whistling as he went into the small offices in East Ham where they ran the loan business.

He smiled as he looked around him; it was obvious that a woman worked in here. For a start it was spotlessly clean and the plants, which were numerous, were well watered and healthy-looking. Even the venetian blinds were dust free. It always made him smile; it was like being in a small home office where the lady of the house did her accounts and wrote to her friends. He always felt too big for the place, especially the oak desk, even though Sharon had replaced the chair with one that allowed for his height and bulk.

He sighed pleasantly. Soon the workers would be in with their usual complaints about late payers and other gripes. But he was well able for them, as his old mum used to say, and deep down he enjoyed his work.

Sometimes the past came back to haunt him, but those moments were getting less as the time wore on. Prison, especially a lump of a sentence, could do that to a man. It was the isolation from the outside world that was the worst. Once you got your head around that it made life easier. Some men became paranoid; others who missed their families became depressed, while men like him just felt that they were in some kind of suspended animation.

He shook the thoughts from his mind and sipped at his thick, strong coffee – careful, as always, to use the coaster provided! He was smiling once more at Sharon and her foibles. Most loan offices looked like a scene from War on Want. As the business of the day began he felt himself relax properly; he loved his work and that was half the battle.

Chapter One Hundred and Ten

Sharon was enjoying having a day off. She had cleaned the house from top to toe and she was about to get into a nice relaxing bath when her doorbell rang. Sighing in annoyance, she slipped on a dressing gown – a thick, warm, towelling one – and went down the stairs to answer the door. It was Big Lenny. She saw that he was well away and letting him in was the last thing she wanted to do. She tried to slam the door in his face but he was already halfway into the house. This was the one time she cursed that no one could see them from the road.

He shoved the door shut clumsily behind him and said angrily, 'Why are you treating me like this? I was there for you after Lenny died and you weren't so fucking fussy then, were you?'

Sharon Scott looked at the man who had often made her feel uneasy but who had also been a great father to Lenny and grandfather to her boys. He was now her enemy, but she had to box clever. She said, as placatingly as possible, 'Please, Len. Will you go?'

Big Lenny was staring at her. She had bewitched him. He fantasised about having sex with her, about them living as man and wife, about having her whenever he wanted her. In the fantasy, though, she was a willing participant. She was groaning with pleasure and egging him on to bigger and better performances. But the reality was very different.

'I am warning you, Len. If you don't go I am going to tell Lesley what's going on.'

He continued to stare at her and she felt fear washing over her.

'I'm not joking. Reggie and Ray already know what the score is—'

It was hearing Ray's name that seemed to send Big Lenny over the edge. His hand shot out and he grabbed the front of her dressing gown, pulling her towards him and causing it to fall open. She was naked underneath but before he knew what had happened, she had slipped out of the sleeves and was making a run for the back door. He was on her in seconds and, when he forced her to the floor, she could feel the coldness of the wood, and the pain as he lay on top of her. She was fighting not just with fear but also with disgust. She could smell the alcohol on his breath, and the sweat from his body. It was making her gag.

As he held her arms above her head with one large hand, he shoved her legs open with his knee, all the time fumbling with his zipper, and she screamed out. He was forcing himself inside her. With one last surge of strength she bucked her hips and forced him off her. She turned, bringing her knee up with all her might, and caught him perfectly. Now it was he who was screaming in pain.

As he rolled away from her she was up and running. She ran up her stairs and didn't stop until she was in her bedroom. She locked the door and picked up the phone.

She rang Jack Johnson, assuming rightly that he was the best person at this time. Ray would do murder. As would Reggie. As would her father.

As she whispered urgently into the phone she could hear Big Lenny coming up the stairs and she was almost hysterical with fear. She could still smell him on her. It was making her want to vomit. She placed a chair under the handle of the door and then ran into the en-suite bathroom, locking that door behind her. She stood there shivering in fear as she waited to see what was going to happen next.

Chapter One Hundred and Eleven

Jack Johnson was in shock but he was a man who worked well under pressure. He racked his brains for someone he knew in the area where Sharon lived and he came up with a huge bouncer called Dougie Stewart.

Dougie was a big Scottish lump from Glasgow who had married a very pretty and available Essex girl. She had produced two beautiful children – and then run off with Dougie's best friend. Dougie now brought his kids up with the help of an au pair and spent his spare time hunting down his errant wife.

He listened carefully to what Jack Johnson said, kissed his kids and smiled at the au pair. Then he left the house and was on his way in seconds. He was disgusted with what Jack had told him; that a man could go after his son's widow was just about the lowest of the low. Reading between the lines it seemed that Big Lenny, the piece of shite, was looking for a right-hander. Well, he would not have to wait for long.

At Sharon's house, he parked the car, walked around the back and kicked the door in with one swift movement. He could hear the commotion upstairs and made his way up the stairs with great speed considering his bulk.

He was still hammering Big Lenny when Reggie arrived. It took all Reggie's considerable strength to pull him off.

Chapter One Hundred
and Twelve

Gerry was sitting with Sharon, refilling her wineglass when needed and just listening to what Sharon had to say. Gerry was scandalised at the horrific treatment of her friend. And by her own father-in-law! *That* was what she had trouble getting her head round. She had tidied up as best she could, disposed of the dressing gown, helped her friend into the bath and arranged for the boys to go to Sharon's mother's house.

Big Lenny had been taken away by Reggie and Dougie, and they had heard nothing from anyone since. The girls agreed that the last person Sharon needed now was Ivy. She would just tell her husband what had happened to their daughter and that would cause even more aggravation. She would have to be told but not yet.

The other person in the dark about the night's events was Lesley, though why Sharon was trying to spare that religious maniac, Gerry didn't know. But Sharon could be funny like that; she knew how much the boys meant to Lesley since the murder of her son. Sharon was a better person than she would ever be, Gerry knew that much.

She still could not find out what exactly had happened. Gerry would lay money that he had managed to rape the girl; she had seen the bruises on her in the bathroom. But that was something for Sharon to say yes or no to. She was the victim and it was her call. Gerry shuddered, trying to imagine the horror of your dead husband's father trying to have sex with you. It was gross, unnatural – especially with a man like Big Lenny Scott.

Sharon knew that it would be pointless trying to keep the attack from Ray, but what she knew she *had* to keep secret was that she had been raped. He had managed to penetrate her, and the thought of it made her feel physically ill. The smell of him was still in her nostrils and she wondered if it would ever go away. She could still feel his hands on her breasts, between her legs and his tongue probing inside her mouth. She felt like gagging again and she tried to stifle the reflex.

She could see poor Gerry watching her, and she knew her friend had guessed a lot more than she was letting on. It was strange because Gerry was normally full of inane chatter, but now she was quiet and calming. Sharon was pleased she was there. She knew that she would go along with whatever Sharon wanted to do about the situation. She would need someone watching her back –

none of the people she was dealing with were fools.

She had to lie, because as bad as what they thought Big Lenny had done was, if they knew he had actually succeeded in his quest to take her, he would be a dead man. As much as Lesley Scott irritated her at times, she was still her boys' grandmother, still Lenny's mother. She didn't know why it mattered so much. But it did. The boys needed family in their lives and that meant she had to lie for their sake, not for her own. She hated Big Lenny, but she did not want his death on her conscience, however much she craved it. Because, God knew, she wanted him dead more than anything.

The last few months had been a nightmare for her with the late-night visits and the drunken lectures that she needed a man to take care of her and her father-less sons. She had known she had to be careful but she had also been frightened to tell anyone about it. She lived in a world where certain things were only settled with extreme violence, and trying to take on your dead son's wife was definitely up there with the lowest of the low.

Now, of course, she realised she should have told Jack Johnson when it started. He would have discreetly sorted it out for her, she was sure. Jack Johnson was a good man, and he had her best interests at heart. But it had been hard to tell anyone what was going on. She had felt so ashamed, as if she was somehow at fault and, because of what had happened to Lenny, she had assured herself that his father was suffering from some kind of stress over his son's death. She had tried to sort it herself and where had it got her?

It was strange what you did for the people you cared about – like keeping Lenny and Reggie's secret because of her sons. Like allowing Big Lenny to terrorise her – because that is exactly what he had done – and all for family unity. Fucking family was overrated in so many ways. Her husband had preferred another man to her and her father-in-law seemed to think that she was willing to enter into some kind of sexual relationship with him. Because that is basically what he had wanted from her, no matter how he tried to justify it. Using her sons as an excuse to try and have sex with her. It would be laughable if it wasn't so fucking sad.

She knew that, despite the secrecy surrounding everything, the cat would well and truly be out of the bag and she would have to face everyone: her mother and father and, worst of all, Lenny's mother, who she knew would blame *her*. Lesley Scott had a blind spot when it came to her son and her husband. They were, and always would be, beyond reproach. Sharon wondered how long it would be before she had Lesley swooping down on her like the Avenging Angel, and how she was going to handle it.

Chapter One Hundred and Thirteen

Del Conway was like the Antichrist – that was the only way that Ivy could describe him. It took both Reggie and Ray Donovan to keep him from going out and killing Big Lenny. No one wanted him to go after the man more than Ivy did, but she could see the logic in stopping him doing something he would be banged up for. Jack had assured them that it would be dealt with and that was enough for her.

As she looked at her poor daughter, she wondered at a world where one girl could be given so much grief in such a short time. Ivy had great hopes for her daughter and Ray. She liked him, and she could see that he adored Sharon and the boys.

Now that fucking madman had nearly raped her child, and that had to have an effect. Wait till she saw that fecker Lesley Scott! Always acting like her shit didn't stink and they were better than everyone around them, going on that the boys were being dragged up and needed her influence to keep them on the straight and narrow. After what she had bred – a fucking criminal of the first water – she thought she was in with a chance with those two? The woman was deluded.

Ivy felt a small glimmer of shame at her secret delight that Lesley had been brought so low. But it was human nature, she supposed. Lesley had always acted so superior, with her church-going and her refusal to have a drink or a laugh, as though it was all beneath her somehow. She busied herself making endless pots of tea as she waited for her husband to calm down enough to be freed from the two men's grip. But she could understand his anger for she felt it herself. What she *couldn't* understand was why her daughter wanted to be alone and had asked her mother to let her get herself settled a bit before she saw her again. That had felt like a slap in the face.

Ivy wished things had turned out different for her child, but one thing that she knew from experience was you had to roll with the punches. Learn to accept whatever life threw at you. It was the only way to survive.

Chapter One Hundred and Fourteen

Lesley was sitting alone in the dark. Nothing could have prepared her for what she had been told by Jack Johnson. He had been so calm, and insisted she had a brandy, which she had to admit she was grateful for; she could feel the man's sympathy for her plight. But as she looked at him now, she felt the urge to tear his face apart with her well-manicured and prettily painted nails. She knew he was telling her the truth – even though she tried to deny it.

She had seen the way her husband had looked at that girl; it was like he had a hunger in him – a hunger she had never been able to arouse or indeed provoke. He had watched Sharon's every move, even when their son had been alive. The too-long embrace goodbye, the way he had always chatted to the girl as if they were long-time friends. She felt the bile rising up inside her at the words Jack was saying.

'He never managed to actually . . . You know.'

Oh, the shame of it. That's all she could think of now, the shame. Knowing that he had tried to . . . She pushed the thought from her mind and concentrated on the brandy that Jack Johnson had poured for her.

Jack was heart-sorry for the woman, but she seemed devoid of emotion and he had a feeling it had nothing to do with shock. Clearly there was a large part of her that resented her daughter-in-law and the way she managed to keep those boys away from their grandparents. Lesley, being the woman she was, didn't think that it might have had something to do with her husband.

She was already formulating a scenario where this was Sharon's fault. The girl had not waited long before taking up with another man, after all. That it had, in truth, been a couple of years, Lesley conveniently overlooked. Oh, she knew whose door to lay the blame at and it wasn't her poor husband who would have been caught up in that whore's web of lies.

Lesley was gulping more brandy now, trying to convince herself that she was right in her assumptions. But, even in her drink-fuddled mind, she still couldn't quite manage it. That, she knew, would take time.

Chapter One Hundred
and Fifteen

Ray Donovan was like a man possessed. To think his Sharon should have to put up with *that*, even after Big Lenny had been warned off, was unbelievable. Well, as far as he was concerned, it ended now. He was in a small lock-up garage in West Malling in Kent, waiting patiently for Reggie and Barton to bring the guilty party to him. There was no one living close enough to hear anything, which is why he had chosen this exact spot.

He opened a bottle of Chivas Regal whisky and poured himself a stiff shot. He was almost excited at the prospect of what he was going to do. He had thought this was all over for him, but now that he had to avenge the woman he loved, he was pleased to bring this part of his life back to the fore. He had been good at what he did – an artist at it really. He glanced at the workbench with the array of tools laid out and he smiled nastily to himself. Big Lenny 'the fucking Big I Am' Scott was going to regret his actions for the rest of his days, or his name wasn't Ray Donovan. This was personal now and Big Lenny Scott was going to find out that some urges were best left unexplored. Trying to fuck your dead son's wife was one of them. Ray was as disgusted as he was angry. Poor Sharon had not asked for any of this. She'd had her fair share of heartbreak and, if it was in his power, she would not be getting any more.

Ray rubbed his hands together in glee. It had been a while since he had had to teach someone a lesson. There was a time when this had been his forte – not that he would tell Sharon that. He was looking forward to the pleasure that using his instruments would bring him as he showed that cunt Big Lenny just what the fuck he was dealing with. Just exactly *who* the fuck he was dealing with.

In his former life, his rep had been The Torturer. He had worked with a gang for a long time. He had made his bones and done his time. But he had enjoyed his sojourn as the main man in his field. He had known that he was born to harm people who stepped over the line. Back then his activities had been the subject of more than one fucking documentary. He had been forced to take a back seat. It had been safer for him to keep a low profile.

Now, for the first time ever, his particular skill set was going to be used for his own good. Well, bring it on. He was looking forward to giving that cunt the worst night of his life.

Chapter One Hundred
and Sixteen

Sharon was trying to sleep. The fact that she had not seen Ray yet that night spoke volumes. Why would he want her now? She had been the object of her father-in-law's desires. She must have somehow made the man think that he was in with a chance when that had been the furthest thing from her mind. Big Lenny was the father of her husband. She wondered if he knew that Lenny wasn't the man they had all thought he was. Either way, she could not help feeling responsible for what had happened, as if all that had befallen her was somehow her own doing. Big Lenny's actions had completely destroyed the family, even more than his son's had, if she was honest. He had made her feel unsafe in her own home, fearful for her safety and as if it was all her fault.

He had destroyed his own family too. Sharon wasn't Lesley Scott's biggest fan, but she would never willingly wish this situation on her. She had a knack of making everyone around her feel just that bit inferior. Who could compete with her, with her church-going and her belief that she had the ear of Christ Himself? Lesley was a hard woman to get close to, especially when she didn't want you to get too close. Sharon had never really stood a chance with her. Her dad had always said that Lesley Scott could start a fight in an empty house and that pretty much summed her up. After Sharon had buried Lenny, she guessed that his mother had sensed that everything wasn't right with her, but she had assumed this for entirely the wrong reasons. Lenny had been the be-all and end-all in Lesley's life – and when he had been murdered no one recognised that as much as Sharon.

Sharon was well aware that as a wife for her son, she had always been lacking in Lesley Scott's eyes. But then, as she told herself over and over again, no one would have ever been good enough for him. At first, Lesley seemed to like her but that had changed as the years went on. Now she seemed to blame Sharon for Lenny's involvement in the Life – for leading him astray somehow. She always had a reason to criticise Sharon these days. She had tried to rise above it. When Lesley Scott had basically questioned her parenting skills to her face, and found them sorely lacking, Sharon's natural kindness had come to the fore and she had tried her best to build bridges. Well, Isambard Kingdom Brunel couldn't build a bridge strong enough to cover this latest fucking aggravation and no one could dispute that. Least of all Lesley, Hail Mary, fucking Scott.

Now it seemed to Sharon that she had lost Ray. He was a man of few words, not really given to public displays of affection. She feared that he would see her as damaged goods, and who could blame him? Certainly not her. But she loved him and she could not deny that it would devastate her to lose him. The shock was wearing off and the enormity of the situation was sinking in. She had to try and make something good come out of this but how she was supposed to do that, she really didn't know. She cried bitter tears.

Chapter One Hundred and Seventeen

Reggie and Barton King delivered Big Lenny to the lock-up garage. None of them were happy about it, but what could they do? Sharon was Ray's squeeze and the man needed to be taught a serious lesson. He needed to be shown that he could not use everyone around him for his own ends, least of all his son's widow.

As they walked into the lock-up they were without any idea as to what Ray was contemplating. Then they saw the array of tools on the bench and, despite themselves, they were worried. This looked far too professional. Clearly Ray was a man who had done this before, a man who was at home with his surroundings. A man who looked more than ready for whatever was going to happen.

But they delivered Big Lenny Scott nonetheless.

Chapter One Hundred and Eighteen

Lesley Scott was mortified. How could she admit that her husband, who, despite his faults, she loved, had been lusting after her son's wife? She had believed the girl would be good for her boy, would make him into a better person. Lesley had long concealed a fear that her son, Lenny, wasn't everything she hoped he was. She had been frightened by his natural leanings, fearful of where they would lead him. She would never voice it but she had known him better than anyone else ever would or could – especially that girl he had married. He was her baby, her only child, and she had always looked out for him.

Big Lenny had fucked up big time, and there was nothing she could do about that. But she was determined her grandsons would always be within her fucking orbit, no matter what she had to do to achieve it. She had to think and make plans for the future. Her grandsons were never going to be in the hands of that northern cunt, she would make damn sure of that as long as she lived. They would never forget their father. Her son. Her baby. Her life.

Chapter One Hundred and Nineteen

Big Lenny had been picked up from a pub in Bow. The landlord had been happy to serve him up just to get him off his premises. He was also pleased with the large drink he had been given for his trouble. Big Lenny was not a man who endeared himself to people.

As they went into the lock-up, there was an air of worry. It felt stifling even though it was a cool night and there was something about the look on Ray Donovan's face that seemed almost demonic. Reggie and Barton had expected him to be angry, to mete out a punishment, but this seemed wholly inappropriate.

Barton took in the instruments, so lovingly set out, and said loudly, 'Oh, for fuck's sake. Jack Johnson will not be pleased.'

Ray shrugged, unconcerned. 'I don't give a fuck what Jack or anyone else thinks.'

Reggie sighed at the inevitable. In all truth, he wasn't

that bothered what would happen to Big Lenny; he had asked for it, as far as he was concerned.

As drunk as Lenny was, he wasn't so far gone that he didn't take in what was going on around him, and it took Reggie and Barton a few seconds to restrain him. He was begging now, his fear making him almost incoherent. He was forced to sit on an old wooden kitchen chair and he was then restrained. He felt the gag being forced into his mouth, then Ray Donovan was duct-taping his mouth tightly. Lenny was absolutely terrified now and he felt a warm trickle as he wet himself. He was drunk, but he sobered up quickly as he saw what he had got himself into. Ray was humming as he put a light to a small blowtorch and looked his enemy straight in the eye.

'You, Lenny, won't be raping anyone again. I can promise you that much.'

Chapter One Hundred
and Twenty

Big Lenny had been missing for two days and Lesley Scott was at her wits' end. She had swallowed her pride and, finally, here she was at her daughter-in-law's house. As she stepped over the threshold she had to admit that Sharon looked very pale and wan.

She followed her silently through to the big kitchen that overlooked the back garden. It was a pleasant room and the garden itself looked wonderful. Lesley thought of all the good times she had experienced there with her son and her grandsons. She was not including Sharon in any of her reverie; Sharon was now the enemy as far as she was concerned. In a way she had always been that. After all, she had taken her beloved son from her at a young age. Sharon seemed to breed controversy and trouble. Now she had bewitched her husband, her own father-in-law, and therein lay all the hurt and upset.

Sharon sat at the wooden table and waited patiently

for Lesley Scott to seat herself. Lesley was eyeing her, and Sharon could feel the controlled jealousy coming from the woman in invisible waves. Sharon noticed that she was holding a rosary in her hands, and fingering it absently. She could imagine all the prayers and demands that were being sent heavenwards by this woman before her. Lesley set great store in her relationship with God. She felt she had unlimited access to the man in question and that she lived her life by His lore. Hypocritical old bitch that she was.

Sharon waited patiently. There was no way she was going to start this conversation. Lesley Scott seemed to understand this, and she was thrown by the girl's calmness and detachment.

'You know why I'm here.'

Sharon still didn't answer her; all she did was shrug her slender shoulders indifferently.

'I want to know where my husband is.'

Sharon shrugged once more. 'I don't know and, quite honestly, I don't care.'

Lesley had aged overnight and Sharon was sorry for what had befallen the woman, but she saw her as her enemy. If Lenny had not died like he had, this woman would still be dictating her life in some way, looking down her nose at them.

'You caused this, Sharon.'

Sharon Scott looked steadily at the woman before her and swallowed down the anger that was building

347

up inside her at an alarming rate. Lesley had to know the truth of it as there was no way anyone could pretend otherwise given the circumstances, no matter how much she might want to.

'Have you nothing to say to me, Sharon?'

She shook her head slowly, afraid to speak in case the canker inside her burst and she completely lost the plot.

Lesley Scott sat back in her chair now, sure of her ground and that she would get her ten-pence worth in if it was the last thing she did in this life of hers.

'Since I lost my son, you have done everything in your power to keep me away from those boys. You have practically ignored me these last few years, and now you have that Ray in your bed I suppose that will be the end of us, won't it? They will be calling that northern ponce "Dad" before we know it.'

Still Sharon didn't say a word.

Lesley carried on – as if she was chatting about the weather, so calm was her voice.

'I know you set your cap at my Lenny. Your own husband's father. What happened? Got fed up with him, did you? Wanted a newer model, a younger man, is that it? Not content with taking my son, you wanted his father as well . . .'

The blow that came nearly took Lesley Scott out of her chair and the shock and the pain was almost overpowering. Sharon was out of her chair and, unzipping her tracksuit top, she pulled it off and showed the woman the purple bruises covering her arms and back.

'Does this look like I wanted it, like I wasn't resisting? Does it? He raped me—' She swallowed noisily before saying quickly, 'Your precious fucking Lenny tried to rape me . . . I've had murders with him for ages. Always round here telling me how I needed a man to look after me. I wouldn't have touched that filthy old cunt if the bomb dropped and he was the last man on earth, you stupid, *stupid* fucking woman!'

Lesley Scott was staring at her daughter-in-law with such venom and hatred that Sharon took a step away from her.

'You must have encouraged him! He's old enough to be your father. He was a decent man, a good man, until you set your fucking cap at him.'

The fight left Sharon suddenly. She picked up the tracksuit top and put it back on wearily. This woman, this deluded woman, was a waste of space. It was pointless talking to her.

'I have no idea where Big Lenny might be. Pissed somewhere, probably, frightened that he might get found out. He wasn't that complimentary about you and your sex life – or lack of it shall I say. He's probably shacked up with some young Tom somewhere.'

Sharon couldn't resist the last barb even though she knew it was a cheap shot. She was well aware that Big Lenny was getting his just deserts and she was glad of it. She wanted him to hurt as he had made her hurt. She was toughening up at last and that was no bad thing; in fact it was about time. The world was a scary place for women, she understood that now. Oh, how she would like to burst that sanctimonious bitch's bubble about her son's real leanings. But she wouldn't do it. She had to at least leave her some illusions. She just wasn't about to admit that she knew Lesley's husband was being paid out for his deeds. Pleading ignorance was the byword these days and she would abide by that rule.

'I hope you never know another day's peace, you vicious little whore. That will be my prayer, morning, noon and night – that you get your fucking comeuppance, young lady.'

Sharon laughed bitterly. 'I might have known you would bring God into this. Well, He hates hypocritical old bags just as much as everyone else does. Now fuck off out of my house before I pick you up by the scuff of your scrawny neck and turf you out myself.'

She watched the woman walking away and she felt the urge to plant her foot firmly in Lesley Scott's skinny, bony backside. Who the hell did she think she was?

When Lesley had left, Sharon went to the phone and rang her mother's house.

'Bring the boys over, Mum. The sooner we all get back to normal, the better.'

She felt better then, stronger. It was as if Lesley Scott had healed her somehow with her vitriol and her delusions. She knew she had to get her life back, for the sake of her boys and for herself. She remembered how once, at school, the English teacher had said that it wasn't what happened to you, it was how you dealt with it. She couldn't remember where the quote was from but it was apt. She wasn't going to let this latest trouble destroy her. She was going to get on with it, make a good life for her and her boys, and she would get even with Lesley Scott, not by fighting with her but by putting this behind her and not letting it define who she was to become. Anger, she was finding, could actually be a good thing.

Chapter One Hundred and Twenty-One

Jack Johnson was talking to Ray Donovan alone. Ray was not too bothered; he knew he had right on his side and, in fairness, Reggie and Barton had stopped him before he had done too much damage to Lenny Scott. He had done what he had set out to do: made sure that Big Lenny Scott never touched another woman as long as he lived. That seemed just and fair to him, though what had happened to his Sharon would not be so easily remedied. Now he looked calmly at Jack, a half-smile on his face. He had had his retribution; he felt better for that anyway.

'What can I do for you, Jack?' He spoke quietly and respectfully. He had no quarrel with Jack Johnson and he had a feeling that Jack didn't have any quarrel with him.

'Feeling better?'

Ray shrugged nonchalantly. 'A little, if I'm honest. But it still doesn't change anything for Sharon. What he did was brutal and frightening and soul-destroying.'

Jack nodded in agreement and sympathy. 'True. But at least she hasn't got to contend with him ever again. That in itself has to be a blessing. One thing, though. I've realised who you are, or rather who you were.'

Ray was immediately alert and he sat up straighter in the chair as he said, 'I don't know what you mean.'

Jack smiled then. 'Oh, your secret's safe with me, son. I won't say a dicky bird. Do you still keep in touch with the Wheelans? I know them well. Todd and Dingo were old muckers of mine many years ago when we were all starting out.'

Still Ray didn't say a word.

'Listen, if I really want to, I can find out another way, Ray, but I would rather hear it from you.'

There was a hint of a threat, but only a hint, and Ray relaxed somewhat.

'They are fine. Obviously I don't see that much of them now they are banged up. I hear the odd word, of course.'

He was challenging the man and Jack knew it and admired him for it.

'Why are you so interested?'

Jack shrugged gently. 'Curiosity. No more and no less. I knew that their torturer was an unknown – that he did the job well and that when it all went tits up they kept their traps shut about who you were. Wise men. Everyone is vulnerable in prison. Not the safest place to make enemies.'

Ray held his large hands up in a gesture of supplication. 'So, now you know. What happens next?'

Jack Johnson smiled quietly. 'Nothing. Why pick at a scab? I just wanted to know for my own gratification. It was the blowtorch that alerted me. I heard that was your forte. That and pliers.'

Ray laughed delightedly. 'Those were the days, all right. No one knew who I was, see? So no one saw me coming.' He coughed quietly before continuing, 'I stalked my prey and I caught them. I tortured them and I left them to be found by relevant parties. I was good at my job and the fact that no one knew who I was worked in my favour when it all fell out of bed. I came South and the rest is history.'

Jack nodded. 'You were lucky, Ray. The Wheelans kept schtum.'

Ray shrugged once more. 'It was in their interests to keep quiet about me. I did what they asked and I know where the bodies are buried. They would never have seen the light of day again if I had turned.'

'Which, of course, you never would!'

Ray laughed again as he said nonchalantly, 'But the Wheelans didn't know that, did they?'

'Have you told anyone? Reggie or Barton?'

Ray shook his head. 'And I am not going to. That was another life.'

Jack understood his logic and applauded it. 'Sharon can never find out. You do realise that, don't you?'

They held eye contact for a few seconds before Ray said casually, 'She won't. I can assure you of that.'

Jack smiled again. 'Ever thought of taking on some private work? All under the table – no one would know who you are. I know a lot of people who would pay well for your kind of expertise.'

Ray was smiling again and Jack knew he had him. Men like Ray Donovan only came along every second or third generation and, when they did, they were worth their weight in gold.

'I will broker for you and never mention your name.'

'I'm game if you are, Jack. I miss my old occupation, if I am honest. A good stress-reliever, much better than the shite they spout on *Good Morning*!'

Jack laughed with him, pleased that he had struck the deal.

'Fancy a quick snifter?'

Ray grinned, and it was as if the sun had come out, as he said happily, 'Why not? Been a great day in many ways. It was good to get back into the swing of things. I didn't realise how much I'd missed it.'

Jack Johnson smiled but a small shiver ran up his spine. Now he knew exactly who he was dealing with, he would use extreme caution for the foreseeable future. This was not a man to cross. Even he knew that.

Chapter One Hundred and Twenty-Two

Sharon was bathed and in a robe when Ray came into the house. She ran to him and he pulled her into his arms, holding her tightly. She smelled of coconut shampoo and Nivea Creme. It was a smell he had begun to love. She looked up into his eyes and he smiled at her reassuringly.

'It's done. We won't ever talk of it, OK? Not unless you want to . . .'

She shook her head quickly. 'No, I don't want to talk about it ever again.'

He hugged her tightly once more, and then she said, in a small voice, 'Is he dead?'

Ray laughed then, and kissed the top of her head. 'No, lass. He's not dead.'

She kissed him lightly on his full-lipped mouth, and he kissed her back. Then the two boys came running down the stairs in their pyjamas and he held out his arms to them so they could join in with the hug. They were thrilled to see him and he was pleased to see them too. They were good kids, but they needed a stern hand and he could provide that for them.

'Who fancies a game of Monopoly?'

His voice was loud and jocular and the two boys were immediately full of excitement.

'I'll make us all hot chocolate, shall I?'

As Sharon watched Ray and her sons setting up the game she felt a glimmer of hope. She had been so lucky when she had found Ray Donovan and she knew that his gentle firmness was just what her sons needed. His love for her was all-encompassing and she honestly felt cherished by him. Finally Sharon could see some kind of future. Christ Himself knew, she'd had enough to deal with in her young life. Surely it was time that she got some good luck? She had earned it one way or another.

She poured a shot of brandy into her hot chocolate and brought it through to the lounge where the boys were arguing over who was having the dog while Ray watched them with a big smile on his handsome face.

Chapter One Hundred and Twenty-Three

Lesley Scott looked down at her husband. He was in hospital and under sedation. He had been badly attacked by assailants unknown. His genitalia had been practically burned away and his fingernails had been removed with pliers, as had some of his teeth. Lesley knew that the police were not going to be investigating this too closely; that bastard Jack Johnson would make sure of that. She was too shrewd to make a scene or even hint that she knew who was responsible. But God was slow and He was sure, and she would pray every day to see that whore got what was coming to her. She would live to see Sharon Scott, her dead son's widow and the mother of his children, brought as low as she had taken her. It was all that was keeping her upright – that and the hatred she harboured in her heart. The only thing she had left her with was this excuse for a man.

Dry-eyed she left the hospital and made her way to the nearest church where she knelt down before the altar and started her prayers for vengeance.

Book Four

Great is truth and it prevails.

3 Esdras 4.41

Chapter One Hundred and Twenty-Four

1995

'Come on, boys. We ain't got all day, you know.'

Sharon looked around her home and felt a swell of pride. The move was the best thing she could have done and she was so pleased that Ray had insisted on it. Getting away from everything had completely changed her outlook on life and she loved the Essex countryside. But, best of all for her, was that the boys loved it here; they were thriving and that was what she really cared about – that and Ray and the child she was carrying inside her.

She was thrilled to be pregnant again and she felt that this new addition would complete their family. Ray was so good; he did not even care if it was a boy or girl. He saw young Lenny and Liam as his own sons and for that she would be forever grateful to him. They called him Dad now and, over the years, Lenny had gradually ceased to exist for them. She knew it was wrong but she was also glad of it. The photos in this house were all of the four of them, smiling and laughing and looking like any other family. She was blessed, she knew that much, and she was grateful for this wonderful life that she had. Sometimes it seemed too good to be true and that was when the old fears would plague her, but those feelings were getting less and less frequent. Ray wasn't living a secret life; she trusted that deep down in her heart. He was the opposite of Lenny Scott. His lovemaking was different; everything about him was different. And that was what she loved about him.

Ray had expanded the businesses over the years and they now had quite a high standard of living. She loved that they had their own pool and enough land to give them privacy. The boys went to a Catholic school that wasn't cheap, but it seemed to keep them out of trouble. As Ray said, you can't fuck with the Jesuits, they were hard bastards. And they were that, all right. Ray prided himself on being a good Catholic and he had insisted that the boys had a proper education. It was paying off though – the boys were worn out with all the sport and they genuinely seemed to like their teachers – even if they did wear what Liam referred to as 'dresses'. They were changing and that pleased her. They had a future now. Sharon had never been happier and it showed.

As Ray left with the boys to drop them off at school, she made herself a pot of tea and sat in her large, sunny kitchen contentedly. Life just didn't get better than this. Not that she never argued with Ray. She could be stubborn, but they were the normal arguments and petty squabbles of family life: where to go on holiday, what they would do at Christmas. Ray always wanted them to go to his mother's but now it was better for her to come to them. Old Annie Donovan loved coming to her son's beautiful home. Sharon adored her. She was a wonderful woman. When Sharon had asked her where Ray got his dark good looks she had laughed delightedly and said, with searing honesty, 'His father was a Turk. He left one day and he took my heart and most of my electrical equipment with him!'

Sharon had laughed with her then, but she could see the woman had genuinely loved the man, whoever he was. Annie got on well with her, and they were a happy family. Sharon's mother thought the sun shone out of Ray's backside and her dad thought the world of him too. So, despite all she had had to contend with, life had taken a turn for the better and she thanked God every day for that.

Chapter One Hundred
and Twenty-Five

Reggie Dornan suspected that there was some business going on between Jack and Ray Donovan. It was obviously just between the two of them, but he wasn't too worried about it. He too had his private deals with Jack Johnson – that was how their world worked. What he felt, though, was that whatever they were doing together, it was not something he wanted a part of. There was a feeling there of an almost unholy alliance. He knew it sounded melodramatic, even to his own ears, but he could not shake the thoughts away. Ray disappeared for days at a time, and no one knew where he was or what he was doing. Again, nothing so strange about that in their world. But Reggie's gut instinct was telling him to be careful and not to pry.

He didn't see that much of Sharon these days and that suited him, though she was civil to him and grateful for his help when she had needed it. His relationship with Lenny would always be there between them. He respected that she had kept it to herself though he guessed that was more for her and the boys' sakes than his. Either way he was glad it wasn't out there. Even in these enlightened times it was still seen as a weakness. Lenny Scott's memory would have been destroyed and everything he had ever done would be suspect. It was wrong, but it was the world they inhabited, simple as that.

Reggie got out of his car and pressed the buzzer at the electric gates and then he waited in his car patiently for Sharon to open them. He parked on the large driveway and walked casually towards the front of the house. It was an impressive place, and he was glad for them.

Sharon had blossomed since she had been with Ray and the boys were not such a handful these days. Lenny had encouraged them to be boisterous, even while he punished them for it. Ray was a more moderate parent. The boys loved him, there was no doubting that, and Ray thought the world of them too. He took them to football and karate – whatever they wanted to do, he was as up for it as they were. Now he had his own child on the way and Reggie supposed that would complete the family.

Reggie kissed Sharon lightly on her cheek and followed her through to the big, bright kitchen that was like something out of *Homes & Gardens*.

She was pouring him a cup of tea as he said teasingly, 'You're getting bigger, girl!'

She laughed. 'Fucker won't keep still. Keeps night-club hours this one. Moving all night and sleeping all day!'

Reggie took the mug of tea and laughed. 'If it's a boy, we'll start him as a doorman!'

Sharon didn't laugh quite so heartily at that quip. Sharon didn't want her sons in the Life, thank you very much. She had great hopes for her boys and being criminals wasn't one of them.

Reggie, realising he had put his foot in it, changed the subject quickly. 'So, Jack tells me you need someone to sort out stuff for a cinema room, I believe?'

He could not help feeling the irony of Sharon's annoyance at her sons' implied criminality and the fact she expected him to provide stolen goods! But he didn't say a word.

She nodded happily. 'Come through, I'll show you what's needed. Jack said someone had a load of home-entertainment systems going cheap. It will be wonderful for the boys, obviously.'

He followed her through the house and she opened the door to a large room and beckoned him inside.

'I'm getting black-out curtains made for the windows. But I don't know what's on offer screen-wise. You should decide really; I'm useless with anything electrical.'

He smiled at her as he surveyed the room.

'So, how was Manchester?'

It was said completely without guile and Reggie

looked at her and frowned. 'What you on about?' As soon as he spoke he realised he had put Ray right in it, but that was not his fault. If Ray needed a fucking alibi, he should have told him about it.

He saw Sharon's head snap back quickly and then she composed herself saying, 'Oh, I probably got the wrong end of the stick. Blame the pregnancy hormones!'

He laughed with her but the damage was done. The sun had gone out of her day and they both knew it. Reggie sighed heavily. He hated personal intrigue – even his sexual encounters were practised well away from his home turf. He would let Ray know he had dropped him in it, but the question had been so unexpected he had no chance. Let him sort his own fucking messes out.

Chapter One Hundred and Twenty-Six

Ray was aware that he had dropped what was known in his world as 'a serious bollock'. It had been so last minute and he had forgotten to tell Reggie he needed an alibi for a few days. Sharon wasn't in and out of the offices any more; they had people to take care of everything and she was more or less a home-body now. Ray could kick himself, seriously kick himself. He knew how dodgy it would look to Sharon, especially as she was heavily pregnant and on a short fuse. And now, on top of everything else, he had to go away again for a few days. He was leaving at five in the morning and he imagined that news was going to go down like a lead balloon. He sighed heavily. Sharon was a good girl, and he loved her, but she could be suspicious at times. His mum insisted it was a woman's thing but he wasn't so fucking sure. Sharon had a radar in her head, and nothing or no one could turn it off.

As he drove through the gates to his home he was amazed that he actually felt nervous. Sharon was the only person in the world who could make him feel like this – that she kept him on his toes was part of the reason he loved her. He hated lying to her but the truth, if she ever found out, would be so much worse. Not that he could tell her that, of course.

Chapter One Hundred
and Twenty-Seven

Jack Johnson was with a small, sharp-toothed man called Micky Biggs. An unfortunate name, considering his reduced size. At four foot eleven, he was just off being a dwarf. But anyone with half a brain would take one look at the short man and know instinctively that he was not to be fucked with.

Jack remembered seeing him attack a huge fellow once in a North London pub. The bigger man had made one too many quips about his diminutive height. It had been a sight to see, that was for sure. Micky didn't so much fight, as bite. He was like a terrier and, like a terrier, he went for throat, ears and face. It was the sheer ferocity of his attacks that laid waste to his detractors. Now he was a small but respected member of the community, not that anyone ever mentioned the former. Not within Micky's hearing anyway.

'You look well, Jack. Time's marching on, boy.'

Jack accepted the compliment easily. He knew this was just the preliminaries before Micky got round to what he really wanted to talk about. It was laughable, but it was social etiquette to get the niceties out of the way, pay each other due respect, before discussing who was going to get maimed or murdered. Jack sipped at his whisky and savoured the burn that accompanied it. Micky was of the strange breed of criminals who did not drink alcohol at all. He claimed he didn't like the taste and that it made him aggressive. As if he needed any help with that!

'How's the wife, Micky?'

Micky sighed happily. He loved his Lynda with a fierceness that frightened everyone but her. She was a tall blonde with the body of a streetwalker. But they worked, somehow, and had one of the happiest marriages in their world.

'She is fucking over the moon with the new baby. Fabulous mother and, now she's breastfeeding, her knockers are fucking enormous!'

Jack laughed with him. 'How many is that now, then?'

Micky's face was tinged with pink as he said, 'Five – all boys too! She wants a girl badly, so I suppose this won't be the last one till she gets her way.'

Jack looked at this strange man with respect. He was a grafter, an earner, and he gave respect where it was due. As long as no one mentioned his height he was a good friend to have. But, like most men in the Life, he could be a bitter and ferocious enemy. Jack was interested to know who had been fool enough to fuck him off or try to have him over. But they would get there in the end. They always did. It was pleasant to chat with Micky Biggs; he was a lovely bloke – a gentleman.

Chapter One Hundred and Twenty-Eight

Sharon was eyeing Ray with suspicion in her blue eyes. He was smiling at her disarmingly and waiting for the onslaught that he was sure would be coming in the near future.

Pregnancy suited her; she had really bloomed, as the old saying went. Her skin looked almost luminous and her thick blond hair seemed to glow like gold. God, he loved this woman.

'Why were you and Reggie in Manchester again?'

He wanted to smile at her words; she really had no guile.

He shrugged. 'Reggie didn't go. I thought he was supposed to but I had got it wrong. Why?'

She screwed her eyes into slits and sighed lightly, trying all the time to calm herself down. If she lost her temper she would blow it, she knew she would.

She shrugged nonchalantly. 'What exactly were you

doing in Manchester? That's supposing you *were* in Manchester, of course.'

He looked her directly in the eyes and he said seriously, 'I can't tell you that, Sharon.'

She was taken aback by his words and the way he had delivered them.

'I beg your pardon?'

She was at the beginning of outrage and they both knew it. He went to her and held her gently by the shoulders and, looking at her, he said in complete honesty, 'I really can't tell you anything. If I did tell you I can guarantee you would regret ever asking me about it. That is as much as I *can* tell you, Sharon. You have to trust me on this.'

She looked up into his beautiful, dark eyes and believed that he was being honest with her. She could not help but be suspicious of his absences. What woman wouldn't be? She had two sons and was heavily pregnant to boot. She had a man she thought she could trust with her life and now the doubt was creeping in. After Lenny she couldn't go through that heartbreak again.

He sensed her uncertainty and, holding her to him gently, he said sincerely, 'I wish I could tell you about these trips, I really do. But there are some things in our world where you are better left in ignorance. Believe me, I'm not trying to play you, Sharon.'

A voice inside her was telling her that she should accept what he said at face value. But another voice in the back of her mind was asking what was so terrible he could not tell her about it? What skulduggery was he involved in that required so much secrecy? One worry just seemed to replace another.

He kissed her tenderly and caressed her swollen belly. 'Like I would want anyone else. Haven't I got everything I need right here?'

She allowed him to hold her and pet her but worry still lingered in the back of her mind.

Chapter One Hundred and Twenty-Nine

Lesley Scott looked in the *Barking and Dagenham Post* and saw her two grandsons' photograph from the boxing. They had been for the ABAs. She drank in the picture of them, and prayed once more that her daughter-in-law would pay the price for destroying her family.

The boys were her Lenny's doubles, especially young Lenny. It was like looking at her beloved son at the same age. When she thought of the trauma and heart-break that bitch had brought into their lives she felt almost capable of murder. She heard her husband calling to her and she quickly poured him a glass of orange juice and went through to her front room.

Big Lenny was a shadow of his former self, and it showed. The weight had dropped off him, and he looked almost skeletal, sitting on the sofa watching his endless video collection. He was like a child now – all the life was gone from him and he was pitifully grateful to her for the smallest kindness. Gone was the vibrant man she had married all those years ago. In his place was this complete wreck who now had a catheter in to drain his urine, who had been left unable to walk without a stick and who had difficulty stringing a sentence together. Another victim of that Sharon Conway. Lesley could not bear to call her Scott; that name was far too good for the likes of her!

That girl had wreaked havoc on her and her family and it was hard to live through each day knowing that. They were pariahs now in their community, and even bingo was a closed door as no one would sit with her any more.

She felt the sting of tears, and forced them from her rheumy eyes. She too had aged dramatically since her husband's accident – she always thought of it in those terms. The shame of his actions ate at her like a cancer. She knew that the rumours about her Lenny attacking his dead son's wife had been rife at the time. Ray Donovan was looked on as a hero now, taking on those two boys and being a father to them. Well, he was not their father and never could be! They were *her* flesh and blood.

She glanced at the clock and was pleased to see it was nearly time for seven o'clock Mass – she liked the evening services and the early morning ones. They weren't as busy and she didn't run into people who were once classed as friends. The loneliness of her life had made her even more bitter towards Sharon; and she had heard a wedding was likely. That had upset her more than she had thought possible.

She absent-mindedly touched her husband's ravaged face and went back to the kitchen. Then, taking the scissors, she carefully cut out the article about her grandsons to add to her scrapbook. They would come looking for her one day, she was sure, and, when they did, she wanted them to know that she had never forgotten them. Then she got ready for church, rosary already in her coat pocket and missal in her handbag. She set out, as she did twice a day, to pray for the destruction of the girl who had brought her family so low. How, she asked her God, could He let that whore prosper, knowing the evil and the damage she had done? But the wheels of God grind slow, and one day He in all His glory would see fit to punish that bitch of hell. All Lesley had to do was be patient and wait.

Chapter One Hundred and Thirty

Micky and Jack were happily reminiscing about the old days, and Jack had forgotten what great company Micky could be when he was in a good mood. Micky Biggs had a wonderful, warm personality that Jack was sure accounted for his success with the opposite sex.

'Then, Jack, fucking Petey Brewer vomited – projectile vomited – all over the poor PC's fucking shoes. I was on the floor! Anyway, suffice to say he couldn't wait to be rid of us, and we walked off towards Vicky Park with all the poor fucker's takings from the betting shop!'

Jack was nearly crying with laughter.

'Foolishness of youth and drink. We took the money back next day and apologised. Nice old fucker he was. Jewish. Forgave us and then let us pick out some sweets!'

Jack was laughing again.

'Couple of years later I used to sell chorred fags to him!'

Jack poured them both more whisky and Micky sipped his gratefully, savouring the smoky taste.

'Anyway, Jack. As nice as this has been, I want to ask you a favour.'

Jack nodded.

'I hear you have access to a man who can settle scores for a price.'

Jack smiled. 'I have. And it ain't cheap, Micky.'

Micky sighed as if to say that he wouldn't expect it any other way. 'It's that cunt George Thomas. He has been on my fucking case for ages to bring him in on a deal, the nature of which you don't need to know. Anyway, I did as he asked and now the cunt has not only tucked me up, but he has also earholed me out. So, as you can imagine, I am not a happy bunny.'

Jack nodded once more but his face was very serious now. George Thomas was not a man to cross unless you had a mob handy, Jack knew that much.

'I don't want to go to war with him. As you know, my old woman's just given birth and I realise that I might be better off disabling my opponent. Which is what brought me to your door.'

Jack was nodding his head once more. His grizzled old features looked concerned but, in reality, he was wondering how much Micky would be willing to pay to disable a Face like George Thomas. He took a large sip of his Chivas Regal before saying quietly, 'As I said, it ain't going to be cheap, Micky.'

Micky Biggs grinned widely. 'I had a feeling it

wouldn't be. I will pay whatever you want. And up front too, to show my goodwill. I want him fucking maimed – unable to carry out his business for at least a year or eighteen months. I also want his eye out. Not both, I ain't a vindictive man, as you know. But I want one eye popped, that is a certainty.'

Jack looked at Micky and then said, 'Old saying, Micky. "In the kingdom of the blind, the one-eyed man is king."'

Micky laughed delightedly. 'Fuck that, Jack. In my kingdom *I* am the fucking ruler and I rule that that ponce needs to be taught a severe lesson. Of course, I had nothing to do with it. Which is why I am coming to you humble and with an open fucking chequebook.'

Jack smiled. 'Leave it with me and I will see what I can do. I need to discuss it with the person concerned.'

Micky Biggs was happy enough with that and he said as much. 'You're a diamond geezer, Jack. I will leave it all in your more-than-capable hands.'

Chapter One Hundred and Thirty-One

Sharon was lying in bed with Ray, listening to him snoring softly. She wondered if she would ever be able to sleep alone. Knowing he was beside her made her feel safe and very happy. He made her feel secure and the love she had for him was so colossal in its intensity that, at times, it frightened her. She had been let down by Lenny; it was hard to accept that your husband had another woman, but another man put a completely different complexion on things. You could fight against another woman, but another man? It was the ultimate insult; it had made a mockery of everything she had held dear. That was something she thought of on nights like this, when she was awake and sleepless.

The baby was moving around inside her and she smiled. Definitely nightclub hours with this one. She caressed her belly and felt a rush of love for this new child.

She could not wait to meet it. That was why she didn't want to know the sex – she wanted a surprise.

She thought back to earlier in the day and Ray's words. He had been sincere, she was convinced of that. He wasn't a good liar, her Ray – not to her anyway. She knew when he was being honest. But his words had chilled her. What was he doing that she was better off in ignorance? Oh, she wasn't a fool. She had grown up in the world they lived in, and she accepted that world. But there had been something in his eyes that had filled her with dread. It was like he was telling her to step away as if there was a bomb in the room.

He turned over in the bed, pulled her into his arms and kissed the top of her head as she snuggled into him. She would not think about it any more; she had him and that was what mattered. Why look for worries where there weren't any?

No matter how much she tried to reassure herself there was still that very real prickle of fear inside her. But, like many a woman before her, she forced it from her mind. Life was good and she had a terrible feeling that knowing the truth might cause her more troubles and pain than forgetting they had ever had that conversation. Finally she slept.

Chapter One Hundred and Thirty-Two

Sharon watched as Ray packed an overnight bag. She was looking at what he was putting in there, to see if he was packing a clean shirt or anything that might make her think he was meeting another woman. She hated herself, but she couldn't help it. Of course he could easily purchase clothes and aftershave if he required them – indeed Ray would be far too shrewd to give her any cause for alarm. But still she found herself watching what he was doing and she knew that he was picking up on her suspicions. That fact alone embarrassed her.

He turned from the bed and smiled at her lovingly. 'Had your look? Want a photograph?'

She forced herself to laugh lightly; she was a fool but she couldn't help herself. She wondered if it actually *was* pregnancy hormones.

'I will miss you, that's all. How long did you say?'

He shrugged. 'Two to three days, depending.'

'Depending on what?' It was out of her mouth before she could stop herself.

He shrugged again. 'Please, Sharon. Not this again, eh? I hate leaving you like this. Upset and suspicious.'

She could hear the underlying annoyance in his voice and that saddened her more than anything. He was rarely impatient with her and, when he was, she knew it was generally for a good reason. She smiled sadly and went back down to the kitchen. She busied herself making a pot of tea and some sandwiches for their lunch.

Ray sighed, and continued to pack his overnight bag. Sharon thought he was going up to Scotland when in truth he wasn't going to leave the county of Essex. But she didn't have to know that, did she? If she guessed the truth, she would be wishing it had all been as simple as another woman. The truth, he had found, did not necessarily set you free. The truth at times could make a prisoner of people.

He walked slowly down to the kitchen with his bag deliberately unzipped as if he had nothing to hide. Which, of course, he didn't. Not where the bag was concerned, anyway.

Chapter One Hundred and Thirty-Three

Jimmy Carter and Jason Palmer were two friends who were as close as they were dangerous. Ray had met them during his stint inside and they had immediately recognised a kindred spirit. Both large men, they were also quiet, close-mouthed and trustworthy. These were the main reasons that Ray had recruited them to work for him on his special jobs. Another was that he genuinely liked them. The Two Js, as they were known in the nick, wouldn't give their names unless they had to. It was apt. They were so very tight with information, especially anything personal. Someone had once said that to Ray and he thought it summed them up perfectly. Though they were hard, they were not affiliated to anyone, and they took jobs on doors and did a bit of collecting as well.

Thanks to Ray, they now had a very lucrative sideline. It was well-paid work and it suited their personalities. They planned each job meticulously as no one could know they were involved. The Two Js loved the element of danger involved and thrived on it. Now, they sat in a white Transit van and waited patiently for their quarry to arrive.

George Thomas was a fool. He was what was known as a creature of habit, and that meant they could watch and wait and plan in peace. Every Monday night, while his wife was at her mother's, he visited a little bird on the Thamesmead Estate. He arrived just before seven in the evening and he left just after midnight. He always parked his car well away from the little lady's block of flats, and he walked back to his car sure in the knowledge he was George Thomas and as safe as houses.

The blow to the back of his head brought him to his knees and the injection in his neck knocked him flat out. He was in the back of the transit within seconds and, just minutes later, was trussed up like the proverbial kipper. All in all a good night's work for the Two Js, who were sensible enough not to spark up a big fat joint until they were well out of London.

Chapter One Hundred
and Thirty-Four

Ivy was staying with her daughter while Ray was out of town. She lived for these visits; seeing the boys doing well and knowing her daughter was settled with a decent man did her heart good.

Del loved Ray with a passion that bordered on mania. He thought he was the greatest living human being since Muhammad Ali and, in Del's world, that was praise indeed. But Ivy had to admit the man was good. Her daughter and her grandsons were living a near-perfect life and that was thanks to Ray's dedication. She had worried for those children even before Lenny had passed on. They were almost out of control, but Ray was so good with them, so kind and patient, that the lads had responded well to him. They adored him as he did them.

But her Sharon was looking a bit peaky and Ivy was worried about her. She knew she fretted about Ray when he went away on business. But Ivy reasoned that was to be expected, after what had happened with Lenny. Here one moment and dead the next – murdered. Sharon had been the one to identify the body. He had been so badly tortured and beaten he had been almost unrecognisable and that had to affect her girl. It would affect anyone, something like that happening. There had never been a whisper of who might have been behind it all, but that was not too unusual in the world he had lived in. Unexpected violence was part of the price you paid for the life you chose.

'You all right, love? Can I get you a cup of tea?'

Sharon smiled tiredly. 'I'm fine actually, Mum. This baby is lying on my bladder and I am going to the loo every ten minutes as it is.'

Ivy laughed. 'I remember it well! Still, it'll be worth it once it arrives.'

Sharon nodded, but Ivy could see there was something ailing her daughter.

'He will be back before you know it, Sharon. Stop worrying. Nothing bad is going to happen.'

Sharon sat up in her chair and said, smiling, 'You are right, Mum. Go on then – I will have that cup of tea after all!'

Pleased to have allayed her daughter's fears, Ivy trotted off happily to put the kettle on. Alone, Sharon let her mask slip. She wasn't even sure what exactly was bothering her; all she knew was that something wasn't right.

Chapter One Hundred
and Thirty-Five

George Thomas woke up and felt a stab of real fear shoot through his body. He had some kind of blindfold on, though he wasn't gagged or duct-taped. He was clearly in deep shit. The question was why? He racked his brain to come up with anyone who might have wanted him outed and could think of no one. All right, he had fucked Micky Biggs over but that didn't warrant this, surely? He had not seen Micky as that serious a problem. He was, after all, a loner, old Micky.

George felt dry-mouthed and realised he had been drugged. He could not move his arms or his legs; he was certainly well tied up, wherever the fuck he was. His mounting panic only added to his anger at not being able to see who was fucking holding him. He could hear a door opening and someone moving around; it sounded like he was in a fucking dungeon or something. He took a few sniffs and he could smell dampness and mildew. This was not making him feel any better about his situation; in fact he could feel himself starting to panic.

Someone took hold of his hand and he felt a fingernail being removed with what he could only assume was a pair of pliers and he screamed at the shock and the fear of what was happening. Whoever it was did not say a single word. That frightened him more than anything.

'Tell me who you are, you coward! You fucking cunt!'

Whoever had him trussed up was not saying a word, but George could hear him humming quietly to himself between bouts of extreme violence. This was a nightmare, except he was more than aware that he was wide awake and this was only just starting. He swore to himself there and then that if he survived, he would hunt this cunt down and pay him back tenfold. It was all that kept him going.

Chapter One Hundred
and Thirty-Six

Ray was impressed by the man he was dealing with. He was screaming all right, but he was also cursing and threatening retribution. Most people begged for mercy or offered to double what he was being paid so he would leave them alone. He had a grudging admiration for George Thomas. But a deal was a deal.

He was hot and sweating so he left the man and made his way up from the cellar to the small kitchen above. He had bought this place for a song, and it was perfect for what he needed. A tumbledown old farmhouse and twenty-five acres of arable land, worth fuck-all in the present climate. Still, there was a chance it might change. If he ever got planning permission this lot would be worth the national debt. Whatever happened, it was perfect for his little earner.

He washed his hands clean of blood and made himself a sandwich – a thick doorstep of ham, cheese and pickle. He was starving. He poured a mug of tea and sat at the table, looking through the holiday brochures he had picked up a few days earlier. The boys would love Disney World again, but he fancied something a bit more exotic. The Maldives, maybe. He would book for when the baby was one year old – Ivy could look after it while they lounged in the sun and his Sharon could have a proper rest. She would need it by then, he was sure. From what he had heard, babies were a fucking nuisance for the first twelve months, then they got interesting. He was excited to think he would have a child in the world, his own flesh and blood. His old mum was over the moon; she had never thought it would happen.

He had bought her a little house nearby so she could move down South, or use it for her visits – that was entirely up to her. But he owed her a great deal and he always paid back his debts. Old Annie had really been good to him, and he had had a great childhood because of her constant grafting. OK, she might not have been there when he came home from school, but she had made sure they had a clean house, good food and all the love he could handle. She had tried her best to put him on the straight and narrow and she had given him the work ethic. He hated it when people tried to portray the Irish as feckless fuckers; they were real grafters. They were all over the fucking world because they had hunted the work down. Did that sound like a race of shiftless fuckers?

He finished his tea and carefully washed up the

crockery. Then he went down to the cellar and started round two. He was in a good mood; this time tomorrow he would be at home with his Sharon and the boys. He would be especially attentive to her, and he had told Jack to hold off with any more of these little jaunts for a while. That might placate his Sharon. After all, she was having his child, and he didn't want her or that baby upset.

He knew that George Thomas could hear his approach because the man was once again vocal with his threats. No doubt about it, he was a game old fucker; he had to give him that. As Ray picked up the sulphuric acid he was sorry in a way that he had to blind him, even partially. He knew the pain would knock the fucker out, and then he would give him a quick shot of liquid oxycodone and Bob was your uncle – as the Southerners said – and Fanny was your fucking aunt. The Two Js could dump him, and then Ray would get the bleach out and scrub his workplace clean. He liked a clean workspace; there was nothing worse than people who left too many clues behind them. It was a fool's game, and could lead to nothing but trouble.

George's screams died down to a faint moan and, when he finally lost consciousness, Ray Donovan was actually relieved. He liked the man, and had nothing whatsoever against him. His final job was to shatter his right ankle and basically hobble him. There was no getting away from it: George Thomas had fucked off Micky Biggs royally. But his was not to reason why, as his old mum used to say.

He rang the Two Js and set about cleaning his instruments. Once George had been taken away he would concentrate on the cellar itself. He checked his watch and was pleased to note that if he got his arse in gear he would be in time to catch *News at Ten*. He liked the news; he felt that people should keep up with current events. It was the sign of a lively mind.

George was groaning in pain, and now the noise was beginning to get on Ray's tits. The sooner he was out of here the better.

Chapter One Hundred and Thirty-Seven

Jack was with Micky, assuring him that the job he had requested had been done. Micky Biggs was over the fucking moon, as he kept saying again and again. He put the fifty thousand pounds in cash on the table in a small holdall, and he knew that Jack Johnson trusted him too much to count it while he was there.

'He did everything I asked?'

Jack nodded imperceptibly. He didn't like the way Micky was taking such a pleasure in George Thomas's downfall. Jack Johnson could be funny like that.

'He was blinded in his left eye, and his right ankle was hobbled, per your instructions. My source tells me they are leaving him on the steps of the Old London, as you also requested.'

Micky was smiling from ear to ear now. He had his business back, and he had meted out a punishment that could in no way come back and bite him on his tiny but well-shaped arse. As Micky sipped his drink he had an almost beatific smile on his face.

He liked the idea of faceless retribution; it appealed to his sense of honour, and Micky, as mad as he could be, was an honourable man. He had treated George Thomas with the utmost respect and that cunt had walked all over him. People needed a lesson in social graces every now and then, and this would send out the word that George had crossed a line and that line had been his downfall. It wouldn't take a blind dog long to sniff out that Micky was probably in on it, but as long as no one could prove it, he was basically home and dry.

This was definitely money well spent. It had solved the age-old problem of 'me or them' – and that was what the world they lived in could often be about. He felt good – his only regret being that he had had to forfeit the bragging rights.

Chapter One Hundred
and Thirty-Eight

Ray slipped into his house at just after midnight. He had decided that coming home earlier than Sharon had expected would please her. She was still up watching *Beaches* with her mother. He liked Bette Midler but there were only so many times he could sit through that shit. He popped his head around the front-room door, and when he saw the genuine relief on his Sharon's face he felt almost as if he could cry with happiness. He could be a very emotional man, and sometimes he felt that the great love he bore for this woman and her boys was a weakness. He accepted that it was his nature to be sentimental – he was the same with his old mum; watching her sometimes brought tears close to the surface. She had looked out for him his whole life, and she was a decent woman and an exemplary mother.

'I managed to get away, darling.'

She was straight into his arms and Ivy looked on

happily. This was a real love job and she was so pleased for her girl. She said her goodnights and left them alone.

Sharon was thrilled to have him back a day early and she knew then that he had come home just to be with her – just to stop her worrying – and she felt bad about her thoughts. Ray loved her and he loved her boys. She was blessed with this man, and she would put her fears out of her mind in the future.

Ray was happy to see the relief and pleasure on Sharon's face. He knew that he had done the right thing and, as he held her to him lovingly, he wondered absently how George Thomas was getting on at the hospital. Then he put the matter completely out of his head. The one thing a man should never do was take his work home with him.

While Sharon made him a late-night snack, he checked on the boys. They were both asleep; one good thing about that school was that they concentrated on sports and, for boys like these, that was important. He remembered that they had another boxing night soon, and he was determined to take them with him. They always enjoyed meeting some of the older boxers. It was a nice treat for them; Lenny was a good fighter, but young Liam was a natural. If he chose to, he could go far in that world. He had the temperament needed for a professional fighter and he could parry and dance with the best of them. Most of his opponents had been hard pushed to even land a punch, let alone dodge the boy's right hand. Ray was proud of them both; they were turning into nice young lads. Very polite to their mother and helpful to him when he asked. They were asking cheeky questions about the businesses as well. He knew that Sharon was not too pleased about that, but those two would go their own roads.

Ray went around and locked up the house. He loved this place; it was everything he had ever wanted and more. Best of all, he knew that Sharon was happy and content here. Once the baby arrived they would be complete as a family. He hoped for a boy, but a daughter would be almost as good, and his mother, he knew, secretly wanted a granddaughter. She had stepped in as nan to the boys and they adored her just as much as he did.

As Ray settled back into his life he was well pleased with how much he'd achieved and how much he had to be grateful for. He knew that there were a lot of men who would kill for what he had. He also knew that he would kill anyone who tried to take it all away from him.

Chapter One Hundred and Thirty-Nine

George Thomas was in the operating theatre for five hours. He had lost an eye, and his ankle had to be reconstructed using metal plates and pins. His handsome face was ruined for ever, and he would never be the same man again. When he eventually awoke in intensive care, he gradually pieced together a timeline.

For the next two months in the hospital, only one thing kept him going and that was how he would find out who had harmed him and, more to the point, who had ordered it. He had his suspicions, and every time Micky Biggs visited him, all solicitude and compassion, he was more and more convinced that he had found the culprit.

Chapter One Hundred and Forty

Lesley Scott was listening to her husband's laboured breathing and she knew that he was not long for this world. She looked at the man she had married all those years before and felt her futile tears as they finally ran down her wrinkled face. She had aged considerably since her husband's attack, but that didn't bother her too much. It was seeing Big Lenny brought so low that had really affected her.

As he lay there breathing his last, having already received extreme unction from his priest, she remembered the huge, handsome man she had married. She had looked beautiful that day and she had felt hope for her future. Some of those hopes and dreams had come to fruition. When she had given birth to Lenny, her husband had been like a dog with six lampposts. She could see him now in her mind's eye, holding his little son in those enormous hands and laughing with delight. She thought of her son on his first day of school, all scrubbed and smart with his satchel and his packed lunch. He had been such a handsome boy, and tall for his age; he had towered over all the other kids in his class.

Everything had been perfect, until Lenny had brought that whore among them.

Not content with just having the son, after he had been brutally murdered she had then set her cap at his father. Lesley shook her head at the very thought of it. It was a disgrace!

That Sharon could walk around like she did, while decent people were vilified and ostracised, was beyond her comprehension. Why couldn't people see her for what she was? See through her veneer of goodness to the putrid filth that lay beneath those sparkling blue eyes.

Big Lenny Scott's breathing was getting shallower now and she knew the time was nearly upon them. He had been left less than a man, and he had never got over it.

The police had not even really given a flying fuck as to why or how it had happened to her husband – but why would she expect any more? That witch had everyone around her under her spell and she was protected on all sides. She was living a charmed life now in her mansion in Essex with its electric gates and swimming pool. Where was the justice in that?

At least she had sent the boys to a good Catholic school, run by Jesuits; that meant they had a chance of getting away from her. That had been the hardest thing to accept: being separated from her son's children, her blood relatives. Not to be able to see them or talk to them had been a form of torture in itself, especially for her husband. He had adored those lads as much as she had.

She realised that Big Lenny had finally gone to his great reward and, drying her tears, she set about putting a rosary into his hands. She wiped his face with a damp flannel and tried to brush down his unruly hair. At least he would have the comfort of being with his son, and she would bide her time until it was her turn to go to them. She had nothing now, no one to call her own. The knowledge frightened her. How would she live without human contact? It had been hard enough when Big Lenny had been by her side, but he had become like a child to her. Looking after him had brought a focus to her days. Now it would be just her and her alone.

She felt a hand on her shoulder and looked up to see the priest, Father Gordon, smiling down at her. God was good. No matter what happened she would always have the church.

'Come away now, Lesley, and we will get you a cup of tea.'

The nurses were grateful to him for taking her away so they could deal with her husband's body. Standing up, Lesley kissed her husband's forehead and meekly followed the priest to the hospital canteen. It occurred to her that the funeral was yet to come, and that would show her just how alone she really was.

Chapter One Hundred
and Forty-One

'I am pushing, for fuck's sake!'

Ray Donovan was deeply regretting being present at the birth. Sharon was irritable in the extreme and he felt that he was getting in the nurse's way. But he plastered a smile on his face and tried to look as if he was enjoying the experience. He had no idea how brutal and bloody giving birth was. Real life was nothing like it was on the TV where the women had full make-up on and smiled serenely. He had never heard language like this coming out of Sharon's mouth before. She was sweating like a pig and he was well aware that he was getting on her nerves, but what could he do? She had refused the pethidine and was on gas and air; and every time she was about to scream another obscenity he was covering her mouth up with the breathing apparatus – and that was making her even angrier. If he was honest, he could do with the fucking pethidine himself!

The midwife was a nice lady, a big Jamaican woman

who stood no nonsense from either of the nurses or her charge. 'Come on now, Sharon. A few more pushes and your baby will be here.'

Sharon was glowering at her but the midwife was not taking a blind bit of notice. He felt Sharon tensing up and knew another big contraction was on its way. She was squeezing his hand as she bore down, sounding like a dog in pain as she tried to squeeze this new life out of her body.

'You're crowning, girl! I can see the head coming.'

Sharon was panting once more and getting ready for another big push. When the child's head emerged, Ray Donovan understood why women gave birth and not men. No man would do this more than once. Once she heard the baby cry, Sharon laughed with delight and demanded to know if it was all right. It was as if all the hours of labour had been nothing.

The cord was cut and tied and the child was wrapped in a blanket. It was covered in vernix and blood and he had never seen anything so incredible before in his life. He had a daughter – a beautiful, red, angry-looking, screaming daughter – and, as she was placed in his arms, he felt a rush of love so intense he thought he would actually pass out. Never before had he felt such emotion. He showed her to Sharon, who was laughing and crying at the same time.

'Oh, Ray, she's beautiful! Give her to me.'

He watched as his Sharon gazed at their child and didn't even murmur as they put in a few stitches. The whole experience had been a complete awakening for Ray Donovan. He looked at Sharon as she cradled their child, and he felt he could never love her more than he did at this moment.

'Kathleen. Kathleen Donovan. What do you think, Ray?'

He smiled his agreement. She had a head of black hair like his, and startling blue eyes like her mother.

'Kathleen it is, darling.'

The afterbirth had been one step too far for him – especially when it was mentioned that in some cultures it was actually eaten. Thank fuck Sharon wasn't peckish; he could not have coped with that. It was a messy business this giving birth, but it was also a miracle. He would go to Mass with his mum and Ivy later and give thanks for this safe delivery. They were keeping her in for twenty-four hours, so they would be home with him tomorrow and he could look after them both properly. He was impressed with Sharon, and so pleased that her travail was over. He knew that one day they would look back on this and laugh at her antics.

When he finally took his leave of his daughter he knew that life had changed irrevocably. This was the day he had officially become a father. It was a good feeling.

Chapter One Hundred
and Forty-Two

Jack Johnson was listening with half an ear as Ray described the birth. Reggie was all ears, apparently genuinely interested in the blood and gore; Jack wasn't that enamoured with women's shit, personally, but he laughed out loud as he heard Ray saying seriously, 'Honestly, guys, if someone on the street put you through that much pain and suffering, you would want them to get ten years!'

'Women's work, Ray. My old mum used to say, if men had the first child and women the second, there would never be a third!'

Ray grimaced as he said in disgust, 'Wouldn't be a fucking first! I don't know how they do it!'

Reggie grinned. 'I delivered my own little brother. I was fascinated by it.'

Jack and Ray exchanged worried glances and Jack broke the mood by saying loudly, 'So, are we agreed then? I will put in an offer for the Carlton brothers' loans and bets? They ain't coming home for a fucking long time – their probation officer ain't even been born yet! Poor fuckers. Definitely a grass there, I reckon. But, either way, it adds to our holdings.'

Ray laughed with delight. 'I don't see a problem myself. Do you, Reg?'

Reggie shook his head slowly, but he didn't look too convinced.

Jack noticed and said seriously, 'You have any reservations, Reg, then you should share them with us.'

Reggie sighed deeply. 'Honestly? The Carltons have a big family network – cousins, et cetera, the whole fucking shebang. I think they will want to leave it in the hands of the family. I would, wouldn't you? Both of them have families that still need to be taken care of. If they get a huge lump, they will want ongoing businesses, not a one-off sum. The court costs at the Bailey will be the national debt alone. By the time they have bumped a judge for a guaranteed sentence they will be practically boracic. That, Jack, is *my* worry. I don't think it will be quite as cut and dry as you seem to think.'

Ray could see the logic of what Reggie was saying but he also knew that Jack didn't like the Carlton brothers in the least. He saw them as boors and bullies, which they were. Ray was well aware, though, that Jack had set his heart on taking over from them.

'Fuck them and their extended family.' Jack's voice was hard now. He had never liked to be contradicted even though he asked for honesty from his entire work-force, no matter how high or how low.

Ray looked askance at Reggie and then waited for Jack to speak again. Ray could see what Reggie was saying and he thought he had made a very valid point.

'I want those fucking businesses. And the sooner you pair realise that, the better. This is not about asking, it is about *demanding*. Those pricks are gone for the duration, no matter how much they weigh out for a reduced sentence. The Crime Squad wants them because they were stupid enough to take out a Filth. Even a bent Filth is still one of the blue line, and they were cunts if they didn't remember that. As for the family members, if you put all their IQs together they would be hard pushed to write their own names and addresses! Fuck them.'

Reggie and Ray shrugged nonchalantly. Jack Johnson had spoken and he was the main man.

'We'd better get planning then, Jack.'

Jack smiled at Reggie; this was what he wanted to hear. Ray agreed that Reggie had more than a point and that Jack Johnson, old war horse that he was, should have given what he said more consideration. He might not like the Carlton brothers but they were still a force in South London, and they had their creds. But all they could do was go along with what Jack wanted – that, unfortunately, was the way of their world.

Reggie tried one last time. 'Well, we can but try.'

This was not what Jack wanted to hear, but he overlooked it because, deep down, he too knew that there was an element of truth in what Reggie had said.

Chapter One Hundred and Forty-Three

Kathleen Donovan was a good child and she was an outstandingly beautiful baby. It had surprised and pleased Sharon that even her older brothers were enamoured of her – especially young Lenny. He would hold her for hours and just gaze down at her in abject amazement. He would ask questions about babies, and be genuinely interested in Sharon's answers.

Sharon knew that his daughter's effect on the boys pleased Ray no end. He made even more of a fuss of them than usual to compensate for the new arrival. All her worries were gone and she was determined just to enjoy her new daughter, who she was absolutely thrilled with.

Ray, her darling Ray, was even more besotted than she was. He was fascinated with the different aspects of child rearing and he was making a point of getting home as soon as possible so he would not lose any time with this new daughter of his. The fact that his mother was as mad on the child as he was seemed to be the icing on the cake. He worshipped his mother and Sharon had to admit she was easy to be around. Unlike Lenny's mother, who had pushed her way in, Annie was quite happy to just be there and do whatever was required.

Ray was still concerned for Sharon's welfare even though she felt fine. He seemed to think that what she had gone through, what he called her 'travail', had been far more taxing than she was letting on! But she loved him even more for this caring of her and his family, because that is what they were – a wonderful family. She thanked God for him every day of the week.

'Dad? Is it still OK for you to take us to football and that?'

Liam was worried that, now his sister had arrived, they would not be able to do as much stuff as usual. Not that he minded – he loved the little thing – but he liked his clubs and he would be quite happy to find his own way to wherever he needed to go. Like his brother, he was chomping at the bit to get a touch more freedom from his mum and dad.

Ray smiled understandingly. 'Nothing will change, Liam. I promise you.'

Sharon was listening quietly, waiting to hear what was being said.

Liam tried again. 'The thing is, I am quite happy to get the bus or trains, like. So is Lenny.'

Sharon saw Ray stifle a smile as he said forcefully, 'No, that's all right, son. I will still accompany you, don't you worry about that.'

Annie had to leave the room. Sharon followed her, and together they laughed at Liam's attempt to get a bit more freedom.

'They are good lads, Sharon, but you can't blame them for trying!'

'I suppose. I'm more pleased that they have accepted little Kathy so easily. I mean, they really do love her.'

Annie smiled and Sharon could see the traces of her former beauty, though she still looked good for her age, there was no doubting that.

'Thing is, lads especially need to be let off the leash, you know? Not that I am criticising, mind. But I do think that these days children are mollycoddled. I read the other day that young ones were leaving university after having gone great guns with their studies but they didn't know how to look up a bus timetable! Have you ever heard the like!'

Sharon was suitably shocked but she understood that Annie was telling her it was time the boys were let free. She knew she was right, but it was hard just the same. She decided she would let them travel to school with their friends; that would be a good start. Annie had decided to move to the house in the village to be near her grandchild although Sharon would happily have her living with them. Annie was a calming presence in the home, and she was still young at heart.

Sharon guessed it would be hard for her to give up her life and friends in Gateshead where she seemed very settled and happy.

'Instead of moving to the village, Annie, why don't you move in to the gatehouse here? That way you would have your freedom but you would be nearer to us. Then you could commute – you know, spend time at your home up North and time here.'

She saw the relief in Annie's eyes and she knew that, for all her talk, she was just doing what her son wanted.

'You have a great life up there with lots of friends. I would love you here, Annie, you know that. I just worry you are giving up too much.'

Annie hugged this wonderful girl her son had been lucky enough to find and said seriously, 'We don't deserve you, Sharon. You are a wonderful and insightful woman who is far too good for that hooligan I raised!'

Sharon hugged her back tightly and she felt choked up as she said honestly, 'That hooligan you are talking about was the best thing that happened to me and my boys.'

'And you, lady, are the best thing that could have ever happened to him.' Then she said quietly, 'He did nine long years, and that affects a body. When he came home he was like a rudderless boat. Then he met you. I thank God every day because you and those boys gave him a purpose. From day one it was like he was on a mission to make you happy and I think he managed

417

that. But, more to the point, you made my only son into a happy and contented man.'

They were hugging again and that was how Ray found them and, embracing them both, he said loudly, in a thick Geordie brogue, 'Why-aye, ladies, why you bubblin'?'

And Annie, laughing loudly, said, 'We are crying with happiness, you big streak of piss!' feeling that she had finally come home.

Chapter One Hundred
and Forty-Four

Bobby Carlton was visited while on remand by a young man called Elton Mills. Elton was black, cockney and had a way with him that Jack Johnson felt was going to get him far. He was handsome, easy-going and he could fight like a paratrooper if the need arose. As young as he was, he was already making a name for himself. He had that wonderful combination of attributes that would take him a long way in his chosen occupation. He was intelligent and he could suss a situation within nanoseconds. This was why Ray and Jack had given him the job of approaching Bobby Carlton; the boy had never even been cautioned so he could move from nick to nick relatively easily.

'He fucking wants *what*?'

Elton smiled easily, his sweet face belying the steel trap of a mind that it hid from the people around him. Elton already had two bodies under his belt. One was personal: the man who had hammered the fuck out of his mother for years and then mysteriously disappeared one night, to the amazement of everyone. He was buried on the Essex marshes, beaten to death with a crowbar. The second body was an honest-to-goodness job. Elton had been paid handsomely – in fact, he had bought a house for his mum with the proceeds – to remove a gang member who had fallen foul of the boss he had been involved with. Like Elton's stepfather, the gang member had never been found. Elton believed – rightly – that if there was no body, how the fuck could there be a crime? He was a very cool, calm and collected young man. He had the handsome face of an angel and the mind of a demon.

Ray was already keen to make him his protégé. Elton was a good kid and, at nineteen, he understood more than men three times his age did. Like Ray Donovan, he had no conscience whatsoever – it was just work to him. Ray was painfully aware that people like them were few and far between. Oh, there were the lunatics who made a splash by being vicious and vindictive, but real violence wasn't personal. It was something that needed to be done quietly, unobtrusively and with the maximum of secrecy. You did not advertise serious lunacy; the person involved was astute enough to guess that their particular forte would eventually be discovered by the relevant parties.

But those cunts who told all and sundry the ins and outs of their vicious dealings were no more than cunts to themselves. They were inevitably caught and banged up within a few years, when even their contemporaries breathed a sigh of relief. No one around them could ever trust them – they were the original loose cannons and they always shat on their own doorsteps. They would attack a local boy they thought looked at them sideways, or batter the mother of their children. They always fucked up big time – it was the nature of the beast. They went away for years, stuck in the nick on temazepam or Dolmatil or, worst-case scenario, they were drugged up until they couldn't string a sentence together. Not that they were that great at it before their capture.

No, young Elton Mills was a find, and Ray understood that, and that was why he had sent him on this job. It was Elton's trial and no one knew that better than Elton himself.

He smiled that winning smile that got him laid on a regular basis and said earnestly, 'It is a genuine offer. Mr Johnson, *Jack* Johnson, is willing to purchase your holdings for a serious amount of poke. He wishes you well, and he just wants to make your latest difficulties a bit easier for you to bear.'

Bobby Carlton sat back in his seat and stifled the urge to laugh at this little black fucker who thought he could talk to him like he was a cunt.

'A genuine offer, is it? In case you haven't noticed, I'm on remand in Funky Brixton. There's a lot of your people in here – that is why it's called Funky fucking Brixton.'

'And that is relevant because?'

Elton looked at the man before him with a real arrogance that was not lost on Bobby Carlton. He actually felt a shiver of apprehension at the boy's demeanour; it occurred to him that this kid didn't give a flying fuck either way.

Elton looked suitably bored as he said quietly, 'I'll take that as a no then, shall I?'

'Tell *Jack* fucking *Johnson* that he can stick his *fucking offer* right up his jacksy.'

It was said loudly and Elton knew that people were watching them, so he stood up and, offering his hand to Bobby Carlton, he said in a neutral voice, 'I will do that, sir. It was an honour to meet you. I wish you well in your future endeavours.'

He walked away without a backward glance and Bobby Carlton had the terrible suspicion that he had been well and truly mugged off. He was also feeling very unsettled, as if he had just made an enemy for life. Which, of course, is exactly what had happened.

Elton Mills would not forget that visit for a very long time. He was a man with no conscience and the urge to harm people he saw as beneath him and those he respected. Elton Mills was the new generation.

Chapter One Hundred and Forty-Five

'A cunt of cunts, if you will excuse the expression. He had no interest in even listening to the proposal. He just made a big drama out of it for the benefit of the people in the visiting room.' Elton's disgust at the treatment he had received was evident to everyone in the room, as was his disappointment at Bobby Carlton's stupidity.

Jack Johnson was impressed with the lad, and he knew that Ray was intending to mentor him. Elton Mills was a one-off; that would always be his strength *and* his weakness. Jack thought the lad was very lucky to have been discovered by a man like Ray Donovan. He had a feeling that young Elton Mills thought along the same lines. He was a shrewd young man with a bright future ahead of him if he used his loaf of bread.

'Well, Jack?'

Ray looked at Jack with a neutral expression and he was pleased to note that Elton was watching his every move. He really liked this kid and he knew that Barton had introduced them for a reason. They were kindred spirits.

Ray continued, 'Bobby Carlton was always a cunt. Let's talk to Teddy before we go any further. He is already Grade-A, even on remand. They have him in Belmarsh, treating him like a fucking IRA terrorist. He is the brains of the outfit – and I use that term loosely – so I think we should pay him the courtesy of a call. That way, there can be no recriminations or comebacks.'

Reggie thought that was an excellent idea, so he said as much. They had to cover their backs with this latest escapade, even though things needed to be *seen* to be done. 'You are right. We need to approach both the main players.'

Jack knew when he had a *fait accompli* on his hands, but he had taken umbrage and that was never a good thing for anyone involved, least of all the person who had been the cause of Jack Johnson's ire.

Ray Donovan bowed to Reggie's superior knowledge of Jack and his foibles. Reggie had been part of Jack's crew far longer than he had and he respected the man's opinions. He would go with the flow and then see what the upshot was going to be. Personally, he thought the Carlton brothers were wankers; they might be named after the Kennedys but they had a long way to go to fulfil that potential. But he didn't say a word. This was out of his hands until such a time as Jack decided what he wanted done. Then he would do everything in his power to make sure it all went as smoothly as possible.

Ray looked at young Elton and said jovially, 'Looks like you will be having your first taste of Belmarsh! Let's hope it's the fucking last!'

They all laughed at the joke, even Elton, who evidently believed he was far too fucking shrewd to ever get caught out. The arrogance of youth, thought Jack Johnson. Well, many a man before him had thought the exact same thing. Young Elton was not the first to think he was invincible; it was part of the territory when you were green and foolish. Not that anyone pointed that out, of course. He was willing and that was to be encouraged. If it all fell out of bed for him they would look after him, that was par for the course.

Jack Johnson poured out his eighteen-year-old Scotch and he was amused to see that young Elton was apparently not much of a drinker. Well, he would soon learn to enjoy life while you had it. In their game, it could be over before it had even really started. He had seen that happen time and time again. Youth, as Oscar Wilde had once said, was wasted on the young! If only they knew that it was just a hop and a skip to a life tariff. But he kept his thoughts to himself. Why fuck with the lad's head? But the truth was, he had now irritated Jack with his youthful arrogance and that did not augur well for the future. Jack would happily have him on the payroll, but that did not mean he had to like him. Now, though, he would feel honour-bound to watch him, which was a different thing altogether. Jack had the final word, and the sooner this little fucker realised that, the better off he would be.

Ray understood the situation immediately; he would lose no time in explaining all that to young Elton Mills, who he liked, but would never really trust one hundred per cent – not until he had proved himself anyway.

Young Elton realised that he had somehow made a faux pas. He would use that knowledge to make sure that this never happened to him again. He was ready to follow Ray Donovan as far as he wanted him to. Elton also knew that Jack Johnson was not as enamoured of him as he would have liked him to be. But he understood that this was something that he could not control. His best shot was with Ray Donovan and he was pleased about that. He knew he was still very young and that he had an inflated opinion of himself. He had read all the books on psychology and psychopathy – he knew better than anyone did what he really was. He also knew that he had to feign humility and he was willing to do that if the circumstances needed it.

He remembered being in care as a young lad, and learning early on that no one was going to look out for you – you had to look out for yourself. And that was exactly what he was determined to do. He would rise above the shit he had been born into. He had killed for the right reason and for the wrong reason. Now he would do whatever it took to make his mark on the world and give himself a life that he had only ever dreamed of.

Reggie watched the changing expressions on the boy's face and had a feeling that, once he was permanently allied with Ray Donovan, there would be no stopping them. For some reason that knowledge bothered him.

Chapter One Hundred
and Forty-Six

Elton Mills was thrilled to be visiting Belmarsh. As far as he was concerned, it was the prison of prisons. And to visit Teddy Carlton, who was Grade-A even on remand, was the highest honour! He had been subjected to a complete rigmarole to get in. First he had to have passport pictures taken, then apply to the Home Office for visitation rights, and finally he had been put through the indignity of having the local police come to his home to ascertain that he was indeed the person he said he was. Out-fucking-rageous was his feeling on the subject. But he swallowed his anger because he knew this was part of a bigger and better plan. The one good thing that *did* come out of it was that, for the first time, Elton Mills understood the real fucking world of having a capture. It could mean the best years of your life in a six-by-twelve cell, and to visit it meant aggravation of the highest fucking order. His mum would be hard pushed to sort that out without help. But then she would be hard pushed to pass a GCSE; he loved her, but she wasn't exactly fucking *Mastermind* material. This shit would frighten her and he had always made sure she was protected from the truth.

This was a learning curve for sure, and he would remember just what was at stake – the main thing being his fucking freedom. There was no way any of Jack Johnson's lot were going away – if it all fell apart, *he* would be the one to suffer. On the other hand, if he used his fucking nous then he would be a very rich man and some other poor cunt would one day be sitting where Teddy Carlton was. It was a chance he was willing to take.

He was searched and he was made to wait for long periods. Belmarsh was peopled with the best of the best – not that he felt the POs were in any way worth the proverbial wank. But he was sensible; he needed to look as benign as possible and get through the visit with the minimum of aggravation. There was a very aggressive vibe here that shocked him. It was bad enough that people were locked away – why would anyone want to make it harder than it already was? Young Elton was having his first taste of the British judicial system. He was not impressed. He was also more determined than ever to make sure that this would never be his life.

When he was finally ushered into the presence of Teddy Carlton he was tired and fed up with the whole process. If only he knew how many women went through the same thing on a regular basis just to see the man they had married and keep him in contact with his children. Elton was still too young to know about the *real* economics of prison and the reality that it forced on everyone involved, including the POs. They were either ex-army and fucking arseholes, or they were looking for an extra bit of income; who could blame them? True, some were of the opinion that the men were entitled to be treated as innocent until proven otherwise. They, though, were few and far between, as Elton was finding out for himself.

Teddy Carlton could not have appeared to be more different to his brother. He was dark to Bobby's fair; he was handsome, very handsome. He was also enigmatic. He was a man who could command respect – as long as he didn't try to express an opinion. After ten minutes though, Elton knew that this man was about as much use as a fucking chocolate teapot. He was a handsome, useless fuck. Now he was well and truly banjaxed. It had apparently never ever occurred to Teddy that ending up in prison might actually be a possibility in his fucking life. Elton was simply disgusted Teddy Carlton had not allowed for the fact that he was going away for longer than his kids had actually lived. Elton had hoped that that might make him more amenable to what was being said to him.

Teddy was like his brother in many ways, though he had more nous than Bobby did in that he seemed more aware of his surroundings. But that could be down to the Grade-A conditions in Belmarsh, of course, which were a bit different to the norm. Grade-A had been brought in for terrorists, mainly IRA, but it was eventually used for anyone the prison system felt was a danger, or who they wanted to teach some kind of lesson. Even the thickest cunt in the world would be hard pushed to miss *that* much.

Elton knew immediately that he was dealing with a narcissistic prick who had a bit of a brain, but not too much; he knew he wouldn't pose a problem. In the world of the Carltons, Elton realised, this man was the *real* intellectual. And that wasn't saying too much. He treated him as such because he knew that was what was expected of him. It didn't mean he liked it, of course. What Elton didn't allow for was that, for what Teddy lacked in intelligence, he more than made up for in cuteness; you did not get as far as he had by being a complete fucking wanker. He had heard all about the visit to his brother, and he was not impressed. He also knew that Jack Johnson wanted what they had. That wasn't exactly something he was shocked about – some fucker was bound to; he just had not thought it would be Jack.

He liked Jack Johnson; he had always been good to them. But Teddy had never seen Jack as a fucking scavenger, scraping around for other people's fucking downfalls. That was wrong! Jack was a fucking man to emulate and to aspire to. But, Teddy reasoned, that was before he and his brother had been the victims of the capture of a lifetime. Life was running away from them both. They were fucked on so many different levels.

Teddy was also man enough to admit that once they were sentenced, there was no real hope for their enterprises. They had more chance of getting a wank off Pope fucking Gregory than they did of keeping the businesses in their orbit, not least because there wasn't one person in the family he would trust enough to run it all.

But young Elton had his own agenda. Especially now that he had a serious grudge against the Carlton family, thanks to Bobby and his bad attitude. The brothers had looked at him like he was a cunt of Olympian standards. But they were the ones behind bars; all he actually was was the broker for them to get a terrific deal. Because what Jack was offering was far more than anyone else would have.

Elton smiled widely at Teddy and Teddy, being Teddy, smiled widely back. It occurred to Elton that if they had met under different circumstances they would probably have been friends. He liked the look of the man, his natural friendliness that was so like his own; it was warm and loving though it actually meant nothing. He sensed that Teddy Carlton had sussed him out as easily as *he* had sussed *him*. Shame really that they were at odds, but such was the life they lived. He had a job to do, and he was determined to see it

432

through. After all, he worked for Jack Johnson. His wages had been paid and he saw that he was well compensated for his time.

So, he sat down and he tried to sell Teddy Carlton the deal, even though he knew as well as Jack Johnson, Reggie and Ray did that this was an insult of epic proportions. But, at the end of the day, businesses didn't run themselves. And what Jack Johnson wanted he usually got – by any means necessary.

Chapter One Hundred and Forty-Seven

Liam and Lenny were out and Sharon was lying down on her bed trying to get a few hours' sleep. The baby was out for the count and the tiredness had caught up with her. She lay in the darkened room waiting for sleep to claim her but it didn't come. She sighed and tried once more to get comfortable, but her mind was racing and she couldn't switch off.

It was a throwaway remark that Reggie had made that had set her thinking. He had bought the baby a beautiful bracelet – white gold set with tiny diamonds – and Sharon had been thrilled with it. Her relationship with him was better than it had been for years; she could look at him now and not think of him with Lenny. But, as she had made him a cup of tea and they had chatted about the baby and Ray's elation at his daughter's birth, Reggie had laughed and said in a jokey voice how Ray was the opposite of Lenny and that could only be a good thing. He had remarked how timely Ray's arrival had been in her life, and how he seemed to have wanted to look out for her and the boys from the moment he had laid eyes on her. At the time she had not thought much about it, but now it bothered her for some reason that she could not explain. It was silly, and probably nothing to worry about, yet it did worry her for some unknown reason.

She pushed the thought from her mind and tried to relax herself enough to sleep for a little while. She knew it was important to try and grab a nap when the chance arose because babies and sleeping did not always go together. She was expressing milk so that Ray could do his share of the night feeds and, in fairness to him, he was a natural parent. She could hear Annie moving about in the kitchen and she guessed that she was cooking the evening meal – she really was a fantastic help to her. Ray adored his mother and she couldn't blame him; the woman was amazing. She felt closer to Ray now that she had spoken so much about him with his mother. Annie lived for her son, and she regaled Sharon with stories of his youth and his childhood. She felt she really knew Ray better than she had before. Annie thought the world of the boys too, and they both loved her but, then again, what was not to love about Annie? She was kind, easy-going and she never interfered. She was a world away from Lesley Scott.

Sitting up, Sharon lit herself a cigarette and took a long pull on it. If she wasn't going to sleep, she was determined at least to rest. Someone had told her that it was often as good as a nap. She smoked and thought, her mind continuing to race. Why she was worried about something Reggie had said in complete innocence, she didn't know. The truth was, sometimes she felt that Ray's entrance into her life was *too* providential somehow. A real man was exactly what she had needed – especially after the revelations about Lenny had come to light. Ray arriving on the scene had brought her nothing but good. So why did she sometimes feel it was all a little *too* perfect to be true? Why was she worrying about something that had only ever been beneficial to her and her sons? Why was she making problems where there weren't any?

She sighed heavily and pulled herself out from under the blankets. As she drew back the curtains and light flooded the room, she looked around her, seeing the evidence of her life with Ray everywhere, and smiled sadly. She was a very lucky woman – she had so much and she was so happy. Why did she feel at times that this was all built on quicksand? She believed that Ray loved her dearly, and she loved him with a ferocity that sometimes surprised her. Sexually she had never felt like this before, and the intensity of her emotions still surprised her. They were compatible in every way; why was she plagued with these doubts?

She pulled on jeans and a T-shirt, and ran a brush through her hair. She was still in good shape even after three kids; if anything, Ray desired her more now than he had before little Kathy's birth. It had seemed to bring them closer than ever. She shook herself mentally and left the bedroom. She would go down and have a cup of tea and a chat with Annie. She needed to rid herself of these feelings, because they were without any real foundation. She ran lightly down the stairs and wondered if she was suffering from some kind of postnatal depression.

Chapter One Hundred and Forty-Eight

Elton Mills had tried his best. Ray believed the lad had done all that was asked of him, and he knew in his heart that it would not have mattered who had gone to see the Carlton brothers – the outcome would have been the same. Henry fucking Kissinger could not have made a dent, and that was that.

Now it seemed Jack Johnson had what he really wanted: a reason to hold a grudge and therefore to take the businesses without a second thought. Ray personally didn't give a fuck either way, but one thing he was sure of was that one of the Carlton brothers needed to be taken out. All that was left to them now was years of waiting out their lives in a series of different cells. Ray had done nine years and that had not been easy, but time inevitably passed even though it might seem to be crawling.

Ray had become addicted to Radio 4 in the nick. He had used the gym to wear himself out physically, and the radio to educate his mind. It had still been a fucking hard old road, because it was the boredom that often caused the worst lows. Depression was rife in prison environments, and the taking of life – either your own or someone else's – was always a possibility. Petty arguments could quickly become massive feuds, as everything was heightened. Coping in prison was all about a mindset, and he wasn't sure that Teddy Carlton had the balls for what he was about to endure. Bobby, on the other hand, would probably fare better. He was, at least, a realist, whereas Teddy Carlton didn't have the savvy to see what the future actually held for him.

Ray stretched and yawned noisily. He was at the smallholding, and he wanted this latest job over with as quickly as possible; he didn't like to keep away from his family longer than he had to. It was amazing, really, when he thought about it, just how much his life had changed for the better. It was as if he had finally come alive when he had fallen in love with Sharon Scott. Now it was time for them to get married. The boys wouldn't mind – they would want it as much as he did. Sharon would relish the chance to arrange it. It wasn't like they had never discussed it, they had just never got round to it.

It would be a church wedding, of course, and it could be as large or as small as Sharon wanted. He relished the thought of taking the name Scott away from her, and making her a Donovan. He wondered if he should ask the boys if they wanted to change their names; after all, he was, to all intents and purposes, their father now and they called him 'Dad'.

He heard a deep groaning coming from the basement and sighed. He finished his tea and, after washing up the mug, he made his way down into the cellar. The smell of blood was overwhelming but he didn't really notice it. The man he was dealing with was watching him with frightened eyes. Ray ignored him. His victim had raped a serious Face's young daughter, and that needed to be paid for by the man responsible. The police were never called in, and this was to be kept hush-hush. That was fine with Ray. All he needed to be told was the name of his victim and that Jack Johnson wanted to see the ponce suffer and suffer. And so he would.

As Ray picked up a small pair of pliers, he saw the man attempting to break free of his bonds. It was a futile gesture, of course, but Ray reasoned it was the human need for survival that kept the hope in his victim's eyes alive. He was whistling between his teeth and decided to wrap this up quickly. He would take a photo of the man's body, to be passed on to the relevant parties, and get himself home to that lovely woman of his. He set about his task; he was getting bored now.

Twenty minutes later the man was breathing his last, and Ray watched the light leaving his one good eye, the other eye having been removed earlier by Ray himself. Then he set about the clean-up operation and the disposal of the body. This had been a lucrative and enjoyable few hours. Now he hoped to get back in time to give his little Kathy her night feed.

Chapter One Hundred and Forty-Nine

Lesley Scott could not sleep. Ever since she had heard about the child born to Sharon and that Ray she had felt utter devastation. No matter what she did, Sharon Conway was somehow still blessed. Lesley had been praying on a daily basis for that whore to be taken down in some way but all she seemed to do was go onwards and upwards. Her son's children called this man 'Dad'; it was as if, between them, they had edited her handsome son out of their lives altogether. She felt the tears of anger and frustration constantly.

They lived behind gates in a huge house and they seemed to have endless supplies of money while she was hard pushed to stretch her meagre savings to pay all her bills. Her husband might have died but she still used the same amount of gas and electricity. Lesley felt like she was being thwarted on every level. Her life was getting worse, while that whore's was getting better by the day. There had to be some kind of retribution, surely? God could not, in all conscience, let that bitch prosper. He would *have* to punish her. That was what kept her going: knowing that at some point Sharon would get her well-deserved comeuppance. And, when she did, Lesley would feel that her son's death had finally been paid for.

She had lost so much, so very much. Her family had been decimated and that whore seemed to be replenishing *her* so-called family all the while. Her family was growing, getting bigger – they even had that man's mother living with them. She felt the sting of tears thinking of her handsome grandsons calling another woman 'Nanny' and another man 'Dad'. Life could be so raw, so cruel and so unfair. But she was determined to see the day her daughter-in-law finally paid for her actions.

Chapter One Hundred and Fifty

Jack Johnson was unable to sleep and that was annoying him no end. He had lost a measure of respect for going after the Carlton brothers. His anger was beneath him in many ways, but the brothers had always irritated him; if he was honest, it was because they had achieved against all the odds. They were thick as shit, and twice as stupid, as his old mum would say, and yet he had always coveted what they had.

Years ago he had been given first refusal on their businesses and he had declined the offer. Turned out that was a really stupid fucking thing to do. A fucking retard could have made money off it, which is why the Carlton brothers had done so well. He knew that he was being petty but he could not help it. They were so fucking stupid but they had seen something he had not. Now they were looking at such a big lump, they would have paid for their burial plots long before they got parole.

He heard the door open; it would be Ray Donovan telling him that he had fulfilled his latest job. Ray was a fucking Brahma. He was that strange mixture of nice bloke and raving fucking nutcase. Jack had sensed his forte the first time he met him – he had crossed paths with people like him before, even though they were a rare breed. Frankie Fraser had had it – the aura of danger that told you that the person you were dealing with wasn't on the same page as everyone else. If he was honest, Ray frightened him, because he was capable of doing damage to anyone – even people he liked. He enjoyed his work, and that was why he was so good at it.

'All right, Jack?'

Jack Johnson forced a smile on his face. He didn't want to talk to him tonight. Jack wasn't squeamish but he knew that Ray, the new father, the man who acted like Dad of the Year, had spent a lot of time torturing someone for money. Tonight that bothered Jack and made him wonder what else he was capable of. He still poured him a drink, though; he knew what was expected.

Jack picked up a holdall and passed it to Ray and saw a smile of satisfaction cross his face. Ray loved money – cold, hard cash. Jack knew he had no right to feel so disgusted with this man; after all, he was his broker. He made sure he had work. But tonight, seeing the pleasure on Ray's face made him feel uneasy. No one should enjoy inflicting pain that much. But, then again, the fact that Ray could do what he did was why they were earning fortunes. Lenny Scott had

had his fucking problems – Jack knew that better than anyone – but seeing Ray with Sharon and the kids genuinely frightened him. Someone once said, you can know too much about people, and never was a truer word spoken. The more he got to know Ray Donovan, the more he worried that Sharon Scott had made the biggest mistake of her life. They seemed happy – they had a child and they were getting married, by all accounts. He wholeheartedly believed that Ray would never turn his particular talents on his wife-to-be and her children, but there was still that niggling worry that he'd been wrong to encourage Sharon and Ray in the first place.

He sighed heavily. He was getting old, that was the trouble. As you aged, you saw problems where none previously existed. But he couldn't shake the feeling that Ray was changing somehow and Jack wasn't so sure it was for the good.

'I wrapped that cunt up early, Jack.' Ray grinned good-naturedly. 'I can't wait to get home to the new baby! Honestly, if someone had told me I would feel like this, I would never have believed them! It's like I've finally grown up or something.'

Jack smiled at the man he was beginning to think wasn't as stable as he had first thought. He shook himself mentally. This was Ray Donovan, who was a good worker and who was also a terrific earner.

'You all right, Jack? You look like you're sickening for something.'

Jack shook his head and poured them both another glass of Chivas Regal.

Ray noticed that the man's hands were shaking, and he was nonplussed for a few moments. This was Jack Johnson, the hard man, the London Face. Recently he had not seemed himself, though, and that was getting noticed by others as well. Reggie had said he seemed to be getting frail and Ray thought that was a very accurate description. But looks, as Ray knew better than anyone, could be deceiving.

'Oh, I nearly forgot, Jack. Here are the Polaroids for the client. Tell him I had that fucker screaming for mercy.'

Jack took the photos but he didn't look at them; he placed them in a drawer of his desk and shut it firmly.

'It was a really easy one this time. Bloke didn't see it coming. He actually got in the car without a murmur. Fucking nonce. I tell you, Jack, I was tempted to do that one as a favour.'

Jack sipped his whisky and watched as Ray chatted. He was always on a high after a kill like this; the man was a natural-born predator. Jack was old-school: a good hiding, or even the removal of someone you needed removed, was part and parcel of their livelihoods. As was extreme violence, but to prove a point, not torture. Violence for the sake of it didn't appeal to Jack – not on this scale anyway.

Ray was now back on the subject of his family and

Jack could hear the genuine adoration in his voice for those boys who he saw as his own. It was funny, but Jack would not have believed a man of Ray's temperament could be capable of real love. To listen to him, you could be in no doubt that he worshipped his family. Again, Jack was attacked with a stroke of conscience, because when he listened to Ray talking it all sounded wonderful. It was when you looked into his eyes that you realised there was blankness there that was not evident to anyone who didn't know him very well. It occurred to Jack that Ray was like an actor playing a part and, in fairness, he seemed to be playing this particular part very well. But what would happen when he decided he didn't want to be the big, benevolent father and husband any more?

Jack was pulled from his reverie by Ray's words and he said quickly, 'Say that again, Ray.'

Ray Donovan flashed one of his blinding smiles that made him look very handsome and very easy-going – women loved that smile.

'I said, both the Carlton brothers will be gone by tomorrow. They are committing suicide, apparently.'

Ray watched carefully for Jack's reaction; he had taken this on himself for no other reason than he wanted it over. Jack was getting on his nerves with his dithering.

Jack swallowed down his whisky and forced a smile on to his face as he said blandly, 'Well, that certainly will put the proverbial cat among the pigeons.'

Ray grinned easily as he said, 'I've also sent out warnings to the extended family. We won't have any trouble there.'

'Seems like you have thought of everything.'

Ray shrugged and changed the subject. He had made his point. But this had rattled Jack Johnson more than he would ever admit. It was tantamount to fucking mutiny, and *that* was something he would never countenance. The atmosphere in the office was charged and Ray was watching Jack Johnson every bit as closely as Jack was watching him. The gauntlet had been thrown down. It was time this firm had a revamp and Ray knew that, if he wanted to get on, this was necessary. They were at the top and, if they wanted to stay up there, they had to move with the times. Jack Johnson, he was sure, would eventually bow down to his way of thinking. And if he didn't, then that was his lookout.

Chapter One Hundred and Fifty-One

The demise of the Carlton brothers was a nine-day wonder, and no one except the prison service believed their deaths were suicides. Somehow it was rumoured that Ray Donovan was behind it all, ergo, that meant Jack Johnson had ordered the brothers to be removed. Reggie Dornan didn't comment either way. No one commented, in fact. Ray had presented them with a *fait accompli* and there had been no stopping that. But Reggie could tell that Jack Johnson wasn't a happy man, and that he no longer trusted Ray Donovan as he once had. These were trying times, especially for Reggie whose allegiance obviously lay with Jack Johnson, his mentor. In truth, Reggie could see things from Ray's point of view as well. They had to fucking get with the times and that meant great changes. Thanks to Ray, they were now undisputed kings. People asked their permission before they did certain things, and even the northern Faces were offering allegiance.

Reggie's other worry was that young Elton seemed to be joined to Ray at the hip. Ray was obviously grooming him for a top job. That in itself wasn't a problem, but it should have been discussed, especially as everyone – including Elton Mills himself – knew that Jack Johnson didn't like him. Elton was very like Ray – there was something off about him even though he came across as a nice guy and was always very respectful to everyone. He was lucky in that he had never even had a caution from the Filth, so he was still able to travel to prisons all over to talk face to face with men they needed to contact for whatever nefarious reason.

It wasn't good to overlook Jack Johnson though, and that is what Ray was doing. He was readying himself to take over and everyone, including Jack Johnson, realised that. But by the same token, that wasn't a bad thing. Jack was getting on, and he didn't understand a lot of the new villainy. He didn't know that you could rob people with a fucking computer and that massive deals could be done online with overseas partners so that no flights were involved. It was a new world and people like Jack Johnson were rapidly becoming dinosaurs.

Reggie watched as Elton and Ray stood chatting for a few moments before coming into the offices. Jack wasn't there yet, so Reggie put the kettle on for their early morning tea. One good thing about Elton Mills was that he made a blinding cup of char.

Reggie was meeting Sharon and his sister Gerry later to talk over the wedding plans. It was going to be held in a few days and, though it was small, it would be very tasteful – all handmade suits and expensive hats. He was pleased to be so included in the plans as it proved to him that Sharon had finally come to terms with his relationship with Lenny. She was moving on, which, for him, was a good thing. Once she married Ray she would be a Donovan, and that, as they say, would be the end of it. Lenny Scott, who he had loved deeply, would finally be forgotten. His wife and sons had gradually airbrushed him from their lives. The only way Lenny would live on was through Reggie and his memories.

Chapter One Hundred and Fifty-Two

Little Kathy was nearly six months old and a real beauty. With her huge blue eyes and jet-black hair she caused a stir wherever she went. She could crawl at an Olympic pace so she kept everyone on their toes.

Lenny and Liam were locked in their respective bedrooms and so Sharon had an unaccustomed quiet few hours ahead of her. Kathy was ensconced in her lobster-pot playpen with her toys and a drink of juice and Sharon poured herself a nice cold glass of Chablis and sat down gratefully to drink it. She looked around and felt the pleasure her surroundings always brought to her. Why wouldn't they? She had an exceptionally beautiful home that looked like something from a Sunday supplement. Ray gave her carte blanche when it came to the house, the boys or his new daughter. He never baulked at the prices she paid for anything. He was good to her and she knew that he loved her above all else.

So why was she feeling so nervous about the up-coming wedding? She sipped at her drink, and watched her new daughter playing with her toys and talking baby talk to herself. She had everything any woman could want and she could not understand why she was questioning it. She felt like this periodically and she put it down to the fear of losing what she had again. When Lenny had been brutally murdered it had left its mark on her, and that was to be expected. Even though she had had to confront his other life, she had still been left a widow with two young, fatherless chil-dren. It had been so hard to pick up the pieces, and then she had met Ray. More to the point, Ray had entered her life and he had been at her side from the moment she had met him.

Making love with Ray was a completely different experience to Lenny; how could she have known that the sex they'd had was always more about him than her? She realised now that Lenny had been scratching an itch – she could have been anyone. He had been possessed of a high sex drive and he had basically fucked her. No one had ever made love to her until Ray Donovan, and the change had been amazing. He made her feel treasured, loved and desired. He adored her and the kids and they never really had a cross word. The nerves about this wedding were a melon scratcher all right, there was no doubt about that! There was a niggling little voice telling her not to go through with it.

The gates were buzzing and she heard Gerry's voice through the intercom. Opening the gates, she waited patiently at the front door to welcome her friend. The worst thing was she couldn't tell anyone her fears because they sounded so silly and were not really grounded in any specific reasoning. Ray had never put a foot wrong, and she realised that was what was bothering her. That, and his habit of seeming to be somewhere else at times, especially after he had been away on one of his business meetings. It was like he was in his own world, a place where she could never go, and where she felt she couldn't reach him.

She shook the thoughts from her mind. She was being silly and she knew it. This was just the pre-wedding nerves that all brides experienced, no more than that. Her sons were excited by the idea of the wedding, and were talking about getting their names changed so they would all be Donovans. She knew that thrilled Ray, but there was a part of her that didn't think they should lose the name Scott. They were, when all was said and done, Lenny Scott's flesh and blood.

Gerry looked amazing as always and, as she walked into the house, Sharon said brightly, 'How did the blind date go last night?'

Gerry was laughing and said loudly, 'Oh, pour me wine, please. He looked like he had fallen out of the ugly tree and hit every fucking branch on the way down!'

Sharon was laughing with her; this was exactly what she needed – some light relief and some easy fun. She had to stop these dark thoughts before they took over her life.

Chapter One Hundred and Fifty-Three

Ray looked good and he knew it as he stood with his stepsons, waiting for his wife-to-be to arrive. They were outside the local church where they took Communion and worshipped regularly; it was a beautiful old building decorated with huge bunches of white roses and white orchids. There were not that many guests – only close family and friends. The reception later on would have more people but, for the actual ceremony, Sharon had wanted it small and intimate. She had got her wish.

When Sharon arrived in a black Bentley, Ray was so proud of her. She looked fantastic. Her dress was like a cocktail dress, cut just above the knee, and it fitted her perfectly. Her thick, blond hair was swept up and she wore a short veil. She looked like something from *Vogue* and he felt the pull of her as she smiled at him tentatively.

'You look absolutely stunning, darling.' His northern

accent was always more pronounced when he felt emotional.

He entered the church to go and wait by the altar and, greeting all their friends and family, he felt like the happiest man on the planet.

Walking down the aisle with her proud father to the opening bars of Joan Armatrading's 'Love and Affection', Sharon looked about her and felt that maybe, just maybe, she was doing the right thing. Her sons were smiling at her, her mum looked like she would burst with happiness and Annie was already in tears. Little Kathy was dressed in salmon pink and she was grinning widely as Gerry held her in her arms. Reggie Dornan winked at her as she passed him and it made her smile. Then the priest was marrying them and Sharon wondered at how different this wedding was to her first one.

Chapter One Hundred and Fifty-Four

Jack Johnson was drinking his usual Scotch and, as Sharon walked by him, she stopped and kissed him on the cheek. She had always liked Jack and she knew that he had always had her best interests at heart.

'Well, girl, the dirty deed has been done! I hope you will be very happy, darling.'

She smiled at him, but she felt there was an underlying question in his voice.

'I think we will be happy, Jack. Don't you?'

He grinned his usual easy grin as he said nonchalantly, 'Only you know what's in your heart, girl.'

She hugged him suddenly and he hugged her back, amazed at the emotions she was causing him to feel.

'I will be all right, Jack. He is a good man.'

Jack smiled, but he was wondering to himself, who was she trying to convince – him or herself?

Ray came up and placed a proprietary arm around her waist and smiled, his big, handsome face looking pleased and proud, as he said happily, 'Mrs Donovan, eh, Jack! Sounds good, yes?'

Jack laughed at the man's obvious delight and he found himself looking deep into Ray's eyes. He was relieved to see he seemed genuine. As they moved off on to the dance floor together Jack felt a terrible urge to weep. Shaking his head to clear it, he wondered if he was going senile in his old age. Then, seeing Reggie and his sister, he went over to them for a chat.

Chapter One Hundred and Fifty-Five

Ivy and Del Conway were over the moon at the way the wedding had gone off. Ivy had never seen her daughter looking so beautiful. They were in a nightclub on Southend seafront that they had taken over for the night, and the food and drink was outrageously good. They had champagne on tap – anything anyone wanted was on tap. It must have cost Ray a fortune, and Ivy was pleased that her daughter had got herself a man who was so good to her. Those boys were well behaved these days, and they obviously loved Ray as much as he loved them. It did her heart good to see them all happy. Little Kathy was going to be a heartbreaker with that black hair and those blue eyes. The place was packed and, as she watched her own husband getting steadily pissed at the bar, she smiled to herself ruefully. Her Del would never change, but even she could see that he was pleased for his daughter, and so he should be.

Annie made her way over to Ivy, and the two women, who were very friendly with each other, chatted happily together. This was a wonderful day, and they were both pleased with how it was turning out. In fact, they were both of a mind. They saw that the children they had produced had finally found the soulmate that eluded so many other people. They were rightly pleased with the day and saw nothing in the future except happiness for these two who were so much in love.

Chapter One Hundred and Fifty-Six

Gerry and Reggie were both half-drunk and sitting together in one of the small booths that dotted the nightclub.

'Strange venue for a wedding, Reggie, don't you think?'

Reggie grinned and she was aware of how painfully handsome her brother was. Of course, she knew he was gay – and that it was still something to be kept as quiet as possible. Even now that was a no-no in the criminal underworld.

'He's just bought it. Well, the word "acquired" is probably more apt.'

Reggie knew that he was talking out of school but at this moment he didn't really give a shit. He had felt it was wrong what Ray had done and he had said as much to him.

Jack Johnson agreed with him but, as Jack said, what could they do? It was over with, finished and done.

Maybe if they had known about it beforehand they could have intervened, but Ray had a habit of working on his own and that was always going to cause friction. His attitude had been: this is a personal matter, why would I involve anyone else? He had a point, but it was the principle. Young Elton was in on it, of course, and that was another bugbear. Elton Mills was in on everything these days.

Gerry didn't know what to say but she could sense her brother's discontent and she hoped that it would not blow out of proportion. She knew how easily that could happen in their world, and how brutal it could be.

'Well, you do have separate businesses, Reg.' She was striving to be fair.

Reggie sighed and said honestly, 'And I mention them before, during and after the transactions. I don't just fucking spring them on everyone.'

Gerry's smile lit up her beautiful face. 'Well, he is a Northerner. They do things differently up there!'

She was trying to lighten the mood; Reggie just shrugged and changed the subject. 'Saw you eyeing up that Barton earlier and him eyeing you back. I don't think his wife noticed.'

Gerry looked suitably ashamed as she whispered, 'I've been seeing him for a little while, Reg. I know it's wrong, but I can't help it.'

Reggie sighed heavily. 'You are hardly in the first flush of youth, Gerry! Why don't you look for a proper bloke? One who hasn't got more baggage than fucking Heathrow Airport.'

His words stung and, in a rare act of retaliation at her brother, she said snidely, 'I might say the fucking same to you, bruv.'

But Reggie just smiled as he said benignly, 'That is different and you know it. Though I have got the Italian-looking waiter's number!'

They were friends again and she hugged him quickly as she said in a whisper, 'You like them big and manly, just like I do. Must be a family trait, eh?'

They watched as Ray led Sharon on to the dance floor and, as he pulled her into his arms, Reggie saw that she wasn't as happy as she was making out. He knew her better than she realised and he hoped against hope that life had not thrown her another fucking curveball. She had had more than enough to contend with over the years, and she deserved a slice of happiness. Whether she would find it with Ray Donovan remained to be seen.

Reggie clapped with everyone else and watched the pair dance in silence.

He hoped Sharon would be happy; he could never look at her without the guilt almost choking him. He had loved her husband very much and, the saddest part of it all was, so had she.

Chapter One Hundred
and Fifty-Seven

Sharon had danced with her new husband, both her sons, her father and Jack Johnson. Now she was dancing with Barton, aware of the huge strength he possessed as he held her to him tightly.

'He is one lucky man.'

Sharon felt herself blush and laughed to hide her embarrassment. He really sounded like he meant what he said to her. But he was a womaniser and he looked on all of the female sex as potential mates. Although he was already married to her friend, she knew that, as much as he loved Jamella, he would always need a bit of strange. It was the nature of the beast.

'Your eyes look sad, Sharon. Sparkly, but still there's a sadness behind them.'

'Hark at you!'

He looked down at her face and he said seriously, 'You thinking about your first wedding to Lenny?'

She nodded almost imperceptibly and then she said

honestly, 'I can't help it. I feel terrible but I suppose it was inevitable, really.'

He nodded but continued to look into her face and she wished the Stylistics record would end so she would be free of his scrutiny. Barton was a shrewd man and that was not just her opinion – it was the opinion of anyone who came into contact with him.

'Human nature, Sharon. I would be surprised if you didn't think about it. You had a prosperous union by most standards. Two lovely boys. And then him being taken so viciously. Bound to have an effect, darling.'

She sighed. 'Well, that was then, and this is now. I know we are going to be very happy together.'

Barton could hear the uncertainty in her voice but he did not remark on it. After all, who knew what she had heard about Ray? He could guarantee that anything she did hear from certain people would not be to the good. Ray was making a few enemies and that was something Barton understood, because in their game it was part of living the Life.

'He loves you, Sharon, more than anything. He adores those boys, and that little girl you've given him has made him happier than I have ever seen. Remember that. He ain't like me. I'm always on the lookout for a bit of strange, as you have probably heard. Let's face it – my old woman ain't exactly quiet about my foibles, is she? But never him. Ray has eyes only for you and that counts in his favour, surely?'

Sharon forced a smile, feeling her face ache with

the effort of looking as happy as this man wanted her to be. And she *was* happy – she was determined to be.

'I'm glad to hear that, as you can imagine!' She made her voice light and full of fun and that was good enough for Barton, who decided that he had said his piece and that would be the end of it.

Chapter One Hundred and Fifty-Eight

Ray caught young Lenny smoking outside and he saw the worry in the boy's eyes at what Ray might have to say to him. He removed the cigarette from the boy's mouth, crushed it out beneath his huge foot and, smiling his easy smile, he said quietly, 'A mug's game. Look at me and your mother, both hooked! If you are determined to do this then please make sure you don't get caught in the future, OK?'

Young Lenny could not believe his luck; he had expected to be read the Riot Act. Ray wondered at why this boy didn't irritate him; after all, he was the living image of his father. Yet that wasn't an issue because he knew the boy was more his than he had ever been Lenny Scott's. These lads of Sharon's had needed a male presence and he had provided that. And he actually did care for them.

In the beginning he had courted them to get to Sharon, but now he looked on them as his own flesh and blood. He knew they adored little Kathy, and that pleased him because he really did not want them to be jealous of her. He had great plans for these boys and it did not involve university or any of the other shit that Sharon wanted for them; he had just said that to go along with her in the early days. They had a natural cunning and he felt that should be utilised. Also, as they had grown, they had expressed a desire to be a part of his world and that suited him down to the ground. Not that he would want that for his child, of course, but then Kathy was a female and, as such, would have no value to him in any way. But these were the offspring of Lenny Scott and that would never be forgotten.

'Do you ever think of your real dad, Len?'

It was a question he had always wanted to ask, but there never seemed a right time to do it. Now he felt he could ask it without fear of the answer.

Young Lenny screwed his eyes up. It appeared that he was seriously considering the question, and then he said sadly, 'Not really, Dad. It was so long ago and, even though he used to do things with Liam and me, he wasn't doing them like you do. You know, just us together, laughing and that? It was always with Uncle Reggie.'

He held Ray's eyes now and the unspoken truth was there between them. Liam had obviously told his older brother what he had witnessed and the boy had believed him. Which, considering the circumstances, spoke volumes. Young Lenny had sussed out that both he and his brother were used as a blind for the two men to spend time together. There was a small part of Ray that felt sorrow for Lenny Scott and the fact he had to live a lie for all those years. He was also sorry for this lad who had to come to terms with knowing what his father was.

'Honestly, Dad? If he'd not been murdered, I think that I would have ended up killing him myself.'

It was so honest and so heartfelt that Ray could do no more than pull the boy into his arms and hug him tightly, and young Lenny returned the embrace with fervour.

'Listen to me, Len. Your father was from a different world. He could never really be himself, you understand? Not in the world *we* live in, anyway.'

Young Lenny liked that he had said 'the world we live in'. That seemed to seal their relationship. He liked that Ray thought he was worthy of being included in his life. His work life. It was what he wanted more than anything else.

'He was a liar, Dad. To my mum and to us, and I hate him for it.'

Ray didn't answer the boy; he didn't know what to say. He was certain of one thing though: young Lenny had what it took – of that there was no doubt whatsoever. He hugged the lad again. Liam had come looking for them; noticing him, Ray opened his left arm widely and the boy walked into the embrace without hesitation.

That was how Sharon found them, and, far from being happy about it, she felt for a few seconds that she was looking at an unholy alliance. Her two handsome sons and Ray Donovan together seemed sinister somehow and she wondered once more what she was doing. Then Ray motioned for her to join them and, shifting Kathy on to her hip, she did. Years later she would come to realise that by then the damage had already been done. But she gave herself up to the love of her new husband and her sons because she felt that she had no choice. The decision had been made and she had to fulfil her destiny, whatever that might be. One thing was for sure: there was no going back now.

Book Five

A man's foes shall be they of his own household.

Matthew 10:36

Chapter One Hundred and Fifty-Nine

2012

'Sixteen years! Who would have thought it?'

Sharon laughed at the incredulity in her friend's voice. Gerry Dornan had not aged well; her lifestyle had taken its toll and she looked what she was: a good-time girl. She had systematically worked her way through every Face or wannabe-Face in London but she had never found the happiness she hoped she would. Gerry's trouble was she thought that everyone she met had the same capacity for loving that she had. The repercussions she was confronted with when the people she took up with were liars and thieves never occurred to her – she believed every word they said and then she was disappointed. It was always the same: she gave them her heart overnight and the passion was gone as quickly as it had arrived. Reggie had once said to Sharon that his sister was in love with the idea of being in love. Sharon had a feeling that he was right. She wished, in some ways, the same could be said for her.

She had spent the last years living a complete and utter lie. Nothing had been the same since the wedding; the fears she'd tried so hard to ignore had only multiplied. Oh, she loved Ray, especially when he was making love to her. That would never change – he was the only man to ever ring her bells. But it was their day-to-day existence that frightened her with her husband. Because she didn't trust him as far as she could throw him. She had come to terms with the fact that he took a flier now and again these days. But then she wasn't exactly in the first flush of youth and she was well aware that men like Ray had women throwing themselves at him all the time. He seemed to have a penchant for young blondes – he always liked the fair-haired women. She supposed it was because he was so dark himself – dark-skinned, dark-eyed and dark-haired, though his lovely, thick hair was streaked with grey these days. But, wouldn't you know it, it just made him look more distinguished. Sod's law, she supposed.

As for Sharon, she was rattling around in her big house – there was plenty to keep her busy. At weekends she cooked for the family and they sat and ate together as usual. She still washed their clothes and ironed for them all. She knew that even Ray felt she should have a hobby or something, but she wasn't sure there was anything she really wanted to do. She couldn't see herself going to flower-arranging classes or learning

French, it just all seemed pretty pointless to her. She was knocking on fifty, her sons were grown men now, and her daughter was nearly eighteen. She didn't think she was going to stagnate just because she no longer had them to look after constantly.

'Why don't you come out with me one night? Have a girlie one, Sharon?'

Sharon was laughing, imagining Ray's face if she told him she was going clubbing. She said as much to Gerry and when Gerry didn't laugh with her, Sharon understood that it actually wasn't funny at all. She rarely went out without Ray, and that was something that had just occurred to her.

'Do you know what, Gerry? Let's do it.'

Gerry was grinning now as she said saucily, 'Might find yourself a bloke!'

Sharon flapped her hand in embarrassment and said sadly, 'Who would fucking want me at my age?'

Gerry shook her head as she answered her seriously, 'You would be surprised, girl. It's a different world out there now and women have as much right as men to do what they want.'

Sharon had moved from Lenny straight to Ray and she had never really 'gone out' as such. She had been in a relationship since she was thirteen years old. It was a sobering thought.

Chapter One Hundred and Sixty

Chrissie Jennings was twenty-two and built like a Playboy model. Although she was not the most intelligent girl that had ever walked the earth, she possessed a shrewdness that belied her years, and she saw herself and Ray Donovan as the lovers of the century. She liked his foreign good looks and his big cock; and it was big, there was no doubting that. He was hung like a fucking horse and she was relishing that fact.

She climbed off him and lay beside him, happy that she had given him the fuck of a lifetime. She knew exactly how to fuck; it was second nature to her. Great sex was what would get her what she wanted. It didn't occur to her that the women men fantasised about and the women they married were two different things. She was, after all, as thick as paint.

Ray lit a joint and toked on it deeply. Now he had fucked Chrissie she held no real interest for him any more.

Chrissie snuggled into him and did her usual little-girl laugh and baby talk as she said happily, 'That was the best ever!'

Ray extricated himself from her arms expertly as he said, 'I'm sure you have said that on more than one occasion, Chrissie. But it won't wash with me, sweetheart.'

Chrissie might not have been the Brain of Britain but she knew when she was being mugged off. After all, this would not be the first time she had been unceremoniously dumped by a man she was fucking. She stood up, naked and sure of her allure. She did have a killer body – no one could dispute that – and she knew how to use it as well.

'You can't treat me like shit!'

Ray Donovan laughed then – a real, genuine laugh at her antics.

'Oh, but I can, Chrissie. You are just a fuck – a *good* fuck, I'll give you that – but that is it, lady. I have a beautiful wife and I will never leave her for a skank like you.'

Chrissie could hear the viciousness in his voice now and she was hurt. She really thought this was it for her. She believed she had hit the jackpot.

'You can't talk to me like this! I love you, Ray.'

He grabbed her arms as she went to fight him, and pinned her to the bed.

'I think I'm pregnant, Ray. You have to look after me now.'

Ray registered her words, but he could not believe what he was hearing. Was she really that fucking stupid? Chrissie thought he was going to fuck her again and tell her what she wanted to hear. Instead he put his face close to hers and said nastily, 'I would not love you or allow you to have my child if you were the last fucking female on earth, Chrissie. You are a fuck, pure and simple. My wife is getting on a bit, I admit that, but she is worth a million of you. You're a whore, and that is all you will ever be to me or any man you take up with. Get over it.'

Chrissie knew then that she had lost not just the battle but the whole war. 'Get out.'

Ray Donovan held her down and fucked her once again before he got up and, as he dressed, he said quietly, 'I will go. No man in his right mind would even consider you as a mate of any kind. You were born to be a mistress, darling.'

Chrissie had been putting it about since she was sixteen years old, and this was not the first time a married man had said as much to her. She felt an enormous anger welling up inside her and she shouted, 'Well, let's see how your precious wife feels when I tell her what we have been up to the last few months, shall we?'

That was when the beating started, which was what she liked, if she was honest – at least it proved they cared. But when he grabbed her throat and started to squeeze, it dawned on her that she had picked on the wrong man this time.

Ray choked her to death. When he realised what he had done, he was annoyed with himself. This was the last thing he needed right now. He rang Elton – he would sort out what needed doing. Ray knew that he needed to calm himself down. It wasn't the first time this had happened – he should have been prepared for the girl's threats. At the end of the day, that is all they were – girls. Sharon was the love of his life, his wife, and, as such, she *would* be afforded respect. Even by the women he fucked. What kind of husband would he be if he allowed them to bad-mouth the mother of his daughter? He fucked them but they were never going to be contenders to Sharon's crown. What made them think they ever could be?

He smiled as he waited for Elton Mills to arrive; he was good, was Elton. He always made everything go away. Ray was relying on him more and more.

Chapter One Hundred and Sixty-One

Elton Mills had been in bed with his girlfriend, a good-looking Jamaican girl called Abigail, when the phone rang. She was stunning, with big brown eyes and a shaved head. She really embraced the African look – it suited her and she knew it. She believed that Elton Mills was going places so, when he took the call, she was sensible enough to smile and act like she thought it was perfectly normal for a man to leave her halfway through making love to her.

'I need to leave, baby.'

She kissed him deeply, using her tongue to its best advantage. 'Come back soon. I will be waiting for you, baby boy.'

He knew she meant every word, well aware that she was after the main chance, but he did not say that, of course. Instead he got dressed and left as quickly as humanly possible.

Ray was starting to bother him. He respected the

man – in truth, he was the reason he had such a fabulous life. Elton was his number two and everyone knew that. But lately, Ray had been like a loose cannon. Now he had taken out that silly Chrissie. She was a fucking prat, but she was only twenty-two and had been used by everyone in their orbit, so her disappearance would be noticed by all and sundry. It wasn't as though Ray had hid his relationship with her either; he was pretty fucking blatant. Elton wondered if he wanted Sharon to find out, if he was trying to get some kind of reaction from her. That was just speculation, of course.

One thing Elton knew for sure was that Ray worshipped his wife and his infatuation with younger women was nothing in the grand scheme of things. Now Elton had to take the girl and make her body disappear into thin air, and that was really not what he wanted to be doing.

Chapter One Hundred and Sixty-Two

Sharon couldn't sleep but that was nothing unusual. She had not slept an entire night since her wedding to Ray all those years ago. Her sons were both now firmly embedded in the Life, and that broke her heart every bit as much as it pleased them. They were both thrilled to death to be villains, and what could she do? They had been determined and Ray, whatever he tried to pretend otherwise, had encouraged them to follow his example. He saw their rise in that world as a reflection upon himself. It was only young Kathy that he wanted to stay outside the Life – should she ever embrace it, it would kill him. Ray wanted his daughter to be a doctor or a scientist. It did not occur to him that, for all her expensive education, she wasn't academic in any way, shape or form. She was a nice, normal girl, who didn't see herself as some kind of fucking intellectual needing to prove herself every second of the day. But that was how Ray treated her.

Sharon was aware that it worried her lovely daughter. Kathy simply wanted to please the people around her. She was seventeen and she was still finding her feet. Why did Ray need her to act like she was only put on this earth to please him?

She heard young Lenny come into the room and she forced herself to face him, but she'd had a large glass of wine and she could feel the animosity coming off him. He hated that she needed a few drinks to get her through the day, but who the fuck was he to tell her how to live her life? He was Ray's son now, and they both knew that.

'Where's Kathy?' His voice was clipped and she could tell he was angry at her. He saw her as just someone who wanted to drink and nothing else.

'She is staying at her mate's. Was she supposed to ask your permission?' She was angry and it came across in her tone.

She watched young Lenny look her over and find her wanting. It was a deliberate rebuke and she had seen it many times before. Oh, he was Ray's boy now, there was no doubt about that.

'Can I help you, son?' Her sarcasm was evident.

'Who is she staying with?'

His lack of respect for her was hard to live with. Even her own mother had told her that he needed a right-hander, but what would it achieve?

'Who the fuck do you think? Where does she usually stay, Len? At Maria's. Maria, the girl she has been friends with for years. Going to check up on her, are we?'

It would not be the first time. Kathy had been in high dudgeon when he had turned up there before. In fact she had been livid. And she'd had every right to be; after all, Sharon trusted her, so why couldn't her father and her brothers? If she didn't look out for her daughter, the girl would be on lock-down.

'Are you going out or not, Len?'

She dismissed him, unable to bear the antagonism between them. It broke her heart, because she loved her sons, whatever they might think of her. They were more Ray's boys now than they had ever been hers.

Chapter One Hundred and Sixty-Three

Kathy was at her friend's house and she was laughing her head off when Maria's mum knocked on the bedroom door and said that her brother was downstairs wanting to talk to her.

Maria rolled her eyes in exasperation as her friend left the room to put her brother's mind at rest. She knew that Kathy expected nothing different from her family, but she felt that if her brothers were so fucking insistent on knowing her whereabouts it would drive her insane. Her own brothers were normal – i.e. they had no real interest in her. That was how it should be, surely?

Kathy went out into the front garden so they would not be overheard and, looking at her older brother, she said in exasperation, 'Why do you do this, Len?'

Lenny felt bad but he knew that he had to look out for this girl; she was completely naive where men were concerned. Ray thought she was a fucking brainbox but Lenny knew the truth. She'd only ever been an average student at best. She needed looking after, whether she agreed or not. She was his sister and he would protect her with his life if need be.

'I'm just looking out for you, Kathy, that's all.'

He could see the sadness in her eyes and he wished he could tell her something different. But then he would be a liar.

He tried to justify himself as he said, 'Be fair, Kathy. Mum drinks a lot and she can't always be trusted to say what is actually going on, can she?'

Kathy didn't even bother to answer; she just turned away and walked back into the house, closing the front door firmly behind her. She had been there and done that, and it was getting boring as far as she was concerned. Her brothers were a pain in the arse. As she went back up the stairs to where her friend was waiting, she wondered when she would ever be free of them. It was like being in prison.

Chapter One Hundred and Sixty-Four

Jack Johnson was watching his daughter pouring him his nightly Scotch. She looked out for him, even though he had been an absent father at best. He was getting on, but he still had Reggie onside and he would always be his trump card, because what Ray had never allowed for was Reggie's determination.

He smiled at his daughter. She was a good girl, if not the prettiest woman he had ever seen – unfortunately she looked too much like him. That was a shame, as her mother had been beautiful in her day. Jack regretted how he had treated her mother. In his own way, he had loved her very much, but the Life had taken him over as it had so many men. Hindsight was a wonderful fucking thing.

He waited with bated breath for Reggie to arrive; he knew that he did not have long for this world, but before he went, he would fuck up that cunt Ray Donovan. He was determined to do it. He had swallowed his knob over and over again because he'd had no choice in the matter, but he was on his last legs now and that meant he had fuck-all to lose. How good that felt. He had the knowledge that could ruin that cunt's whole life and he was now willing to use it, no matter who it hurt. He had sussed Ray out from the first and he had kept his own counsel. Now he was dying, he felt it was his duty to put the cat among the pigeons. That was all he could do really. After all, he had always been a man who left his mark. Why should he change the habit of a lifetime?

Chapter One Hundred and Sixty-Five

Elton Mills looked at the dead girl in front of him and sighed heavily. 'You must learn to control your temper, Ray. This isn't good for business.'

Ray smiled that easy smile of his and said seriously, 'As soon as they threaten to talk to the wife, I lose my temper. Be fair, Elton – I never proposed marriage.'

Elton could see his point, but he also knew that Ray Donovan was getting out of control. This was not good sense; whatever Chrissie was, she was well liked, especially by the men who had fucked her, and they were legion. Elton shook his head, his anger at his friend more than apparent.

'This is the last time, Ray. You fuck up again, *you* can fucking sort it – and I mean that.'

He felt the animosity coming from Ray Donovan in waves but he didn't care any more. This had gone too far. Ray was a loose cannon.

Chapter One Hundred and Sixty-Six

'You OK, Sharon?'

Ray was watching his wife closely. He could see she was pissed but he overlooked it. After the night he'd had, he could hardly say a word.

'I'm fine, Ray. You all right?'

She was giving nothing away. Sometime in the past sixteen years she had found out that he wasn't kosher, that he was a fucking liar and a fucking fraud. It had made him sad because he really did love her, but she hadn't been the person he had expected. She always felt she had to be his moral compass. He wanted a wife, not a fucking judge. It had driven a wedge between them.

'I have never been better, darling.'

With his eyes on her, she felt the pull of him, of his sexuality. No matter how bad she might feel, she would always want him like that. Even though he took his fliers she knew they meant nothing to him. Ray was a man who would never love lightly – and one thing she knew for sure was that he loved her with a vengeance. That was the most frightening thing as far as she was concerned.

'Glad to hear it, darling.'

He could hear the sarcasm in her voice and he hated himself for making her feel so bad about herself. But she was no longer the girl he had met or married. She had aged. Women could never age like a man – he looked better as he had got older, whereas she was battered round the edges. She had lost that firmness he had so enjoyed, and when they made love, it wasn't the same. He wanted a younger woman, but that did not mean he didn't love her with all his heart – of course he did. He just didn't want to fuck her any more.

Chrissie came into his mind. She was another one who thought that he would actually leave his Sharon, the mother of his child, to be with someone like her. It was laughable.

He pulled Sharon into his arms and tried to hold her to him but she wriggled away. Laughing, she said, 'I'm not sure that Chrissie would like this. She is your latest, isn't she? And from what I've heard you are leaving me for her. She is pregnant. Really, Ray, another child, at your fucking age? Congratulations.'

Ray felt the first tingle of fear. If Sharon knew then it must have been common knowledge. He could see the hurt and the anger in his wife's face.

'Please, Sharon, you have to believe me. There is no one in my life but you, darling.'

Sharon Donovan used all her strength to push her husband away from her as she bellowed, '*Fuck* you, Ray Donovan. *Fuck* you to hell! You have fucked everyone else and pretended that I didn't know! Have you no fucking *respect* for me? Pregnant? Are you fucking sure?'

Ray had never loved her more than at this moment. She looked like an Amazon warrior. This was the woman he had fallen in love with.

He grabbed her hands and shouted back angrily, 'I know this much, lady: you need to remember that I am your husband and I fucking love you more than you know.'

Sharon pulled her hands from his and said quietly, 'You didn't answer my question, Ray.'

They stood there like antagonists, both trying to stare the other out. She was aware that Ray was stronger than her in these situations, but she was determined not to back down. She had always backed down; all her married life she had moved away from what had been a worry.

'You are, and will always be, the love of my life, Sharon.'

She laughed with complete disgust, and he was more than aware of what she was really thinking.

'Fuck you, Ray. Fuck you and your little girls. If I am too old for you, don't you think you might be too old for them? And this new baby. Are you going to tell Kathy or shall I?'

'There is no fucking baby, Sharon. Take that from me.'

She could hear the fear in his voice and it hurt because she knew that he was more worried about Kathy's reaction to his adultery than he was about hers. But that was him all over. The Big fucking I Am. He acted the big man to his daughter but Sharon knew that Kathy was not as gullible as her husband believed.

'That's not what I heard. That skank has been broadcasting it to all and sundry. So I say again, Ray – congratulations. Now get the fuck out of my house.'

Ray laughed and, grabbing his wife by the neck, he said angrily, 'I think you will find that this is *my* house, darling. If there is any throwing out to do I will be the one doing it.'

'Oh, really? So I have no say at all then, Ray? No say over the house I have taken care of for years, the home that I made for you. That means nothing? Is that what you are telling me?'

Ray was so angry he looked like the Antichrist and he was screaming at the top of his voice as he said viciously, 'You, Sharon, may be my wife but I tell you now, you will get fuck-all from me. It's benefits for you, lady. You will not fucking ever get the better of me. Never forget that. I will never let you go. You are my fucking wife! I gave you my name.'

He was so angry, Sharon knew then that if she was

ever going to go it had to be now. This was the man who professed his love for her day and night – yet he was quite happy to threaten her like this.

Sharon shrugged as if what he said had not broken her heart. 'If I go, Ray, think on this: your daughter will come with me, even if it is to a bedsit. She is my baby, no matter how much you tried to make her yours. You took my sons, but I didn't understand you then. I still trusted you. More fucking fool me, eh?'

Chapter One Hundred
and Sixty-Seven

Reggie was waiting for Ray in a little spieler in Canning Town. It was a dive but it was safe and it was filled with Faces of one sort or another. Elton was getting them drinks at the bar, and Reggie wondered what this meet was about. This was neutral ground so it couldn't be about work in general; that was all dealt with at the breakers yard.

Ray finally arrived and, after ten minutes of being hailed by the clientele, he finally got to sit with them at the table. Reggie waited for him to settle down and tell them what was on his mind. He knew Ray well enough by now to know that he would not say anything until he was good and ready. They made small talk, and asked after each other's respective lives – not that any of them were really interested in the answers. This was just getting the preliminaries out of the way.

The bar stank of cheap aftershave and lager. Reggie

loathed the place but he knew it was Ray's choice so he was lumbered with it. Ray knew how much he disliked the dive and Reggie guessed that was why it had been the chosen venue for whatever was going on.

Eventually Ray said seriously, 'This is about Jack Johnson.'

Reggie nodded. There was no way he was going to commit himself to anything until he had heard the whole story. He wasn't a fool and he knew as well as Jack did that the man's days were numbered. Jack was old and frail now, but he was still a powerful Face and he had much respect from everyone in the Life. Even Ray knew that no one would countenance Jack disappearing as so many others had done. Jack Johnson was an institution and, more than that, he was well liked.

'It's hard to say this, Reggie, but we think it's time Jack stepped down.'

Reggie looked from Ray to Elton Mills, who at least had the grace to appear a little bit ashamed. Jack had never liked Elton but he had afforded him the respect; that meant a lot to Elton who, in his own way, looked up to the likes of Jack Johnson. Jack was one of the last of the old guard. He had known all the Faces from Jack 'Spot' Comer right through the card.

What Reggie didn't like was the 'we' part of what was said. The 'we' meant Ray and Elton, and it was another fucking way of saying he was being gradually rowed out. He had seen this was coming – he wasn't a fool.

'So you think that Jack will just retire, do you?'

The sarcasm was not lost on either of the men and he looked at them both with open hostility. It was a fucking diabolical liberty to spring this on him like this, especially as they had clearly already discussed it between them and made up their fucking minds. All they wanted was for him to go along with their plan and probably do the fucking shit work – like mentioning it to the man he looked on almost like a father.

Ray Donovan held a hand up in a gesture of peace. 'Hey, come on, Reg. You know this makes sense. He's nearly fucking eighty, for fuck's sake. Let him spend his last years with his old cronies. He is about as much use as a fucking pork chop in a mosque. Barton agrees with us about that.'

Reggie felt a real anger now, a white-hot fury that seemed to be consuming him. 'So, even Barton has been brought in on these talks about Jack, has he? How about young Lenny and Liam? They in on this too?'

Ray realised he had just put his big foot in it and he would have to try to placate Reggie as best he could. But Reggie was determined to have his say.

'I'm amazed that you have discussed this outside the firm, even with fucking Barton! Jack Johnson always said keep your fucking trap shut – only talk to those in your know. I wasn't aware that Barton was on our fucking payroll.'

'Look, listen to me, Reggie . . .' Ray was getting angry himself now but he was still trying to talk Reggie round as best he could. He needed him onside and he knew that Reggie was as aware of that fact as he was.

Reggie stood up and, looking at Ray like he was a piece of shit, he said, loudly enough to be heard by the other people in the small bar area, 'No, Ray. *You* fucking listen to *me* for once. You are making a big mistake because Jack might be nearly eighty, but he ain't a cunt. My advice to you would be to remember that.'

He left them then. He was so angry he felt capable of anything. He was burning up inside with it. Ray had his rep, but Reggie wasn't exactly a fucking moron where the criminal underworld was concerned. He had his own fucking creds, and Ray Donovan needed to remember that. Reggie was shaking with anger as he got into his Mercedes and he was still seething when he arrived at Jack's house. Jack needed to hear about this, sooner rather than later.

Chapter One Hundred and Sixty-Eight

Kathy Donovan was lying in bed with her father's good friend Barton. Both were well aware that there would be murders – literally – if this ever came out.

Barton, who loved youth and enjoyed the chase, was in a quandary. He had taken this girl and then he had made the mistake of letting it go too far; now she was in love with him. He didn't know how to tell her that good sex did not constitute love in any way. She wasn't like the usual girls he took into his bed; she was the daughter of his close friend and known fucking lunatic Ray Donovan. This was going to explode in his face at some point and, as hard as he was, Barton knew he was no match for Ray – especially not the Ray who would see his friend's death as a natural consequence of him having taken his daughter's virginity. Not that she'd needed much persuading.

He sighed in exasperation. She was snuggled into him and, as he looked down at her perfect skin and her beautiful blue eyes, he wondered how the fuck he was going to out her from his life with as little fuss as possible. She was all woman on the outside, but inside she was still a little kid. Sometimes her incessant chattering made him want to lamp her one; she talked utter shite and she assumed he was as interested in celebrities and fucking bands as she was. Once again he asked himself, what the fuck had possessed him? But he knew what had happened. He thrived on the dangerous and the illicit – it was what excited him, and this young woman, with a killer body, had the added attraction of being his best friend's daughter. The daughter, no less, of one of the most feared men in London.

Now she was in love with him, and he had to try and extricate himself as best he could. But she was a clinger and, like most girls in love for the first time, she would turn on him if he didn't handle it properly.

Kathy Donovan, for her part, was happier than she had ever been before in her life. Kathy, who wasn't the most academic of people, had discovered sex. Pure, deep, down-and-dirty sex. She believed that her attraction to this huge, handsome, black man was love, and she was deluded enough to think that he felt the same way. She fantasised about them getting married and living in a nice house somewhere. It didn't occur to her that the fact he was a married man already and her father's best friend to boot could be a problem. After all, her father had always given her what she wanted. Her mum said she was a spoiled little princess and Kathy took that as a compliment. Why shouldn't she get what she wanted? It also didn't occur to her that this might be the one time her father would not humour her and let her have her wish granted. She had not only inherited her father's beautiful, thick, Turkish hair, she had also inherited his stubbornness.

She stretched like the cat that got the cream and Barton felt himself hardening again. As her mouth clamped on to his, he knew that he had to finish this and finish it soon. But Christ Himself knew this felt fucking good.

Chapter One Hundred and Sixty-Nine

Young Lenny and Liam were in Romford picking up loans. They were both big lads; Lenny was his father's double whereas Liam had more of his mother in him. The one thing the two boys shared was that they were both completely ruthless. Ray Donovan had seen to that and he was proud of them.

As they walked through the market they were chatting amiably, aware that people were looking at them, that people knew who they were. There was a blonde girl on one of the clothes stalls, Emma Nuttall, that Liam liked so they made their way over to her and, as always, he gave her one of his winning smiles. Today, though, there was no answering smile. She looked away and pretended to be sorting through the clothes on the rails all around her.

'Hey, Em. No smile for me today?'

As he spoke to her a large blond man came around the side of the stall and said gruffly, 'No, there ain't no fucking smile. She is engaged to me, you cunt, and I don't want to see you sniffing around her again.'

Liam and Lenny were studying this bloke who they both believed must be on drugs, at the very least, to take them on. Then, glancing at Emma, Liam saw she had bruises around her eyes that make-up had not fully concealed.

'Has he given you a fucking right-hander?' He turned to the man and bellowed, 'Have you fucking clumped her, you cunt?'

The baseball bat came out of nowhere, but Lenny and Liam disarmed the man in seconds, and then they set about giving him a lesson he would not forget. Emma Nuttall, the girl who had inadvertently caused all this aggravation, was still screaming when the police arrived. Her boyfriend, Andy Bedford, died on his way to the hospital.

The two Scott boys, it was being said, had finally gone too fucking far.

Chapter One Hundred and Seventy

Sharon was in pieces but the police would tell her nothing. It seemed that even the name Donovan didn't hold much weight with the Old Bill when there were that many witnesses to a murder. A female DI took Sharon through to the canteen and got her a cup of tea as she waited for Ray to arrive and sort the mess out. She was terrified. If they went down for this it would be a serious lump, and she didn't know if she could cope with losing both her sons to the prison system.

A deep, abiding hatred for Ray entered her mind that night, because *he* had brought them to this. He had given them an in to the same world that had left their father murdered in cold blood in a filthy alleyway. And now that is what they were too: murderers. She felt the sting of tears and, taking out her mobile, she started ringing around.

She wasn't surprised when Reggie got there before

anyone else. Ray could not be traced; his mobile was turned off and she guessed rightly that he would be with some girl somewhere. The one time she needed him – *really* needed him – and he had turned his phone off on her. That bothered her more than she could believe.

Within ten minutes of Reggie arriving, she was finally led through to the back of the police station to see her sons. Reggie had arranged a brief for them and was already working on damage limitation. Suddenly she felt like she could breathe again. What the fuck were they thinking of? But that was the trouble with her sons – they didn't think. They thought the name Scott and the tutelage of Ray Donovan was enough to keep them out of prison. They were a law unto themselves, and now their young lives could be over for the foreseeable future. For that, she would always blame Ray. She'd had such high hopes for them once, but she had gone along with Ray, as she had always gone along with Lenny before him. She knew deep down that the person she should be blaming was herself. She should have stopped the boys becoming too involved with Ray and the Life, but they had been determined to follow in both their fathers' footsteps. Lenny and Ray had been the reason they were now sitting here waiting to go to court and, as a best case, get bail. She hoped that they would get special concessions, but she also knew they would not get a walk.

Reggie was already talking about trying to get the

charge reduced to manslaughter for self-defence and people would be paid handsomely to keep that fiction going. Her boys had wanted to do what they had done – they were both impetuous and they were both arrogant.

Her phone rang and she answered it quickly. It was Jack Johnson telling her that he had already started things moving and he would use his vast contacts to try and resolve the situation for her. She began to cry; she was so grateful to him. She knew that she could count on Jack Johnson to come up trumps for her; he had always had her best interests at heart. She rang off, feeling much better about the situation now Jack was on board. Then she looked at her sons, and her anger flared. They were not in the least bit contrite and seemed to think that this was nothing more than a formality. That is when her heart finally sank and she knew that the best thing for these sons of hers would be a short, sharp shock. If they didn't take this seriously, what fucking hope was there for them in the future? She had lost them; she had lost them a long time ago. And the knowledge broke her already fragile heart.

Chapter One Hundred
and Seventy-One

Ray arrived the next morning after a particularly heavy night of passion with a Swedish girl he had met in one of his clubs. She was tall, thin and had little tits that fascinated him. She also had the strength of a lion, and when she wrapped those long, slim legs around his waist and squeezed he honestly thought he had died and gone to heaven. She looked like the blonde one from ABBA in their heyday. She was a real looker, all right.

Now, though, he knew he was well in the doghouse and he needed to have a bit of a grovel. He was shocked at how rough Sharon looked; she seemed to have aged ten years overnight.

'You finally got home then?'

He could hear the accusation in her voice, and he looked suitably contrite. But how could he have known those stupid fuckers would do something so fucking idiotic?

'I'm sorry, all right? But I'm here now and I am sorting it. So don't worry.'

Sharon pushed past him and, shaking her head slowly, she said loudly, 'Jack and Reggie have already done what's needed, thank you. Get back to your fucking whore. You are not welcome here.'

Kathy had heard the exchange and she was amazed to witness her mum talking like that to her dad. She could see the look of utter incredulity on her father's face and realised that her mum had won this battle – but that did not mean she would necessarily win the war. Her respect for her mother shot through the roof and, taking Sharon's lead, she walked into the kitchen and gave her father a filthy look.

Ray Donovan stood in his state-of-the-art kitchen and swallowed his anger. He knew that Sharon was entitled to be annoyed today – as long as she understood that he would not put up with this treatment for too long, she was quite safe.

Chapter One Hundred and Seventy-Two

Sharon was tired and she wasn't in the mood for any mind games. She could hear Ray in the kitchen and she sighed with annoyance. This was his new habit – making a point of coming home at a reasonable time, acting like a new man. But it was too little too late. She had got used to him not being there and now his presence irritated her beyond belief. He was like some kind of fucking ghost, wandering in and out of the rooms and trying to make small talk.

The boys were on remand and they had been denied bail – something that had really got up Ray's nose. But it seemed that Andy Bedford's father was a magistrate and a pillar of the local community. The boys would have to toe the line on remand and that, it seemed, was that. Ray was more annoyed by the fact that she knew that he had not been able to secure their bail, and that it was killing her visiting them in

Funky Brixton. But there was a big part of Sharon that felt they might learn a lesson or two by having their freedom curtailed – not that she would tell Ray that, of course. Let him fucking grovel and worry about her reaction; it was about time he had a taste of his own medicine.

Kathy had been giving him the cold shoulder too but Sharon had a feeling that it was not so much because of his latest squeeze. She knew in her heart that there was something else bothering that beautiful daughter of hers. But one thing at a time; she had enough on her plate with the boys' situation and, given Kathy's penchant for dramatics, she wasn't interested in a boyfriend dispute. She knew that her daughter was spoiled, highly strung and selfish as fuck but she loved her nonetheless and she wanted the best for her. Once she had this lot off her plate she would find out what was wrong with Kathy. Until then the girl could just sort it herself as best she could. Sharon guessed she had been dumped by her mysterious boyfriend and she allowed herself a little smile at the perils of young love. If that was her only problem how happy she would be!

She sighed as Ray brought her in a glass of white wine and seated himself beside her on the sofa.

'This is a beautiful room, Sharon. You always had great taste.'

She shrugged. 'You always had plenty of money.'

Her voice was flat and Annie, who could hear the

conversation from the kitchen, felt a deep sadness at what had befallen this family. They didn't speak again, and that alone told Annie all she needed to know.

Chapter One Hundred
and Seventy-Three

Jack and Reggie were ensconced in Reggie's flat drinking the usual Chivas Regal that Jack had always favoured as they caught up on recent events.

'I'm so sorry, Jack.'

Jack knew he meant it and he sighed in resignation. 'It'll please Ray, anyway. Save him finding a way to take me out that looks like an accident. Even *he* couldn't be blamed for my cancer!'

'What's the outlook?'

Jack shrugged again and Reggie was amazed at the man's stoicism.

'Few months. Thing is, I'm not really that bothered. I can get my affairs in order, sort a few things out. If I'm honest, I am ready to go, son.'

Reggie really didn't know what to say to that and they drank in silence for a few moments.

Then Jack said sadly, 'I do feel sorry for Sharon.

That girl has had no luck with the men in her life, has she?'

Reggie nodded. He knew that Jack wasn't berating him. He was just stating a fact, and a true fact at that.

'You and Lenny were very close, weren't you?'

Reggie nodded, not trusting himself to speak.

'Shame you had to live a lie, the two of you. Nowadays no one bats a fucking eyelid. I don't pretend to understand it myself, mind.'

That was the nearest Jack would ever get to saying he didn't mind Reggie's sexual preference and Reggie felt a real affection for the old man.

'Got them on the telly and everything now.'

Reggie had to stifle a laugh. 'So I hear!'

They were both laughing now and, when Reggie replenished their glasses, Jack said seriously, 'I will miss me old drop of gold watch, I know that.'

'I'll slip a bottle in with you, mate. I will do you a bet, and all. A hundred-to-one outsider!'

It was an old Irish custom and they both laughed as Jack said jovially, 'If the fucking horse comes in, I will be disinterred the next day! So, what's the state of play with Happy Harold then?'

Reggie shrugged. 'Ray is Ray, and he won't change while he has a hole in his arse.'

'He's a fucker, that's what he is. Now, I am going to tell you something else and you can do what you like with this information after I am dead and gone, OK?'

Reggie nodded and that's when Jack told him the story of the Wheelans and of Ray being their hired torturer. He also told him that he was his broker as Ray still liked to keep his hand in. Once he had finished his tale, Reggie was quiet for long moment. Then he said viciously, 'The snidey cunt. The Wheelans? Are you sure?'

Jack nodded and he looked suitably serious, even though he knew he had given potentially explosive material to a man who would not hesitate to use it.

He watched as the colour slowly drained from Reggie's face.

Jack sat back in his chair, satisfied he had done what he had set out to do: bring down Ray Donovan. He had lit the blue touchpaper. Now all there was to look out for was the explosion. And this particular explosion would be earth-shattering for a lot of the people involved.

Chapter One Hundred and Seventy-Four

Sharon had been to see the boys and she was tired out. It had not been a good visit. She had lost her temper with them, and they had been suitably chastised. They still seemed to think that it was a big joke and that they would be out and about in no time. Nowhere in them did she see remorse for taking another man's life and that was what had tipped her over the edge. Her shouting had bought the POs running and the other prisoners on their visits had enjoyed the cabaret. She knew her sons would be livid with her for making them a laughing stock, but at this moment she didn't really give a flying fuck about that. They frightened her.

As she poured herself a much-needed glass of wine, Ray burst in through the front door and she heard him screaming Kathy's name, following with heavy footsteps as he crashed up the main staircase. Putting her wine down, Sharon started to walk out of the kitchen when she heard the screaming. When she got up to her daughter's room she could not believe her eyes. Ray – Kathy's dad Ray, who worshipped the child – was battering her. She forced her body between them and finally managed to push Ray away. He looked like a man demented.

'What the fuck are you doing?'

She was hugging her terrified daughter to her now, trying to make sense of what she had seen.

'Tell her, Kathy. Go on, tell her what I found out today!'

Kathy was sobbing too much to make any sense and, looking Ray squarely in the eye, Sharon said quietly, 'You tell me what this is about, please.'

Ray laughed then, a nasty, vicious laugh. 'It's a fucking whore we bred, Sharon. A whore who is shagging Barton. Fucking Barton, the cunt! The two-faced, dirty, fucking bastard of hell that he is.'

Sharon was so shocked she could not form any words. All she could think was that her lovely girl had lowered herself to sleep with a man old enough to be her father, and whose wife had always been a friend to them. Ray could see the shock and the horror on Sharon's face and found it in himself to feel a moment's pity for her.

She turned to her beautiful daughter and, pulling her face up to look her in the eye, she said calmly, 'Is this true?'

Kathy was nodding, the tears were overflowing and

she had strings of snot hanging from her nose. She looked twelve again, just as she had when she could not get her own way as a little girl. Her tears would always guarantee that Ray would eventually relent and give her whatever she wanted.

'I will fucking kill him!'

Then Sharon started laughing.

'What the fuck is so funny?'

She could see the bewilderment on Ray's face and that just made her laugh harder. She knew there was a tinge of hysteria in her voice and she used all her willpower to try to keep from screaming out loud.

'Like father like daughter! You know, I was always frightened that one of the boys would be gay like Lenny. But now that means nothing, does it? No one has to hide who they really are any more. Except you, of course, eh, Ray?'

He was looking at her in complete and utter amazement.

'She obviously inherited your lying, scheming, fuck-anything-with-a-pulse gene. Because she sure as hell didn't get it from me! You fucking hypocrite. As for Barton, she is seventeen – he could be her fucking grandfather! Another fucking whore, like you. Did it ever occur to you that he might have taken advantage of her? How many little girls have you chatted up, Ray? They were all someone's daughter or sister. This isn't about our Kathy, this is about you! Barton has pissed on you from a great height and you can't fucking stand it, can you? Well, now you know how I feel.'

He stormed from the room and she shouted after him, 'Smash him up, smash his fucking face in. Go on! That's your answer to everything!'

When the front door was given a resounding slam, Kathy sat up and, putting her arms around her mother, she waited to be comforted.

Instead, her mother gave her a stinging blow across the face and threw her away from her. Behind her, Annie gasped.

'Oh no you don't, lady. You slept with the husband of one of my dearest friends, a woman who has always shown you nothing but kindness and respect. You little whore. Your father was right about that much, anyway. What have I bred? Two murderers and a fucking whore. Not much to show for a lifetime of love, is it? That was my only job, loving and caring for you all. The only thing that mattered. And how have you repaid me, eh? You have trampled on my love and thrown it back in my face. Well, do you know something? Fuck you! Fuck you all!'

She turned into an embrace with Annie, putting her head on the old woman's chest and she cried like she had not cried since the night she had found out about Lenny and Reggie. This time, though, she wasn't crying for her sons, her children. She was crying for herself and the abortion her life had become.

Annie was a wise old bird and she held Sharon

tightly until the crying subsided. Then she slowly walked her down the stairs and through to the kitchen and, pouring her a brandy, she urged her to drink it for the shock.

Kathy lay on her bed feeling desolate. For the first time in her life her mother had turned her back on her. And that hurt more than she would ever have believed possible.

Chapter One Hundred and Seventy-Five

Reggie had heard that Ray was looking all over the Smoke for Barton and that there had been some kind of altercation. Ray had been everywhere, demanding if anyone had seen that 'cunt and ex-friend Barton'.

Reggie turned up at the house and Sharon was evidently pleased to see him. She filled him in on the latest developments and saw the genuine shock on his face when he heard that Kathy had become embroiled in something so sordid, and with Barton of all people. He understood Ray's ire – he would feel the same; it was a double whammy. He sat at the table with Sharon and Annie and tried to calm Sharon down.

'He was a man demented, Reggie. I have never seen him so angry before.'

Annie was quiet; she knew when silence was the best medicine. Let the girl get it out of her system.

'When I met him he was so different to how he is now. He was the sweetest, most gentle man I had ever been with. But then, what did I know? I had only ever had Lenny and we know how that turned out, don't we?'

She was crying again. Reggie motioned to Annie to leave them, and she gratefully went back to the gatehouse and her own front door. As for Kathy! Well, she could hang as she grew for the time being. She was disgusted with the child.

'I fucking hate him now, do you know that, Reggie? He made my boys into what they are: murdering fuckers who have no remorse for that young lad whatsoever. That was Ray taking them into the Life at such young ages. But I am as much to blame, because I let him. I let him!' She was sobbing once more.

Reggie took a deep breath and said, 'There is something you need to know, Sharon.'

The timbre of his voice relayed his seriousness to her and she stopped crying and, looking into his eyes, she said quietly, 'What? What now?'

Reggie Dornan held her hands in his and said gently, 'Ray worked for the Wheelans. Remember Lenny and his outside deals? Well, Ray was their hired torturer. He was the one who took people out if they had crossed them.'

His words were sinking in and she was shaking her head in denial.

'No . . . No, not that. I can't believe that . . .'

But she was remembering some of the things that had bothered her over the years, the little things that Ray had said that had hit a nerve. Once they were discussing Lenny's death with the boys when they were teenagers, and Ray had said that their dad had been wearing a dark-blue suit. At the time she had thought he had read the police report, or she had mentioned it, but deep down she must have registered that he had known more than he was letting on and she had assumed he was trying to protect her.

Now, looking into Reggie's eyes, she realised that what he was saying was the truth. She had brought her husband's murderer into her home, she had mated with him and she had handed him Lenny's sons on a plate. She could not believe that her whole life had been built on another lie. A big, fat, stinking lie that made so much sense even as she tried to deny it to herself. She put her hand over her mouth and she groaned in actual pain.

'What have I done, Reggie! Oh God, what the fuck have I done?'

He stood up and hugged her to him and he said sadly, 'That's just it, Sharon. You haven't done anything, darling.'

She was staring ahead as if in a trance and he poured her another brandy and helped her to take a swallow as her hands were shaking too much to hold the glass herself.

'You know what is going to happen now, don't you, Sharon? You understand that this has to be redressed?'

His words penetrated her brain and she nodded.

'He is a murderer for hire, Sharon. He tortures for money but, from what I can gather, he loves every second of it. He tortured Lenny and took him out, darling. Did you know Lenny had been paralysed – that he couldn't move while he felt every cut and every blow? Jack paid off the Filth so it was reported as a mugging. He had to, I understand that. It's part of the game. But, to think that Ray came to you, to all of us, as a wilting fucking virgin, like butter wouldn't melt . . . And, all the time, he knew what he had done.'

Sharon felt physically sick at that knowledge. She had slept with Ray – she had given him rights over the sons of a man he had murdered. She had borne him a child, a daughter that he had infected with his fucking filth.

'I am going to fucking kill him. I am going to remove him from the earth, Sharon. I don't care that he is Kathy's dad. She is better off without him.'

Sharon looked at the man she had alternately loved and hated over the years, but who she knew would always be a true friend to her and her kids. She had been duped twice in her life and each time by a man she had adored with all her heart. Was it her? Did she attract this trouble to her door? She had slept with two men who had both been living fucking lies. God, what was wrong with her?

She grabbed the front of Reggie's shirt and said seriously, 'I want to be there. This time, I *need* to be there. He destroyed my boys – Lenny's boys – and his own daughter. He blamed *her*, not fucking Barton. I want him dead, I want him fucking gone from our lives. I need him gone now, before he infects us even more with his viciousness and his fucking hate.'

Reggie nodded and she could see that he understood her. He kissed her gently on the forehead and said quietly, 'You can have that, darling. You deserve it.'

Then, calling Kathy down to look after her mother, he slipped out of the house. He had had to tell her; she had a right to know the truth about the man she had been married to for sixteen years. He had been the cause of her living a lie once – Reggie was not going to be the cause of that again. He owed her that much.

Chapter One Hundred and Seventy-Six

Sharon had waved her daughter away eventually and gone to her bedroom where everywhere she looked there was evidence of Ray and their life together. She made it into the en suite just in time to throw up into the toilet, heaving up everything she had eaten and drunk that day. She really did feel as if her heart had been irrevocably broken. How could he have lain with her, played with her sons and laughed and joked with them, all the while knowing that he had taken Lenny away from them? That was the hardest thing for her to understand. How he could have loved those boys. And he did love them, she knew that much. Yet he had beaten their father to death with a crowbar. He had murdered him without even any malice. He had been paid to do it.

She remembered reading about women who had found out that their husbands were rapists or paedophiles and she had always thought: how could these women not know? How could they not know the men they lived with, slept with? But now she understood that it was quite possible to live a lie and not be in the least bit aware of it.

She looked at Ray's clothes in the wardrobe, at his shirts that she had washed and ironed and hung there ready for him whenever he needed them. She used to worry that she had too much, and that it couldn't last. That, somehow, everything had to be paid for. Now she knew that it wasn't fanciful thinking or her Catholic guilt at having so much when others had so little. God, at times, did pay back debts without money.

Now it was Ray's turn to pay and she hoped he paid out well. She'd had two men in her life, and neither had been what they had seemed. She had been fool enough to fall for them and love them and give them children. So what the fuck did that say about her?

She went downstairs to wait for the phone to ring. When the call came, she listened to the person at the other end without a word before she dressed carefully in jeans, a T-shirt and a cheap jacket. Then, smiling, she got into her car and drove away from her house with a calmness she had not felt for years. In fact, she felt as if she had been released from something that had been dragging her down and would have eventually been the death of her. She was playing The Eagles, 'Hotel California', and she felt lighter than ever before. She was in a wonderful mood when she reached her destination.

Chapter One Hundred and Seventy-Seven

Ray Donovan turned up at Jack's yard. It seemed that Elton had come up trumps and brought Barton there to await his punishment. And what a punishment it was going to be. Ray was demented at the thought of his friend with his daughter – his extremely young daughter – who he now felt was sullied and dirty. He would never feel the same about her again. She had been his sunshine, his happiness. Now she was putrid, filthy to him.

He had loved her, given her the world on a fucking plate, and what had the little whore done? She had humiliated *him*, of all people. He was so angry he knew that he would not be responsible for his actions. He had even thought about removing his Kathy from this earth, such was his anger at what she had done to him – Ray Donovan, the man of the fucking hour! How Barton must have laughed at him behind his back, the black fucker must have thought he had got away with it. Well, no one humiliated Ray Donovan and lived to tell the tale.

Inside the office he felt his guts turn to ice water. There was Jack sitting in his usual seat. There was Elton, trussed up like a Christmas turkey. And there was Barton and Reggie with sawn-off shotguns. But the worst thing of all was seeing Sharon – his wife, who he had raised from the gutter after she'd been married to that queer cunt Lenny Scott – sitting there, looking at him with a smile on her face.

Before he could say a word, Reggie said angrily, 'Been sussed out, mate. How does it feel to be on the receiving end for once?'

Ray knew now that he was beaten. He saw the other men with shotguns covering him, and he knew that he could not get out of this one. So he laughed – his arrogance knew no bounds – and Sharon watched his face as it finally dawned on him that this was it. There was anger and there was resignation, and she felt nothing for his dilemma at all. She laughed gently and it was a pleasant sound in a room full of tension. It also told Ray all he needed to know about his wife and his demise.

'I gave you the life you fucking dreamed of, Sharon.'

She knew that he really meant what he said and, for a split second, she felt a great sorrow for him. But not for herself. She realised now that he had a completely warped view of the world that he inhabited.

'I raised you to be my wife. I dragged you out of

the gutter. I gave you what you fucking craved. A *real* man. But you got old, darling. You knew it could never really last, surely? No man wants the same dinner every night, love. And, as for you, Jack! I was the best thing that ever happened to you.'

Jack shook his head and said loudly, 'You are fucking scum, and northern scum at that.'

Ray Donovan found it funny. He knew it was over for him and he was determined to go out with a big fucking bang.

'I took out the queer who was fucking the arse off Reggie, his so-called best mate, Sharon. I did you and your boys the favour of a fucking *lifetime*.'

He opened his arms wide as if in absolute wonderment and grinned. 'You were a good wife, darling. Like I said before, the only mistake you ever made was getting old. It was like fucking my mother in the end. You were always a mum, never a lover. But I would have stayed with you. You can't help getting a bit long in the tooth. I would never have abandoned you. Even though you bred me a fucking whore.'

Reggie knew that it was time to shut Ray up. It was clear that, even on his own deathbed, he was determined to cause as much hurt as possible.

Sharon shook her head in abject disbelief. 'You never made me feel like Lenny did. You never *really* touched me, Ray. You were a means to an end. As for Reggie, he is closer to me and mine than you could ever be.'

Her lies hurt him, as she knew they would. She had

loved him once with all her being and she'd believed that he was the answer to her prayers. Now she hated him with every bone in her body.

'I want you dead, Ray. I want you gone from my life and my kids' lives too. Especially my kids' lives. You really thought you were something else, didn't you? Something special. You fucked like an amateur, Ray. You were just a pay cheque to me, darling. And now, I'm afraid, you have been sacked.'

Reggie pulled back the barrel of the gun and slipped the cartridges into their place. Then he said pointedly, 'This one's for Lenny.'

He took Ray's legs from under him and, as he hit the floor, pain exploding through his body, Reggie was reloading again. Holding the barrel to Ray's face, he said, 'And this one is for Lenny, too. And his kids and his wife for that matter. And for me, as well. Fuck you, Ray Donovan. Fuck you to hell.'

Sharon watched as her husband and the father of her daughter died before her eyes. She could hear the gurgling as he drowned in his own blood. It seemed to her to be a fitting end for the man she loathed with every fibre of her being. She was amazed at how calm and collected she felt. For the first time in years she was free, and she knew that this was a good feeling. One to hang on to for the future. She needed to remember this moment, the death of her daughter's father, the man she had married with such love and such hope. Would she never learn?

Across the room, Elton groaned – he knew he was next.

Barton grinned at him happily. He had dodged a bullet and he was in a wonderful mood. 'You backed the wrong fucking horse there, son.'

Then he took Elton out with one shot.

Jack was laughing. Their ears were ringing from the gunshots and they were all relieved that the night was over. Jack stood up and, bending over Ray's body, he spat on him.

'Who would have thought I would have outlived you, eh?'

They laughed again.

'Burn this place down with those two still in it. I have removed everything of value. Fuck them. Let the Old Bill sort it, useless cunts that they are.'

Barton and Reggie did as they were asked and, as they drove away in their separate cars, they knew that it had been a good night's work. They felt justified at what they had done and they all breathed a very heavy sigh of relief.

Chapter One Hundred and Seventy-Eight

When the police came to inform Sharon of her husband's death, she was very calm. Too calm, they thought, but they didn't comment. She was very polite and she made them a cup of tea, thanking them for letting her know.

Annie and Kathy, on the other hand, were in bits and Sharon did what was necessary, even though she felt like laughing her head off. For the first time in years she was light of heart, even with everything that had happened. Knowing that Ray was gone was the catalyst she needed to start the healing process. He would never be coming back and for that she would be eternally grateful to Reggie Dornan. He was now her hero, and that in itself was strange, considering the history between them.

That night she slept better than she had in years, and she turned a deaf ear to her daughter's sobbing. Kathy still had a way to go before Sharon would forgive her for her latest escapade. It occurred to Sharon that she had changed in the last few days; she was harder inside, but she supposed that was to be expected. She didn't know what the future held, but one thing she did know: Ray was gone for ever and he would not be there to corrupt her sons any more, or invade her life. That alone was worth all the pain and suffering in the world.

But Barton wasn't getting off with anything either. Sharon rang his wife and told her everything about Kathy and her handsome husband's affair. Sharon may have lost a friend, but she had also taught her daughter a valuable lesson in life. Never shit on your own doorstep.

Chapter One Hundred
and Seventy-Nine

Lesley Scott was in a nursing home when she read about Ray Donovan being murdered. She was over the moon with joy. Her prayers had been heard at last. Sharon's husband was dead – another one murdered. Now she felt she could die in peace. Her prayers had been answered and God had turned His face to her. Her Lenny's death had been avenged somehow. She felt that all the hurt and the heartache that Sharon had brought to her door had been returned to her three times over. Lesley could now let go and see her family once again.

She passed away that night with her ever-present rosary clutched in her hands. She had a smile on her face and the nurses remarked that it looked like it had been a happy death.

Epilogue

Nunc scio quid sit Amor.
Now I know what Love is.

Eclogues, Virgil (70–19 BC)

2014

'You look amazing, Sharon!'

She laughed at the awe in Gerry's voice.

'Not bad for a couple of old dears, are we?'

Gerry was glad to hear the deep laughter of her dear friend. It had been a long time coming and she was pleased to see her enjoying her life for once. Kathy was smiling at them all – she knew she looked beautiful, so she didn't need any reassurance. Her boyfriend, a money broker from Camden, was looking at her like he had never seen a woman before, and that made Sharon smile to herself.

'Who would have thought we would be here today, eh? Look at all the people who have turned up for it. Times have certainly changed. Every Face in the country's here, by the looks of things.'

Sharon smoothed out the peach silk dress she was wearing, and adjusted the matching hat. She was looking forward to this wedding. She didn't know why, but it felt like the start of something new for them. She had finally started to live a life of sorts, but it was a different one now – a calmer, happier existence for her. It was hard visiting the boys in prison; they had got seven years each and they were in separate nicks. But they would be out before they knew it. Kathy had grown up, and what had happened to her had given her plenty of food for thought. Sharon wasn't too worried about her any more. Annie had passed away shortly after Ray's funeral. And what a funeral it had been! She shuddered as she thought of it and pushed the memories from her mind. This was a happy day and she was determined to enjoy it. Knowing Annie was in the gatehouse had always made her feel safe somehow. She missed her.

A white Rolls Royce pulled up and everyone cheered as Reggie and his intended got out, smiling widely. Both were in morning suits and they made a beautiful couple. Reggie had met this man and fallen in love on a holiday in Mykonos. Geoff Tranter was tall, handsome and absolutely gorgeous. He was also a hard man. He was from Liverpool and he was fifteen years younger than Reggie. They were a perfect match, and Sharon adored him. It was funny, but she and Reggie had become very close and now she really relished his friendship and his humour. He was the number one now that Jack had passed away, and he was wearing his crown well. She wished him all the best.

The sun was shining brightly and, as they made their

way into the registry office, Sharon felt the first ripple of excitement she had felt in years. It was as if, with Reggie's wedding, his obvious happiness had rubbed off on her. She knew one thing for sure: she never wanted another man. Never put your happiness in someone else's hands. She had read that recently and she had felt a strange urge to cry. There was such a truth in it that it had hit her like a thunderbolt.

What she wanted now was to live her own life to the full. She had money, she had property and she had her family. First stop was Australia with Gerry, and then they were going to see where the fancy took them. One thing she knew was that no matter what happened to you, no matter how bad life got, happiness – true happiness – was a state of mind. She had paid out everyone who had ever hurt her and now her new mantra was quite a simple one: *don't get mad, get even.*

'I think anyone who grew up on or near a council estate like I did understands my books, the background.'

Read on for more about Martina Cole . . .

> *'I've always been a book fanatic from when I was a little kid…'*

- Martina is the youngest of five children.

- Her nan taught her to read and write before she went to school.

- She secretly signed her mum and dad up to the library and borrowed books in their name.

- Her dad was a merchant seaman, away on the boats for long stretches. He'd come back for Christmas and bring the books that were big in America at the time.

- She used to bunk off school to go and read in the park.

- She was expelled from school – twice – and left school for good at 15: 'They said, don't come back.'

- She was expelled from a convent school for reading *The Carpetbaggers* by Harold Robbins ('They were nuns, how did they know what was in it?!')

- Her first boyfriend was a bank robber. He was really handsome, he had a Jag. 'We're still really really great friends.'

- The first book she remembers reading is Catherine Cookson's *The Round Tower* – she borrowed it from her nan.

- She reads on average two or three books a week.

- Martina wrote her first book when she was 14. It was about a girl who was at a convent but secretly worked for the CIA.

- Her first paid job as a writer was for her neighbour – a Mills & Boon fanatic who paid Martina in cigarettes to write her beautiful stories where they kissed on the swings at the end. Her neighbour's son used to steal the exercise books from school for her to write in!

- Her books are the most requested in prison – and the most stolen from bookshops.

- She sells hugely in Russia, and sometimes thinks it's because the Russians think it's a handbook to the London underworld.

- She has her own Film/TV production company with Lavinia Warner, the woman who produced *Tenko* – the first TV series with really great female characters.

- Alan Cumming did his own hair and make-up and singing for his part as Desrae in the TV adaptation of *The Runaway*.

- *The Faithless* made her the first British female adult-audience novelist to break the 50 million sales mark since Nielsen Bookscan records began.

- *The Take* won the British Book Award for Crime Thriller of the Year in 2006.

- Her fans include Rio Ferdinand – he was snapped with a copy of *Revenge*.

'I'm a great believer in anything that gets anyone reading…'

MARTINA COLE was just 18 when she got pregnant with her son. Living in a council flat with no TV and no money to go out, she started writing to entertain herself.

It would be ten years before she did anything with what she wrote.

She chose her agent for his name – Darley Anderson – and sent him the manuscript, thinking he was a woman. That was on a Friday. Monday night, she was doing the vacuuming when she took the call: a man's voice said 'Martina Cole, you are going to be a big star'.

The rest is history: *Dangerous Lady* caused a sensation when it was published, and launched one of the best selling fiction writers of her generation. Martina has gone on to have more No. 1 original fiction bestsellers than any other author.

She won the British Book Award for Crime Thriller of the Year with *The Take*, which then went on to be a hit TV series for Sky 1. Four of her novels have made it to the screen, with more in production, and three have been adapted as stage plays.

She is proud to be an Ambassador for charities including Reading Ahead and Gingerbread, the council for one-parent families. In 2013, she was inducted to the Crime Writer's Association Hall of Fame, and in 2014 received a *Variety* Legends of Industry Award.

Her son is a grown man now, and she lives in Kent with her daughter – except when she chases the sun to Cyprus, where she has two bookshops.

Her unique, powerful storytelling is acclaimed for its hard-hitting, true-to-life style – there is no one else who writes like Martina Cole.

> *'I'm not educated but I'm very well read…*
> *I read anything and everything. I can read*
> *a book a day. For me reading has been*
> *my biggest pleasure all my life.'*

Martina's Top Books And Favourite Authors:

Hatter's Castle by A. J. Cronin – 'The book that stayed with me all my life'

Wedlock by Wendy Moore – 'A true story written like a novel'

The Godfather by Mario Puzo – 'The book was so much more powerful than the film'

Brighton Rock by Graham Greene – 'the book that changed my life'

Hollywood Wives and *Hollywood Husbands* – 'I was always a big Jackie Collins girl – these are two of my favourite books of all time'

The Hitchhiker's Guide to the Galaxy by Douglas Adams – 'Certain books are like old friends and this is one'

Room by Emma Donoghue – 'I thought it was so good – I read it on a flight to Cyprus and made sure we ordered copies for my bookshop as soon as I arrived'

Hermann Hesse – 'For pure beauty of writing. *Steppenwolf* had a big effect on me'

George R.R. Martin – 'He's given me back my love of fantasy'

Val McDermid – 'Love a good serial killer'

> *'She felt that all her Christmases
> and Birthdays had come at once…'*
> (Get Even)

Keep your eye on Facebook
f/OfficialMartinaCole to be the first to
hear when the next Martina Cole
is coming out.

And if you don't want to wait, treat
yourself to a nice bit of vintage Cole.
Here's a reminder of those blinding bestsellers
that have made Martina Cole the undisputed
matriarch of crime drama – and some quotes
from the lady herself to help you choose
which one you fancy reading…

> *'When I did* Dangerous Lady, *they told me it was too violent and I said – she's hardly going to hit them with her handbag!'*

The book that first made Martina Cole's
name – and its sequel
DANGEROUS LADY
MAURA'S GAME (Dangerous Lady 2)

The only time Martina's written from the Old Bill's
perspective: her deadly DI Kate Burrows trilogy
THE LADYKILLER (DI Kate Burrows 1)
BROKEN (DI Kate Burrows 2)
HARD GIRLS (DI Kate Burrows 3)

You might have seen these on TV – but that doesn't
mean you know what happens in the books!
THE TAKE
THE RUNAWAY

> *'I love the fact that my books are the most requested books in prison and the most stolen books in bookshops, I love the whole concept of that!'*

Martina writes brilliantly about what it's
like on The Inside. For gripping novels
that tell the truth about prison, try
THE JUMP
FACELESS
TWO WOMEN
THE GOOD LIFE

'Your family is either the best thing that ever happened to you or it's the worst thing that ever happened to you.'

Family life is always at the heart of Martina's storytelling: loyalty, protection and how the ties that bind us can also sometimes choke the very thing we want to protect…

FACES
THE FAMILY
THE FAITHLESS
And coming soon … BETRAYAL

'I deal with the mums, the wives, the girlfriends, the sisters, the grandmothers whose children or family are caught up in this life.'

Anyone who's ever read Martina Cole knows her women are the best: strong, resilient, vengeful – nothing will get in the way of these ladies when they know what they want

GOODNIGHT LADY
THE KNOW
CLOSE
GET EVEN

'My books are very anti-violence. I say this is what happens to you if you get caught up in the violent life.'

With her unflinching talent, Martina's stories reveal a world that many would rather ignore

THE GRAFT
THE BUSINESS
THE LIFE
REVENGE

'I wrote what I'd like to read and as luck would have it other people liked to read them too – they either love them or they can't read them, they find them too shocking to read.'

Coming soon . . .

BETRAYAL

*'When a friend betrays you it's
awful, it's terrible – but when a
close family member betrays you,
it's devastating . . .'*

'She's from the Essex darklands, and so are her books
– a brutal world of petty crime, and put-upon women,
and violent men. The voice on the page is her voice
in real life . . . She's a total one-off' *Guardian*

MARTINA COLE
THE KNOWLEDGE

For an indepth interview with Martina, and sample
chapters from all of her books, download the free
ebook – search The Knowledge.